THE SLYPE

ARTHUR RUSSELL THORNDIKE was born in Rochester, Kent in 1885. Although his sister, Sybil Thorndike (1882-1976), was the better-known actor, Russell Thorndike also acted both on the stage and in a number of films, but his first love was writing books. Thorndike finished his first novel, *Doctor Syn: A Tale of the Romney Marsh* (1915), around the same time he enlisted for service in the First World War. After being severely wounded at Gallipoli, Thorndike was discharged and returned to acting. Perhaps surprised at the perennial popularity of the first Doctor Syn novel, Thorndike revisited the character several times in the 1930s and 1940s, in addition to publishing a number of other novels, of which *The Slype* (1927) is probably the best.

In the final twenty years of his life, Thorndike wrote no new novels, but continued to act, appearing frequently as Smee in productions of *Peter Pan*, and made a few film appearances, including minor roles in Laurence Olivier's *Hamlet* (1948) and *Richard III* (1955). Russell Thorndike died in 1972.

Thorndike's *The Master of the Macabre* (1947) is also available from Valancourt Books.

MARK VALENTINE is the author of several collections of short fiction and has published biographies of Arthur Machen and Sarban. He is the editor of *Wormwood*, a journal of the literature of the fantastic, supernatural, and decadent, and has previously written the introductions to editions of Walter de la Mare, Robert Louis Stevenson, L.P. Hartley, and others, and has introduced John Davidson's novel *Earl Lavender* (1895), Claude Houghton's *This Was Ivor Trent* (1935), Oliver Onions's *The Hand of Kornelius Voyt* (1939), and other novels, for Valancourt Books.

Cover: The cover reproduces the scarce jacket art of the first edition, published by Robert Holden in 1927.

D1489764

By Russell Thorndike

Doctor Syn (1915)

The Slype (1927)*

The Vandekkers (1929)

Herod's Peal (1931)

The Water Witch (1932)

Jet and Ivory (1934)

Doctor Syn Returns (1935)

The Further Adventures of Dr. Syn (1936)

Dr. Syn on the High Seas (1936)

The Amazing Quest of Dr. Syn (1938)

The Courageous Exploits of Dr. Syn (1939)

Show House—Sold (1941)

The House of Jeffreys (1943)

The Shadow of Dr. Syn (1944)

The Master of the Macabre (1947)*

The First Englishman (1949)

* Available from Valancourt Books

THE SLYPE

RUSSELL THORNDIKE

With a new introduction by
MARK VALENTINE

VALANCOURT BOOKS
Richmond, Virginia
2013

The Slype by Russell Thorndike
First published London: Robert Holden & Co., Ltd., 1927
First Valancourt Books edition 2013
Reprinted from the "Author's Edition" published by The Dial Press in 1928

Copyright © 1927 by Russell Thorndike
Introduction © 2013 by Mark Valentine

The Publisher is grateful to Mark Terry of Facsimile Dust Jackets, LLC for
providing the reproduction of the original jacket art used for this edition.

Published by Valancourt Books, Richmond, Virginia
Publisher & Editor: James D. Jenkins
20th Century Series Editor: Simon Stern, University of Toronto
http://www.valancourtbooks.com

ISBN 978-1-939140-64-7 (*trade paperback*)
Also available as an electronic book

All Valancourt Books publications are printed on acid free paper
that meets all ANSI standards for archival quality paper.

Set in Dante MT 11/13.2

INTRODUCTION

THIS marvellously rich and satisfying story is set in Rochester, the cathedral city on the Medway estuary in Kent that was also the scene for Charles Dickens's great unfinished book, *The Mystery of Edwin Drood* (1870). Dickens had a strong affection for Rochester and asked to be buried in the cathedral, but this was thwarted by the public demand that he be honoured by interment in Westminster Abbey: Rochester has to be content with a memorial plaque. In both Dickens's and Russell Thorndike's tales, the city is a strong presence, a character study in its own right. The ancient hallowed stones of the cathedral and its close, the rambling inns and little narrow passageways, the great walls of the castle, all feature.

But whereas Rochester was an adopted home for Dickens, it was Thorndike's birthplace. His father was a minor canon at the cathedral, and Arthur Russell Thorndike was born on 6 February 1885 in the cathedral precincts. He later recalled that for him and his sister Sybil (who became a much-loved actor) as children the cathedral and its quarter were not solemn and sacred, but a wonderful playground, "our scenes for plays and romances."

No doubt because of the Rochester connection, Thorndike was a great enthusiast of Dickens, adapting seven of his books for children in a series published by Raphael Tuck between 1944-1946, each named for a lead child or youthful character: David Copperfield, Little Nell, Oliver Twist, Barnaby Rudge, Little Dorrit, Paul Dombey, and Pip from *Great Expectations*. Thorndike followed Dickens's example in making the hero of *The Slype* a street child, an engaging ragamuffin. And, also following his master, he recognised the importance of providing a sinister, strange and macabre villain, in this case the memorable Paper Wizard.

The Slype, first published in 1927, was not Thorndike's first success. He is best remembered today as the author of *Dr. Syn* (1915), a swashbuckling adventure in which the ruthless but charming rogue of the title rides with his eerie horsemen across the Romney Marsh at night, ever eluding the watch of the Excise men. Yet Dr.

Syn has a secret: during the day, the smuggler, it transpires, is the village's courteous and pious clergyman, tending to the spiritual needs of his parishioners. Thorndike went on to write six more adventures in the series in the 1930s and '40s. *The Slype* borrows a character or two from the Dr. Syn novels, and picks up a thread from one of them: the idea that there might be a secret treasure hidden in the city of Rochester. However, you do not need to have read any of the Dr. Syn books to enjoy *The Slype*, which is an entirely self-contained mystery of its own.

It was the first of nine novels that Thorndike wrote that were not in the Dr. Syn series. They included *Herod's Peal* (1931), another fine mystery, *The Master of the Macabre* (1947, also available from Valancourt), a ghostly tale about an occult detective living in an old abbey, and Thorndike's last book, *The First Englishman* (1949), a historical romance about the Saxon rebel Hereward the Wake. All of them have a sense of great gusto, a panache in the plotting and storytelling, strong pace and vivid colour. Russell Thorndike also grew up, like his sister, to be an actor, as well as director, impresario and author, and the theatrical qualities are well to the fore in *The Slype* and these other books.

This instinct for storytelling and theatre had started early. The precocious boy's earliest literary productions were religious plays, showing how his imagination mingled the matter of the church with a delight in the theatre. This could only have been nurtured further when he became a chorister at St. George's, the Chapel Royal, Windsor, accustomed not only to holy services but also to regal and state occasions, full of elaborate costume and ritual: he sang during the magnificent obsequies of Queen Victoria's funeral in 1901. Thorndike later wrote a history of the Chapel and the choir, *Children of the Garter* (1937; the title reflects that St. George's is also the chapel of the Knights of the Garter).

In their early twenties, both he and his sister, who had been training for the theatre, joined a Shakespearean company touring North America, and they were away for several years. Later tours took them also to India and South Africa, and they performed in London over the next ten years. During the American tour, on the road to a rather volatile Southern town, Russell span a fantasy to his sister about Dr. Syn: she later recalled she was "rigid with fear and thrill, open-mouthed" as he unfolded "horror upon horror." As both cleric and thoroughgoing pantomime villain, Dr. Syn epitomises, with a grand flourish, the two great impulses of Thorndike's life, the religious background of his upbringing, and the two siblings' devotion to the stage. And *The Slype* similarly mingles the gentle, stately rhythm of the cathedral city with the sly villainy and mystery going on in its secret passages and dark old houses.

The First World War intervened in their lives, and it brought sorrow: their brother Frank was killed in action, and Thorndike, who had joined up in the First Westminster Dragoons at the outbreak of the war in 1914, was badly wounded at Gallipoli and invalided home in 1916. He had used some of the time at the front to complete the book he and Sybil had planned so long before, and in 1915, *Dr. Syn: A Tale of the Romney Marsh* was published by the young and adventurous firm of Robert Holden (they also took early work by Claude Houghton and Australian fantasist Vernon Knowles).

Thorndike married Rosemary Dowson, a daughter of an actress, in 1918, resumed his acting career and was soon in demand as a leading man, though he was also involved in theatre management and directing. Amongst many major roles, he took both lead and character parts in Shakespeare productions, appeared in the English premiere of Ibsen's *Peer Gynt,* and was also in demand for modern plays. In film, he often portrayed characters much older than himself, including Dickens's miser Scrooge, and he could also be relied upon to provide what actors then called "a bit of the 'old'", in a different sense, meaning the grand, melodramatic style of Victorian theatre.

He also became an industrious writer, perhaps sometimes simply because he needed the money: not all his theatrical projects were a financial success. As well as his adventures and mysteries, amongst his miscellaneous books were a biography of Sybil, by then even better known and more adored than he was, and two guides to Shakespeare's country. But he remained best known as the creator of the Dr. Syn books, which are still celebrated in regular festivals in the Romney Marsh country today. Wonderful though they are, there's no doubt the Dr. Syn books have cast a long shadow over Thorndike's other work; it is high time the best of this had another chance to beguile readers, and *The Slype* is probably the book of his that has the strongest claim to be reread.

   Though he wrote no more books in his last twenty years, from 1950 onwards, Thorndike continued to work in the theatre and cinema, with a regular seasonal role, aptly enough, as Smee in *Peter Pan*, and a few last film appearances in cameo roles in the 1950s. Russell Thorndike died at his Norfolk home on 7 November, 1972, aged 87, after a colourful and somewhat hectic career. Sheridan Morley wrote affectionately of him that he "remained devoted to his wife, sister, and overacting, in approximately that order, across more than half a century of greasepaint touring," and he will always have a place in theatrical history. But it is likely that he will be remembered just as much as a fine, full-blooded teller of tales, as much a master of the "old" in his storytelling qualities as he was as an actor.

MARK VALENTINE

July 20, 2013

THE SLYPE

AFFECTIONATELY INSCRIBED

TO MY SISTER

SYBIL THORNDIKE

IN

MEMORY OF

MANY HAPPY YEARS SPENT

TOGETHER IN AN ANCIENT CITY

"A path of the vineyards, a wall being on this side, and a wall on that side . . . a narrow place, where there was no way to turn either to the right hand or to the left."

Numbers xxii. 24-26

SLYPE (from which we get the English "slip")
An Anglo-Saxon word meaning
"A narrow passage between buildings."

Webster's Dictionary

"A secret path, covered way or passage. A space very frequent in Abbeys, intervening between the transept and the entrance to the chapter-house, often called by the expressive name of the Slype."

New Oxford Dictionary

"The Slype was the passage which led to the cemetery, lying usually between the transept and chapter-house."

1865 *Ecclesiologist* xxv. 207

CONTENTS

THE SLYPE

CHAPTER I

DANIEL DYKE GOES DOWN TO DULLCHESTER

IF I have any diffidence in setting down the facts concerning the Mystery of Dullchester it is certainly through no lack of faith in the story. I have it from Detective-Inspector Macauley, that in all his experience at Scotland Yard, he had never a case showing more complications, more surprising occurrences, or a more unique solution. In our own times that a number of clerics and citizens, whose respectability mattered in a Precincts, should disappear from it, one after the other, into thin air, is surely astounding enough! But when the explanation is as astonishing, here is, I hope, a tale well worth the telling. However, since two of the principal actors in this drama are prominent men of letters, I am sufficiently modest to wish that one or the other had undertaken the story. As this seems impossible—the Dean of Dullchester pleading stress of work, and Mr. Dyke excusing himself as being too nearly connected with the affair, I take up my pen with more boldness on the assurance of their supervision, and go back to the day when Daniel Dyke re-visited his birthplace and accepted hospitality at Dullchester Deanery.

As first impressions are so important towards ultimate appreciation, I should strongly advise anyone pleasurably bent on visiting Dullchester, to approach it from the west, by way of St. Rood's, rather than from commercial Talkham which joins the Cathedral City on the east. Business people don't do this, because it means taking a slow train, for the expresses rush you through St. Rood's Station, show you little or no view of the famous river which divides the Kentish Men from the Men of Kent, spoil the glimpses of Dullchester Castle and Cathedral by placing them behind slummy back streets, and rattle you into crowded Talkham before you are aware that you have passed a Precincts, as picturesque, peaceful and proper as any city could desire. Daniel took a slow train because he knew all this. He also took a first-class ticket because he was in a mind to enjoy the journey to the full. After a long spell abroad, to be in Kent again was glorious. The very slowness of the train pleased him. He only wished it could be slower. There were so many landmarks to look to, so many familiar stations to stop at, and all bringing back well-remembered occasions when his parents had been alive and this part of the country had been his home.

About half-way on the journey—to be exact, just as the train was moving out of Arrowford Junction—a man ran along the platform, jumped on the footboard, opened the door of Daniel's compartment, stepped in and pulled the door to with a slam, as he sank into a corner seat, mopping his face with his sleeve and chuckling, "Near shave that!"

"Yes," laughed Daniel. "You cut it pretty fine."

"I always does," answered the newcomer. "It's my trade, you see. I cuts things fine for a living," and he whipped out a long pair of scissors, and began snicking them in the air as he hummed a quaint tune.

At first Daniel thought that his travelling companion must be an eccentric tailor, for the handkerchief pocket of his great coat was full of pairs of scissors, while the coat itself was covered with buttons of all sizes and descriptions. It was a long coat reaching to the ankles and much too heavy for that hot autumn afternoon. From the side pockets innumerable rolls of paper were sticking out, and on the outside of the scissor pocket was pinned a very startling silhouette cut in paper of a gibbet with a man hanging therefrom. As startling was the hat. A top hat, with paper patterns pasted round it. The man himself looked more the sailor than the tailor, for his smiling mahogany face was clean-shaven, brass rings adorned his ears, his wrists were tattooed, he wore fisherman's boots, and under his arm carried one of those knob-topped sticks called Penang Lawyers.

"He's a character, this," thought Daniel. "I must find out what he is."

The other was evidently as curious, for he suddenly rapped out, "Do you always travel First?"

Daniel smiled. "No. Do you?"

"Always when going Dullchester way," was the answer. "Has my reasons, believe me. Private reasons. So excuse me. Where are you for?"

"St. Rood's Station for Dullchester."

"Same here. Now exactly what might you be, Mister?"

Amused at such direct impertinence, Daniel promptly answered, "A man of Kent named Dyke. Born Dullchester thirty-five years ago. Left it fifteen years ago. Since when, been in most parts of the world."

"What doing?"

"Seeing places and faces and writing about them."

"Author, eh?"

"Well, yes. One lives in hopes."

"Then you've got money of your own. Of course. You're well turned out. That suit now. I likes it, and I knows. Been a gentleman's valet myself. You doubt that, eh? You looks at this button museum on my coat and thinks I has no taste. But in my profession one has to attract attention before beginning work. What's the good of all these buttons that don't do up? Nothing, except to make 'em look. I'd cut 'em all off if I had private means. Nice to have private means. I shall have 'em some day. At present it's a bit of a struggle, but I cuts my way along all right. Parents living?"

Daniel shook his head.

"Same here. Any kids?"

Daniel told him "No."

"Not married?"

"No. Are you?"

"Was, but she's dead. There was a kid. A boy. Staying long in Dullchester?"

"Don't know. Are you?"

"Don't know. All depends. Cathedral towns is good for the silly-wet business. Plenty of sky-lines."

"I see," nodded Daniel. "You cut silhouettes?"

"That's it, Mister. I'm known as the Paper Wizard. Cuts out anything in architecture from a full-blown Cathedral to a bathing machine. Anything in shipping from a battle cruiser to a swinging boat. And that's why I travels. Keeps my eye-lines fresh. Gives variety. Why, I've cut all the buildings of the world what dare to call 'emselves buildings. I've cut the flat-irons of America till they was ashamed of 'emselves, and the temples for the black maria-jars in India. The joss houses of China, the patogas of Burmah, the pyrawits of Egypt what was child's play, and as to mountains—why I've made a speciality in that line from the 'Immilayjars to old Ludgate 'Ill. Anything erected by Gawd or man, what can show me anything of a sky-line—I cuts 'em all. Blokes mugs too. Thousands of 'em from clergymen to criminals including Royalties, white, black and yellow. Been snicking my way up and down Kent lately. Fine county. Full of sillywets. Castles and what-nots. So you're going to Dullchester, are you? Well now, how's this from memory?" The Paper Wizard brought out a roll of paper, folded it in a peculiar manner and began to cut. He then doubled it over and cut again, blowing fragments away with his mouth. He continued doubling, folding and blowing until he held between the first finger and thumb of his left hand a thick paper wad. Trimming the edges of this with great dexterity, he said, "There we are then," and dropped the scissors into his pocket. Then shaking out the paper in the breeze that blew through the open window, he sang:—

> "I cuts you anything out I does,
> With a pair of scissors and a very little fuss."

The Paper was held out against the dark cushions of the carriage and Daniel beheld an exact reproduction of the City of Dullchester as viewed from St. Rood's bridge. "That's how I earns my bits of silver, sir," exclaimed the Wizard. "A decorative art. Very popular for friezing. You don't tire of it. It's simple." He folded the silhouette carefully, slipped it into an envelope which he produced from another pocket and handed it to Daniel saying, "There. I makes you a present of Dullchester."

After Daniel had expressed his thanks and pressed half-a-crown on the artist, he suggested that such an art must call for a great deal of practice.

"Ah. And that reminds me to practise now," nodded the Wizard. "There's this picture here"—and he touched the gibbet on his pocket. "I've got to practise cutting this as quick as lightning. I've reason for it. Private reason. That's why I'm going to Dullchester. Excuse me. Can't explain."

So for the remainder of the journey he snipped rapidly with his scissors, cutting scores of gibbets, and from each one the same little fat man was hanging. By the time the train screeched into the tunnel outside St. Rood's the floor was white with them. Then the Wizard was forgotten, for Daniel was piercing the darkness for the first view of Dullchester at the other end. Yes. Here it comes. The faint light growing on the thick smoke. A loud whistle and the tunnel opens. There they are: Castle, Cathedral, River and ships, and the voice of a porter calling out, "St. Rood's. Change here for Dullchester."

Daniel got out, nodded good-day to his companion, collected his luggage and sent it to the hotel by the Bull Bus. No. He wouldn't ride himself. Preferred to walk . . . and he strolled down into St. Rood's and made for the great bridge, beneath which the waters of the Kentish river sluggishly curl and lap, where the breeze blows down from meadowed valleys, turning the clumsy sails of old-fashioned windmills, filling the red and brown sails of laden barges, dispersing the clouds of smoke from the cement-works' chimneys, and bringing perfumes of seaweed drying on the muddy banks; a bridge, hot and glaring in the afternoon sun, but leading to the shade of the High Street on the further side. He sauntered to the middle of the bridge, leant on the balustrade and gazed down on the river. "I wonder how many people will remember me?" he asked himself. "Amongst those who matter in the Precincts to-day, are there any who mattered when my father was a parson here and I was born in Minor Canon Row?"

He looks along into the cool and narrow High Street, where the sun only manages to gild the golden full-rigged ship that serves for a weather-cock on the lofty pinnacle of the Town Hall. He sees again the great white clock that sticks out over the pavement from the walls of the Corn Exchange, and as its black hands point to half-past three, the sleepy bells from the old Cathedral ring out for Evensong. "I'll obey the bells. I'll go to the Precincts and see." But he gives one more look over the balustrade and sees something white floating out on the tide from the darkness of the bridge. It is a paper gibbet. He turns and looks at the other side of the bridge. Yes. There is the Paper Wizard, with his back turned towards him, looking at the water. Not wanting to be interrupted in his reverie, and not wishing to enter the city with such a conspicuous companion, he hurries on to the hotel, books a room, identifies his luggage, strolls out again into the High Street, and turning under a large gate-house, which separates a dilapidated churchyard from the shops, Daniel Dyke enters once more into Dullchester Precincts.

CHAPTER II

THE PRECINCTS

Now there was one person in the Precincts of Dullchester that really mattered. Mind you, there were lots of people that mattered. Let us describe them first.

Potter mattered. We begin with Potter because he was seen most in the Precincts. So much of the Cathedral work was carried on by Precincts folk in private. Not so Potter's. His work was all public. He required no book-lined study as the parsons did. He was not called to scratch his way through life with pens and ink. His study was a wheelbarrow, and with brooms and scraper he traced his record in the dust.

Potter was a jovial old humorist who swept up chestnut leaves outside the Cathedral and picked up dilapidated hymn-book leaves inside it. His face was like a russet apple, and it shone between white whiskers. You could not walk through the Precincts without encountering him upon the way. Little was done in the Cathedral circle without approbation from this sweeper of botanical and literary leaves. He was venerated by all, from the Dean to the tiniest choir-boy, his ready tongue had always the right word for the right person at the right time. When any of the clergy chanced upon him, you would hear the pass-word of the Precincts, "Ah, Potter, busy as usual?" and on the strength of that salutation he would wipe his brow with his dinner-cloth, sit himself down amongst the brooms in his barrow and fall a-wondering whatever the Precincts would do when the chestnut leaves were falling on his grave instead of round his brooms and he would be no more seen in the Precincts "a-pickin' of 'em up." When the bells rang for Matins and Evensong Potter left his barrow, descended into the Crypt and changed into his best suit. Over this he put a black gown with bobbles on it and became the second verger.

Styles was the Head Verger, with one foot in the grave and a chronic cough on his chest, contracted from a life spent in a dank Cathedral. Styles carried the silver poker before the Dean, ushered the Canon-in-residence to the lectern, and methodically tripped over the same piece of cocoanut matting every time he showed visitors round the Nave. Styles, who in the midst of daily Matins would wink encouragement at the officiating Minor Canon, as if he would say, "Findin' it dull? So am I. But cheer up. It ain't Litany Day, thank God, and it won't seem so long when you've finished with the Royal Family and the Parliament." Styles, who augmented his verger's salary by waiting at the Deanery table—Styles mattered.

Of course the Dean mattered. If he hadn't mattered to anyone else he would at least have mattered to those responsible for the compiling of *Crockford's Clerical Directory*, for they have a great deal to say about him. His name was Jonathan Jarndyce Jerome: Dean Jerome, D.D., a mighty man in every way. Apart from his breeding roses and pigs, and being an ardent collector of mechanical toys—of which Crockford makes no mention whatever—you will learn, if you take the trouble to run around to the nearest parson's house and borrow a Crockford, that he has resided in the course of his ministry in four Curacies, five Vicarages, one Archdeaconry, one Rural Deanery, and one genuine Deanery. The analytical mind will therefore have jumped to the conclusion that Dean Jerome is an authority on moving house, dilapidations and fixtures, to say nothing of the complications contained in Queen Anne's Bounty, glebe fields and tithes.

Since Crockford does not describe the character and appearance of this worthy Clerk in Holy Orders, let me.

The hair on Dean Jerome's head was grey. A veritable mane on a head like a lion. In stature a Colossus: big boned rather than fat.

A great bronzed face, clean-shaven, that looked the more rugged by being framed in such a mass of grey hair, the pride of the local barber, who knew exactly what to do with it to please the ladies of the Precincts. He had the kindest, cleverest eyes, with crows' feet that twinkled in their corners. His heart was that of a comedian. He enjoyed the hearing of a good story just as much as the telling of one. A voice of thunder, but in such perfect control that it could "roar at you as gently as any sucking dove," and yet be heard in the remotest corner of the Cathedral. This voice, backed by a striking personality and carefully studied oratory, made his eloquent sermons unparalleled, so that he could draw from his congregation laughter without offence or pocket handkerchiefs without disguise.

Dean Jerome rarely left the Precincts, save when he charitably occupied a neighbouring pulpit, but divided his time between his library, where he rehearsed his sermons to the furniture, his Cathedral, where he delivered them to his great following, his rose-gardens, where he invented new blooms and named them after his friends, his styes, where he petted his stock, and the polished floor of his large hall, where the rugs would be kicked aside to afford a happy manœuvring ground for the rapid revolutions and eccentric gyrations of wound-up mechanical toys.

It was a lesson to any nursery to watch the Dean, crawling on all four after these playthings, as they gambolled and whirled around the floor. He would have them all out together, thirty, forty, or fifty at once, and the great idea was to get as many as possible wound up at the same time, and he would scream with panic when a motor car was going to bump into a servant-girl sweeping with a little broom, and roar with delight when all twelve dancing fiddlers were moving together and playing the same tune in practically the same tempo but in very different keys. This String Band, as he called it, was the star turn of his collection.

His love of pigs had developed quite by chance, or as Mrs. Jerome put it, quite by mischance. A farmer of miserly reputation had been so moved by one of the Dean's sermons that he had sent him a litter of six. An awkward gift, but not to be refused under the circumstances. So styes were set up in a remote corner, and the pigs prospered, increasing exceedingly. Pigs are an economical proposition, but the Dean did not bother about that. He found them comical. He grew to like them, and when it became necessary to turn any of them into pork, he grew very sad. He trained them to chase him round the drive, and if one of the squealing porkers succeeded in pushing his clammy snout against the agile decanal gaiters, that athletic one was given extra rations from the pig-buckets. To a stranger an odd sight indeed to meet a Dean, renowned for scholarship and learning, running a mad Marathon against a herd of swine.

The poetical side of the Dean came out when he was amongst his roses. He tended the trees carefully, grafted and pruned them gingerly, and when in doubt left them to his wife while he made love to her and held the scissors. The large garden was attractive, antique and rambling, flanked by the grey walls which in former centuries had stood for the outward defences of the Castle, and there were other walls of red brick, mellow with moss, that ran to meet the grey ones, and all the chinks and crannies were gay with wallflowers, for every jutty, frieze and buttress had been commandeered by these garden sentinels for coigns of vantage. And the ivy ran its great scaling ladders here and there over the top, whilst below were ranked the giant guards of the flower world, the gaily uniformed hollyhocks. And from bloom to bloom the monotonous hum of the red-hipped bumble bee carried the news of the garden. On the red walls were peaches, pears and apricots, and these in such profusion and fine condition that the Dean had not the heart to move them to make room for more rose trees, "For after all," he would say, "it's jolly having fruit amongst the roses, for one can eat the fruit and tend the flowers at the same time, and you know, in an orchard where there is nothing but fruit I become a dreadful schoolboy again and make a terrible pig of myself, but when the roses are watching, I always mind my manners."

So if the reader has taken into consideration half of these particulars, he will not be surprised to hear that in this ancient Precincts the Dean mattered.

Then there was Norris.

Although he did not live in the Precincts, but some yards out of the Precincts, Norris was always in the Precincts, and Norris mattered, for he kept the Old Curiosity Shop in the High Street, printed the local newspaper once a week, and as a side-line wrote books about Dullchester Castle. When any Precincts folk went into Norris's shop to buy a pewter plate, a blunderbuss, a coffee-pot or candlestick, not only did the floor shake under them by reason of the printing press in the cellar, but the antique when purchased and taken home would carry with it an overwhelming reek of printer's ink. A learned ancient smell, well adapted to learned ancient noses that hovered in antiquated corners over venerable books. And a smell that proved the antique genuine, for no fakes came out of Norris's. Norris had a very sweet-looking Mrs. Norris for a wife. She was gentleness itself, and only got excited when a customer asked the price of an antique. She never knew, but would seize the article in question, rush into the print-room, push it under her learned husband's nose, and cry, "How much?" If it were a blunderbuss, a poisoned arrow or a fowling piece, Norris would look alarmed and say, "Careful, dear; thirteen and three." He always quoted odd prices, giving customers full value with the minimum of profit for himself.

And so, by reason of his large stock of weapons, his unlimited supply of brass, his ungovernable love of old china, his versatile achievements with bric-à-brac, and his educational novels on Dullchester Castle, which teemed with romance and historical data from cover to cover, it is small wonder that Norris mattered.

Another person who did not live in the Precincts, but was always in and out of the Precincts, was Miss Tackle, who associated herself with bees, sold honey to the Minor Canons' wives, and attended all the services at Cathedral in a large hat fitted with green anti-bee netting. From the hives to Cathedral, from Cathedral to the hives, with no time to change her hat, was Miss Tackle's mode of life. She took a great interest in the clergy, and a Minor Canon had only to affect a hoarseness in the Exhortation to find a gratuitous pot of honey waiting for him on his doorstep in Minor Canon Row. No doubt she attended Cathedral entirely on religious principles, but Mr. Styles thought otherwise and told Mr. Potter why he thought so. "She regards this old vault as a giant beehive, where she can listen to them lazy Minor Canons droning away in the distance, and the deep notes of the organ a-buzzing in the roof. She's bee mad, I tell you. Bee mad."

If one happened to meet Miss Tackle in the Precincts on her way to Cathedral or the hives, there was no point in saying, "How bonny you look," or "It seems to me that you want a holiday," because you could not see her face, for this same green veil was impenetrable and looked capable of withstanding an aerial torpedo, let alone a bee. So nobody ever knew Miss Tackle, but everybody knew the veil. It was a thing that had to be reckoned with; as much an institution in the Precincts as Potter's wheelbarrow, or the silver poker of Mr. Styles. No function was complete without it; no service in the Cathedral too insignificant for it. It attended not only the Churchings of Women, but the Special Addresses to Ordination Candidates and other services for Men Only, which the Dean considered tactless, the Minor Canons laughable, their wives unmaidenly, and Mr. Styles "nothing less than disgusting!" And so, Miss Tackle, or rather Miss Tackle's green veil, could not possibly create all this stir in the Precincts and not matter in it.

Canon Cable can certainly be chronicled as mattering. Learned Canon Cable, who knew so much of the dead languages that he not only said his prayers in them but thought in them, entirely neglected the vulgar tongue, and never said Good morning to anyone, because he had forgotten the English for it. Little Canon Cable, who was so blind that he could never see the Cathedral clock, and so deaf that he could never hear the Cathedral bells, and consequently always imagining himself late for service, ran three steps, walked two, and bumped into everybody in the Precincts. Withered Canon Cable, so wrapped up in the Ancients that he never acknowledged the Moderns, nor apologized when he bumped into them. Oh yes, Canon Cable, the mummied biblio-maniac—he mattered.

Then there was Arnold Watts, mattering partly because he was Chapter Clerk and had an office in the Precincts, but chiefly because he had been Mayor three times in succession. As Constable of the Castle he was privileged to wear a sword, which he did on state occasions, and people used to take it quite seriously, even when he fell over it. He lived in an Avenue named after one of his ancestors, who had been a great benefactor to the city, and whenever Potter met him in the Precincts, he would crack the same feeble old joke, "Well Mr. Watts, and what's doing in Watts

Avenue, what, what?" To which Mr. Watts would answer cheerily, "Ah, Potter. Busy as usual?" Mr. Watts was a portly man with a rubicund face, small eyes and a large black moustache. His ancestors had all been famous lawyers in Dullchester. Many had been Mayor, and quite a number Chapter Clerk, so that the present Mr. Watts did not consider it necessary to dress the part. He didn't look like a lawyer, even when he wore his silk gown and wig. Indeed then he looked exactly like a "super" in a town pageant. He took a great interest in Cathedral matters and played the double bass in Mr. Trillet's Amateur Orchestra.

Mr. Trillet was the Organist and a great composer of services. What he hadn't done with such material as the Te Deum and the Jubilate wasn't worth doing. He couldn't let them alone. Most people have heard them in Trillet in B Flat. He did a great deal for them there, as he made them easy enough to be popular with parish choirs. Also he did a lot for them in C Major, in a more ambitious way. But nothing could be compared to what he did for them in F. It marked an epoch in the History of the Canticles, and needed a Choir Festival and a Massed Band to do it justice. But Trillet did very well with it on the Cathedral organ, for during the Te Deum he did his best to hold himself in reserve, but before the choir had got to "never be confounded" he had found his feet as it were, and the whereabouts of his feet seemed to be all over the pedals, and his irritation at having to stop in order to give the Second Lesson a chance burst forth with pent-up fury released on the first chords of the Jubilate. "Oh be joyful," shouted the choir, and the gusty organist implied with some hurricane passages that if they weren't going to be joyful, he'd blow the whole congregation out of the Cathedral; and this rage for compulsory joyfulness increased with every verse, and reached such a musical maelstrom as the time accelerated into the Gloria, that at the conclusion of the service, Mr. Gony, the Chapter Architect, had to be called in to look to the fabric of the roof. A small man with a mincing walk, who throughout the week wore Sunday clothes. Insignificant he may look when walking to Cathedral, but get him on the organ seat, and you have either got to listen to him or go and live in St. Rood's. And so, because of the noise of his organ pipes, Mr. Trillet mattered.

Now if you look up Canon Beveridge in Crockford, you will not find that he was the most courtly cleric that ever sat in a choir-stall. But he was. And he had a large family of sons and daughters and stepsons and stepdaughters. And whenever the sons met the step-daughters they raised their hats and were courteous. And whenever the stepsons met the daughters they raised their hats and were courteous. In fact the brothers and sisters and stepbrothers and stepsisters vied with each other in friendly competition to be as courteous as the Canon. But that was quite impossible, for he was too courteous for words, and therefore his courtesy was such that it cannot be described. Crockford, after laying great stress upon the scholarship of Edward Beveridge, D.D., should have added that here was a fine type of English Gentleman whose goodness was reflected in his children. Between families and stepfamilies we so often find rivalry and dissension. Not so with the Beveridges. The joys of the stepsons were just as much the delight of the sons as the delights of the daughters were the joy of the stepdaughters. A jolly family, generally laughing and always happy, who saw the humour of the Precincts and could crack jokes about the Cathedral and their father without losing respect for either, the chief reason being that the saintly canon could always be the first to see a joke against himself. Though maintaining a lively interest in current events, modern literature and living people, he would allow nothing to eclipse in his mind the death of General Gordon, Law's Serious Call and the Prince Consort, though the latter was hotly rivalled by the Iron Duke, as witness the ponderous collection of Wellington steel engravings in his dining-room at Prebendal House, his Precincts residence. Therefore Canon Beveridge mattered because his courtesy was of the right breed, and he made the Precincts sweet with his presence.

The general opinion of the Archdeacon was that he didn't matter, because he was never there. He always had a cold and couldn't come here or go there, and when he hadn't got a cold he was recuperating from one, or building up his strength to tackle another, so "regretted his inability to attend." In fact the Archdeacon was a constant source of income to Doctor Rickit.

There were two doctors in the town. Dr. Rickit mattered; the other did not. Dr. Rickit attended the Cathedral clergy and was responsible for keeping the canons on their legs and the minor canons in voice. He had grey side whiskers cut close, and could bend over a sick-bed in an elegant fashion; owned a brougham and two top-hats, a grey one for the summer and a black one for the winter; was Conservative and Church of England—broad. Consequently he held the monopoly of patients in the Precincts.

Dr. Smith, possessing none of these attributes, damned himself with the Cathedral folk by attending Chapel, hob-nobbing with the defeated Labour Candidate, who was regarded as a Bolshevist, and by wearing a football trophy on his watch-chain. He also frequented skittle alleys, and won the majority of prizes at the local rifle range. Cathedral folks thanked God that the odious man was not an inhabitant of the Precincts, but of North Square, a dingy colony on the further side of the High Street. Miss Tackle, who unfortunately lived next door to him, said that he should not be allowed to put up a brass plate anywhere. His coarse face boasted a black moustache, waxed so sharply at the ends that the Precincts ladies declared it was a blessing the fellow was a bachelor, for had he a wife to kiss, she would find herself impaled upon the point like one of Fox's Martyrs. It was whispered amongst the spinsters that he had a horrible habit of winking at women, and a rumour was afloat that he was head over ears in love with Jane Jerome, the Dean's grand-daughter. Certain it was that whenever she came to stay in the Precincts he followed her about. He had not proposed. Of course not. How could he? A doctor who attended nobody in the Precincts, nobody in Talkham Dockyard, and nobody in the Officers' Quarters facing the military lines; whose only patients were a few second-rate tradespeople, and Nonconformists at that; a doctor who was not known to the élite of Dullchester, and yet dared to set up a plate in rivalry to their own Rickit—how could such a one think of pretty Jane Jerome? The fair recipient of this undeclared and undesirable passion scouted any idea of his admiration. She said it was idle gossip; but for all that whenever she saw him she found some excuse to hurry away in another direction, which was unlike her behaviour to anyone else, for Jane was talkative and friendly, and as catholic in her choice of acquaintances as the Dean himself.

Jane Jerome spent her holidays at the Deanery. Since her mother's death she had looked upon it as her home, for her father, the

Dean's son, was a Captain in the Navy and stationed in China. But a Precincts life not satisfying her, she had found herself a job after her own heart. Inheriting her father's love of ships, she had gone to live on Dingy Ness, a wind-swept, sea-battered promontory of the Romney Marshes. By the purchase of a good motor van which she could drive herself, and the price of a trawler which she soon learnt to handle, she acquired a working partnership with an old fisherman named Jubb, and so successful were they that in a year they had bought up every tub and hand on the beach, and those who had at first resented her as a rival were pleased to work for her when they found that they could earn more money than they had ever dreamt of as independent owners. The firm of Jerome and Jubb thrived quickly, for the motor van was always first at the market. Of course there were Precincts folk who didn't approve. "Was it ladylike to sell fish?" But the Dean silenced that argument by saying, "If the fish trade were good enough for Zebedee's sons, it's good enough for my grand-daughter. Girls will have professions these days, and why not fish? If Miss Tackle can keep bees and sell honey, why can't Jane deal with dabs?"

So because the head on Jane's shoulders was pretty as well as business-like, she mattered to the Precincts. Besides she was the Dean's grand-daughter.

The Minor Canons mattered very much to the choir-boys, for the Minor Canons set the pace of the services, could hang the thing up no end, if they had a spite against the boys, by dragging the long prayers, by getting flat in the Responses (when Mr. Trillet, not being able to punch the Minor Canon's head, would punch theirs instead), and by shoving in unnecessary bits, like the prayers for Ember Days, whereas if they hadn't mentioned them, nobody would have been any the wiser.

Minor Canon Quaver was Precentor and honorary secretary to the Madrigal Society, where he was immensely popular amongst the Sopranos, the Mezzos and Contraltos. He hummed in the Precincts more than all the lay-clerks put together, and every morning sang the Hallelujah Chorus in his bath.

In order to acquire "absolute pitch," he attached himself to a tuning-fork which lived in a red leather case in his side pocket. This would be produced and set humming upon every bit of furniture he encountered, and was rather more convenient than the silver pitch pipe which lived in his waistcoat pocket, for this instrument, having no red leather case, would fill itself with dust from the Minor Canon's pocket, and when the said Minor Canon drew in his breath to test a note, his throat would become a vacuum-cleaner and be put out of action for the next half hour.

Minor Canon Dossal was not so musical, and sucked eucalyptus lozenges instead of a pitch pipe. If you heard Mr. Dossal singing and then looked at him, you received rather a shock, for the voice was alto, the voice of a Cherub, while the man was a species of Zulu. A fat man, with a crop of woolly black hair, dark eyes and a yellow complexion. Admirably suited had he been Bishop of Mashonaland, but something out of place in Dullchester. As Sacrist he superintended a voluntary band of ladies who cleaned the altar vessels and set up the flowers.

On the vexed question of voice-production the Minor Canons nearly came to blows, for while Mr. Quaver maintained the only method to be "nasal resonance and placing it forward," Mr. Dossal was positive that "open vibration and striking it back" was the true singing.

So these two clerics also mattered in the Precincts of Dullchester. Mr. McCarbre mattered in that he had restored the Cathedral—that is to say, his money had done so, for he was not an architect, but a wealthy invalid. Finding himself growing older and the more liable to general debility, he had become uneasy about the sort of reception he was going to get in the next world. Naturally he wanted a comfortable one, but was afraid he wouldn't get it because of his past life which he seemed to review as terribly vicious. So he had come to Dullchester, had taken a house in the sacred Precincts, where he had shut himself up, admitting only two visitors, Doctor Rickit and the Dean. To the former he had paid stiff fees to look after his physical health, and to the latter he delivered extraordinary sums for the Chapter treasury, in order that the Doctor of Divinity might use his influence for the comfort of his spiritual health.

"Come along then, my dear sir," the Dean had said. "Let us hear the worst that you've done, and I daresay we shall be able to find you some rest and comfort."

When McCarbre had recounted his past life, and had valiantly tried to exaggerate a heap of little faults and failings into crimes, the Dean, thinking that his penitent was making rather a fuss about nothing, burst out heartily, "Upon my soul, I don't see what you are getting agitated about. If you make such a 'to-do' over your little shortcomings, what would you do if you were possessed of mine? We should have to put you in a padded cell."

McCarbre was a thick-set little man. He had a very short neck, so short that he seemed to have no neck at all, for what there must have been was hidden by a scrubby black beard. Before he spoke, he looked as if he were about to burst, and his words were gnashed through clenched teeth with a ferocity only surpassed by the humility of his utterances. When Sergeant Wurren of Dullchester Police first set eyes on him, he said to himself, "That man's a criminal." When the Dean first heard him talk, he said to himself, "This man's a saint." But Saint or Devil, there was no doubt about one thing—he was most peculiar.

And now having catalogued all those who mattered in the Precincts, we will introduce the one who really mattered. He was known as Boyce's Boy. A queer quizzical little urchin. When wearing an expression of injured innocence, which he invariably did when he was in the wrong, he looked twelve years old, but when he chuckled at anyone's discomfiture he was an old devil of seventy. In reality he may have been anything between twelve and seventeen. He was called Boyce's Boy because in his official capacity he ran errands from Boyce's shop, a greengrocer's establishment with one window devoted to delicate fruits convalescing themselves in baskets filled with cotton-wool; a fine old timbered house, built at the corner of an alley-way that ran up into the Precincts, and with a shop front on the High Street, facing the Guildhall.

Shady on the hottest day, the sensitive productions in Boyce's always looked cool and tempting, and following the doctrine that the people should pay for falling into temptation, the sagacious Boyce put exorbitant prices on his fruit baskets, which the public paid because it was the best greengrocer's in the town, just as Boyce was the best bass in the Cathedral choir, where he regularly shook all nations in long Handel runs, to the spiritual edification of the Canons' wives, and the perpetual terror of the choir-boys.

Unless you heard it for yourself, you could never believe how Boyce would shake things. He did it so thoroughly, and in order that there should be no shadow of a doubt as to what he was shaking, he would mention his targets by name. If the Lord really shook the Heavens, the Earth, the Sea, the Dry Lands, and all Nations, as Boyce led one to suppose, well—one can only hope that these delightful objects had the gumption to hang on tight.

Boyce's Boy was as shady as Boyce's shop. Precincts folk were glad that the Guildhall was also the Police Station, for being opposite Boyce's shop they liked to think that the Police could keep an eye on Boyce's Boy. As a matter of fact Boyce's Boy spent most of his time keeping an eye on the Police. The Sergeant used to get most uncomfortable when he sat writing in the window of his office, making notes about criminals, for Boyce's Boy would sit himself down on Boyce's front step and make notes about him. But Sergeant Wurren did his best to conceal his annoyance, for there were too many rumours about Boyce's Boy. Wild stories of people who had tackled Boyce's Boy and got the worst of him. But in an old-fashioned place like Dullchester things do get exaggerated, and the cronies who frequented Cathedral seemed to have nothing better to do than to foregather in the Precincts and discuss the latest exploits of the young rogue.

Mrs. Norris was honest enough to confess that she was downright afraid of him, for he would flatten his nose against the window of the Curiosity Shop till she couldn't see any resemblance to a nose, and then with rolling eyes he would suddenly stare at the little fat blunderbuss in the window which nobody would buy and then at Mrs. Norris until she felt that she must either scream or take the weapon out of the window and perhaps lose a good offer for it from a person with a taste for blunderbusses. However, she generally took that risk, and hooked the weapon on the wall behind the counter, when Boyce's Boy would stand on tiptoe and flatten his nose sideways as much as to say, "I see where you've put it. Don't try to deceive me." And there he would stop until Mrs. Norris would run to the print-room and call her husband "for to drive away that horrid boy," but by the time Norris had reached the pavement, there was no sign of Boyce's Boy in the High Street. He was one too many for Norris.

Canon Beveridge had once spoken to him in the Precincts, inquiring with great courtesy how he found himself that fine day. Boyce's Boy looked at him, and then looked away, with the air of one who could not be bothered to answer anything so silly, and when the kindly Canon, with the sweetest intention, repeated his question, Boyce's Boy called to Jim Stalk, the butcher's boy, who was passing, "'Ere, cat's-meat, want to see an old cove what's gone dots upstairs?" Courtesy cut no ice with him. He would not allow himself to be influenced by civility. But the Canon would not have courtesy hindered by rebuff, so he tried again with, "I think it's going to blow up for rain, don't you?"

Boyce's Boy answered, "I'm sure I don't know what it's goin' to blow up for. Ain't thought about it. But it wouldn't do the town no 'arm to blow up a stray Canon or two, I'm thinkin', or failin' that, if it cared to blow along a stray lunatic asylum it might come in useful."

It was therefore not to be wondered at that Canon Beveridge gave him up as a very bad job, and when next he met Boyce's Boy he pretended not to see him.

The sayings and the doings of Boyce's Boy monopolized the conversation of Dullchester tea-tables, and although Sergeant Wurren stated that the boy's importance was grossly exaggerated, he owned to himself that there were many points in his connection which he himself failed to understand.

In the first place, what was the boy doing in Dullchester? He did not belong to that city, for if he did, who, what and where were his parents? Nobody seemed to know. It was all very well for Sergeant Wurren to criticize the Precincts for taking more stock of Boyce's Boy than was warrantable, but he had fallen into the general spell to the extent of making careful inquiries upon this absorbing subject, and when all was said and done he had not arrived at any conclusion other than these generally accepted facts:

That he was employed by Mr. Boyce to run errands.

That until recently he had slept in a disused knife-house behind Boyce's shop.

That recently he had been known to sleep in a hammock which he had slung up in Potter's tool-shed in the Precincts.

That he was supposed to be paying Potter for this privilege, but that great secrecy was maintained by both parties in this transaction, as it was a moot point whether Potter had any right to sublet Dean and Chapter property, even though that property were nothing but a tool-shed, sadly dilapidated, in the corner of an ancient burial-patch.

That he was conducting negotiations with the proprietor of that Bull Hotel for renting a disused stable that jutted an impertinent end into the Precincts.

That he was obviously in receipt of more money than Boyce paid him for errands, as he was paying money regularly into the Post Office Savings Bank and never drawing any out.

That this money was entered in the name of Boyce's Boy.

That amongst other errand-boys of the town he reigned supreme, for even Jim Stalk, who was a fine upstanding ferocious young giant, did all he could to keep on good terms with him.

So Sergeant Wurren watched the mysterious suspect from the window of the Police Station, and although cats would spit at him and High Street dogs growl when he amused himself by shooting unripe gooseberries at them from a catapult, the animal world followed mankind and gave Boyce's Boy as wide a berth as possible. He had a something about him.

Just as there were many people in the Precincts of Dullchester who mattered, but only one who really mattered, so amongst its buildings and enclosures, its nooks and its corners were there many that mattered but only one that really did.

The Cathedral mattered to the clergy, and to those members of the Established Church who dwelt within its purlieus.

The ruined Castle, with its walled gardens, mattered to the antiquarians, to the tourists, and the local nursemaids with prams and children, and to the thousands of pigeons and seabirds that nested in its walls.

The Gate-houses mattered, East, West, North, South; the Deanery, the Canon's Residence, the Minor Canon Row, and the King's Grammar School.

On the side of the Precincts opposite to the Castle Gardens another pleasure ground, enclosed and called "The Vines," mattered. A place where ancient Abbots had cultivated grapes from France. This one-time vineyard had been approached in olden days by a walled and narrow way, just as the vineyard through which Balaam rode on his ass with the Princess of Moab was approached by a walled path. This narrow way was now but a fifth of its original length, for generations of builders had pulled down its stones to erect houses in the Precincts, and what was left of those mighty walls was left perforce, as other mighty buildings abutted on them on either side.

Now this narrow passage—the fifty yards of it that remained—really mattered.

It was called the Slype—and it was haunted. A hooded woman—name, age and date unknown. A highwayman. Two duelists who had fought there and killed each other. A woman burnt there as a witch. A sexton who had sold his soul to the Devil and had eventually been claimed by his master in that sinister passage. Not to mention a couple of nuns, a lady-abbess and a monk. In more recent days there had been suicides within the Slype. A sailor, three gypsies and a circus clown. They haunted it too. Whether this uncongenial party ever met together and held Walpurgis Night no one could say, but certain it is that each of them had been seen severally at one time or another by Precincts folk.

Take any cynic who will not believe in ghosts and let him meditate alone in Dullchester Slype, and that foolish soul will wish he had not boasted.

Even in the daytime there is something fearsome about the place. To begin with, it is so entirely out of proportion, with its thirty-foot walls built six feet thick, and all to flank a passage through which it is difficult to walk two abreast. This alone creates in the normal mind a sense of the peculiar. The summer sun never penetrates to the bottom of the Slype, and by reason of its suicidal tendencies, the iron-studded oak doors at either end are locked by Styles or Potter after Evensong, so that anyone wishing to do away with himself after dark and desiring the Slype as a setting for his last act, is forced to scale a thirty-foot wall, or ask for the key.

Naturally the weird aloofness of the place has attracted happenings sinister and evil, and its reputation is feared in the Precincts. Nursemaids frighten their naughty charges with, "If you don't stop it, I'll lock you in the Slype"—a terrible threat when one real-

izes that the wickedest gargoyles in the Precincts look into it from
their lofty perches.

Approaching from the cheerful Vines down hill to Minor Canon
Row, you come to the top door of the Slype, let into the Deanery
wall. You open this and are surprised at the isolated gloom that lies
before you, culminating in thick darkness at the far end, where the
way descends by some twenty steps worn and broken, down into
a tunnel cut out of the solid wall, which at this point increases in
thickness to sixteen feet, and as this tunnel turns a corner in the
wall itself, the way is made the longer and the darker. When you
reach these steps, supposing that the bottom door is shut, which
is the usual practice, you cannot see your hand before your face.
It is pitch dark, and even if you know the steps and are acquainted
with the exact position of the handle of the door, you cannot
fail to feel for it in panic and find relief when you swing the old
door back and perceive the sunny patches on the lawn of Canon
Beveridge's tennis court. The opening of the bottom door is like
the awakening from a nightmare, so terrible is the passage.

CHAPTER III

THE AMAZING BEHAVIOUR OF MR. McCARBRE

THIS was the Precincts to which Daniel Dyke returned, and the
first person he met in it was the Dean, who no sooner recognized him as the son of an old colleague, than he hurried to the
Deanery, called for Catharine his wife, had the guest chamber prepared, and ordered Daniel's luggage to be sent round from the
Bull Hotel.

On hearing that Daniel had proposed staying a week, the Dean
showed great delight, crying out that he hoped some occasion
would detain him longer, and to this Mrs. Jerome added her hos-
pitable assent. Had they known what dreadful occasion would
necessitate Daniel's stay, they might have thought twice before
putting it in that phraseology.

The old-fashioned Deanery, a large house, antique and comfortable, was so delightful that Daniel stayed a fortnight, and then

announced over the breakfast table that he really would have to return to London, find rooms and settle down to work.

"My dear Catharine, what do you think of that?" exclaimed the Dean. "I always thought you, my love, the most selfish person in the universe, but this Daniel Dyke will give you a run for your money. My dear boy, you cannot be serious. Go back to London? And after all your professions of regard for us. Are you going to leave me to the tender mercies of that terrible woman opposite? Fancy putting me off my breakfast in this way. There. I cannot finish my scrambled egg"—pushing his plate away and rising—"and look"—pulling away his wife's plate, "my dear Catharine cannot finish hers. But look here, all joking apart," he laughed after restoring the plates, "you can't possibly leave us yet, as I'm sure you'll both agree, when I've read you a very exciting letter that I've received by this morning's post."

"It's Jane's writing," said Mrs. Jerome. "She's coming to see us? I hope she is."

The Dean put on his spectacles and propped the letter in question against the toast-rack.

"Yes, it's from Jane. And when Daniel has heard the special message which my grand-daughter entrusts me to give him, he will either abandon all hope of returning to London, or all claim to the title of English gentleman."

"MY DARLING GRANDPA"—(you perceive that she likes me.)

"Am coming up to Dullchester on business re Talkham Fish Market. Won't bore you with details. Arrive either to-morrow or next day. Will wire Holt's for cab. May have to stay, so please put up with me and put me up. Play on words not intended. No decent clothes, so don't ask people to dine. If you have, put 'em off or I shall meal in the kitchen. But you have to be so polite in the kitchen. Love to Granny and old Tackle. Your loving grand-daughter,

JANE.

"P.S.—I got yours. Fancy Daniel Dyke being at the Deanery. How killing. What's he like? Ask him if he remembers bowling a hoop round my pram in the Castle Gardens and telling me that I should be terribly freckled when I grew up, 'worse than the smallpox.' Also tell him not to dare to go till he's seen me. I want to show him what a true prophet he was. Is Potter still busy as usual? My love to him. Also to Trillet in B Minor, the roses, pigs and toys.

"P.SS.—Has Boyce's Boy been convicted of murder yet? And if not, why not? Yours, J. J. J. of Jerome and Jubb, Dingy Ness."

"There now, Mister Dyke, and what do you make of that?"

"Why, sir," replied Daniel, "that as Miss Jane has done me the honour to remember me in all these years, I must do myself the honour and you the inconvenience of obeying her commands."

"Splendid!" laughed Mrs. Jerome.

Just then the front door bell gave vent to an ecclesiastical tinkle and the Dean was summoned to the study to interview Mr. James McCarbre.

A quarter of an hour later Daniel was introduced to this gentleman in the hall. Daniel shook him warmly by the hand and asked: "How are you, sir?" McCarbre winced with pain, withdrew his flabby hand, turned purple in the face, and hissed through his teeth: "So sweet of you to inquire, sir. Sadly and sickly, I fear. Sinking, some say. Anyhow, sir, there is no doubt I am seedy. But I am very, very pleased and very, very proud to meet any friend of his Reverence. Very, sir, indeed."

"Well, it's more than you look," thought Daniel, who was afraid that Mr. McCarbre, for all his peaceful overtures, was contemplating murder and sudden death.

"We are just going along to the Cathedral, my boy," said the Dean. "Mr. McCarbre has not seen the new Memorial Window, and he is the very man who should see it, as he paid for it. By the way, McCarbre, I hope you will be satisfied with it. My Committee, although unanimously declaring that the designs could not be better, expressed their regret that you would not examine them on approval, and by the way, they are passing you a vote of thanks for your munificence and also one to Mr. Burgoyne, the artist, who has so faithfully carried out his orders. The scaffolding has been removed from the inside of the Lady Chapel, so you will get a good view of the window. The outside scaffolding remains up till to-morrow, I believe, and the Bishop will consecrate your gift some time this month."

"Then that is all satisfactory?" asked Mr. McCarbre. "You are pleased?"

"Yes, indeed," replied the Dean. "Except for the fact that the work, being completed, will be difficult to alter if you are not pleased."

"My dear sir," exploded Mr. McCarbre, "what right have I to be pleased or not to be pleased? How can I criticize ecclesiastical sketches? When the Cathedral was restored at my expense, I hope I was not guilty of any suggestions? I don't remember making any. Isn't it enough for me to supply the funds? Why should I make suggestions? If *you* are pleased, I am more than satisfied. If I were a saint," added Mr. McCarbre, looking ferociously at the Dean, although he was endeavouring to convey his admiration for that gentleman, "why then, perhaps I might be called upon to criticize stained-glass windows. As it is, if I seem to be scanty in my praise of work that you have approved of and sanctioned, please attribute it to the fact that I am excessively seedy, sir."

By this time the three were walking down the Deanery Drive towards the Cathedral. Daniel suddenly heard somebody singing. It was a man's voice, but coming from the direction of the High Street—not from the Cathedral.

"I thought for the moment that Mr. Boyce was shaking a Handel run," he remarked, laughing.

"He wouldn't thank you for the thought," retorted the Dean. "Boyce, with all his faults as a greengrocer, and God knows their name is legion, has precious few in the art of singing. This noise reminds me of Quaver and Dossal demonstrating voice-production. Whatever can it be? See, there's quite a crowd."

Indeed, through the lofty palings that divided the Deanery Drive from the High Street could be seen a crowd of townspeople clustering round somebody who was apparently the singer of the song.

"Good gracious!" exclaimed the Dean, "it is astonishing what trifles will collect a crowd in this old town. It is a bad sign when people have so little to do. What is it, Daniel? Can you see? Perhaps we could all see if we step across the grass, clamber on to the coping-stone and hang on to the railings."

The Dean accordingly trotted across the grass, followed by Daniel and Mr. McCarbre.

"By Jove, I know who it is," cried Daniel, as the Dean was hauling himself up. "I've heard that song before."

> "I cuts cafedrals out I does
> Wiv a pair o' scissors and a werry little fuss."

"It's the Paper Wizard. He cuts paper patterns," and he thereupon recounted their meeting in the train.

At this Mr. McCarbre became peculiar. He seized Daniel's leg and pinched it. "Cuts *what*, did you say?"

Daniel looked down at Mr. McCarbre from the coping-stone. That gentleman looked more than ever as if he were going to have an apoplectic fit.

"If you don't mind, sir," said Daniel, wrenching his leg from the other's grasp, "but I got a Turkish bullet in my right calf, and so I have to object to people pulling my leg."

"Aren't you pulling *my* leg?" hissed Mr. McCarbre. "What do you mean by *cutting paper?*"

"I mean that this old chap in the crowd here cuts buildings and shapes out of paper—with scissors, you know. Climb up and have a look."

"I'm too sick a man, sir, to climb anywhere, and Dr. Rickit has warned me against standing on grass. I'm standing on it now, and I'm feeling very queer."

The Dean promptly jumped down and apologized, and the three hastily walked towards the Cathedral.

"Funny-looking chap in a long coat and a high hat, and he manipulates his scissors like an artist; and the tragedy of it is," added the Dean, "that I don't suppose he earns in a year half the income that Hogham the barber earns in a month, and both of them work with scissors."

"Cutting the hair of serious-minded men is more useful than cutting silly shapes out of paper," snarled Mr. McCarbre.

Daniel thought, "I wonder why this man McCarbre is driving himself into an apoplectic fit over nothing."

The Dean looked at Mr. McCarbre and thought, "Who on earth would imagine that this man is a saint? But he is a saint, because he goes to such pains to hide his halo."

They reached Deanery Gate and passed Potter's barrow of

brooms. Potter himself was having a heated argument with Styles in the North doorway. Boyce's Boy, with an empty basket over his arm, was smoking a cigarette in the shade of the Cathedral wall, and watching them.

"Ah, Potter, busy as usual?" remarked the Dean. "And what's the trouble with you?"

"The trouble, sir, was in my barrow, but now is in my hand, and I wants to know who put me in the way of putting it in my barrow. There's enough to put into the barrow without such foolery as this," and Mr. Potter held up a paper pattern. It was cut into the shape of a gibbet, and there was a little figure of a fat man hanging from it. In its way it was a triumph of workmanship. As Potter held it up the gentle breeze blew the little paper man backwards and forwards in a most realistic fashion, and Daniel could not help thinking that were Mr. McCarbre to be silhouetted on a scaffold, he could hardly expect a better likeness. Perhaps Mr. McCarbre thought the same, for he took the paper gibbet from Potter, scrunched it in his hand, dropped it, and then kicked it viciously down the drain at the corner of the pavement.

"It's a great shame that Mr. Potter should be so annoyed," he said. "The committer of such a nuisance should be handed over to the police. It's that cheap-jack in the High Street. I should give orders, Mr. Dean, that such characters are debarred from entering the Precincts."

"Is that bloke with the top-hat, long coat and scissors back again?" exclaimed Potter. "I ain't set eyes on him for a tidy time. He always litters paper in my Precincts. He's a suspicious one, he is. Styles, keep your eye on the Dean's plate-basket if he's around. Let the Dean put it under his own bed. The Paper Wizard wouldn't think twice when it come to plate-baskets. That's him right enough. He cut that gibbet, and I'd made up my mind to give that there rascal there a bit of the broomstick."

Everyone turned to look at the rascal indicated. But Boyce's Boy merely blew a cloud of smoke from his mouth, threw away his cigarette-end into the graveyard, and lit another. Potter couldn't unsettle Boyce's Boy.

Now, although the Dean was always amused at Boyce's Boy, he considered it impolitic to let him know it, so assuming a severity which he was far from feeling, he said, "My dear lad, if you smoke so many cigarettes, you will never grow to be a big man."

"Exactly why I smokes, so there!" responded Boyce's Boy. "I don't wish to be a big man. It's little 'uns what does things in this world. He's my fancy"—and Boyce's Boy pointed at Mr. McCarbre—"I lay he's done things in his life what you, Mr. Dean, would shrink from. He looks knowin' to me."

Mr. McCarbre, evidently not knowing what else to do, threw away his cigar and, followed by the Dean and Daniel, allowed himself to be piloted by Mr. Styles into the Cathedral. Boyce's Boy, grinning at Potter, threw away his newly-lighted cigarette and picked up the remains of Mr. McCarbre's cigar, pushed it into his mouth and sauntered off along the Precincts.

"Cigars, too," muttered Potter, sitting down in his barrow, and nodding to the Cathedral for want of any other old friend to be matey with at the moment. "Depend upon it, old fellow, that boy won't come to no good."

Although it is a debatable point whether Mr. Potter should have been so familiar as to address the Cathedral as old fellow, there can be no doubt that the Cathedral in question is old. Round the solid Norman pillars of the Nave hangs the mist of ages which the sun's rays, softened in clothes of colour by the stained glass, could never seem to disperse. Mr. McCarbre enjoyed the peace of it all. In this haven of sanctity he felt more hopeful about the next world. After all, sin and sanctity were only matters of proportion, for in this world wherever two or three are gathered together in the name of any god or no god, it has been found necessary for the most Mosaic gentleman of the party to draw up a list of rules and regulations, in order to prevent the community imposing on each other, and therefore sin and sanctity taken as a whole resolve themselves into unknown quantities, for what is perhaps right and proper on some remote reach of the Congo River will probably be termed immoral at Maidenhead. Thus reasoned Mr. McCarbre for his soul's edification as he walked past the recumbent figures of cold Abbots and stony Knights who reclined on clammy tombstones. These solemn ones were probably no more perfect in their days than Mr. McCarbre had been in his. They had lived in an age when murder and plunder were common talk, just as he lived in an

age when murderers and burglars were made adventurers in pic-
ture-papers. The crimes of these old saints were now forgotten by
their generous and whitewashing successors, and all because they
had given money to the monks to have their haloes advertised to
the generations to come. What the monks had done for them the
Dean could do for Mr. McCarbre. He had confessed everything to
the Dean and had received absolution. He had detailed his life most
carefully to that sympathetic sin-layer. He had omitted nothing of
importance except a certain three minutes of his life, and much as
he would have liked to have thrown the weight of those infernal
three minutes on to the Dean's responsibility, he had not dared, for
even Deans might have nightmare and talk in their sleep. Besides,
he had lost more than he had gained—so far, for he had not yet
realized one penny-piece from the three minutes' work. The terrible business had so preyed on his mind that he had expended
thousands on charity to make amends. Here was the proof of it. A
real Cathedral rendered safe for hundreds of years by his money.
Moreover, was he justified in considering himself responsible for
the work of those three minutes? It was all so long ago. A man's
body changes every seven years, they say. Very well, then, Mr.
McCarbre had changed at least four times since then, and it was
unjust that this one thing should spoil his life. In the peace of this
old Cathedral, as he walked with the Dean to view the memorial
window which his money had raised to the glory of fallen heroes
in the war, it was monstrous that the past should obliterate everything but those three damnable minutes. Voices from the tombs
whispered "murder" as he walked. The twelve famous abbots of
Dullchester, whose effigies he had paid for and who now stood in
their niches under the organ screen, ranged themselves into a jury
breathing "Guilty" against him as he passed, while the coloured
bust of an Elizabethan Watts was wearing the blackest of black
caps and seemed to be saying, "May the Lord have mercy on your
soul." It was useless to equip himself in argument with these, for
this judge, this jury, and this old court of dead bones were employ-
ing the most terrible of all methods of trial; they were calling upon
him to reconstruct the crime. Away went the solid Norman pillars
of Dullchester Nave, and in their place appeared the poles of a
Burmese tent. Away went the musty smell that crept up from the

crypt, and in its place the spicy scent of the Irrawaddy flats. Daniel saw that the Dean was raising the tapestry curtain that hung across the entrance to the Lady Chapel, and hurried forward to assist him, but Mr. McCarbre saw something quite different. His accusers were holding back a tent-flap and signing for him to enter. So Mr. McCarbre entered because he could not refuse. To refuse would be to proclaim his guilt to the pitiless jury behind him and that stony-eyed judge above.

The water-bottle on the credence table was the first thing that Mr. McCarbre noticed on entering what to the others was most certainly the Lady Chapel. The water looked yellow, for the sun was shining upon it through an amber-stained window, and yellow was the colour that he hoped yet feared to see.

The central figure in the memorial window, to which the Dean was pointing, represented a young officer in khaki lying dead upon a field-stretcher. The Dean was speaking: "I think the face of that dead soldier is the most beautiful thing in the Cathedral." Mr. McCarbre was still looking at the water-bottle. "Is he dead?" he whispered.

"Surely," answered the Dean, "there is no doubt about that. I have seldom seen death so beautifully expressed on a man's face."

Daniel, looking at Mr. McCarbre's face, thought he had never seen fear so vividly expressed on a man's face. His eyes were glassy. His teeth were clenched. His lips were twitching far apart, the upper lip drawn so high that it showed the red gums. Altogether his behaviour was singularly amazing. Had they known what was passing in Mr. McCarbre's mind they would have been more amazed, for Mr. McCarbre saw himself as a young man, a rich young man with a taste for entomology. He was exploring the Irrawaddy for certain insects, and young Henderson, who had six weeks' leave from his regiment, had accompanied him to replenish their larder with his gun. The two young men got on well together and would have continued to do so, had they not quarrelled over the quaint little manuscript book which Henderson had picked up in the native market at Penang. They had explored the pages of this MS. together. Henderson did not believe a word of its contents. McCarbre did. The book pointed the way to a famous treasure which had long ago been lost, and McCarbre was all for removing this in secret and going shares with Henderson. The young officer, although pooh-poohing anything so fantastic as a treasure-trove, insisted on the search being made openly, with the authority of the law to back them up. McCarbre, jealous of sharing the spoils with anyone else but Henderson, tried to get the MS. into his own possession. Henderson would not give it up, and here was Henderson dying of fever, with the book in his pocket. The stricken man was groaning in the tent. McCarbre was poisoning insects outside in the shade. His medicine-chest was lying open before him on the ground. Henderson's servant was asking for his master's medicine.

"Is that it, sir, in the bottle? One spoonful to two of water, ain't it?" But the man had picked up the insect poison, a yellow mixture which McCarbre was about to administer to one of his vicious little victims. McCarbre, thinking of the MS. book, made up his mind in one second. He nodded; and in three minutes Henderson was dead.

There were no dangerous questions asked, for Peterson of the Irrawaddy Navigation Co. had dined with McCarbre the night before in the camp, and had testified at Rangoon that young Henderson was dying of fever. The servant, Flagget was his name, put his master's body in the earth that night, and McCarbre put the MS. book in his own pocket. They stayed by the grave until the Rangoon boat came down, and McCarbre studied the MS. while Flagget amused himself by sitting on the pile of stones above his master's grave and cutting patterns out of some old magazines they had brought with them. McCarbre did not like Flagget. From the moment he had entered the tent to see Henderson lying dead, he had feared him, for Flagget pointed to the camp table, over which he had spilt some of the medicine, and there was the body of a large grasshopper lying dead.

"That there grasshopper is a lucky thing for me, ain't it?" he had said.

"Why so?" demanded young McCarbre.

"Because," leered Flagget, "when a poor man has a rich man's life in his hands, it means that the rich man has to make the poor man rich."

"Are you trying to blackmail me?" snapped young McCarbre.

"Blackmail's an ugly word," replied the servant, "but murder's a worse one."

From that moment Flagget attached himself to McCarbre, getting money out of him at every turn and irritating him with his incessant habit of cutting shapes out of paper. McCarbre gave him the slip once. It was at Rangoon. Flagget had a drinking bout and McCarbre got on to the Calcutta steamer. But as they were going up the Hooghli, McCarbre saw bits of cut paper blowing about the ship and perceived Flagget at his eternal pastime in the steerage. McCarbre hid in his cabin till they reached the landing-stage, and then would not go ashore till after dark. The quay looked deserted as he went down the gangway at midnight, but Flagget appeared from behind some barrels and followed him to his hotel. He stayed for weeks with him in Calcutta, and finally journeyed on with him to Bombay, giving out that he was McCarbre's servant, which McCarbre dared not deny, though he repeatedly tried to give him the slip. All the while, this unwelcome shadow cut patterns out of paper. Finally Fate favoured him, for Flagget had a fight with a man in a bar, was arrested and put in prison. McCarbre sailed for England immediately, and then went to America, where in the course of time he made a large fortune. Years later he came back to England, and settled in the retired Precincts of Dullchester. And here, it seemed, he was run to earth, for there was a man cutting paper in the High Street, a stone's throw from the Lady Chapel in which he was now standing. McCarbre shuddered; pressed his hand against his forehead, then drew it down over his face, at the same time looking from the water-bottle to the window. For a few seconds his eyes remained riveted upon the face of the dead soldier, then they appeared to start out of his head. With a peculiar reeling movement he took two paces forward, and leant against a chair for support. On the chair was a hassock and a hymn-book. McCarbre picked up the hymn-book and put it furtively into his breast pocket. This annoyed Mr. Styles beyond bounds, for he whispered to Daniel, "One might think as how he couldn't read, and 'Not to be Taken Away' is stamped large all over the cover, even more important than Hymns Hatche and Hem. Still, if he thieves under the Dean's nose, it's the Dean's look out." Although Daniel agreed with Mr. Styles that Mr. McCarbre's behaviour was rather odd, he excused him by saying that when a man pays several hundred pounds for a memorial window, the pocketing of a cheap hymn-book might well be winked at.

At this particular instant Mr. McCarbre turned away from the window with a shudder, and looked towards the curtains that marked the entrance to the Chapel. Then he uttered a scream that pierced the lofty arches of the Triforium, ran round the Nuns' Walk, echoed into Mr. Trillet's organ-pipes and sank at last through the dark stairway that led into the Crypt. As he screamed, he raised himself on tiptoes and then fell with a crash, unconscious, on the Chapel floor.

"God bless my soul!" cried the Dean, as he stooped down to raise McCarbre's head from the stone. "Give me that hassock, Daniel. Now, Styles, the water-bottle from the credence table."

While the Dean administered water to the stricken man, he bade Daniel and Styles respectively go for a doctor and a cab. Daniel, knowing the whereabouts of the cab-office, left the doctor to Styles and hurried from the Lady Chapel. Indeed, he went through the curtains that hung across the arch so speedily that he nearly fell over a man who was kneeling on the cocoanut matting on the further side. He muttered a hurried apology before he recognized the Paper Wizard. Mr. Styles, thinking that Daniel would reach the cab-office and return with horse, cabby and cab before he reached the doctor's, had hurried too, and as he invariably did trip over the cocoanut matting whenever he could, it was not very surprising that he fell flat over the unexpected worshipper on the other side of the curtain.

"Now what's all this nonsense?" he said, scrambling up on to his feet. "What do you mean by kneeling about like this in the Nave? Get up and out of it at once."

Although the occasion demanded haste, Daniel was horrified at the attitude of the Dean's verger, and at once remonstrated with him, pointing out that it was a pity more people did not avail themselves of a quiet Cathedral in which to meditate.

"Oh, yes; all very nice, I daresay," replied Mr. Styles. "But I ain't been verger here for forty years for nothing. Once let 'em start this kneeling-about business out of service hours, and where will it lead 'em? I knows. Independent bits of prayers all over the Nave, and they won't be satisfied then till you'll find 'em flopping down higgledy-piggledy all over the Chancel, and then I won't be responsible for the altar-plate; no, nor yet the poor-box neither."

"Old man took queer in there?" asked the Paper Wizard of Daniel. Mr. Styles, not quite accustomed to being ignored in this fashion, gave the Paper Wizard a sharp rap over the knuckles with his silver poker, exclaiming, "If you don't get out of this, you'll be took queer, I promise you."

"All right, old 'un," muttered the Paper Wizard. "I'm a-goin', and don't you be so free with that there magic wand of yours, or you'll find me snickin' about your knuckles with *my* stock-in-trade," and suiting the action to the word, he whipped his long scissors from his buttonhole and clacked them savagely up and down the verger's staff, which so flabbergasted Mr. Styles that he moved hurriedly away, mumbling something about "running for the doctor."

Daniel followed his example and left the Cathedral for the cab-office. But the Paper Wizard did not leave the Cathedral. He tiptoed back to the entrance of the Lady Chapel, and peeped carefully through the curtains.

Everyone familiar with Dullchester knows Holt's. Holt's is the cab-office situated on the further side of the High Street that is on the side furthest from the Cathedral. To reach Holt's, you leave the Cathedral from the North Transept door, pass Deanery Gate on your right hand and go down a cobbled alley-way which is flanked by the Post Office. You then cross the High Street and see a large window, which is darkened by a dingy-looking window-screen across which is written one word—Holt's—in large and respectable type. Holt's is eminently respectable. The cabs of Holt's have taken Precincts folk to churches, to parties, to concerts, to stations, and to hospitals for generations. These old-fashioned growlers, by dwelling so near the Cathedral and rumbling so close to it, have assumed a Cathedral atmosphere. You breathe the same air in a Holt's growler as you breathe in the Cathedral Crypt, and you sit upon wonderful plush seats that seem to have been upholstered from discarded dossel curtains. Holt's cabmen are known personally to every lady in the Precincts as sufficient chaperon for any young thing going to a party. It is no using asking a Holt's cabman to have a drink, for he would look at you as much as to say, "We never drink at Holt's." Holt's stables run down a slope behind the office, and the smell of straw and horses floats into the office itself. This office has more the appearance of a Bank than anything else, for it is filled with large desks as if it employed many clerks and cashiers, and there is a highly-polished brass rail running along the front of the counter to keep you from looking at the books. The books at Holt's are enormous, and there are many. What they are all for nobody quite gathers, but Miss Holt knows and enters names in them according to her own fancy. Boyce's Boy was of the opinion that if you were very popular with Miss Holt, she would enter your name in a dirty white vellum book which was as large as the Bible on the Cathedral lectern, and this theory has spread through the town, so that one left the office with disappointment if his order was copied into one of the brown calf volumes. The firm of Holt's consisted of Miss Holt. At least, that is all the firm that the citizens of Dullchester ever knew about. Miss Holt was the firm, and firm was just the word for her. To know Miss Holt was to love her, but to meet her suddenly in the office was to fear her. She gave you the uncomfortable impression that she was sizing you up in her mind and considering whether or no you were sufficiently solvent to order one of Holt's cabs. Yes, she was a capable business woman, and as Boyce's Boy remarked, she was the only nut in this old town that he had never cracked, though he hoped there would come a time. Miss Holt was not tall; but then Napoleon was not tall, and they say that Napoleon could frighten you when he liked. She was a handsome woman, with a florid complexion and brown hair strained back into a neat bun at the back. Her voice was deep, but not unpleasant, although Boyce's Boy described it as "three tones deeper than old Boyce when he rumbles and grumbles in the choir." This was the lady that surveyed Daniel Dyke as he entered the office.

"May I have a cab at once, please, at the Cathedral?"

Miss Holt raised her eyes and then her eyebrows, surveyed Daniel with a show of severity, and then resumed her writing in one of the brown calf books.

"I daresay you may," she said after a pause. "I don't see why you shouldn't. But you must wait."

Daniel remembered Miss Holt of old. Her cabs had taken him to many a jolly party in the Christmas holidays, and he fell to wondering at the little change that time had effected in this Dullchester lady. She was just the same. In fact, had not altered a bit. Neither had the picture of the first coach ever built by Holt's which hung over the clock above her head, and yet the chestnut horse and the dappled horse, the black horse and the lemon-coloured horse that were attached to that famous first coach that Holt's built had heard that clock go round a deal.

"You may remember me, Miss Holt," said Daniel. "I am Daniel Dyke, and I used to live in Minor Canon Row."

Without looking up, Miss Holt answered abruptly: "You wore sailor suits, sang a song one day at a bazaar, and always forgot to remove your hat when entering the Cathedral."

Daniel laughed. "You seem to remember the worst about me. I've been away for nearly twenty years. But I don't find the place much changed."

"Trams in the High Street," snapped Miss Holt, as she continued to write.

"Yes," said Daniel. "That's a pity."

"It doesn't matter much," replied Miss Holt. "Nobody takes 'em. What was that you said about wanting a cab? Date, time, address, style of conveyance and mileage, if you please." This last sentence rapped out like a word of command as the Napoleon of cabs moved to another book.

"I want it now. That is to say, as quickly as possible," urged Daniel. "Mr. McCarbre—you know him, I suppose?"

"Only officially," returned the lady. "Supply him with conveyances, but do not take tea with him. I am a spinster. He is a bachelor. I couldn't know him."

"Well, Mr. McCarbre," continued Daniel, "has been taken ill at the Cathedral and the Dean sent me. Shall I pay now?"

"No," retorted Miss Holt, as if the very mention of the Dean and payment in one sentence was abhorrent. "Where are you staying— I was going to say Master Dyke, but I suppose it's Mister now?"

When Miss Holt heard that he was staying at the Deanery she said, "Oh," and moved directly to the white vellum book. "Landau, victoria, brougham, or fly?"

"I don't think it matters so long as it's quick," replied Daniel. "They're all very much the same, aren't they?"

"Entirely different," said Miss Holt, banging her hand sharply upon a large brass push-bell that stood upon the desk.

"Hallo," replied the shrill voice of some invisible djinn within the four walls. Miss Holt unhooked a speaking-tube from the wall and replied, "Fly. Closed. Red plush. No luggage. Tipple. Cathedral."

"Is Tipple still with you?" asked Daniel.

"Tipple is still driving for Holt's," replied the lady.

"And Snelling?"

"Gone all to pieces. Drives a taxi-cab for Trace & Clockett's."

Daniel had touched a dangerous topic, for this was the rival vehicle firm. More up-to-date perhaps, but lacking the tradition of Holt's. They possessed no picture of their first coach, and their manager did not matter in the Precincts.

Daniel replied sympathetically, "That's bad."

"Is it?" answered Miss Holt. "Have a cachou?"

Daniel had forgotten all about cachous. In his wanderings and adventures he had never met such a thing since he left Dullchester, but he now vividly remembered that Miss Holt had always eaten them from a little paper bag upon her desk. He took one, and then said:

"I must get back to the Cathedral now, Miss Holt. I hope I shall see you again. You'll send that along, won't you?"

"If you mean the bill, I understand it's to be sent to the Deanery, but it can't be sent until it's made out."

"Quite right, Miss Holt; but I really meant the cab."

"They're washing the fly down now," replied the lady, as she returned to her brown calf book.

Daniel re-entered the Cathedral the way he had left it, by the North door. As he pressed down the iron latch behind him, he heard strange noises coming from the direction of the Lady Chapel. It is astonishing what an unnatural voice can do in an empty Cathedral. The place seems so tuned to solemnity in monotone and chords, that an unecclesiastical voice sounds not only all wrong but downright ugly. Therefore the unnatural screaming of Mr. McCarbre filled Daniel with more horror than the situation demanded, and he hurried across to the Lady Chapel. But for all his hurry the Paper Wizard did not hear him coming. He was still peeping through the curtains. Daniel came up behind him and stopped. The Paper Wizard stood in the shadow of the archway, with an expression of fiend-like glee on his face. Daniel looked over the man's shoulder and saw the Dean and Mr. Potter, who had been summoned meantime from the Precincts, bending over Mr. McCarbre, who seemed to be stark staring mad. His collar had been loosened, his tie was all awry, and his face diabolical, for his eyes were wide open and staring up at the memorial window. His screams echoed to the roof, and at each scream the Dean remarked, "God bless my soul! All right. All right," and at each scream the watcher at the curtains showed himself to be more delighted. Daniel took the Paper Wizard by the shoulder, demanding roughly what he saw that was so funny, and quickly entered the Chapel.

"He's very bad," said the Dean. "All right. All right. God bless my soul. Do hurry up the doctor."

Daniel ran back to the entrance, and saw the Paper Wizard going down the Nave. "Instead of laughing," he called out, "why don't you go for a doctor, you idiot?"

At that moment the West door banged and Styles came hobbling up the aisle, followed by Dr. Smith.

"Where is he?" asked that gentleman as he hurried after the verger. "In there, by the noise."

"Rickit was out on rounds," explained Mr. Styles to Daniel, "so we'll have to put up with *him*."

Dr. Smith went into the Lady Chapel. Just then Mr. Trillet entered the Cathedral, with a pile of Anthem-books under his arm and a string of choir-boys in his wake.

"Oh tra-la," said that brisk little man to Daniel. "What in the name of Sebastian Bach have you got in the Lady Chapel?"

"Old McCarbre in a fit. D.T.'s, I should think," remarked Styles.

"He's making enough noise about it," replied the organist.

"And if you've any respect for the Cathedral," went on Styles, "you'll go up to the organ-loft and drown him with the pipes as the Dean's a-trying to do with the water-bottle."

Another piercing scream came from the Chapel. Mr. Trillet hummed four notes and said, "A flat. I could teach him to sing."

"When was he taken like this?" asked Dr. Smith of the Dean.

"The moment he set eyes on his memorial window."

"Not very complimentary to the artist, whoever he is," laughed the doctor. "I don't see anything to have a fit about. It looks to me quite a good window."

"It is," replied the Dean. "The face of the dead soldier is one of the most beautiful bits of stained glass I've seen."

Mr. Trillet, who had gone upstairs to the organ, suddenly put his foot on a very bass pedal, and the deep note of the Tuba rolled out. This had an amazing effect upon Mr. McCarbre. He sprang to his feet and cried out, "It's the siren. By God, if I miss the steamer, I'm done!"

It was all so astonishing that nobody moved. The silence was intense, for Mr. Trillet, excessively alarmed at the effect of the Tuba stop, had bounded off the organ seat to look over the parapet. Daniel said afterwards that he didn't know how long they would have stood there had not Mr. McCarbre's terrified eyes glanced away from the window to the curtains at the entrance. There, in between the curtains, was the face of the Paper Wizard, who had returned again. Mr. McCarbre saw him, and his upper lip rose, showing his teeth like a mad animal. He staggered to a chair, which he seized by the back, and tried to swing it over his head. But the chair was joined to its row by a wooden stay, which is customary in churches. He wrenched at it to no purpose and then, with a scream of rage, seized a brass candlestick which stood on the harmonium and dashed at the curtains. Down went the Paper Wizard, with a cry and a sickening thud, and down went McCarbre on the top of him, striking at him frantically with the candlestick. Daniel flung himself on the madman's back, gripping his arms tightly, while the doctor secured them with a red rope that the Dean had promptly unhooked from the altar rails. Just then Boyce's Boy came round the corner of a monument and announced that one of Holt's growlers was awaitin'.

"Then in he goes and home with him," panted the Dean, who had sat himself down on McCarbre's legs. "And, gentlemen, you will please say nothing about this. There is no use in causing a scandal, and if this gentleman" (to the Paper Wizard) "will come home with me, I will see that he is attended to."

So Mr. McCarbre was lifted by Potter and Daniel and placed in the cab beside the doctor; and the Dean, after watching the cab depart round the corner of the Precincts, accompanied the Paper Wizard through Deanery Gate.

"Well, I'm dashed," said Mr. Trillet, sliding back on the organ seat and treading on some mysterious pedal that shot all the stops at once into the terrified faces of the choristers. "Now, boys, open your Elijahs and your mouths and all together, page ninety-two:

> "'Baal, we cry to thee,
> Baal, we cry to thee,
> Hear and ah ha ha ha hanswer us!'"

So the full organ roared, the choir-boys screamed, and Holt's cab jolted Mr. McCarbre to his house.

Now all this was evidently very unusual and puzzling to Mr. Potter, for he pushed his hat to the back of his head and mopped his brow with his dinner-cloth. This he continued to do until the cab stopped at Mr. McCarbre's front door. He then seemed to sum up the situation, for he said in something the tone of a head juryman, "I tell you what it is. I sees it as clear as daylight. This 'ere benefactor of ours, this 'ere peculiar old gent what gives so much money to our Cathedral, and has such a wonderful regard for his reverence the Dean, has gone, lock, stock and barrel, off his rocker."

"Hush," cautioned Dr. Smith in a whisper. "Our patient is coming-to."

"I hopes so, heartily," said Mr. Potter, "for I ain't very enthusiastic about carrying him upstairs. For although he's a little 'un, he's as thick-set as a buffalo and about as weighty as one of Canon Cable's sermons."

But Mr. Potter and Daniel did have to carry the stricken man upstairs, where they left him to the tender mercies of Dr. Smith and Mrs. Sarle, the housekeeper.

"Well," muttered Potter to Daniel, on the way downstairs, "I don't grudge doin' nothin' for nobody, but when he does come to up there on his bed, I hopes as how somebody tells him who took him there, for when you has dealings with a rich merchant like him, I don't suppose you or me will be too proud to take a tip from off him."

Somebody else was evidently thinking of tips, too, for Holt's cabman, Mr. Tipple, was waiting to know if that was all that was required of him, as he was nearly due at a job elsewhere.

"Well, if you're going for the London train, mate," volunteered Potter, looking at his watch, "you needn't worry, 'cos you've missed it." A vibration shook the house as he spoke. A dull roar was heard as of distant thunder, and hundreds of pigeons rose screaming from the Castle gardens opposite. "There you are," he continued, "that's the twelve o'clock gun from Talkham Fort, and my watch and chain says it's exactly to time."

"I ain't goin' to meet no London train," returned the cabby. "No, nor yet the Constantinople train, nor yet the Jerusalem express, nor the Bagdad special. In fact, I ain't goin' to meet no train at all, but a boat. The Dean's grand-daughter is what's on the boat, if you wants to know, and Holt's was wired to be on Dullchester Pier at noon, and it's noon now and Holt's ain't there."

Daniel thought this a very good piece of news, for he knew how eagerly the young lady was looked for at the Deanery, so he dismissed Mr. Tipple with half-a-crown and injunctions to emulate Jehu the Great and drive furiously. Down the Precincts, past North-gate and round to the right along the High Street went the cab, and shaking himself free of Potter, Daniel went in the opposite direction, and yet not opposite for far, for he turned at the top of the Precincts and strolled into the shady path that led back to the Castle and so, incidentally, to Dullchester Pier. As he went down the sharp incline on the further side of the Castle, he perceived the cab coming along the esplanade beneath, and at the same time a fishing trawler, that had been furiously tacking up the wide river against the wind, lowered her mast to get clear under Dullchester Bridge. And a stiff fight she had to make it, for the long oar whirled and skirled in her wake, and a firm hand was needed in the stern, but she got through at last, and up went the mast, and the rattle of the tackle ceased as the trawler shot across the muddy waters. Then back again she tacked and tacked again and then again, and at every tack her red-brown sail made nearer for the Pier.

CHAPTER IV

JANE COMES TO DULLCHESTER

DULLCHESTER PIER is very attractive because it is so very surprising. People who live in Dullchester invariably forget that there is such a thing as a pier in their midst. Although these very same citizens will go to the seaside and say amongst themselves, "What shall we do? Shall we go to the pier? I'll pay"; yet with a pier of their own to hand, and free gratis admission, they never go on it. If it is true that a prophet is not without honour save in his own country, the same thing may be said about piers, or, at any rate, of Dullchester pier. It is tucked away at the end of the esplanade, right under the Castle wall. It is as neglected as the swimming bath which lies to one side of it. A dismal tank, this swimming bath, which accommodates ladies on Mondays and Thursdays, and devotes its dirtier days to Gents Only; for the water is changed for Ladies' Days, and as Boyce's Boy once remarked, "What they do to it I don't know, but mind you, if you are fond of diving into pea-soup you'll find it to your liking, only you ain't allowed to tease the jelly-fish what you'll find there."

But although Boyce's Boy had a bad impression of the bath, he was mightily fond of the pier. "Here is a place," he would say, "for a feller to get right away from things. You forgets all your troubles on the pier; especially when the tide's up and water sparkles between the cracks of the boards; and you can get a rare splashing if you like, by going down the slippery iron steps and seeing the old river squirt itself up through the diamond-shaped holes. Then there's lifebuoys, what you can throw over the rails when no one's looking, and don't worry if they sinks, 'cos there's ropes attached. Oh, yes, for a fresh whiff of seaweed, dead dogs and tar, Dullchester Pier is the place."

As Daniel went down the Castle hill towards this institution, he wondered why he had forgotten its very existence. But then, there is the attraction of it. When you did see it, it surprised you because you hadn't expected to see it, for the simple reason that you had forgotten all about it.

Holt's cab had just reached the pier and was turning round preparatory to going back to the Deanery. Mr. Tipple was perhaps a little hurt to find Daniel there as soon as he, for he said, "Now why didn't you tell me you was a-coming? I could have saved you all that run."

"It's not very far," explained Daniel. "I came the short cut."

"But I got here first," grinned Mr. Tipple, resolved that Daniel should not boast that he had raced Holt's. "And I'd have been here minutes ago if one of them dilapidated trams hadn't lost itself in the narrow part of the High Street. Shall I come along and get the luggage?"

"Yes," said Daniel. "I expect we can manage it between us. Will the horse be all right?"

"Ah," replied Mr. Tipple doubtfully, "that I can't say. Miss Jerome don't bring much luggage as a rule. Generally it's one conveyance only, a sort of suit-case, so if you can manage that alone, I don't say as how I shouldn't be much relieved"—and Tipple looked nervously towards his sleepy horse, at the same time dropping his voice to a whisper—"for one never knows, with the Thunderer there. He has a trick of feeling lonesome when I leaves him, and once he feels lonesome, no matter where you wants him to go, or where you happen to be, he'll make no bones about it but will walk straight back to Holt's, and that's apt to give Miss Holt a turn, for she starts a-worritting as to what part of the country it might have been where I fell off the box."

"Well, then," said Daniel, smiling, "you stay on your box and look after the Thunderer, while I go and look after Miss Jane and her box," saying which, he sauntered down the pier. Just as he reached the railings at the far end, the little trawler was making her last tack. There were two fishermen in the stern, and both were in oilskins. One, an old fisherman whom, by his likeness to St. Peter, Daniel put down as Jubb, and the other a fair-haired girl, whom he knew to be Jane.

Jubb made a funnel of his hands and sang out, "Dullchester. Landing, Ahoy!"

Daniel glanced down the iron steps, expecting to see a watch-

man, but there was no one. Jubb was evidently warning the pier
that he was about to run into it, which accordingly he did with a
lusty bump.

"Steady on, you beauty," laughed Jane. "You ought to have
more respect for good timber and iron. I wonder you haven't sent
pier and all to the bottom."

"Not while you be on board, miss," chuckled Jubb. "It 'ud be a
sorry thing for me to introduce you to Davy Jones in a river. Tie
her up at the bows, and don't slip when you jumps."

Daniel at once descended the iron stairs to lend the girl a hand,
but this was unnecessary, for before he reached the water's level,
Jane had sprung ashore, with an attaché-case in one hand and the
bow-line in the other. As she made fast the rope, Daniel raised his
hat.

"Hallo," said Jane, looking up. "I know who you are. You're
Daniel Dyke, and—how absurd—you haven't altered a bit. Have
I?"

"You used to have freckles. I don't see them now," answered the
young man as they shook hands.

"No, they're gone, most of them," laughed the girl. "Here,
Jubb, give us the fish-basket, and come ashore."

As they walked along the pier towards the cab, Daniel took occasion to observe the girl more closely, although he was engrossed in
conversation with Jubb.

Jane Jerome was slim and fair, and she gave the impression of
being taller than she was because she carried herself well and had
a graceful, rhythmic walk. She had blue eyes, a retroussé nose,
and her female detractors gave her a large mouth, which, however, looked remarkably pleasant when she laughed and showed
her teeth. Her expression was honest and penetrating, which is a
look common to those who occupy their business in great waters.
Her hair was bobbed, golden and untidy, for she had pulled off her
sou'wester and there was a lively breeze blowing on the river. She
wore a red-brown jumper which might have been made out of
an old sail, a brown skirt and brown silk stockings which showed
off her ankles to perfection, and her shoes were brown, thick and
small. All this Daniel observed as he chatted with Jubb about fish.
The old fisherman would not be persuaded to enter the cab but

clambered aloft with Tipple, and consequently Daniel had the gratification of being alone with Jane in the cab. It is very strange what little things go to make up romance, but it seemed to the young man that the smell of Holt's cabs must always have been the essence of romance. He was marvellously happy, and although it never occurred to him to say to himself, "I am in love," yet he found himself thinking that he was a lucky dog to be going to stay under the same roof as this attractive creature by his side, and luckier still to be sitting so close to her in the cab. The ride to the Deanery was all too short, and Daniel wondered if he would ever sit so close to the girl again, for Holt's cabs had a delightful habit of squashing their passengers; and then there were so many amusing things to point to out of the window, with, "Oh, do you remember so-and-so happening there?" and "Look, there's Rhodes', the toy shop; there's Huntley's, the gun shop; and, oh, of course,—do look!—there's Boyce's." A minute later the Thunderer was jerked back from a trot into a crawl, for Deanery Arch was narrow and a menace to the axles.

"Oh, but look there," cried the girl, leaning across Daniel and pointing out of the window. "There's the most important thing of all."

"What's that?" said Daniel, who was more interested in the golden hair that was brushing against his face.

"Why, Boyce's Boy, of course!" laughed the girl, as she was jolted by the cobblestones back into the cab. "The little pig had his arm right down the drain!"

"Really?" answered Daniel, and he remembered the little paper figure of the gibbet which Mr. McCarbre had kicked into it half-an-hour before.

CHAPTER V

BOYCE'S BOY CHAMPIONS A LADY

MEANTIME Mr. McCarbre had been put to bed and had gone to sleep, as the result of a draught administered by Dr. Smith, while Mrs. Sarle the housekeeper, after providing the doctor with lunch in the sick-room, had been dispatched to the chemist's for further medicine. The draught which the doctor had administered resulted in giving the invalid a bad nightmare (if it is possible to have such a thing in the afternoon). The stricken man gibbered in his sleep, and looked more hideous than usual, and the doctor, who had promised the housekeeper to await her return, sat at the foot of the bed, listening to the most extraordinary ravings, mutterings and whimperings. But ere long he found himself becoming interested in what was said, so he drew out his pocket-book and made notes. And as he wrote he became more interested, and heartily prayed that Mrs. Sarle would be a long time at the chemist's.

In point of fact, that good lady, finding that the chemist required half-an-hour to compound the drugs, took her basket and herself along the High Street to purchase some fruit at Boyce's. It was the heavy time of afternoon, between three and four, when the shops pulled down their sun blinds and went to sleep; when by mutual consent the shopkeepers hid themselves in little rooms behind their counters to indulge in forty winks, feeling confident that the forty would not run into higher figures, as the Cathedral bells were bound to ring for Evensong. Yes, you can run steam railways into Dullchester; you can shake her narrow streets with motor-lorries and electric trams; but you cannot stop the old Cathedral bells any more than you can stop the cawing of the rooks, the cooing of the pigeons, or the excitable screams of the seagulls who pass the latest news of ships and shipping to their feathered friends ashore who have never seen the lower river where it meets the sea in deserts of mud and marsh.

Mrs. Sarle found the Precincts end of the High Street entirely deserted. Nobody else was walking there, and in the narrow street her footsteps echoed against the overhanging houses as if she were a regiment of foot, and the sun-blinds in their sleepy way filled themselves with what breeze they could conveniently gather, and snapped at her angrily for disturbing them. "Flip-Flap-Flop," they said; which ejaculations, translated into the vulgar tongue, obviously meant, "What right has *she* to go shopping at this hour, when nobody else is doing it, and when even the trams, ashamed of showing their emptiness to this select part of the town, give up this part of the town as a bad job, and don't come here?"

There was only one conveyance stirring, and that was the water-cart, which advertised itself in large letters as being the Corporation of the City of Dullchester. There was no mention of the Mayor, but if the driver with a wooden leg was meant to represent him, he was a very sleepy representative, for although he held the reins, he allowed the long-tailed mare to take him where she would, which appeared to be the very narrow stretch of the High Street which was always shady. Consequently the rest of the High Street was left like a glaring Sahara to bake itself in its own dust, and the Corporation cart, by making many processions over the same ground, turned the part of the street into a miniature Medway.

Mrs. Sarle gathered up her skirts and stood aside to let the water-cart get ahead, and then followed it to Boyce's. On the front step sat Boyce's Boy, with a notebook on his knee, an empty fruit basket on the pavement, and a catapult in his hand which he was fingering dangerously. His cap was pulled down over his left eye, which rendered his right eye the more ready for rapid fire. The objective towards which the right eye of Boyce's Boy was focussed was the water-cart, for he awoke the silence of the street with shouting, "Now, you old timber-legged camel driver, wake up. If that there four-legged six-humped dromedary with a wart on his nose gets much nearer and splashes my boots, what I cleaned last Thursday, I'll turn his wart to water and shiver the mizzenmast of your right leg."

The wooden leg in question pressed a lever and the full rage of the Corporation of the City of Dullchester gushed forth in a sound of many waters; but the miniature Niagaras seemed more attracted to Mrs. Sarle's stockings than to Boyce's Boy's boots, for they caught her from the knees to the ankles and rushed down both legs and filled both boots. That lady, trying to avoid the flood, stepped aside into Boyce's Boy basket and fell over on the pavement.

"All right, miss," chuckled Boyce's Boy. "I'll learn the Corporation Tank to mistake old ladies for Aunt Sallies outside my shop," and putting his hand into a handy basket of nuts that stood on the floor of the shop, the catapult twanged and the faithful nut struck the driver behind the left ear. He uttered a yell of pain and jumped up on his box, preparatory to descending and giving Boyce's Boy "what for," but Boyce's Boy, reloading his infernal machine with a hoary-headed old Brazil, twanged it straight at the mare's hind leg. The terrified animal immediately took fright, upset the driver into the tank at the back, and disappeared with the whole bag of tricks round the corner of the High Street into the sun.

Sergeant Wurren, who had witnessed the whole event from the office window of the Police Station, felt himself called upon in the name of the city to avenge the discomfiture of one of her paid officials, so seizing his truncheon, he ran to the door, crying, "Now, you young monkey, what do you mean by it, assaulting the Corporation's best water-cart?"

"Stop where you are now," shouted Boyce's Boy, without getting up, but in a tone of such authority that Sergeant Wurren obeyed. "You've seen as how I'm pretty deadly with the best Brazils; well then, don't you aggravate me to introduce your nut to another what's as hard," and without taking his eyes from the sergeant's, he reached behind him and took a cocoanut, which he balanced ominously in his hand.

"I'll have you up to-morrow before the Mayor," spluttered the sergeant.

"Oh, no, you won't," replied the urchin. "Not unless you wants me to call this pretty lady here as a witness. I'll lay you half-a-dozen best apples to your tin whistle that we would make the dirtiest story of the two. What'll the Mayor say when he hears how his water-cart has been squirting ladies' stockings in the High Street, and how his Sergeant of Police was laughing at it?"

"Wasn't laughing," said the sergeant.

"You was. I saw you," replied Boyce's Boy. "And now, lady, what can we do for you?" he asked sympathetically, ushering Mrs. Sarle into the shop, but pausing on the threshold to loose a final shaft at the policeman. "As for you, my man, any time you wants to intro-duce me to the Mayor, I shall be delighted. In the wrong end of my little orderbook here I haven't half got some notes about you. I'm thinking of selling the copyright to Mr. Norris for the local paper. It should fetch a bit, I'm thinking, and it won't half set the gossips' tongues a-waggin' either."

"You young scoundrel!" exclaimed the sergeant. "You shall hear from me!"

"Any time," answered Boyce's Boy airily. "And you shall have an answer by return of post," and he twanged his empty catapult at him. Sergeant Wurren rushed back to the office window and made some furious notes, while Boyce's Boy filled a large basket with delicate fruits and followed Mrs. Sarle's still squelching boots first to the chemist's and then to the Precincts, which were now vibrating with the echoes of Cathedral bells.

CHAPTER VI

CATHEDRAL BELLS

AT the first sound of the Cathedral bell, Mr. McCarbre, who for the last quarter of an hour had been tossing about under the bedclothes, peeped out of them, and nodding to Dr. Smith, asked him if he heard the bell.

"Certainly," replied the doctor, nodding back.

"That means 'Any more for the shore?'" explained the sleeper. "We've caught the boat by the skin of our teeth, and now it won't be many hours before we are safely there."

The doctor, who was still busily engaged in making notes, asked exactly where their destination was likely to be.

"Rangoon, you fool," replied the sleeper (for McCarbre was all this time talking in his sleep). "Where else should we be likely to go, idiot?"

Although Rangoon was just about the last place in the world that Dr. Smith was expecting to visit at that moment, he managed to conceal both his surprise at the news and his resentment at being called fool and idiot, and mentioning that he hoped they would get there safely, made a note of the fact in his loose-leaved diary.

Now loose-leaved diaries sometimes have a habit of showing that they are loose-leaved and going on the loose when not required to do so. As Dr. Smith wrote, he inadvertently touched a spring, which had the same effect upon his book as ever Ali Baba had upon the entrance to the Robber's Cave when he shouted "Open Sesame!" for the fastening flew open and pages of months and weeks mixed with pages of Post Office directions, orders to chemists, patients' addresses, and memoranda, fluttered in the breeze from the open window, jumped off their steel clasps, and flew all over the bedroom.

Although the doctor was exceedingly irritated at perceiving January mixing with December and November becoming sociable with May, not to mention patients' addresses pairing off with directions to Inland Revenue, and chemists' orders being matey with memoranda, his irritation paled before the unparalleled rage of Mr. McCarbre.

"You sneaking hound!" hissed that gentleman. "Isn't it enough that you hold my life in your hands? Ain't you satisfied with frightening and threatening? Or must you irritate me too? If you must cut paper with those infernal scissors of yours, for God's sake go on deck, where the bits and scraps will blow away to sea. Don't litter my cabin with your paper-peelings."

All of which gibberish Dr. Smith put down in his notebook, when the loose leaves had been collected and handcuffed once more with their steel rings.

The Cathedral bells were responsible for other inconveniences on this same afternoon. They took Minor Canon Dossal from his strip of garden to wash his dirty hands for service. They stopped Minor Canon Quaver playing clock-golf with one of Canon Beveridge's pretty daughters. They woke up numerous scholars in the Grammar School who were slumbering over their books, with the glad tidings that in another quarter of an hour a shriller bell would ring in the school hall and they would be free to repair either to the School House to roast chestnuts at their study fires, or to the Paddock to kick innumerable footballs at one wretched goalkeeper; or, if the waking student happened to be a day-boy, or "day-bug," as he was contemptuously called by the boarders, he could collect his home-work and run as fast as his legs would carry him over Dullchester Bridge to catch the four o'clock train home from St. Rood's. The bells also reminded the cook who "did" for Canon Cable in more ways than one, that it was time to go into her master's study and impress upon him that the bells were really ringing, though perhaps he was too deaf to hear them, and that the sooner he shook himself free of the dead languages the more chance there was of his being able to read the First Lesson in the vulgar tongue of Miss Tackle and the choir-boys. The bells also sent Mr. Potter from the Deanery garden to the vergers' cupboard in the Crypt, where he disguised himself in a black gaberdine with bobbles on it, and shouldered a silver wand only inferior to the silver wand borne by Mr. Styles, who had already gone to the Deanery in readiness to escort his reverence to the Cathedral.

In fact, during the half-hour that the bells rang, a great many people were reminded that it was necessary to repair at once to the Cathedral, but it was a curious fact that for twenty-five minutes none of them exactly did it, but dawdled about until the five-minutes bell went monotonously clanging all by itself, quicker and quicker, as if nervous at finding that his companions in the belfry were holding their tongues and leaving him to perform a solo.

And as the huge minute-hand on the Cathedral clock got nearer to the top of the hour's hill, so the bell went quicker and quicker, and many a quaint front door was opened and banged as quainter Precincts folk fled to the old building. The Minor Canons went running along, with their gowns blowing out like the wings of the rooks that flew over their heads; and the Canons, who robed at home and scurried through their back garden gates to the vestry door, were only restrained from following the example of the Minors through fear of tripping over their cassocks and dirtying their surplices. The Precincts seemed alive with hurrying lay clerks sucking lozenges and humming snatches of the anthem they were billed to perform; and driven like a flock of frightened geese before the Precentor went the choristers, clattering down into the bowels of the Crypt, where their surplices were hung in a large linen-cupboard that could hardly be expected to keep out so much damp.

Mr. Trillet just climbed into his organ-loft in time to introduce the theme of his voluntary as the clock struck four, and as it was necessary to keep the organ on the quiet side, in order that he could hear when the choir got into their places, down on their hassocks and up again on their feet, this voluntary was generally a tame affair, lacking the volume, punch and "go" of Trillet in his noisier and happier moments.

The Exhortation was intoned with that rapidity in which only Minor Canons excel, and after losing a whole tone in the Confession, which was made apparent to the whole congregation by Mr. Trillet sounding on the Tuba the note on which they started and should have finished, and saying quite audibly, "One tone; that's bad," the Psalms for the Day were worried through, and Canon Cable groped his way behind the silver poker to the lectern, where, putting on a large pair of horn spectacles and following line by line with his nose touching the print, he recounted to the exhausted choir-boys how Abram's name was changed to Abraham, and Sarai's to Sara, which the choir-boys thought was so slight a change that had the lady and gentleman in question never mentioned it, nobody would have been any the wiser.

Then followed Trillet in B Minor, and a fine impersonation of St. Paul by the Dean, whose rich voice woke everybody in the Cathedral and put them into a fit state to listen to that famous anthem, "Wesley's Wilderness," in which a fat falsetto "blossomed as the rose" in such a timid voice that Mr. Boyce, who was the next to get going, exhorted him in stentorian tones to "be strong and fear not," which covered the falsetto with confusion. Then, after a fiercely-moustachioed tenor had made a "lame man leap like a hart" and all in one line of recitative, the full choir let themselves go in a mad fugue in which every voice tumbled over every other voice, and the Decani side tried in vain to drown the Cantoris and only succeeded in being put out of the fray by Boyce, who, opening his mouth to the fullest extent, drowned the lot of them and defied Mr. Trillet to drown him, although that gentleman was pounding away with both feet at once, both hands and every one of the stops shooting in and out like buffers on a steam engine.

And as after the storm the hush, so after the fugue the quiet quartette, and the glad message that though life may be mad and loud and something hard even in a quiet Cathedral town, the day would come when "sorrow and sighing would flee away," but Mr. McCarbre, who came to his senses as the message floated through his open window, found no relief or comfort in it, for Dr. Smith was holding in his hand a little book which he had taken from a wooden case clasped with brass.

"What are you doing here—and with that?" cried McCarbre,

trying to get up; but Dr. Smith was one too many for him. He put the book down on a table at the foot of the bed and picked up a bottle marked "Chloroform." He took out the cork and saturated his handkerchief with the contents, crossed to the sick man and pressed it over his nose and mouth. McCarbre struggled, but soon lay still and became unconscious of the fact that the doctor had again picked up the little book and with greedy interest was continuing to read.

CHAPTER VII

BOYCE'S BOY OBTAINS A KEY

ONE of the many old shady lanes leading into Dullchester Precincts was known as Bony Hill. The name had nothing whatever to do with the great Bonaparte. In early Norman days Beaunais, a wealthy favourite of Odo, Bishop of Bayeux, had built a palace there, of which only the great walls remain, but as very few people knew of this, it had become the common but erroneous belief in Dullchester that the hill was called Bony because it was between two portions of the Cathedral churchyard. The house which McCarbre rented from the Dean and Chapter had been built in early Tudor days behind the great wall of the Beaunais palace, and was completely hidden by it. Indeed, the only indication of an abode beyond the lofty wall was the old oak doorway cut into it, closing tight against the pavement of the lane.

Mrs. Sarle reached this front door, which was nearly hidden by the ivy that drooped from the old wall, and having handed her basket to Boyce's Boy, rummaged in her purse for her latch-key. It seemed as if it would be necessary to possess a number of latch-keys to open this old door, which published its age to the Precincts in a history-book of keyholes. There was a great hole through which a very great key must at some period have been fitted to admit some great man through the little heavy door, when it served as postern to the Precincts defences. Then there was a little brass keyhole, like an inverted capital T, where a flat key had fitted into a flat slit and then been lifted up another slit, which raised a latch within. This keyhole was caked with congealed brass-polish, while the large one was choked with green paint and dust. In another part of this wonderful and keyholed door there was an ordinary keyhole, through which a long thin steel key must have fitted, and above that there was a neat but irritating brass circle of a Yale lock, which after a great deal of coaxing admitted the Yale key that Mrs. Sarle had been diving for in her purse. Having been condescending enough to admit the key and allow it to unlock the door, this lock utterly refused to release the key in order that it might be put back into the purse, so Mrs. Sarle lost her temper and ejaculated, "Dash the key!"

"Allow me," said Boyce's Boy, dumping both baskets on to the pavement, much to the peril of the medicine bottles.

"Bless the boy!" cried Mrs. Sarle. "I hope you haven't bust them bottles."

Boyce's Boy wrenched the key out of the door and picked up the fruit-basket, for Mrs. Sarle had already taken to her bosom the basket of medicines.

"I'll bring the fruit in, miss, and shut the door." Boyce's Boy had a particular reason for being polite.

"You're very kind—for a boy," replied the housekeeper, as she stepped into the passage and turned to put the key away. But Boyce's Boy, who had a peculiar need for that key, cried out, "Oh, miss, do look at them boots of yours. They're wringing. That's what they be. Wringing worse than them Cathedral bells. If you don't take 'em off and put your stockings in the oven and your tootsies on the hob, they'll about murder you, will them boots, and there's only me to take action against the water-cart and the Town Sergeant, which I would do, and win, though that ain't much compensation to you in your coffin."

Mrs. Sarle was so alarmed at this prospect that she forgot about the key, and headed straight through the hall to a green baize door, which led to the kitchen. Boyce's Boy closed the front door after him and followed her, carrying the fruit-basket. When he reached the kitchen, she was already unlacing her boots.

"Put that kettle on, boy, and you shall have a cup o' tea."

"Tea is just the thing for you, ma'am. You keep on a-sitting yourself down there, the whiles I get it ready."

Mrs. Sarle, who was a spinster, but called herself Missus to make her position in a bachelor's establishment the more permissible, taking pleasure in being thus waited on, took off her boots, changed her stockings and warmed her feet, while she directed Boyce's Boy where to find the various implements for tea.

"What more do we want?" asked the boy, performing a roll call of cups, saucers, teaspoons, caddy, knives, bread, butter, jam, sugar, plum cake, plain cake, hot water and milk. "Why, I knows. You don't tell me the drippin' wouldn't do you good. A friend of mine that was a doctor once said to me when he met me in a rainstorm, 'Boy,' he says, 'go home to tea, and if your mother's a good housekeeper she'll have some drippin'. Take some, and whenever you're drippin' again, take some more drippin', and continue the practice all through life.'" Dripping being a favourite relish of Boyce's Boy, he went this tactful way to find some, which he did, at Mrs. Sarle's direction, in a white pot on the larder shelf. The dripping was no sooner on the table than Boyce's Boy began cutting rounds of bread, two of which he impaled severally with the bread knife and the toasting fork, betting Mrs. Sarle that he'd race her "toasting" for tuppence.

Whether Mrs. Sarle would have taken him at his word or not will never be known, for at that moment the Cathedral bells ceased ringing for Evensong, and in the silence thus suddenly produced a shrill voice rang out, crying, "Shrimps!"

Now shrimps being another weakness of Boyce's Boy, as indeed they should be to every individual who lays claim to taste and relish, he exclaimed, "Shrimps? My eye! That's what you wants to follow drippin', miss. Another friend of mine, what was an army doctor, told me that the salt contained in one shrimp was enough to pickle a whole regiment on the march, and it stands to reason that if you be pickled, you can't catch cold. Shrimps, is it, miss?"

"I'll find a sixpence," said Mrs. Sarle, picking up her purse. Boyce's Boy was quick to see that he had blundered. If Mrs. Sarle opened her purse, she might miss the key of the front door, which was now in his pocket, so he made a grab at her hands, wrenched the purse away and put it behind a coffee tin on the mantelpiece.

"Shrimps is with me, miss," he said in a pleading voice. "Catch hold of the toast and do both, while I fixes the shrimps."

Mrs. Sarle, who rarely had company in the kitchen, began to look upon Boyce's Boy as something of a treasure, so she took the toasting fork and bread knife, while Boyce's Boy took himself into the hall to open the front door. "Lucky she didn't look into her purse. I never thought I'd be able to get the front door key so easy. The gods is with us to-day, my fine fellow, and no error."

Talking thus to himself, he opened the front door, just as an old lady carrying a fish-basket called "Shrimps!" in a loud wail from the pavement opposite.

"Here!" shouted Boyce's Boy.

The old lady smiled and crossed the road, while Boyce's Boy drew himself up proudly in the hope that she would think he had just acquired this fine house in the Precincts.

"Do you want any shrimps, sir?" she asked.

Boyce's Boy, who was very pleased at being called "Sir," looking into the basket with a lordly air.

"Well, it looks to me, mother, that if I did happen to want winkles, it 'ud be precious little good, 'cos I don't see none, nor mackeril neither, but as shrimps is what I do happen to require, it's very convenient all round, ain't it? Sixpennorth of the best, and not too many of them little khaki ones."

"What shall I put 'em in, sir?" asked the old lady.

Boyce's Boy took off his cap in order to scratch his head. "Why, there now, if my servants ain't forgot to give me a plate! I don't know what servants is coming to nowadays. Here, put 'em in my cap."

"Won't it spoil it, sir? Shrimps is smelly things."

"A little niffy, certainly, but not so strong as the hair juice I wears, and a dash of shrimp oil in the hat makes the hair grow, mother. I had that tip straight from the stables what knows. Ogham's the barber, what shaves me every morning, in the High Street, and Ogham knows more about hair-oils than you know about shrimps, I can tell you."

The shrimps were spooned out of the basket by a pewter measure till the cap was filled. "Here, 'old 'ard, old 'un. She won't carry no more, and I ain't had full weight yet." Boyce's Boy looked round for some utensil to come to his aid, and perceived an ancient soup-tureen on an old oak dresser. Accordingly he shovelled the shrimps into that, and took back his cap for more.

"I hopes all the same as how it won't spoil your cap, sir," remarked the old lady as she pocketed the sixpence. Boyce's Boy regarded his cap with as much gravity as ever a Hamlet bestowed upon Yorick's skull.

"If this cap expects to have such fine things as my head in it all its life, it's a-flattering itself. It might do worse than shrimps. Hallo. It's blowing up for rain. Look at that sky. You run along, mother, and get them little shrimps under cover, or they'll be swimming away."

CHAPTER VIII

TEA AND SHRIMPS

A GREAT gust of wind swept down Bony Hill as Boyce's Boy closed the door. The giant trees at the foot of the Castle opposite creaked and swayed, and then, determining that autumn was well advanced before they had realized it, threw away thousands of leaves at once, lest winter should stalk round the corner and find them dressed for summer still. Squadrons of leaves flew everywhere. High up round the old Keep. In at old ruined windows and out of others. Up to giddy heights round the spire of the Cathedral and down through dark gratings to the dusty depths of the dark Crypt. They danced about the deserted graveyard before the West door, with no respect for the worthy ones who were advertised as remaining there. "Come on, lazy bones," they seemed to say, "here's another winter coming, and we'll be skeletons too. But is there any objection to skeletons having a dance? Come and join us if you can." And a cloud of dust would arise from the old graves and out of the crevices of family tombs, and who can say if some remains hadn't taken the leaves at their word and were not now setting to corners with them round the Castle walls?

Three brown old leaves tumbled into the hall as Boyce's Boy shut the door. They were evidently too old to cope with the excitement. They had no stomach for the frolic. "Here, outside, you!" he cried, picking them up and pushing them through the letter-box into the street. The wind screamed in derision, and carried them off to the top of the Castle. Boyce's Boy tried to shut the letter-box, but the hinge was faulty and it kept rattling in the wind. A little red leaf crept through and lay in the wire letter-rack. "Well, you can stay here, miss," said Boyce's Boy, picking up the tureen of shrimps. "You're a pretty little leaf, you are, not old and crinkled like them others and my mind's too full of shrimps to bother about you. Besides, you've as much right to make yourself at home here as I have, and I only hopes you'll do it half as well. So long, Miss Leaf."

Mrs. Sarle was buttering the toast as Boyce's Boy re-entered the kitchen with the shrimps. "Why, bless the boy!" she ejaculated. "If he hasn't brought in one of the master's best bits of china. He won't half go mad if he finds out."

"I should say he must have gone mad already, to put a soup-tureen in a front hall," replied the boy. "These so-called gentlefolk puts the silliest things about in the silliest places. In my business as Errands, I sees the insides of most houses, and the way they furnish halls fair beats me. Now in every hall in this Precincts I'll say you'll find things about what ain't no use in a hall. Most of 'em has old dressers full of plates what nobody eats off of; for who wants to eat half an inch from a front door? Then you'll mostly find a warming-pan, which is as out of place, to my thinking, as if you was to hang up hot-water bottles in red jackets. They'll be bringing in hip-baths soon, and hooking 'em up in halls, and you'll be asked to leave your visiting cards on a washstand what used to be in the cook's bedroom. Do you know what I shall have in my hall, when I gets rich?"

Mrs. Sarle, who had poured out tea and spread dripping on the buttered toast, which she peppered and salted, said, "Shrimps."

"No," replied Boyce's Boy, helping himself. "I would not have shrimps in my hall, though it ain't a bad suggestion; but the boy what 'ud open the door to my visitors would be a boot-black boy like them they have in London in red coats, and he'd clean my visitors' boots before he showed 'em on to my drawing-room carpet."

He looked up, with his mouth full of toast, and regarded Mrs. Sarle critically. "Here, if you peel off the skins of all them shrimps I shall simply leave you nowheres. Catch 'em by the head and tail, so, and chop 'em with your front teeth, so."

"I might swallow a whisker," said Mrs. Sarle.

"Oh," replied Boyce's Boy, eating a shrimp whole just to see what swallowing whiskers did for you. They tickled. He coughed. "Miss Tackle been doin' much in the honey line lately?" he asked.

"Would you like some?" asked the housekeeper, falling innocently into the trap.

"Since you mentions it, I would," replied the boy. "I thought I noticed a new comb in the cupboard, and if it's fresh it should go down very grand."

The honeycomb was accordingly stood upon a plate.

"Miss Tackle's?" suggested the boy.

"Yes," returned the housekeeper. "Hearing as how the master was took queer, she brought it round. But I don't think he'd better have it, in case it makes him sick."

"It would," agreed Boyce's Boy. "Very sick. Don't you give him none. Take my advice. Keep him on physic and slops for a week or so, and see how he gets on."

Lonely Mrs. Sarle, who had been so entertained with her guest, suddenly remembered that she had not gone up to the sick-room to relieve the doctor.

"Why there, now!" she cried, fussing about the kitchen. "I've been so taken up with getting your tea that I never thought of the doctor. I must take him up a cup of tea, and see how master is."

Two trays hurriedly filled; one with tea-things for the doctor and the other with fruit and medicine for the invalid.

"I'll carry one for you, missus, if you'll lead the way," and Boyce's Boy followed Mrs. Sarle upstairs.

"Hope the doctor ain't angry at being left so long," whispered Mrs. Sarle as she stopped with some trepidation outside the bedroom door.

"I'll bear witness that the chemist took hours mixing the stuff."

"Well, he was a longish time," retorted the housekeeper. She knocked at the bedroom door.

CHAPTER IX

THE TWO DOCTORS

At the same moment a private brougham drove up Bony Hill and Dr. Rickit gave a professional "rat-tat" at the front door.

"I should know that silly knock anywhere, Mrs. Housekeeper," said Dr. Smith, opening the bedroom door. "I am not alluding to your knock, ma'am, but to the summons at your front door. Unless I am greatly mistaken, it is Dr. Rickit. Open the door to him, ma'am, and show him up immediately."

Mrs. Sarle was so alarmed at hearing one doctor wanting to see another doctor that she would have dropped the tea-tray had not Dr. Smith been reminded that tea would be more acceptable to him than to the carpet. Accordingly he seized it greedily and bade Boyce's Boy bring in the medicines.

Mr. McCarbre was sitting up in bed, propped around with pillows, and on his knees was a blotting-pad, and on the blotting-pad was balanced an inkstand with a pen sticking out of it, and beside the inkstand lay a cheque-book.

Dr. Smith put the tea-tray on the edge of the bed, and began pouring himself out a cup.

"Where shall I put this tray of medicines, sir?" asked Boyce's Boy.

"On that table," replied Dr. Smith, sitting himself down on the end of the bed and folding himself a piece of thin bread and butter.

"There ain't no room on that for this," observed Boyce's Boy.

"Then make room, you damned little idiot," was the curt rejoinder.

Boyce's Boy put the tray on the floor. Then he removed one by one the books and magazines from the table to the dressing-table, and then one by one the bottles of medicine from the tray to the table. He purposely made a lengthy business of all this; indeed, so long did he take that Mrs. Sarle had mounted the stairs and announced Dr. Rickit before Dr. Smith thought of dismissing

66

him. In fact, Dr. Smith was so intent on keeping his eye on Mr. McCarbre that he had forgotten Boyce's Boy's existence, which suited that young gentleman exactly.

As Dr. Rickit entered the room, Dr. Smith took a little book from his side-pocket, which he showed to McCarbre, and Boyce's Boy thought he heard him whisper, "No nonsense, now," as he put the book back in his pocket.

Mrs. Sarle, thinking that the two doctors were about to operate upon her unfortunate master, took two clean towels from the linen-cupboard, hung them over the bedrail, and then, overcome with emotion, tiptoed out of the room and waited developments on the landing. Boyce's Boy, being a true Athenian and loving to see and hear new things, hoped that they were going to operate, and wanting to be in at the death, busied himself with arranging the medicine bottles in rows, as if he were contemplating a game of chess.

Dr. Smith looked Dr. Rickit up and down with some contempt, while Dr. Rickit scratched his side-whiskers, conjured up his most professional manner, and said, "Well now, and how is our patient getting along? I heard you had had a bad turn from our mutual friend Miss Tackle, and was most distressed that I was not at hand. However, this gentleman"—with a nod towards his rival—"has, no doubt, loosened the first knots of trouble, and will leave me to unravel the rest of the tangle. Now, where are you in pain?"

"Tell him," said Dr. Smith sharply. Boyce's Boy thought he was going to produce the little book again from his side-pocket; instead of which, he took out a little wooden case with brass bands, which he rubbed against his nose.

"Of course he will tell me," said Dr. Rickit. "I need no more help with this patient, thank you," and taking Mr. McCarbre's wrist, he added, "We understand one another, don't we? Now, tell me all the trouble."

McCarbre took away his wrist irritably.

"Oh, no, now!" persuaded Dr. Rickit. "We must feel the pulse in order to locate the seat of difficulty."

"Oh, go on," ordered Dr. Smith, pouring himself out another cup of tea. "Tell him at once, or shall I?"

Mr. McCarbre took up the cheque-book, tore off a written

cheque and folded it carefully; then cleared his throat and said, "Dr. Rickit, on your last visit you had the goodness to leave the account for your services. I have written you out a cheque to that amount, and wish you now to understand that your visits can be discontinued. I have changed my medical adviser."

Dr. Rickit took the cheque without looking at it, stared at the invalid, then glared at his rival and was speechless.

"Now, my dear sir," said Dr. Smith, with a slight imitation of Dr. Rickit's persuasive manner, "do not put us in an awkward predicament. I am not in the habit of stealing patients from my colleagues, but in this case I feel justified in acting upon the express wishes of Mr. McCarbre. He wants me and he don't want you, and that is putting it bluntly. If I, in my turn, fail to give satisfaction, I can assure you that I shall accept defeat with philosophical resignation, and I trust, sir, that you will do the same."

Boyce's Boy could see that Dr. Rickit was getting very angry but was trying to compose himself, for he said with studied calmness, "Mr. McCarbre, I must really entreat you to think this matter over a little more carefully. I am sure you cannot wish to insult me, sir, like this."

"Nothing will alter my decision," exclaimed the invalid, with an uneasy look at Dr. Smith, who had again produced the little wooden case.

"Well, I'll be blowed," ejaculated Dr. Rickit, whose expressions were as obsolete as his methods. "I really will be blowed if I have not this day proved a very pet theory of mine, and for which I have to thank my colleague here." (This with a bow to Dr. Smith.) "I have ever maintained that if the true *esprit de corps*, etiquette, decorum and, shall I say, cricket of our profession are to be guarded, the medical ranks must not be recruited from the lower-middle-classes."

"Or left in the hands of doddering snobs," replied Dr. Smith, "who think that because they cut a figure in a Precincts, with their silk hats and private broughams, they are therefore at liberty to strangle any poor medical devil who chooses to practise in the same town."

"I don't know what you mean, you—you——" Dr. Rickit ceased. Either he could not think of the right word, or, if he could, he was afraid of saying it. Boyce's Boy inclined to the latter theory, having a strong impression that he was about to say "gorilla."

"Oh, cut it out now," said the victorious doctor. "The plain truth is always the best, though at times hard to stomach. I like bluntness more than tact, and whether you agree or not doesn't matter a jot. It comes down to this. Mr. McCarbre thinks you don't understand his case, and that I do. Or, blunter still, I'm thumbs-up and you're a wash-out."

"A wash-out! Ah!" cried the dignified Rickit, pocketing his cheque and walking triumphantly to the door. "We shall hear what my solicitors have to say to the word 'wash-out.' You will hear from them, sir. And if you are not blackballed by the profession and the town——"

"It won't be your fault, eh?" laughed Dr. Smith, completing the sentence for him in a very neat way. At least, so thought Boyce's Boy.

Dr. Rickit banged the door behind him, and ordered Mrs. Sarle to show him out of the house before he choked with rage.

Dr. Smith turned to McCarbre and remarked, "Well, that's the first step in our adventure together. So far, so good." He then saw Boyce's Boy.

"What are you doing here?" he cried sharply, raising his voice.

"Arrangin' bottles," answered Boyce's Boy, raising his voice to the same tone.

"Who are you, anyway?"

"Boyce's Boy, that's who I am."

"Then, Boyce's Boy, you can take yourself out of here as quick as you like. That's my advice to you, my lad."

"Didn't ask you for it, did I?" replied the urchin. "But since you've given it to me, here's my advice to you. Don't quarrel with people till you knows how strong they are."

"Strong? What do you mean?"

"You'll know what 'strong' is, if you lets your tea get tannier, and you'll know what 'weak' is if you gets across Boyce's Boy," and he banged the door, in a lively imitation of Dr. Rickit, and took himself downstairs.

Mrs. Sarle had gone into the kitchen, so that Boyce's Boy found himself alone in the hall. Looking carefully about, to see that he was not observed, he drew from his pocket the paper cutting of the man and the gibbet, of which Mr. McCarbre had been so alarmed, and with the help of a piece of sticking-paper he hung the gruesome sign behind the green baize door. He then turned his attention to the inside of the front door, and discovered that neither of the heavy bolts worked, but that there was a large key which apparently aided the Yale lock at night to keep off burglars. He seemed quite satisfied as he drew out this key and put it in his pocket, and then, casting a final admiring look at the paper gibbet, he pushed himself through the green baize door, and so into the kitchen, where he laid himself out to be attentive to Mrs. Sarle. When he grew tired of this, he bade her good-evening, and let himself out of the front door. Having banged the door loudly, in order that Mrs. Sarle might be satisfied that he had done so properly, for he would not hear of her stirring from her easy-chair to let him out, he produced the Yale key, and having assured himself again that it was in reality the key which could open the door, he took himself along the High Street to annoy Mrs. Norris at the Curiosity Shop.

CHAPTER X

THE WIND AND THE RAIN

THE weather forecast, as suggested by Boyce's Boy to the seller of shrimps, had proved itself true. By eleven o'clock that night the rain came down so hard that every corner and crevice of Dullchester was running and splashing and spouting and dripping. The elements were giving the Corporation water-cart a demonstration in how to do it. If you want to get really wet, go down to Dullchester and wait for rain. This city seems particularly designed for wetting people. There are so many overbearing roofs; so many overhanging signs; so many leaning top-storeys; so many bulging walls with so many jutting stones, not to mention a large collection of gargoyles around the Precincts whose anatomies are maliciously joined to water-spouts and gutters, and whose province is deliberately to surfeit surplus rain water clear of lead-rimmed windows and splash it on to the pavements beneath. There are also so many old trees whose autumnal leaves prefer to get blown into gutters and drains than into anything else, thereby causing stoppages and gushes, that if you don't want water down your neck, well, you don't venture out. Hence the Precincts was deserted as the clocks struck eleven, when Sergeant Wurren, buttoned to the teeth in mackintosh, took his last round before turning in. In his right-hand pocket he fingered an electric torch, and round the corner by North Gate-house, right into the sergeant's stomach ran Boyce's Boy, head-first and running hard.

The sergeant seized Boyce's Boy's head with his great hand and flashed his torch in his face.

"Hallo! and what mischief are you up to on such a night as this? Why ain't you in bed?"

"Because I don't go to bed till I'm tired," replied the boy. "And you'll oblige me by taking that hand of yourn off of my head. Your sleeve is a-drippin' drops down my neck, and I don't like it."

"Where are you going?" asked the policeman.

"If you stops squashin' my lid, I'll tell you," answered Boyce's Boy. "What are you playin' at, anyhow? Can't a citizen take a walk around his own town without leave off the policeman? Go'bli'me, you takes too much upon yourself."

"Where are you going?" repeated the policeman.

"I'll tell you something else," answered Boyce's Boy.

"You tell me what I tells you to tell me," returned the police-man, "and nothing else."

"Ah, but this will interest you," was the rejoinder, "'cos it's about a copper I once knew what got hanged. Guess how?"

"Shan't," ejaculated the policeman.

"Why not?" asked the boy.

"'Cos it don't interest me. There."

"Oh, but it should. It's so like this 'ere, for that clumsy copper put his hand down on a young feller's lid in just the hefty way you are doing it to me, and quite sudden something went 'snick.' Guess what."

"Don't want to," growled the policeman.

"The young fellow's neck," went on Boyce's Boy, "and when the cop said to the judge, 'It were only my fun, m'lud,' the judge he said, 'I'm glad you think it fun, my man,' he says, 'because we're a-goin' to have a bit of fun with you,' and that there cop, for all he was a cop, got copped himself; hung by the neck he was, till he was dead—and what's more, serve him right."

The policeman flashed the torch closer in the boy's face and pressed harder with his left hand.

"You answer my question then, and it will save us both that trouble."

Boyce's Boy produced a cracking noise in the back of his throat and, making his eyes start out of his head, he relaxed all his muscles and would have sunk down in the mud, had not the policeman held him tightly.

"None of your tricks with me, young shaver. Where are you going?"

"To the undertaker's, if you don't let me breathe."

"That's all right," chuckled the policeman. "You don't breathe through the top of your head."

"Oh, don't you!" gasped the boy. "Then why does policeman's hats have ventilation holes?"

This was evidently a poser for the policeman, for he laughed and said, "I never thought of that."

"Look here," said Boyce's Boy seriously. "Fair do's, now. You leave go o' me and I'll tell you true."

"Very well," agreed the policeman, taking away his hand. "Now, where are you going?"

"Swimming baths," said Boyce's Boy.

"What?" retorted the policeman, moving towards him. But Boyce's Boy had dodged out of the shelter of the arch and stood in the driving rain.

"It's a lovely night for a swim, ain't it?" he said innocently.

"You can't get in at this time," stated the policeman.

"Then I shall have to stay outside, shan't I? By the way, I suppose you've no objection to my going to the baths?"

The policeman had no intention of letting the urchin pull his leg, so he growled, "You can go to the devil, if you like, so long as you and he don't go gettin' up to no mischief together."

"As to that," returned the boy, "I holds no truck with him. Whenever I meets the devil, I does like the cove in the Bible and turns my back on him. 'Get thee behind me, Sergeant,' I says," and turning his back on the policeman, he trotted off down the High Street, splashing through all the puddles in high glee.

CHAPTER XI

THE KEY IS USED

WHEN Boyce's Boy reached the bridge he turned sharp to the left, out on to the esplanade, and wet to the skin, reached the closed door of the swimming baths. Producing a large key from his pocket, he fitted it into the lock, opened the door and locked it after him. He then whispered, "It's only me."

"All right. Then come along to the deep end. Better not show a light," came an answer from the darkness.

"Better not speak so loud," whispered Boyce's Boy. "The echoes of this place is something awful."

He had pushed his way through a double swing-door and was walking along a gallery through the boards of which could be seen the dark waters in the bath—dangerous walking, for the wood was wet and slippery—when he fell over a pile of towels that had been heaped upon the floor.

"Curse! Show us a light," whispered the boy. "Better be caught here than break my legs."

There was the sound of a striking match, and from a bathing box in the corner of the deep end there came a man in a long coat, holding a candle above his head.

"Who put them towels here?" muttered Boyce's Boy, kicking them through the rails into the bath. "They can fish them out in the morning, and even then they won't be much wetter than me."

"A warm drink will soon put you in a better temper, my young friend," answered the Paper Wizard, for the man in the long coat was he. "I've got the spirit-lamp a-going under the tub."

Boyce's Boy descended the gallery steps and entered the corner bathing box. The Paper Wizard mixed a hot grog over a spirit-lamp carefully sheltered in the tub which was used daily for wet towels, while Boyce's Boy seized a dry towel and rubbed those parts of his anatomy which he thought necessary for his health. Feeling drier, warmer and more cheerful under the influence of the hot grog he produced a packet of cigarettes and invited the Paper Wizard to join him in a gasper. When these were lighted from the spirit-lamp Boyce's Boy sat on the bench, and after a vain attempt to blow a smoke-ring in that draughty atmosphere, he looked at the Paper Wizard, who was leaning against the tub, and began to speak.

"And now, my friend, it is time that we gave each other a little more of our confidence. There are one or two things which you will be pleased to hear from me, and there are one or two things which I should like to hear from you. In the first place, I have received regular sums of money from you for keeping my eye on a certain gent in the Precincts. That eye I have kept faithfully, and you have taken my word for it and faithfully stumped up. There we are quits. So far, so good. I have also this very day got into a certain gent's house in the Precincts, what you always was anxious for me to get into, and what's more I has so arranged things that it is now possible for you to walk in there at any hour of the night or day. I have also to-day taken a little tour of inspection into a certain gent's bedroom and have witnessed a scene what I should call remarkable, so remarkable that I daresay as how it would interest you to hear it." Boyce's Boy then recounted all that had happened between the two doctors and the invalid. When the Paper Wizard heard that Boyce's Boy had seen a little book and a wooden case with brass bands round it, his eyes shone and he urged excitedly that Boyce's Boy would go on and not forget anything.

When everything had been recounted, the Paper Wizard sat thoughtful for a minute before speaking, then lighting another cigarette and jerking his old one into the bath, he stood up and told Boyce's Boy that he must act at once.

"Now you lean back against that tub again and listen to me," ordered Boyce's Boy with such authority that the Paper Wizard obeyed. "You're a poor man, you are, by your looks, you'll own, and though you'll starve on the road and beg for your living by cutting out them funny pictures of yours, earning your money in a hard and difficult way, yet you can afford to pay me regular, at the expense of them boots of yours what have gone to seed in the uppers. What does this prove? you'll say. Well, it proves that you are making something of a sacrifice, and what does that lead me to know? Why, that I am somehow helping you to something what is very important to you. Now here it is straight, old Paper Wizard. I ain't a-goin' on no longer with my eyes shut. You let me know what you're a-playing at, or I don't look after you no more. Where would you be without me, eh? You seem so scared of something that 'pon my word you're quite helpless. After getting knocked about this morning and then taken to the Deanery and fed, you ought to be as happy as a lark. But no. You wouldn't take the room I got for you over the pawnbroker's. No. You must be where no one will see you. I must lock you up here and come and talk business with you when other folk are in bed. Well, here I am. Now what have you got to say? Out with it."

"Look here, kid, I likes you," whispered the Paper Wizard. "There's something of the Nosey Parker about you what I admires."

Boyce's Boy looked rather flattered as he cut in with: "Well, yes. Perhaps. I don't know who Nosey Parker was or is, nor do I much care, but supposing my name was Parker, which it ain't, leastwise not to my knowledge, I don't see no reason why I shouldn't be called Nosey Parker, nosey being just about what I am. I likes nosing around things what don't concern me, until my very nosing long enough makes 'em concern me, see? The general public don't give me credit for being so nosey. For instance, if I goes to Sergeant Wurren and informs him that a Paper Wizard sleeps in the swimming bath, he will come round and put you in the lock-up, and if you tell him it was me what let you in, he won't believe you because he won't think I had the brain to get the key copied, nor the brain to get a lot of other keys copied what belongs to locks of doors around this old town, for between you and me, and no codding, I can get into most buildings quicker than the Dean can, for he has to ask for the key. I uses my own."

"Where do you keep all these keys of yours?" asked the Paper Wizard.

"That's my affair," replied the boy. "I thought my name was Nosey Parker, not yours."

The Paper Wizard laughed. "You're a rare kid, and no mistake," he said.

"Daresay I am," continued Boyce's Boy. "Still, that's no reason for trying my particular game on me. I'll tell you just as much as I think proper, and no more. I'm stubborn, I am. As stubborn as locks, and locks is stubborn things what takes a lot of arguing with. You say, 'Pick 'em,' eh? So says burglars and such flats. I says, 'Hallo, Mister Lock, you are looking after an interesting-looking door what's looking after an interesting building, and you looks to me uncommon stubborn. You has a look of saying, "Now then, move along, please; this ain't your door."' I replies, 'Right-o, old cock. You won't let me in, eh? You denies yourself the pleasure of my company? Very well. I knows the argument to use with you. Mister Lock, if you're a Christian lock, you'll have a key. I'll find him, if he's anywhere knocking about. I didn't say "steal"—I'll find him, I said; and when I've found him, I'll shake hands with him. There's no offence against the Crown in that, I hope. A cat can shake hands with a king, as they say so why can't a trades-boy shake hands with a key? Though we must say nothing, about the bit of wax I has in my hand when I does it.'"

"Very clever indeed," put in the Paper Wizard.

"Oh, there are lots of ways of enjoying yourself, if you only wakes up to the facts."

"So that's how you come to let me lodgings in the swimming baths?"

"That's it, and quite safe. If you was to oversleep and I was to forget to let you out, why, you has only to complain that you was locked in the bath, and then you wants to know the reason of their putting a dud in charge of a public building."

"That's all very well," commented the Paper Wizard, "but suppose, as is most likely, that they confront me with the bath keeper and he says as how I never come into the bath when he was on duty?"

"Which, judging by your face, seems more than likely," remarked Boyce's Boy, surveying the grubby look of the Paper Wizard. "Well, you must bluff it out," he went on. "You must survey him sympathetically and say, 'Give it up, old friend, for drink has been the death of better men than you,' and if he says he don't drink, you say, 'What about last New Year's Eve at the Old Bull?' He'll know. That'll get him."

"All right. Don't go arguing about it," cut in the Paper Wizard. "There's no chance of oversleeping this night, if you've shook hands with a certain key of a certain house."

"By which you mean McCarbre's on Bony Hill, and if so, why not say so?" grumbled the boy.

"Because I ain't waited this long time for this blessed night of reckoning, to spoil all by talking too loud about it."

"Bah!" scorned the boy. "Don't you hear the rain? What but a tadpole would walk out to-night? I don't suppose your little mysteries would interest tadpoles. What the devil are you afraid of?" Boyce's Boy completed his argument by looking at his companion and adding, "eh?" For the Paper Wizard was not looking at Boyce's Boy. He was looking at something behind Boyce's Boy's head, something which appeared to cause him uncontrollable terror. In an instant Boyce's Boy turned to see what horror was behind him, but in that instant the light went out. The swimming bath was plunged into darkness. The Paper Wizard had put one hand on the candle and the other over Boyce's Boy's mouth. The blackness was so intense, and the noise of the rain upon the skylight so impressive that the boy could not cry out, though he wanted to, till instinct told him that the sudden action of his companion had no animosity in it against himself, for although the hand was still pressed over his mouth there was no indication of a knife driving into the back of his neck. Consequently he suffered the hand to remain there, made no attempt to struggle free, but listened to the rain driving a perpetual tattoo upon the skylight, here and there securing an entrance and dripping into the bath or on to the ragged strips of sodden cocoanut matting that ran in a tattered path around the water's edge. As he listened he stared into the darkness, expecting every instant to see—well, he hardly knew what, since nothing would have surprised him. The lonely swimming bath, now black as ink, was an eerie enough setting for the most frightful apparition. And then he saw it. He saw it first in the water. A weird light that flitted like the reflection of lightning in the bottom of a well. Deep down, in and out amongst the wobbly tiles it seemed to dance, for the drippings from the skylight troubled the waters. His first impression was that a luminous sea-fish had lost its way, wandered out of the Pacific and, by taking innumerable wrong turnings, had got up the river, and finding that "No Thoroughfare" to his home, had given up hope and allowed himself to be sucked through the pump-pipes into the bath. However, when the illuminated thing jumped out of the water and slithered over his boots and up his trousers, he perceived that it was no fish, but a reflection from the skylight. Somebody was on the roof and was flashing an electric torch into the bath.

"It's Sergeant Wurren," spluttered Boyce's Boy into the Paper Wizard's hand.

"He's followed you here," answered that worthy. "That's awkward, because he'll go on following us when we leave for Bony Hill."

"He won't follow us," said the boy, removing the Paper Wizard's hand.

"Then he'll lock us up, which will be fatal."

Boyce's Boy chuckled. "No, he won't. You leave it to me. If there's anyone as wants locking up, it's him," saying which, he picked up a lifebuoy that was leaning against the wall and to the astonishment of the Paper Wizard threw it with all his force into the bath, at the same time uttering a shrill cry.

There followed a silence and then a noise of much scrambling on the roof.

"He's bit," exclaimed the boy. "He's coming down to investigate. Quick now, we must unlock the door before he tries it."

The Paper Wizard stood still. He was obviously frightened of the policeman on the roof. The boy, however, was on the alert, and seizing his companion by the wrist he groped his way along the gallery to the swing-doors, which he fastened back, and just as they heard the policeman's steps on the gravel outside, he turned the key backwards in the lock of the main door.

"What have you unlocked it for?" asked his scared companion.

"Get behind that pay-box," ordered Boyce's Boy, unhooking another lifebuoy from the wall and standing it up on the floor like a hoop, holding it tightly with both hands.

The policeman tried the door. It stuck, but he gave it his shoulder, and as it opened he heard something running heavily down the steps and splash into the water. Whoever was in the building was now in the water, he conjectured, so he walked past the pay-box, through the swing-doors and stood for a moment upon the diving platform, flashing his torch down upon the surface of the green water. Boyce's Boy quickly and quietly unhooked a long pole which was used for fishing towels out of the bath, and creeping behind the policeman, deliberately pushed him with it in the small of the back. The policeman lost his balance and fell into the water.

The boy hung up the pole again, motioned the Paper Wizard out into the rain and, following himself with the key, slammed the door and locked it.

"Listen to the splashing," he remarked, stepping briskly along the esplanade.

"Can he swim? Suppose he drowns; why, that's a hanging job," muttered his companion, who had hurried after him and seized his arm.

"It's the shallow end," replied the culprit, "and there's lifebuoys all to hand. It'll learn him not to follow gentlemen about on wet nights. He can't reach the skylight and there ain't no windows else. He won't trouble us till morning, and even then, as he ain't seen us, what can he prove?"

"There's my spirit-lamp in the tub. He may trace it as my property."

"No, he won't," said the boy. "For I ain't quite such a fool as some. Here's your lamp and your bottle and your tin all serene in my pocket, but you may as well put them in yours, as they're bulging mine something horrible, and the suit I stands up in 'appens to be my one and only."

The articles in question accordingly changed hands and pockets. "Of course," went on the boy, "if you was cutting your bits of paper in the swimming bath, he will know who pushed him into the water, because you always leaves the ends about in the most untidy style."

"But I didn't," returned the other. "Was most careful not to. If you remember, I promised you I wouldn't when you let me in after dark."

"All right," snapped the boy. "And now, as we're already in the Precincts, perhaps you'll explain what we are going to do in this house when we gets there."

"Watch."

"What for?"

"Mr. McCarbre and a brass-bound book."

"And what's that got to do with us?"

"Gibbets or justice."

"Here, I suppose that's a polite way of saying 'Gibbets or blackmail,' ain't it?"

"Some folk might put it that way, but I says that if McCarbre wants me to hold my tongue, well, he can pay me to do it, and not give so much money towards restoring cathedrals and such places."

"I daresay that's all right," went on Boyce's Boy, "but I should like to point out that you ain't a citizen of this 'ere town. I am. Everybody knows me, and when I sails too close to the wind, by which I means 'too close to the police station,' I has to sail cautious."

"Well, I ain't going to trouble you no further, Mister Citizen of Dullchester. You can let me into the house and take yourself home to bed. I can do what I've got to do better alone."

Boyce's Boy looked furtively at the Paper Wizard's face and he said to himself, "It strikes me that if your little game ain't murder, it's something uncommon near. Well, I'll be in at the death, for the worst that can happen to me is to get put up in the witness box, and that 'ud be a real treat and not 'alf, that would, with the dance I could lead them lawyers."

The rain was not falling so heavily when they reached Bony Hill, but it was a miserable night. There was nobody about, so that it was safe enough to walk straight for the front door.

The Paper Wizard looked through the letter-box. Boyce's Boy could see a light shining through it on to his thin face. He stood on tiptoe and whispered, "Anybody there?" The watcher shook his head. "No, but there's a candle burning on the oak chest. It ain't in a stick but stuck on with wax, which ain't very safe to leave for long. There's a rug kicked aside, too. They'll be coming soon. Let me get in while I can."

Boyce's Boy produced the Yale key, unlocked the door and put the key back in his pocket. His companion slipped into the hall and closed the door behind him, leaving Boyce's Boy on the pavement, who thus meditated within him: "Well, I'm shut out, but I've got the key and, taking it all for all, I lay I'm enjoying myself more than what old Sergeant Wurren is in that bath." Then, seizing the brass knocker, he pulled himself level with the letter-box and peeped through.

CHAPTER XII

THROUGH THE LETTER-BOX

AT first Boyce's Boy could see nothing but the candle burning on the oak chest, but as his eyes accustomed themselves to the light he made out the rug mentioned by the Paper Wizard, kicked up at the foot of the chest into an untidy heap, leaving the great flagstones bare and uninviting. By the noise of breathing which he could distinctly detect, he conjectured that his former companion was hiding in the immediate vicinity of the front door. His surmise proved to be correct, for presently a black form shut out the light. This for a second only, as the Paper Wizard crossed his line of vision, tiptoeing carefully along the hall. He stopped at the baize door, and with a startled movement put out his hand to touch the little paper gibbet which Boyce's Boy had rescued from the drain and stuck up behind it earlier in the evening. This seemed to puzzle and alarm the Paper Wizard. Boyce's Boy did not know whether he would have pulled it down or not, because at that moment voices came from the staircase and it was obvious that someone was coming down with a lamp. The Paper Wizard slipped through the baize door. The voices came nearer. So did the light, and the boy heard the strident and somewhat cockney tones of Dr. Smith raised in anger. "You are not more ill than I am. You've had a fright, that's all. A bad fright, perhaps, but you'll get over that. I can't do this thing by myself. I wish to God I could."

"I'm coming down, aren't I? There's no need to make such a fuss."

Into the hall came Dr. Smith, carrying a lamp which he put down beside the candle on the oak chest. He was followed by Mr. McCarbre, wearing a pair of trousers braced over his pyjama

jacket, a pair of fur moccasins, and a flowery dressing-gown unbut-
toned. Dr. Smith faced him and spoke with authority: "The first
thing, my friend, is a stout crowbar. We shall also want a chisel and
hammer. Where can we find such things?"

"You mustn't go making a noise," whispered McCarbre. "Mrs.
Sarle, my housekeeper, is a light sleeper."

"She won't be, to-night," grinned the doctor.

"What have you done to her?" asked the other, in some alarm.
"I will not have any violence done to her, mind."

"There's no need to knock her on the head now you've got
me in the house. I put a little something in her gin-toddy and
watched her drink it before she went to bed. She won't wake in a
hurry. Come and find a crowbar. We've got to make haste. Wait
a moment, though. You take the lamp. I'm just going to pull the
curtain across the front door. It looks to me as if the lid of that
letter-box is moving a bit in the wind, and if anyone should pass,
they might see the light and be curious."

Boyce's Boy quietly let himself down on the pavement and,
much to his disappointment, heard the rasp of the rings as the
doctor pulled the curtain along the rod. When next the inquisi-
tive urchin peeped through the letter-box all was dark. The curtain
had cut him off. He began to think quickly. He racked his brains,
putting two and two together, but somehow two and two did not
quite make four. Here were two men apparently up to no good.
By his own confession the doctor had drugged poor old Mrs. Sarle.
(Possibly poisoned her, thought Boyce's Boy.) Now he was going
in search of a crowbar. Perhaps that was it. The rug was kicked
aside. Mrs. Sarle was dead, and they were about to deposit the
remains beneath the flagstones. But then there was his friend the
Paper Wizard. How did he fit into the puzzle? That mysterious
being who for months past had paid him money to keep an eye
on this man McCarbre, with special instructions that if the gentleman in question was to leave Dullchester by train, Boyce's Boy
was to leave Boyce's vegetables literally in the cart and follow the
trail, wiring to the Paper Wizard when and where the goose-chase
came to an end. Well, McCarbre had not gone by any train, so
he had been spared all that trouble. The Paper Wizard had come
back to Dullchester instead. Had spent the morning publicly in

the High Street, plying his curious trade, till Boyce's Boy called him to the Cathedral to have a peep at McCarbre. This visit and its curious results already related had suddenly made him mortally afraid of showing his nose in the town, so that Boyce's Boy had concealed him in a shed until seven o'clock, when he locked him in the swimming bath. But now, here was this frightened individual venturing bravely into a veritable den of tigers. Yes, it was all mysterious. Two and two would not make four, and this exasperating doctor had rung down the curtain in the midst of a very thrilling drama. Boyce's Boy put his hands in his overcoat pockets. His fingers closed on the Yale key. Should he open the door and hide behind the curtain? True, he would have to close the door behind him, but he could keep his hand on the latch in case he had to beat a hurried retreat. It was a risk. In fact, it was nothing short of housebreaking, and that meant the lock-up, and putting himself under the jurisdiction of Sergeant Wurren, who would not hesitate to make it very hot for him, for had not the town policeman a hundred and one wrongs to avenge? However, if he were to risk it, now was the time to do it, while the villains of the piece were hunting for the crowbar. As soon as they returned it would be too late. But then, again, the mere thought of that crowbar in the hands of the unscrupulous doctor who had drugged Mrs. Sarle somewhat damped the ardour of even Boyce's Boy's love of adventure, whose sweet thrills he was quite used to tasting. No, perhaps in this case discretion was the wisest course to pursue. He thought of his own bed in the outhouse behind Boyce's shop. The idea of that seemed cosier than waiting about in the draughts of Bony Hill on such a dirty night. Yes, he would go back and fry himself a kipper over his oil-stove. Old Boyce never troubled himself about the hours that his errand-boy kept. He had given him the key, and he always turned in early. "That's what keeps me in good voice," he would say. "Early to bed every night." If the boy set the outhouse on fire it didn't signify much to old Boyce. It was insured and was getting dilapidated and, being at the further end of the yard, was no danger to the house. Besides, Boyce's Boy, though mischievous even to the borderland of crime, was in no ways careless. He was perfection as an "Errands." He never forgot things and always kept his word when given, though it was often a labour to get it out of him; but when Boyce had given him the oil-stove he volunteered the information that he would not set fire to the outhouse. So old Boyce slept secure in the house above the shop.

Now whether the fascinations of a savoury kipper or the curiosity about McCarbre's front door would have triumphed there is no means of arriving at with any certitude, because quite suddenly Boyce's Boy sprang for the door rather as a haven of salvation than as a dangerous shoal to be avoided. Any port in a storm, for the heavy foot of Sergeant Wurren was on Bony Hill, and coming up fast towards McCarbre's, the electric torch flashing before him in the darkness like the angry searchlight of a battleship.

"Crikey! Has he seen me?" This was the awful thought that made Boyce's Boy's heart pound as he closed the front door quickly behind him and shivered between it and the heavy brocade curtain. The terrible and relentless footsteps came quickly to the door. They stopped abruptly. "Yes, Crikey, he has," said the culprit to himself. The searchlight of the law flashed all over the door. It penetrated the keyholes. It penetrated the letter-box. Boyce's Boy instinctively gave the collar of his overcoat an extra tuck up to hide the whiteness of his face. As he did so he pricked his hand on an emergency pin that was stored behind one of the lapels.

"Curse!" he said aloud.

The lid of the letter-box lifted.

The great ear of the mighty policeman was pressed against it and the part of the opening not filled with ear was bulging with a pink portion of fat cheek. As the sight of an octopus will make the bravest shudder, so did this soft, bulging substance of policeman fill Boyce's Boy with unutterable loathing. In sheer desperation he resolved to attack first. He whipped the offensive pin from the lapel of his coat and with great determination deliberately stuck it into the piece of soft flesh. With an exclamation resembling the squeal of one of the Dean's pigs, Sergeant Wurren stood up and felt with his great hand for the offensive little nerve that had jumped with such effect. "Funny," he muttered. "Teeth are all sound and never in my life 'ad a pain in my ear-'ole. Must be neuralgia. After the wetting I've 'ad, the draught through that darned letter-box completed the mischief. Crumbs! It don't 'alf urt." The aggrieved Sergeant of Police leant against the door. To the eyes of Boyce's Boy, the pink flesh had retreated to give way to a portion of dark-blue uniform, a thing nearly as loathsome, and certainly more dreaded. As an experienced general commanding an inferior force will sometimes use the expedient of attacking a superior foe, and then attacking again before receiving a counter, thus by sheer force carrying the day, so Boyce's Boy, without considering the consequences, again plunged the pin, this time into the blue uniform.

"Golly!" ejaculated the policeman. "I'm blowed if it ain't pneumonia too. Double pneumonia; that's what nearly drowning has done for me, and if it's only double I'm lucky, 'cos it feels more like treble or quadruple to me, and by the time I finishes my rounds, gets back to the station and changes my kit, if it ain't octagonal, I don't know the law. Lumme! Neuralgia and pneumonia. These new-fangled diseases gives one more 'gyp' than the old 'uns. Wait till I lay hold of them rascals that pushed me in the bath!" Saying which, to the immense relief of Boyce's Boy, Sergeant Wurren in his large squelching boots and cold, aching flesh, proceeded on his rounds.

CHAPTER XIII

THE PAPER WIZARD TAKES CHARGE

THE retreating footsteps of the dread Sergeant of Police had scarcely ceased to echo round the walls of Bony Hill when the returning footsteps of McCarbre and Dr. Smith were heard approaching the hall. Boyce's Boy gingerly peeped round the curtain. He was expecting them to emerge from one of the mahogany doors by the staircase, but to his astonishment they came through the baize door from the quarters that were occupied in the day by Mrs. Sarle. They must somehow have passed the Paper Wizard and not seen him. So thought Boyce's Boy, and remembered a great cupboard in the passage by the kitchen. No doubt his friend had found a corner there in which to make himself scarce.

Dr. Smith carried a stout iron bar with a knob at one end. What such a thing could be used for, except as an implement of murder, Boyce's Boy could not imagine, and his hand tightened instinc-

tively on the handle of the front door latch. In so doing he may
have rattled the door, for McCarbre cried out, "What's that?"

"Only the wind against the door," replied the doctor testily. "I
told you that the lid of the letter-box hung loose."

"I believe somebody's there." McCarbre stared at the curtain.
Boyce's Boy stood behind it. He was scarcely less terrified than the
speaker, who got small comfort from the doctor, who snapped,
"Don't be an idiot" and drew out his watch, holding it towards
the lamp. "Now, it wants seven minutes to midnight, and the date
is the thirteenth. From this moment the diary written in the little
brass-bound book will be continued. It's had a rest for over a century, as it's been waiting for me to come along with this crowbar. It
may take us some days to settle the business, and it may take some
weeks, but during the settling, no one must come to this house.
It's a state of siege that we declare from this minute."

McCarbre frowned and moved about the hall uneasily.

"You can't stop people calling at the house," he said.

"I can," replied the doctor.

"They'll all be calling to inquire after my health," continued
McCarbre, ignoring the interruption. "Besides, we shall have trouble with Dr. Rickit, after your treatment of him. The Dean will
call, too. Rickit will stir up the Dean against me. Then there is
Miss Tackle. No one can stop her bringing her nasty honey to the
house. She sometimes sends me blancmange, too."

"And they'll be very welcome," laughed the doctor. "Honey and
puddings thankfully received, and all forwarded on to the lucky
invalid who will be recuperating at the sea."

"At the where?" exclaimed McCarbre. "I shan't be at the sea."

"Oh, yes, you will," went on the doctor. "At the sea, looking
after something that you'll re-bury in the cellar. It will arrive in a
trunk. No, we won't pack it all up together. We'll divide it. Put a
little in this box, a little in that. All wrapped up in your clothes. I've
a little week-end cottage down at Littlepebble. Lovely air and golf-
links. Do you a power of good. You will go down there with me.
You'll write to the Dean and say how well you're getting on, and
what benefits you are deriving from your new doctor. That will
annoy old Rickit."

"You'll be down there with me, then?" asked McCarbre.

"Not really. The Precincts must think I'm there, but you'll be there alone. At least, not quite *alone*," chuckled the doctor. "You will have the old body with you. Mrs. Sarle, did you call her? She'll be on the move all the while—backwards and forwards"—and he chuckled horribly as he added, "with the trunks."

"And leave you here?" McCarbre conveyed in his tone that he wouldn't if he knew it.

"Of course," went on the doctor. "Damned unpleasant, too. All alone in the house. State of siege. Covering up our tracks so that when you come back nobody will be any the wiser. If you go to-morrow in the light of day, in one of Holt's cabs to the station, it will be all over the gossipy town in half-an-hour just where you've gone to, which is all to the good. If you don't like my cottage at Littlepebble, well—you can come back at night, when no one can see you. Closed motor would do it. I'll find a way. The great thing is to keep people away from this house, and the only way to do that is to shut it up *pro tem.*, as they say in the classics. Are you listening? Why are you looking at that door? Haven't I drawn the curtains?"

"You would infinitely oblige me by drawing them back again," hissed McCarbre.

"Oh, what the hell!" snapped the doctor. "There's nothing there."

"Then will you kindly tell me what that is?" and he pointed to the bottom of the curtain.

"What?" asked the doctor.

"It's gone now. It looked to me like a boot. A man's boot."

"A mouse, a rat or a beetle," was the unsympathetic reply. "These old houses are full of them. But if nothing else will satisfy you—well—pull the curtain I will. Needs must when the devil drives, as they say." The doctor took the lamp from the chest with his left hand and, still grasping the crowbar, came towards the curtain.

The courage of desperation seized Boyce's Boy. He swept the curtain aside with one hand and unlatched the front door with the other. "Stay where you are and listen to me," he heard himself sing out in a shrill voice. The doctor started and brought the crowbar up ready to strike. But he stopped where he was. There was a pause. Boyce's Boy could hear his own heart beating. At last the doctor's "Who the hell are you?" came deep and sharp.

"Boyce's Boy," answered the young adventurer.

"Ah, yes, I remember," purred the doctor. "Come here, Boyce's Boy."

"No. I prefer to keep distance between us. You stay where you are. If you take a step nearer, I'll fling this door wide and yell 'Police!' Sergeant Wurren went by just now, and didn't 'alf act nosey. P'raps he saw your light, as he lifted your letterbox lid and peeped through."

"The curtain's too thick. I drew it," commented the doctor. Then, seeing that he was giving himself away, he added loftily, "Besides, we don't mind. There's nothing here to be ashamed of."

"Oh, really!" criticized the boy in a tone of equal loftiness. "Is it usual to put doctor's stuff in old ladies' gin and toddy so that they won't wake up no more? Look out. Stay where you are," warned Boyce's Boy, as the doctor made an angry movement towards him. "Now, then, you two gents, you listen to me. I'm in this 'ere secret of yours. Shall I tell you for why? Not that I wants to be in it over-much—in fact I've not wasted much thought on that—but just because you can't do without me. If you two are going to declare a state of siege here, how are you going to victual yourselves? If you are codding the town that you're away at Littlepebble, you won't 'alf give yourselves away if Mrs. Sarle goes shopping for you."

"Mrs. Sarle won't be here," put in the doctor.

Boyce's Boy thought of the drugged gin and toddy, glanced at the crowbar, conquered a shudder and continued bravely enough: "No? Well, no doubt she's left her larder behind her; but don't you bank on that. I knows something of it, and it ain't overstocked. There's no tinned stuff or bottled stuff wolfed in this establishment. Without fresh veges and well-cooked fish and meat that there McCarbre will die. Now with me you have not got a Mrs. Sarle. If she'd gone out shopping for you she would talk. Not her fault, mind you—but all old girls do. I've not been a shop-boy for nothing. I tells you we gets all the news of the family circles from off of the servants, especially butlers and housekeepers. Can you blame 'em? What's gentry for but to be gossiped about? Precious little else. If your link with the outside world ain't gossipy, which I ain't when it serves my turn, you'll feel safer, eh? Also with me you gets fresh veges and fruit. You gets more besides, 'cos my credit's good with all the errands on the town. If I want to buy a bit o' beefsteak, say—I buys it, not from the shop, but by holding up the bit what was going on Jim Stalk's stretcher to the Deanery. The Dean's housekeeper chooses the steak. She chooses it for the Dean. So it's a good 'un, I argues. So I cuts off 'Errands' and says, 'What's on that label?' (meaning the price). He shows me, and I gives him the money and keeps the steak while he goes back to the shop, which in the beefsteak's case is the butcher's, and young Ray says to old Stalk, 'Same again for the Deanery,' he says, 'extra company, I expects, to lunch but as it's extra, don't put it down, 'cos here's the cash for it.' Old Stalk may think it odd—but cash is cash, nothing's said, and nobody ain't no wiser; no, not even the Dean, who can't think why the steak's so tough that meal."

"There's something in what this boy says, McCarbre. We may find him very useful."

"If I ain't," replied the boy, "I'll give you back the fiver you're going to pay me in advance per week." As he said this, he looked quite generous.

"Five pounds a week," laughed the doctor. "Is that what we're to pay you?"

"Every penny, and that's flat," went on the boy with full conviction. "But you don't finish with me there. I wants also one-tenth of whatever you make out of this shady business, whatever it may be—and something it is, 'cos doctors don't go drugging old gals for nothing, nor ask for crowbars for nothing, nor talk of"—Boyce's Boy sank his voice to its most tragic whisper—"old bodies moving backwards and forwards in trunks for nothing. One-tenth and a fiver a week for as long as I victuals you and throws dust in the eyes of the Precincts for you. Take that, or I'll step out now and whistle for my friend, Sergeant Wurren, P.C. But if you plays fair, so help me God, I don't see why I shouldn't do the same, though I ain't made that promise till I knows more."

The doctor took McCarbre aside and spoke in low tones. "Can we trust this kid? There's no doubt but that he's knocked the right nail on the head. If we've got him, we've got eyes in the town and in the Precincts too, as well as hands to fetch and carry and ears to listen."

"Best of all, he can keep an eye open for that Paper Wizard." McCarbre added this in such an excitable whisper that the boy under discussion heard every word, and this reminded him that he must be loyal to his first employer, who seemed to be one against two. With this in mind he interrupted the conspirators with, "Do you mean a terrible fellow in a long great-coat what's covered with scissors and knives?"

"Yes," assented McCarbre eagerly. "Do you know him? What do you know of him? Do you know where he is now?"

Boyce's Boy, resolving to be true to his former patron, who was probably within hearing, and not quite knowing what to answer for the best, looked at the paper gibbet on the baize door. He recollected the irritation it had caused McCarbre that very morning in the Precincts, and so he drew his bow at a venture. "Precious near, I should guess," he whispered fearfully. "Ain't that his sign behind your head?"

Both men turned and looked at the silly symbol. The effect on the invalid was exactly what Boyce's Boy thought it would be. The shaft had struck between the joints of McCarbre's harness, for he hugged his dressing-gown about him and fairly moaned with self-pity and fear. The doctor, on the other hand, showed small concern.

"What does he matter, McCarbre, anyway? The fellow is out for blackmail. Well, two can play at that game. You can make him fair promises if we do meet him, and leave the rest to me. I'm not going to have our plans spoiled by some itinerant quack who happens to have a hold on your life. Your life is in my hands now, and I am determined to diagnose your case and without any interference, let me tell you."

McCarbre turned his back on the baize door, shuddering. "Do you know where he is, boy?" he asked sharply, adding in a kindlier tone, "I've got money. I'll give you ten pounds if you tell me true."

But Boyce's Boy did not earn it. Curiosity and the first tinges of terror paralysed his greed. He could not speak because he was looking across McCarbre's shoulder at the baize door.

"What are you staring at?" hissed McCarbre. "Can't you answer?"

Evidently not. The boy's teeth were clenched. His eyes started from their sockets. McCarbre turned and looked. With a cry he spun backwards and gripped the banisters to prevent himself from falling, for there, with his back against the baize door, stood the Paper Wizard, with a revolver in his hand.

The doctor was the first to recover from his surprise. In a matter-of-fact tone he inquired, "What have you come here for?"

"McCarbre knows," replied the Paper Wizard. "A little matter of murder—that's all."

"As I thought!" snapped the doctor. "Blackmail."

"Yes," admitted the Paper Wizard pleasantly. "Blackmail is the word. That's what I am here for, and if I get the situation right, blackmail is the word that fits you into this 'ere puzzle."

"What's your price?" asked the doctor.

"Equal to yours," replied the Paper Wizard. "That's more than you should get, considering I've waited years for this, and you've only just shouldered your way in."

"Let's go into the smoking-room, where we can talk," urged McCarbre going to the door in question.

The Paper Wizard nodded assent. The doctor blew out the candle and picked up the lamp.

"After you," he said.

"No, after you, if you don't mind," replied the Paper Wizard, covering the doctor with his revolver.

"Put that thing away," laughed the doctor, and then, turning to Boyce's Boy, he said curtly, "You stay here in the dark, and if you don't want your neck wrung—keep quiet."

"He's coming with us," corrected the Paper Wizard.

"Why?" challenged the other.

"Because Boyce's Boy is in this with me. There's two of you and there will be two of us. In that way things will be fair and square. Now, Mr. Doctor, after you, if you please," and the strange quartette passed into the smoking-room.

CHAPTER XIV

THE DISAPPEARANCE OF THE MS.

WHEN the whole coast of England is one vast Marine Parade—
that is when all the seaside towns are joined together by reason of
the increase in holiday population; when there is not one square
yard of frontage without its large hotels, its "Sea View," Boarding
Houses and its cinemas—there will still be left Dingy Ness. That
will be the last place to go civilized. This Ness, or Nose, owes its
wild state to the extreme difficulty you experience in getting there,
and when you have got there, to the extreme difficulty you have in
moving about there or getting back again, for the whole peninsula
is one vast collection of moving loose stones, rounded and polished by a million seas that have gone before. To move from one
fisherman's hut to another you place boards upon your feet worn
snowshoewise and called by the natives "backstays." If you fail to
take this precaution you have no respect for shoe-leather or the
comfort of your ankles. There is a fine lighthouse on the Ness—in
fact there are two. One of these days there will be a hundred, for
the extremity of the peninsula moves one solid yard per year, and
at that rate how long it will take to reach France we will leave to
the mathematicians. There is no hurry on Dingy Ness. The sea
sets the pace by merely piling up one yard of stone a year, and the
lighthouses wink every night across to their French colleague on
Grisnez, as much as to say, "There's goodwill between our coun-
tries now, thank God, for Boney's dead and Nosey's dead and our
folks no longer cut one another's throat, specially since we've been
having a go at other people's together, and it don't much matter if
our land does join up now, but by the way this old blustering sea is
working it I don't think it will be in our time."

There are three families who live upon the Ness, who always
have lived upon the Ness, and have always intermarried on the
Ness. The Jubbs, the Joys and the Joneses. These are all fisher-folk
or lighthouse-folk, not from choice but simply because there is

nothing else that it is possible to be upon the Ness. If you are not fond of trawlers and mackerel nets, and have not a burning desire to look after a lighthouse, well then—pardon the accusation, but you are a fool to go and live on Dingy Ness. Besides which—unless your name is Jubb, or Joy, or Jones, you could never settle into the life there. Jane Jerome was the only person who ever succeeded in breaking into that ring, and she is exceptional, and when all is said and done her names begin with a J.

Now Jane and the Dean had been putting their heads together and had formed very definite ideas concerning Daniel's future. As the Dean said, "If Daniel wants to be a writer, he must have his own place to work in. But why London? Why shouldn't he stay on in Dullchester? It's more peaceful here. I know many publishers. I can help him to place his work. Now, there's the coachman's house behind the Slype. It's vacant. It's antique. Could be made most attractive. Why not do it up for him, and be his landlords?"

Jane agreed. Mr. Gony, the Chapter architect, approved, for it meant the restoration of an interesting corner of the Precincts. So Mr. Norris was given the contract for repairing panelling, lead-rimmed windows, carved ceilings and ancient fireplaces. While this was being put in hand, Jane suggested a holiday on the Ness. Mrs. Jerome, preferring the comfort of the Deanery, excused herself, but agreed that it would do the Dean good to go with them, and so, the very next day, the wind having changed, bringing with it a sharp frost in place of rain, they borrowed the luxurious car owned by a wealthy Precincts lady named Mrs. Furlong, and set off, Jubb sitting in front with the chauffeur—Jane, the Dean and Daniel wrapped in rugs at the back.

The storm had stripped the trees of all their leaves, and the Dean remarked as the car glided down the Drive that Christmas would be upon them before they realized it. "When I was a boy, one Christmas seemed very far removed from the next, but as one gets older, I'm bothered if the new turkey doesn't pop up his head in the east to watch the old turkey's tail disappear in the west, and hey presto! before you know where you are, the new turkey has not only grown out of all proportion, but he is lying in state, surrounded by sausages, chestnuts and steaming gravy."

The car crept through Deanery Gate and into the narrow Precincts. Jane pointed to a figure, swinging on a chain between two posts at the corner of the churchyard. "I hope *he* won't get up to mischief when our backs are turned," she laughed. It was Boyce's Boy, having a quiet cigarette.

"He's a wicked-looking young devil," chuckled the Dean. "I believe his natural parents were those gargoyles above his head. You know he's no right to smoke among the graves, but I'm not going to tell him so."

The car turned into the High Street. As they passed the Police Station they heard a loud sneeze, and saw the sergeant in the window, blowing his nose. "Wurren's got a cold," remarked Daniel.

It was late afternoon when they topped the old coastline of cliffs now a mile or so inland, and the Marsh below spread itself out before their eyes like a great mellow map in the setting sun. The sea was as calm as a millpond, but the motor leapt down to meet it like a mill-stream. The rough road out to the Ness was traversed slowly, and just when the chauffeur was thinking that it was getting too bad for the health of his tyres, Jane pointed out the elfin figure of a little girl of ten, dressed in a red-brown overall, waving to them from a lofty pile of stones. "It's Mr. Jubb's grand-daughter," explained Jane. "She's brought over some 'backstays' for us to slip home in. She and I will give you all a half-way handicap, and even then I bet we will race you to the inn."

The child had bright red hair and sea-green eyes. "And she knows more about fish and boats than most of her sailor relations," Jane added.

"Hallo, Shrimps!"

"Ahoy, Winkles!" answered Joyce at the top of her lungs. A few minutes later an exhausted party clattered up to the Dog Fish Inn, and were thankful to find an old-fashioned high-tea awaiting them.

Now the Dean, his grand-daughter and Daniel all seem extraordinarily bashful when questioned as to what happened during their first few days at the Ness.

Apparently the Dean neglected his duties as chaperon in a shameless manner. Indeed, from what one gathers from old Jubb he needed a chaperon himself, for having discarded clerical collar, apron and gaiters within an hour of his arrival for fisherman's kit, he spent all of his time with little Joyce, nicknamed Shrimps, and entirely neglected the young couple, until he discovered that they were engaged to be married, which news delighted more than surprised him.

Old Jubb, who always referred to the Dean as His Harness—and when asked why explained that "the harness denoted his gaiters"—maintained that although the said Harness was extremely popular for his own sake as well as for Miss Jane's, "Captain Dyke was even more so." This may have been owing to the fact that Jones, Joyce's father, who was married to old Jubb's daughter, had served as officer's servant to Daniel during the war. He had certainly advertised his former master's many good qualities, which Daniel did not take long in living up to. His readiness to lend anyone a hand, and the charm and skill with which he did it, went straight to their hearts, so that while the sailors were ready to swear that the oldest salt amongst them could learn something from his style of handling a sail or motor engine, their wives were equally emphatic that he could be trusted to bath all the babies on the Ness, and even Old Jubb declared that although young Captain Dyke was always attempting to pick up something new from him, the Captain was in reality teaching him, the Father of the Ness, all manners of things unawares. And Jane, noticing the admiration which the younger women had for him, realized that if she had not fallen in love with him, her own popularity would have been seriously menaced. So although their engagement was not actually announced, it was generally understood that they were "walking out," and were regarded as a most refreshing romance, and the unanimous opinion of the Jubbs, the Joneses and the Joys was that if any member of the Jerome family objected to the match, they—the Jubbs, the Joneses and the Joys—would want to know the reason. But there was no likelihood of any such disapproval, for the Dean always got his own way in family affairs and was never tired of publishing his admiration for Daniel, as his remark to the young people will show on the occasion of their confiding to him the great secret. "If it's only a question of waiting till you've made good, my lad, I don't think there's much to hinder you, for the man who can make my Jane care for him has, in my opinion, made very good indeed. Besides, you've money enough between you to live very comfortably, even if you were not workers, which, thank God, you both are."

Jane had her own quarters on the Ness, a long hut built by the men, a stone's throw from the inn, where Old Jubb held the licence, and around which he had caused to be built many other huts to accommodate his threefold family. Jane's quarters looked like a ship, of course, for it had been fashioned by seafaring men and fitted with ship's furniture, and as Jones said to Daniel on his arrival, "You'll find it upon inspection, sir, full of convenient gadgets, and all of 'em working O.K., A-1, shipshape and Bristol fashion."

Daniel and the Dean stayed at the inn, a not very attractive house architecturally, with its iron-fenced cemented yard, over which the eternal stones got kicked when anyone went through the gate. A pale brick house that looked entirely out of place, giving the impression that it had originally been built as a water-works house, but before taking up its position beside some suburban reservoir, it had taken a sea trip, got wrecked, been washed ashore, scrambled up the stones, crawled inland a hundred yards, found the going difficult, got cramp in its scullery, which it dragged behind it like a broken limb, lost heart and decided to remain where it was. But however unattractive outside, it was comfortable within. Granny Jubb cooked divinely, and there were log fires—wreckage—in all the rooms. Jones was a capital servant—for he insisted upon taking up his old position of Daniel's batman, and he had fixed up a capital study in a room facing the sea, and here Daniel started in on his writing. By the advice of the Dean he began by re-editing a series of essays written in various parts of the world and which the Dean considered marketable.

Now the essays are important to our story, for as Daniel remarked afterwards, "the annoyance that they caused was the first little cloud which arose in the horizon of our happiness"—a cloud which was the herald of the storm of terror that was destined to blacken the first weeks of their engagement.

He had agreed with Jane not to show her his first series of essays till they were completed. This he knew would give him an extra impetus to work, for he considered that his writing was the best thing he had to offer her, and consequently this made him very jealous and fearful for her approval. Now whereas he would never have thought of locking up money or valuables in his room at the Dog Fish, he did lock up his manuscripts and hid the key of his dispatch-case on a nail behind a portrait of Jubb's father that hung over the mantelpiece.

On a certain Friday night the essays were completed, and on the next day he was to read them to Jane. As a rule Saturday was a let-up day on the Ness, but since Daniel had made his appearance miraculous shoals of mackerel had also appeared which the superstitious sailors somehow connected with him. "You've brought the mackerel with you, sir," was another form of saying, "You've brought fine weather," for mackerel meant work, and work money. The *Dog Fish* crew liked to keep the lead for prices in the market, and although many other fishing concerns had less distance to take their goods to sale, Jane's enterprise had provided them with motor-vans with which to outstrip their rivals. On this Saturday the extra work entailed by the miraculous draught of fishes caused Jane to do overtime, and it was tea-time before she was able to hear Daniel read. He went to his room to get the essays. The key was safely hanging behind the picture, but when he unlocked his dispatch-case, he discovered that his manuscript-book was gone. He hunted high and low. Nothing else in his case had been touched. He made inquiries but no trace of it could be found. Even Jones had been ignorant of where the key was kept, so the theft became very mysterious. Not that anyone on the Ness was suspected, for when all was said and done, to what possible use could fisherfolk put a collection of essays? The trouble was that Daniel had taken no second copy, and he feared that he might not be able to recall all the touches he had put into his work.

The Dean had returned to Dullchester that morning, in order to take Sunday duty at the Cathedral, so they would have to wait till Monday evening to get any advice from him. Jane questioned everybody, although she was confident no one on the Ness would rob Daniel of his work. They were too fond of him to do him such an injury.

"Well, it's no use grousing about it," he said, when all inquiries had proved fruitless. "The book's gone, and the only thing to do is to start the job again, before I forget it all. I'll give it till Monday to show up. If it doesn't, I'll burn the midnight oil again."

CHAPTER XV

A MINOR CANON DISAPPEARS

WHEN Monday came, however, Daniel had other work to do, and the essays were left to go on losing themselves, for Monday's mail brought a letter from a famous literary agent in London:—

"DEAR SIR,

"A leading publishing house being desirous of publishing a romance weaved around the Free Traders of Kent, we have ventured to give them your name, as we believe that you could turn out just the thing they want. A good story of smugglers and the smuggling times. If you would care to consider this proposition, an early reply would oblige.

"We are, yours very truly, etc., etc."

With a whoop of joy Daniel forget the troublesome essays, and clinched the smugglers with a wire to the agent.

"It's all very exciting," exclaimed Jane. "I wonder how they heard of you."

"Haven't the vaguest idea," replied Daniel.

"But I'm sick about those essays," went on the girl. "You'll never do them again, now that you've got the new interest. I'll never see them."

"Perhaps they'll turn up," answered the sanguine author. "They don't matter for the moment. Here's a real publisher on the end of a line that I haven't even troubled to bait. Jane, you've brought me luck."

As they were talking they noticed a little man walking over the shingle. Although he was a long way off, they could distinguish him to be a clergyman. He was much too small to be the Dean, who was not expected back till the evening, and the lovers wondered what a little parson was doing on the Ness. The poor little black figure was evidently in great difficulty. He kept slipping forward on his face, and it seemed that he only picked himself up again in order to be ready for his next tumble. It was like watching the White Knight in "Alice Through the Looking Glass." His tumbles became so numerous and perilous that Daniel seized a pair of "backstays" and hastened over the stones to assist the stranger, who was obviously making for the Ness, as there was nowhere else to make for. When Daniel reached the unfortunate wanderer, he found to his surprise that he was none other than Canon Cable, but the ancient scholar was in such distress that he did not at all realize who Daniel was.

"I thank you very much, young man," he said. "I don't know who you are, because I am very shortsighted, but will you tell me why the Dean spends his holiday in such a terrible spot? I have been tumbling about over stones ever since I got out of the train. No wonder they keep no taxicabs here."

"Did you want to see the Dean, sir?" inquired Daniel, giving the old cleric his arm, but thinking it would be a simpler plan to pick him up and carry him.

"Do I want to see the Dean?" repeated Canon Cable. "Well, it's not that I want to exactly, but that I must. He should not have gone away. I am unable to cope with it all by myself."

"Why, sir, I hope nothing has happened in Dullchester?"

"Nothing?" cried the Canon, standing still and blinking at him through his spectacles. "Well, it all depends what you call 'nothing.' If disappearances are nothing, then nothing has happened at Dullchester."

"Disappearances?" echoed Daniel, thinking of his essays. "What do you mean, sir?"

"Never mind," snapped the Canon. "First, get me somewhere and let me sit down, and then fetch me the Dean."

"But the Dean is in Dullchester, sir," protested Daniel. "He left here on Saturday and does not return till to-night."

"He didn't tell you he was going to Dullchester?" asked the canon, with horror on his face.

"I understand that he was due to preach at the Cathedral," explained Daniel.

"Fiddlesticks!" ejaculated the Canon. "Quaver was due to preach in the evening, and I was to preach in the morning, but as Quaver has disappeared, I had to preach twice, and not being a popular preacher like the Dean, it was very trying to me."

Suddenly the Canon threw up his hands and sat down on the stones. It gave Daniel quite a turn, as he thought the old man had been shot.

"Why was the Dean coming to Dullchester?" he gasped.

"Why, sir," humoured Daniel, "perhaps the Dean thought it would relieve you if he read the Lessons when you preached."

The Canon did not listen. He was following his own train of thoughts.

"At all events, this clears Quaver in my mind. Sergeant Wurren tried to persuade me that our Minor Canon had gone on the drink. Well, I don't suppose the Dean would go on the drink too, do you?"

"I shouldn't think he would go on it with one of his own Chapter," laughed Daniel. "It would be difficult to keep discipline if he did that."

"Then where's he gone to? He's disappeared too."

"Who? The Dean?"

"Yes. Where's he disappeared to? He is a most unreasonable man. Doesn't he realize what the province of a dean is? Has he never looked the word out in a dictionary? A dean is the second functionary of a diocese, sir. That means that in all matters practical he is the first, because the Bishop is always running about in a motor-car and one can never rely upon a bishop being on any given spot when he is wanted. Very well, then—why isn't the Dean on the spot? Why does he want to come and stay at a place like this—all stones? Are not the cobbles in Dullchester Precincts enough for him? But when he says he is going to be here, why isn't he? And if he tells you that he is returning to Dullchester, why isn't he in Dullchester? And if he isn't in his stall at the Cathedral, why isn't he in his library or his rose-garden or his pig-stye, instead of tumbling down a well or something after a minor canon?"

"Down a well?" repeated the amazed young man.

"Yes, indeed, sir. A well. Mr. Gony the architect assures me that Dullchester is full of bricked-up wells. Mr. Norris, who knows the place better than all of us, speaks in his books about secret passages and sudden drops with their mouths cemented up. Hasn't the Dean enough to worry him without seeking them out, removing the cement, and tumbling into them? I must now go back to Dullchester and wear out the ferrule of my walking-stick tapping the pavements for hollow sounds."

"But, my dear sir," pleaded Daniel, "if you will come as far as the inn and wait there for a few minutes, you could see Miss Jerome. Perhaps she could set your mind at rest."

"See Miss Jane?" answered the testy Canon. "I'm quite sure I couldn't. When I get worried, I get blinder and blinder, and I should not see her now even if we were rubbing noses like American Indians. Besides, if I did see her, what comfort could an unnatural girl like that give? She is, if anything, more impossible than her grandfather. The right place for a Dean's grand-daughter is the Deanery, and not a stony wilderness like this, a place that reeks of bad fish. Why can't she behave like a Dean's grand-daughter instead of emulating Billingsgate? I don't want to see her. I must get back to Dullchester. As to Quaver, his conduct is outrageous. I am supposed to be correcting Hebraic proofs for the Clarendon Press, instead of which I must spend my time asking an incompetent policeman why Dullchester Corporation does not keep bloodhounds with which to trace minor canons."

In sheer rage he shook himself free from Daniel's arm and began stumbling back towards the mainland.

If he fell often before, he fell oftener now that he was so incensed, and although Daniel resented his harsh criticism of Jane, he could not see an old man knock himself about unnecessarily. Easily catching him up, he begged the Canon to accompany him back to the inn, or, failing that, to allow him to be his escort to the station. This so enraged the little man that he struck at Daniel with his stick and with such force that Daniel's self-preservation made him dodge, which brought the Canon heavily down again upon the stones. This time he cut his nose and broke his spectacles, but before Daniel could give him any assistance he was up again and stumbling off in quite the wrong direction. Daniel followed him, out of range of the walking-stick, resolving to pick him up at his next fall; but the Canon, evidently suspecting something of the kind, kept turning round and blinking about, so that Daniel had to stalk him, keeping out of his line of vision, something as a hunter follows a rhinoceros. It was not long, however, before the Canon slipped again, this time sliding down a deep declivity of stones, and Daniel leapt in on him before he could rise, seized him tightly round the middle, lifted him bodily and ran with him over the stones. When he reached the smooth Marsh road and put him on his feet again, the little cleric still walked as if he were on stones, and was much surprised when eventually he discovered that he was not.

"Here are your spectacles, sir," said Daniel, holding out the broken glasses.

"Thank you," answered the little man. "I've cracked them. But I have another pair. A rough fellow I met on the beach cracked them. However, as you can see, I managed to escape from him, and I am glad to have met you, sir, for by your voice and actions you seem civilly-inclined."

"Won't you let me help you, sir?" asked Daniel, amazed at this sudden change in the old man.

"Yes. Thank you very much. I really need help. I want to see the Dean of Dullchester."

"He will be back here this evening, sir; not before, I'm afraid. It is a pity that his grand-daughter won't do, because she is coming along the road in this motor-lorry."

As he spoke, the *Dog Fish* motor-lorry had pulled up from the beach-head, and came roaring along the road. Jane had jumped up to the box-seat in order to cut off the Canon and Daniel, and she was now waving to them as they drew up.

"Why, it's Canon Cable!" she cried, springing down. "How are you? Did you come to see Grandpa or me? I hope you came to see me."

"Jane Jerome?" inquired the little man, blinking. "Is it really Jane?"

"Of course. Who do you think I am? You're just in time for lunch with Daniel Dyke and me," as she put her arm through Daniel's and pulled him forward.

"Daniel Dyke?" repeated the Canon. "Why, my late colleague Dyke had a son Daniel."

"Of course he did, thank heaven for it," she laughed. "And here he is."

The Canon now turned to Daniel and shook hands heartily.

"You must forgive me," he said, "for not having recognized you at once. But the fact is, I am not quite myself, for I have had some troublesome adventures."

"Where?" exclaimed Jane.

"Where but at Dullchester?" replied the Canon.

"Tell me everything," Jane said.

"Wait a minute," cried the Canon. "To cap it all, I come down here post-haste to get the Dean's advice, and I meet a man who leads me all over some terrible stones, knocks off my glasses, makes my nose bleed, wrenches my arm, tells me terrible lies about the Dean not being anywhere about, and finally chases me, throwing stones at me till I ache all over, and goodness knows what more he might not have done had he not been frightened off by the approach of this gallant young boy Daniel Dyke. Adventures like this at my time of life are too much for me, Jane," and the old man began to cry.

Daniel realized now that the old man had not the faintest idea of what had really happened, so, assisted by Jane, he led him once more across the stones to the safety of the *Dog Fish*, where he was very soon enjoying lunch, after having grease put on his nose by Mrs. Jones, who persisted in calling him "poor old Daddlecums."

Poor old Daddlecums partook heartily of lobster, and followed it with a Dover sole which he managed entirely by himself, with all kinds of vegetables, washing it down with a whole pint of stout, after which he retired to Daniel's bedroom, lay down on the bed and went sound asleep, while Daniel sat on the beach with Jane and related the true account of these extraordinary adventures.

"The fact is, my dear," she said, when she had listened to the whole story, "that the poor dear little man is so old that he doesn't know what is going on around him. He lives much more in the past than in the present, and although he could tell you every king that the Assyrians crowned, the name of the crown-maker and how much the crown cost, I doubt if he knows what king is ruling over him in England to-day. Indeed, as often as not in Cathedral he prays for Queen Victoria or Edward VII instead of King George. He's terribly absent-minded. As to Quaver disappearing, I don't believe it. He didn't happen to notice him during the Vestry prayer or something. Or perhaps Dossal took service to let Quaver go up in the organ loft with Trillet. The same with Grandfather. Dear old Cable got it firmly in his head that there would be no Dean yesterday, and although there was a Dean, he couldn't adapt his mind quickly enough to realize it. I'll have him motored back to Dullchester in the motor-lorry. Grandfather won't come down till the evening train, so it will be in time to bring him along."

After an early cup of tea, Canon Cable was prevailed upon to get into the lorry. Old Mrs. Jubb insisted on lending him her own cushion from her armchair, and to the last the old Canon, wrapped around in a crazywork quilt and a blanket which Mrs. Jubb had taken from the hot-linen cupboard and which gave him more than ever the appearance of a mummy, said that it was astonishing that one who could study the dead languages all night and every night should be made so sleepy by a little piece of fresh fish for lunch. He had forgotten that the "little piece" was a whole fat Dover sole, and that it had been washed down by a pint of strong stout. But, if he had forgotten this, he had not forgotten the villain of the stones, as he called him, and he conjured Daniel not to let Jane out of sight until such a rough customer had been laid by the heels. So, with many farewells, young Jones motored away over the Marsh to Dullchester, while the little mummy at his side fell against his shoulder and went fast asleep again, dreaming of dead kings who talked to him in dead languages, about villains who lived in stony places and ate minor canons for their lunch. At the back of the lorry, on the floor, sat old Jubb. He had insisted on accompanying them, at the last moment, in order to present to the Deanery a large basket of mackerel. Jane had accordingly scribbled a note to her grandmother, which old Jubb stuck in the ribbon of his battered straw hat. As the motor rushed through the bracing air, he also fell asleep, with his arms round the fish-basket and his head on the top of it, but he did not dream of dead kings, but of going down to the sea in ships, as befitted one who occupied his business in great waters.

CHAPTER XVI

ANOTHER MINOR CANON DISAPPEARS

When Jubb and Jones had deposited the sleeping Canon at his little house in Minor Canon Row, much to the alarm of the old cook-housekeeper, by the way, who was very scared to see her master wrapped up in such a bundle and was only pacified when Jubb presented her with a string of six mackerel and a large crab for her own consumption, the two fishermen repaired to the Deanery with Jane's note and their basket of fish. They found the servants' hall in great excitement over the disappearance of the Minor Canon, and when they wondered what the Dean would have to say when he heard about it, Jubb ejaculated, "Why, ain't His Harness in Dullchester?"

"Don't be loopy," exclaimed the cook, growing pale despite her red face, heated and mellowed from a thousand kitchen fires. "Ain't the Dean at Dingy Ness?"

"No, he ain't," asserted Jones. "He ain't, indeed, ma'am. We thought the old Canon what we've just brought back from the Ness was making a mistake. Ain't he really in Dullchester?"

Before they could argue the point further old Jubb was summoned to the drawing-room by Mrs. Jerome, who had just read Jane's note.

"Surely my husband the Dean is with you on the Ness?" she asked anxiously when old Jubb stood in the doorway, twiddling his straw hat.

"His Harness left us on Saturday," faltered the fisherman. "He left us to conduct services at the Cathedral, we understood, ma'am."

"But it's ridiculous," answered Mrs. Jerome. "He wrote to me on Friday telling me that the Ness was doing him so much good that I was not to expect him at the Deanery this weekend."

"All of which is perfectly true, my dearest Catharine." It was the Dean's voice, and there he was peeping over the screen. "Now give me a kiss, my dear. There, you need not be nervous in front of my friend Jubb. He kisses his wife in public. I've seen him do it."

"But where have you been?" exclaimed Mrs. Jerome, throwing her arms round her husband's great shoulders. "Wherever have you been?"

"Oh. Ah," chuckled the Dean, with a mysterious air. "Never you mind. You'll learn all about it in time, but at the moment it's a secret. How are you, Jubb?"

"Better now that I knows your Harness——"

"Is in harness again, eh?" completed the Dean. "No, Catharine. I fear you will have to go on guessing where I've been, because I can't, I mustn't tell you. It would spoil the whole joke."

"I'm mightily relieved to hear that it's only a joke, Jonathan," answered Mrs. Jerome with a touch of resentment. "I suppose Mr. Quaver's mysterious and most inconvenient disappearance is also part of this ill-timed joke?"

"Not a bit of it, my dear," replied the Dean gravely. "As a matter of fact, I have only just heard that news from Potter, and I must go straight round to question Mrs. Quaver about it. Put on your hat and come with me, if you will."

Accordingly the Dean and his wife took leave of old Jubb, giving him a note to carry back to their grand-daughter, and they both there and then set out for Minor Canon Row.

Mrs. Quaver, a pretty, blue-eyed, plump young woman, was looking out of the front window with a very melancholy expression upon her rosy face, but upon seeing the Dean she brightened up and ran to the front door.

"You have brought me news, Mr. Dean. Please, please come in."

The Dean and Mrs. Jerome walked into the front room, a pretty little panelled room with great oak beams showing in funny little corners, and mysterious oak cupboards let into odd nooks by the fireplace. This old-world chamber served as combined study and dining-room to the missing Minor Canon. At the centre table sat Sergeant Wurren, with a notebook before him and a pencil in his mouth.

As soon as the Sergeant had bowed officially to the newcomers and they on their part had taken their seats, Mrs. Quaver turned to the Dean and entreated him to give her some news of her husband.

The Dean was about to reply with the cold comfort that news of his Minor Canon was just the thing he wanted from her, when he was interrupted by Sergeant Wurren taking the pencil out of his mouth with a popping noise and rapping the table with it.

"Excuse me, miss," he said, addressing Mrs. Quaver, "but you must allow me to question his reverence. And, sir"—as he turned to the Dean—"although as yet we know nothing much about this extraordinary disappearance, I should like to warn you that the worst may have happened, and that anything that anybody says may be taken down against them, which might be awkward for somebody if this disappearance turns out to be murder."

"My dear Sergeant," laughed the Dean, "what on earth is the use of talking in that vein? Quaver isn't lost. I'm quite sure he isn't. Why, only just now my wife thought I was lost, and simply because she was under the impression that I was staying over Sunday at Dingy Ness, when I wasn't doing anything of the kind."

"Oh, then where were you, sir?" rapped out the Sergeant. "I happen to know that you were not at Cathedral."

"Where I happened to be," answered the Dean, "concerns nobody here, Sergeant, except my wife, and I have already refused to tell her, on the grounds that it would spoil a silly little surprise of mine, which I have long been cherishing, and in view of the fact that it has no bearing on the matter in hand, suppose we confine our attention to the Minor Canon's disappearance. I am quite sure, my dear Mrs. Quaver, that your excellent husband cannot be lost. It's too ridiculous."

"Then perhaps the Dean is able to inform us of his whereabouts?" snapped the Sergeant, making a note and then glancing suspiciously at the Dean.

"I regret very much that I know nothing whatever about it," said the Dean. "I have had the bare facts from Mr. Potter—namely, that the Minor Canon was not at his post on Sunday morning, but that he was seen by numerous Precincts folk on Saturday night."

"The last I saw of my dear husband, Mr. Dean," began Mrs. Quaver, with tears in her eyes, "was in my own room about——"

"Silence!" shouted the Sergeant. "I am conducting this inquiry, if you please."

"Oh, don't be silly," interposed the Dean.

"Let me tell you, sir," retorted the Sergeant, "that this affair is no longer a matter for the Dean and Chapter. It is a police affair. I am responsible for conducting it properly."

"Oh, shooks," said the Dean.

"What did you say, sir?" queried the Sergeant.

"I said 'Shooks,' whatever that may mean," answered the Dean irritably.

"And what may 'Shooks' mean?" asked the Sergeant.

"As I told you," replied the Dean, "I haven't the faintest idea. I heard Boyce's Boy use it the other day. It is slang, and I rather hope it means 'don't be silly,' because that's what I meant by using it."

"Now, Jonathan, don't quarrel with the Sergeant," urged Mrs. Jerome. "You both have Mrs. Quaver's interest at heart, I know."

"Nothing of the sort," contradicted the Sergeant. "A police officer is an impersonal machine in affairs of this kind. I have known in my own police experience wives who have wept buckets, as the saying is, when their husbands have committed suicide, and buckets more, as the saying is, when I clapped handcuffs on 'em for murder."

"Really, Sergeant Wurren," pleaded the Dean, "I must ask you to abstain from such shocking suggestions as suicide and murder. Mrs. Quaver is naturally worried over her husband's absence, and instead of showing her that it may be easily explained in a thousand ways, you are terrifying her by piling up imaginary agonies. If your calling will not allow you to show the poor lady sympathy, you can at least extend a little consideration."

"Neither consideration nor sympathy, sir!" thundered the officer. "By her own statement Mrs. Quaver was the last person to see the Minor Canon alive, and therefore she is the first person to come under suspicion. After what she has owned to having happened in the bedroom upstairs in the dark hours of Sunday morning, I want to know what became of Charles William Quaver's body."

"What *did* happen in the dark hours?" asked the Dean, involuntarily glancing at the ceiling to see if any blood had trickled through from the bedroom above. "Mrs. Quaver, kindly tell me."

"Mrs. Quaver will kindly do nothing of the sort," interrupted the Sergeant, turning back a page or two in his notebook. "The suspected party has made her statement, which I have taken down

and which will in due course be used against her. In her own interests she must not be allowed at this stage—this early stage—to
contradict herself. It would make her appear very fishy."

"Now, see here, Sergeant Wurren," said the Dean, pulling his
chair up to the table, and setting his top-hat down upon it. "You
and I are coming to an understanding over this affair. This mistake or, as you still prefer to call it, the 'crime'—let's call it the
crime for the sake of argument—the crime has been committed
on Dean and Chapter property. The master of the Precincts is
the Dean. I am responsible for the welfare of the Precincts and
all within it, and I will not give up my responsibility—even to an
officer of State. Church and State, you know, Sergeant. Not State
and Church."

Sergeant Wurren felt flattered at being called an officer of State.
The Dean continued:

"If you refuse to communicate to me, as Dean of Dullchester,
what has happened, or what you think may have happened, to one
of my colleagues, who, of course, may turn up large as life any
moment, I shall be forced in my own interests to put the matter
into the hands of a London detective, who will very soon get to
the bottom of the mystery. But if you prefer to work the matter
out for yourself, why, then, you will do me the courtesy of telling
all you know. If you compel me to call in aid from outside sources
it will place you in rather an *infra dig.* position, I should think."

"There is no need to call in help," replied the Sergeant proudly.
"I am perfectly capable of giving you all the information you
require in this peculiar little mystery."

"Glad to hear it," nodded the Dean. "Then fire away."

Sergeant Wurren, not knowing what else to do, began to read
from his notebook. "Deposition made by Mary Anne, wife of
Charles William Quaver, Clerk in Holy Orders, resident at No.
2 Minor Canon Row, Dullchester. On the night of the 15th inst.
said Mary Anne retired from study-dining-room and ascended to
best bedroom, situated immediately above same. Said Mary Anne
undressed herself and got into bed. Dozed on and off, and read on
and off. Realizing that many criminal instincts are generated from
certain novels of questionable type, I inquired name of book party
was dipping into in bed. She affirmed that she was reading *Thomas*

O' Kempis. I have not yet had time to dip into this book with the Irish name, but shall seize the same book when I go up to examine the bedroom again, so that I can dip into it myself at the Police Station."

The Dean chuckled audibly.

"You laugh, sir?" objected the constable.

"I only laugh," apologized the Dean, "because you are so very thorough. I should never have conceived it necessary to read *Thomas à Kempis* in order to get to the motive of a crime."

"The police has to be thorough, sir," went on the Sergeant, delighted to find what an impression he was making on the Dean. "Indeed, sir, if we were not thorough through and through, why, we should never get through any business at all. We have thousands of neat little tricks, wheezes, and gags, without which the prisons would be empty and the hangman idle."

"Which would be a terrible pity," said the Dean sarcastically.

"It would indeed, sir," answered the Sergeant sincerely. He then cleared his throat and went on. "Said Mary Anne called to her husband, upon hearing the Cathedral clock strike half-past eleven. When I questioned her as to the exact words she used, she answered, and I am bound to state with some confusion, 'Do come to bed, dearest.'" (Here the Sergeant as nearly as possible imitated a female voice.) "'Haven't you finished that sermon yet?' He replied, according to her statement, 'Yes. Just finished. Am coming up now.' Half-an-hour later, he appeared in the bedroom, explaining that he had been filling in his diary. On the mere mention of the word diary I realized that here might be some important information, so I demanded suspected party to produce same, which she did, and I am bound to say reluctantly. This is what the deceased party wrote." He turned to an open Collins' Diary that was lying before him on the table.

The Dean interrupted. "I wish you would refrain from calling my friend Quaver the deceased party. We have nothing to lead us to such a terrible supposition."

"Of course he may not be dead," answered the Sergeant largely. "We shall give him every possible chance to prove himself the contrary. But whether he is dead or alive, this is certainly what he wrote."

"Dated the 15th of this month. Was on duty Matins and Evensong. Looked in on Trillet to ask how choir practice went, as was unable to attend. T. tells me that our benefactor, Mr. McCarbre, was taken with a fit before choir practice, in the Lady Chapel. Meant to have left a card of inquiry, but forgot. Must remember in future not to forget things. Do it now, Quaver. Do it now. Do it now. A good Christian should never postpone doing little acts of courtesy. I am the more ashamed as I recollect telling good Canon Beveridge after Evensong that I would go round to McCarbre's without fail. I blame myself very bitterly. What a memory! Must think whether I can afford Pelman. Remember to talk this over with Mary. Choir got very flat during Nares in F to-day. Have a suspicion that the altos pull us down. Must tell my suspicions to Trillet. How often choirs are troubled with male altos. They are as difficult to keep up to pitch as they are to find. Must criticize Trillet severely for playing that Mazurka for a voluntary. Most unecclesiastical. Little Burton sang his first solo in 'Lead me, Lord.' The little chap looked very nervous, his prominent front teeth reminding me of a baby rabbit, but he did nicely, on the whole. Must talk with him on voice-production. Finished sermon for to-morrow on Lot's wife. What an interesting story, and what timely lessons may be drawn from it. Think I have handled it rather neatly. Am anxious to know what dear Mary thinks of it. Looking back is one of her weaknesses. Perhaps this sermon may enable her to realize what a danger this sometimes becomes. Must now retire. Cathedral bell chiming midnight."

The eyes of the listeners had riveted themselves upon Mrs. Quaver. The family secret just divulged from the husband's diary, namely, that his wife, like Lot's, had the failing of looking back, made the Dean half expect to see her there and then turn into a pillar of salt. In fact, he nicknamed her there and then in his own mind, "Mrs. Cerebos."

When the Sergeant had finished reading the diary, he again turned to his notebook and continued: "Having perused diary, the party under suspicion further stated, 'I had left the bedroom gas turned on, and I distinctly remember seeing my husband turn it out before getting into bed. I then fell asleep, and dreamt that my husband spoke to me, and on my not answering he struck a match, lit a candle that was beside the bed, and then got up and went into his dressing-room. I spoke to him, but he did not answer. This may have been reality and not a dream at all. It was early morning when I woke to discover that my husband was not in bed. I lay wondering whether he had got up to work on his sermon. While I was wondering, the Cathedral clock struck six. I called to him, and receiving no answer, got up and went to his dressing-room. His waistcoat was there, his clerical collar, his watch and chain, his shirt, his money and his glasses, but he was not. I slipped on a dressing-gown and went downstairs. In the hall I found the candlestick that had been at the side of the bed. His cloak, hat and scarf had gone from their peg, also his boots, which he used to put by the kitchen stairs before going to bed. I found his bedroom slippers in the dining-room. My husband had disappeared, therefore, in trousers, pyjama jacket, clerical jacket, scarf, cloak, hat and boots. I sat and shivered in the dining-room till the maid came down. She was as mystified as I. The Cathedral bell went for early service. My husband was on duty there, but, as we learnt after from Mr. Styles, he was not there. I have received no communication from him since. This is the whole truth, as God is my witness.'"

The Sergeant looked up, as much as to say, "There now, what do you make of that? If this ain't a murder, what is?"

The Dean was about to speak when there came a loud knocking at the front door.

"There he is, depend upon it!" he cried.

"He wouldn't knock," sobbed Mrs. Quaver. "He had his key with him. He always kept it in his cloak pocket."

The knocking was repeated.

"But it may be news," cried Mrs. Quaver, rising.

"I'll open the door, if you please," said the Sergeant. "I prefer that you do not hold any conversation with the outside world at the moment." He went towards the door. "If it is the body, or news of the body," he whispered to the Dean as he passed, "I shall be able to break it gently. Bodies often give women hysterics."

It turned out to be Mrs. Dossal, a badly-dressed little woman in black. She had mild eyes, with a long, curved, thin nose which gave her the impression of being a carrion crow converted to a diet of birdseed which was upsetting her digestion. She had no hat upon her head, which was not so surprising, considering she lived only next door, but her hair was blowing all over her face and she showed no signs of putting it straight. Indeed, she showed every sign of being mad. Her face was grubby and tear-stained. She kept gasping and sniffing, and her mild eyes looked scared. Had Sergeant Wurren arrested her for the murder of Mr. Quaver he would have had some justification. Mrs. Quaver sprang towards her and asked, "Have you news? What is it? You look queer."

Mrs. Dossal, dowdy wife of Minor Canon Dossal, looked boldly at the policeman, at the Dean, and then at Mrs. Jerome. With a gesture of despair she burst into tears of hysteria, fell on her knees in front of Mrs. Jerome, and buried her head in that good lady's lap.

"Now come, come, my dear," soothed the Dean's wife gently. "Compose yourself. What is it?"

The hysteria passed as Mrs. Jerome stroked the untidy hair. Mrs. Dossal looked up, blew her nose in a large handkerchief, and smiled an apology at the Dean for her weakness.

"When I saw you here, Mister Dean, in company with Sergeant Wurren, I thought at first that both bodies had been found."

"Bodies?" ejaculated the Sergeant eagerly.

"Both?" repeated the Dean. "What do you mean by 'both'?"

"My husband," sobbed Mrs. Dossal. "He has been untiring in his search for Mr. Quaver, for whom he has a real regard, though they do occasionally quarrel over voice-production, and now he has gone as well. They've both gone. We shall never hear their voices again."

The Sergeant rubbed his great hands together. "This looks to me like a double murder," he muttered.

Mrs. Dossal looked at him and screamed. Mrs. Jerome pacified her.

"No, no," interposed the Dean quickly. "Nothing of the kind. Who on earth wants to murder minor canons? They're the last class of people to be murdered. Dossal disappearing too is the best thing that could have happened. He is a man well qualified to take care of himself. His boxing is quite admirable. His single-stick rough but effective. He would never allow anyone to murder him. Dossal was searching for Quaver, and has probably found him. Wherever they are, you can depend upon it they are together. Now it is far easier to trace two men than one. If Mrs. Dossal will control herself and tell the good Sergeant all about it, I am sure he will make notes of every detail and explain the mystery to all our satisfactions."

"Certainly, Mr. Dean," replied the Sergeant with a show of great importance, and licking the point of his pencil to prove his willingness to make further notes. "In cases of this kind it is often the most insignificant detail that points the road to Justice and places the criminal on the scaffold. Do not be afraid of tiring me, Mrs. Dossal, with what may seem to you the most insignificant details, for, believe me, it is very often what you and the amateur in crime might call the most insignificant details that points—yes—that is——" The Sergeant, becoming aware that he had already given voice to this sentiment, changed his tactics, cleared his throat, frowned at Mrs. Dossal and then, looking at the Dean, added, "But it is my duty to warn this lady, Mr. Dean, that every syllable she utters may be eventually used in evidence against her." He then regarded Mrs. Dossal sharply and added, "Now then, the details, ma'am. Let's have no more prevarication or beating about the bush."

Mrs. Dossal, not being aware that she had prevaricated or beaten about any bush, and feeling very confident that she had not murdered her lord and master, also placing a greater faith in the justice of England than Sergeant Wurren's behaviour warranted, told the company that she was convinced that her husband had disappeared for good, as he had not come in to lunch, and in all their married life he had never been unpunctual for meals, "for, Mr. Dean, whatever faults dear Henry may have as a preacher there is nothing the matter with his appetite."

The Sergeant, utterly forgetting his former sentiments about insignificant details showing the path to Justice, thundered out in great wrath: "Madame, you cannot possibly waste the time of the police with such insignificant details as meals. Why ever shouldn't your husband miss a meal? He might not have cared for what you were preparing for him. I myself care nothing for sago. I would not sit down with a dish of sago. Considering that I myself saw the reverend gentleman in the Precincts this morning, we find that he has only missed one meal, for tea don't count. He may be searching for his colleague, as the Dean suggests, or he may not. It is not for the police to speak until they know, but you must give me more reason for his disappearance than the missing of one meal. If he don't turn up by to-morrow morning, come to me, by all means, and I'll handle your case as well as Mrs. Quaver's. One meal is not a clue, ma'am. You must find us another."

"There, then!" cried Mrs. Dossal, with something of triumph in her voice. "If you want a clue, *there*, and make something of that!" With a theatrical gesture she threw two small gelatine lozenges on the table.

"What are these?" asked the Sergeant, gingerly poking one of them with his pencil.

"Eucalyptus," cried the lady. "My husband always had two of them in his waistcoat pocket. In case he should feel like coughing during service, he would take one of these. They were his emergency lozenges."

"They look very grubby," remarked the Sergeant. "I perceive the dust from the Minor Canon's pocket adhering to the glutinous nature of the sweet."

"You are wrong again," exclaimed Mrs. Dossal.

"Eh?" queried the policeman, who was not aware that he had been wrong before.

"This is not dust from my husband's pocket 'adhering,' as you call it, to the lozenge. I brush my husband's pockets every morning while he shaves."

"Then what is it?" demanded the policeman, as if he had only been trying to entangle her.

"Precincts dust," replied Mrs. Dossal. "I picked these lozenges up at the corner of Bony Hill. They were shining like gems. One had been deliberately stuck on to the railings of the Cathedral and the other lay in the middle of the pavement, three yards away."

"But I don't see much clue in these things," declared the policeman. He did really, only what he did not see was what use he could make out of them.

"Well, I do," answered Mrs. Dossal. "These are a deliberate message from my husband. It means that he is in the hands of ruffians. Don't we read of dreadful things in the papers? Very well; why may not dreadful things have happened to our dear husbands?"

"I agree, ma'am. I agree," acquiesced the Sergeant. "No doubt they have. But these 'ere lozenges——"

"Are an SOS. Believe me, Mr. Dean, that's right."

Sergeant Wurren, seeing that the Dean was being appealed to and determined not to lose the centre of the stage, as it were, made a grand attempt at creating an impression. "You mention the newspapers, ma'am. May I ask if you have read them lately?"

"I glance at the pictures every morning," answered Mrs. Dossal. "Although my whole energies are devoted to the welfare of my husband and the Cathedral, I consider that it is essential to keep in touch with the events of the world. It often gives Henry an idea for his sermons."

"Then perhaps you have noticed that the three capital K's are very busy again." The Sergeant looked round to enjoy the obvious impression he had created.

"The Ku Klux Klan, do you mean?" laughed the Dean. "What on earth should they be doing in Dullchester?"

"Ah. Yes. What?" repeated the Sergeant with great relish, as much as to say, "You don't know, but I have a pretty shrewd idea."

The Dean was not impressed, because he merely said, "Nonsense." This enraged the Sergeant. "Nonsense?" he repeated. "How I wish it were; but the little the police know of the Ku Klux Klan is far from nonsense."

They were interrupted by the bells ringing for five o'clock Evensong.

"Sergeant Wurren," said the Dean, taking his hat and moving towards the door, "this little mystery will probably be cleared up any minute, but until it is we must all keep in touch with one another. If nothing is heard of the Minor Canons before to-morrow morning, I think it is our duty to get into touch with the London police and perhaps the Press; but that is really your department, so you must think over the wisest course to take."

This little speech was so gratifying to the police officer that he bowed, first to the Dean and then to the ladies, saying, "Very well, Mr. Dean." He then dropped his official manner in a genuine attempt to convey his sympathy, addressing the grass widows with, "Believe me, ladies, we shall do all in our power. It is our duty to be stern and suspicious when conducting any case for the Crown, but believe me, our only desire is to see justice done, wrongs avenged, the innocent cleared, and the criminal convicted. As Sergeant of the Police I shall do nothing but towards these ends, but as plain Bill Wurren, dropping the Sergeant as it were *pro tem.*, Mr. Dean, well, I'm sorry to see you all so upset."

The dignity and simplicity of this little speech, in spite of its stupidity, did more than atone for all the offence he had given, and as they all rose from their seats they were glad to have Bill Wurren as Police Sergeant of Dullchester.

"Perhaps you will walk with me as far as the Deanery, Sergeant," suggested the Dean. "No, Catharine, I would rather you stayed with these dear ladies than accompany me to Evensong. I will call for you here on my way back from Cathedral," and linking his arm through that of the Police Sergeant, he departed to the Deanery to robe for service.

CHAPTER XVII

IN THE SLYPE

THEY went by the short cut through the Deanery stable-yard and so past the pigstyes.

"Not killing any pork for Christmas, Mr. Dean?" inquired the Sergeant, smacking his lips with appreciation.

"No, indeed," replied the Dean, bestowing sundry pats upon the wet snouts that were thrust through the fence to greet him. "My pigs are pets. It would seem like murder to kill them."

"Murder, eh?" repeated the Sergeant. "Let's hope that word ain't come to darken the Precincts. But I ain't sure."

"I won't let myself think of such a thing," was the Dean's comment to that. "But these disappearances are odd, to say the least of it. They are odd, because I can see no motive in them or for them. They are indeed so very odd that anything might almost result from them."

"Even murder," responded the policeman. "I'm not at all sure we shouldn't own to the possibility."

"What are you going to do now?" asked the Dean, when they

reached the side door that led from the garden to the Dean's study.

The Sergeant shuffled his great boots on the wire door-mat before replying, and then said, "Well, I don't know as how I won't come in unofficially and hear service. It's soothing listening to singing sometimes, and I want to think."

"Very well," exclaimed the Dean. "Come in, Sergeant, and I'll give you a glass of good old sherry to drink while I robe. It's getting chilly."

In the study Mr. Styles was waiting to robe the Dean. However, first of all an old bottle and three glasses were produced from a cupboard in the bookcase, and the Dean asked them to drink to a better state of affairs in Dullchester.

"Ah," said Styles, with relish. "You may well say that. Most peculiar, your reverence, these 'ere Minor Canons popping off like this. Never heard of such a thing since I've been at the Cathedral. What they think they're after I don't know. Best respects, sir, and, Mr. Wurren, your health." The old man finished his glass at a gulp. "Good, but badly corked," he muttered as he made ready to remove the Dean's coat. The Dean drank slowly, like a connoisseur. Styles did not approve of anything slow when the five-minutes bell had started. He pointed this fact out to the Dean with a tone of reproach. "Five-minutes bell, your reverence, and we are not ready. I hope we are not going to be late." Perhaps this reproof was also meant to convey, "Even though you do give me a glass, I don't approve of sherry-drinking before service."

Accordingly the Dean hurried, and in three minutes was walking through the Slype on the way to the South Transept, preceded by Styles with a lantern and his silver wand, followed by the Sergeant. Now, as has been mentioned in a previous chapter, the doors of the Slype were closed but never locked until after Evensong. They were closed in order to secure privacy to Prebendal Garden, adjoining Canon Beveridge's residence, but they were unlocked to enable any Precincts folk to use the Slype as a quick means of access to Cathedral (this by the courtesy of Canon Beveridge), and they were locked after Evensong to prevent undesirables from using the passage. Now, on the left side of the Slype going towards the tunnel steps there was an archway cut in the wall, with a stone seat let into it. This shelter was used by errand-boys on the way to the Canon's back door. Its seclusion gave them a safe hiding-place for a smoke, and many is the time that the cook had rung up Stalk's the butcher's to know how long the joint would be, when all the time its wooden stretcher reposed upon this comfortable ledge, while Jim, the son of Stalk and errands of that firm, was discussing Dullchester politics with Boyce's Boy. As the little procession passed down the Slype in the gathering darkness, a voice rang out from this sheltered seat:

"My eye. Look! What's old Wurren pinched the Dean for?"

The Sergeant immediately recognized the voice of his enemy, Boyce's Boy.

"Come out of that, you young rascal," he rasped.

"Don't you come near me," came the answer, "unless you wants mud chucked. I've got a fistful and I don't want to dirty the Dean's surplice, which might happen if you ducked."

Styles, also recognizing the voice from the darkness, hastened his dignified steps, gripping his silver poker the tighter.

"Come along, Sergeant Wurren," laughed the Dean. "The young rascal doesn't mean any harm."

Sergeant Wurren, not wishing the Dean's surplice to be bespattered while in his company, was only too glad to let well alone, and accordingly followed them down the Slype. It was not until he had safely descended the steps and turned the corner through the tunnel that he gave vent to his feelings.

"That young rogue will come to hang in my time, I do believe."

"I hope not," replied the Dean. "I really don't know what Dullchester would do without him. He's a worthless scamp, but there's something attractive about him."

"Attractive, sir?" queried the Sergeant. "Whatever makes you say that?"

"I don't know," replied the Dean. "But it's the sort of quality that makes children go on loving Mr. Punch even when he's murdered Judy, thrown the baby out of the window and beaten Dog Toby. It's because there's something naïve about him."

"Oh, he's a knave all right, but I don't see no attraction in knavery, myself. And I don't approve of Punch and Judies. It's soft-soaping crime. It's dreadful to me when Punch hangs the hangman."

"It's very revolutionary," admitted the Dean.

"As to Boyce's Boy," went on the Sergeant, "you can take it from me, sir, that if them Minor Canons of yours have really disappeared, that Boyce's Boy knows more about it than we do."

The Dean left the Sergeant in the South Transept in order to attend the Vestry prayer. The policeman was making his way towards the Chancel gates when he met Mr. Potter, clad in his gown, coming out of the Lady Chapel.

"Rum things been going on lately, Sergeant Wurren," he said. "What with old McCarbre's screaming fit, that there Paper Wizard popping up again, and then two Minor Canons popping off, I don't know what the Cathedral ain't coming to."

"Dullchester ain't dull these days, Mr. Potter," acquiesced the policeman.

"Dull! Why, do you know, nothing wouldn't surprise me, it wouldn't. There goes Vestry prayer. Hear it? Well, if instead of them choir-boys clattering along in the candlelight, I was to see the Deanery pigs in surplices, I wouldn't even say, 'Well, there!' No, not even if Miss Tackle took a swarm of bees out of the big organ-pipe. Such goings-on we've never had in this Cathedral, Sergeant Wurren. Why, I've not even acted surprise at seeing you here, though now I comes to think of it, what are you doing here?"

"Divine Service," explained the Sergeant. "Can you find us a seat for it?"

This whispered conversation was interrupted by the scraping and pattering of innumerable boots approaching from the darkness. Then the organ-pipes above began to blow a dismal obbligato.

"Find you a seat? Take as many as you like, and put your legs up," answered the amazed Potter. "I can't come with you. I picks up the procession as it rounds this bend."

The Sergeant hurried to the chancel, walking like a ballet dancer on the tips of his toes, to convey reverence and at the same time to prevent, as far as possible, his boots from squeaking.

"Surprises and surprises!" muttered Potter. "Thought nothing else staggering could happen, and now, 'Find us a seat,' says the policeman! Now, what in the name of all that's holy does he want to come poking his nose into Cathedral for?" And, picking up the procession, or rather, pushing himself in front of the two little leading choristers, Mr. Potter allowed the stream of white surplices to float him up the steps under the organ-loft, through the chancel arch into the candle-lit choir, where he continued to stare at the policeman, who had sat himself next to Miss Tackle in the stalls, much to that lady's embarrassment.

There being no Minor Canons for duty, the Dean himself began the service. *"When the wicked man turneth again from his wickedness that he hath committed and doeth that which is lawful and right——"* "Yes, when," thought Sergeant Wurren—*"he shall save his soul alive. Dearly beloved brethren——"* "Have them two Minor Canons got sick of all this and just cut and run, or what?"—*"sins and wickedness."*—"It ain't right for them to desert all this any more than a soldier ought to desert the colours or a policeman his beat."—*"should not dissemble or cloak them"*—"On the other hand, are they innocent? Have they been done away with? Who would want to do away with a pair of Minor Canons? I know. Atheists. But we don't hear much about them lately. Hallo. We kneel down here."

Sergeant Wurren's thoughts were running riot. "Of course, they may turn up large as life and just as natural as the saying is. To-morrow morning perhaps. Or perhaps they have turned up already. If they haven't—if they don't—the world will look to me to find them. Hallo. I ought to be standing up again. Astonishing how one forgets one's church. If they don't turn up, what will their wives say?" *"O God, make speed to save us!"*—"If they don't, where the hell am I going to look for 'em?"—*"O Lord, make haste to help us."*

The Dean was giving out the Psalms for the day when there came a clattering up the aisle. "A late comer," thought the Sergeant. "Very brave, whoever it is. I should be nervous to walk in here when they've all begun. I couldn't face them little boys all a-staring."

Boyce's Boy walked through the chancel gates, his cap in his hands held before him, tiptoeing to a seat. Although he looked the picture of innocence and reverence, several of the choristers, knowing Boyce's Boy, sniggered and were duly poked in their backs by the lay clerks. Boyce's Boy selected a seat opposite the Sergeant.

The choir began the Psalms. They were tricky ones. Everyone's attention was therefore riveted upon the psalter. Had the pointing not been so difficult they might have looked at Boyce's Boy. On the other hand, they might have looked at Sergeant Wurren. If they had, they might have seen a great light of understanding shine from that gentleman's eyes as they stared at the reverent Boyce's Boy. Sergeant Wurren did a rare thing. He made up his mind quickly. He forgot that he might be nervous if the choir stared at him. He turned round in his stall. He grabbed his peaked cap from under the seat and deliberately walked, not like a ballet dancer but like an ordinary individual, down the chancel, between the staring choir-boys, past the Dean's stall on his left and Canon Beveridge's and Canon Cable's on his right, and disappeared into the darkness of the nave.

Mr. Potter walked across to the Dean and whispered, "I'll go and see what's the matter with him. Perhaps he feels sick. He mustn't be sick in the nave." He nodded at the Canon in residence as much as to say, "Don't worry. I'll deal with this," and followed the Sergeant into the gloom. The Psalms went on irresistibly for the benefit of Miss Tackle and Boyce's Boy, and drowned the excited conversation that passed between the underverger and the policeman.

Throughout the whole service the behaviour of Boyce's Boy was exemplary. He followed the prayers in a prayer-book. He even followed, or pretended to follow, the Lessons in a Bible, and never did he raise his eyes to look about. The choir-boys were quite disappointed at this good conduct. They had banked on something funny happening and they went back to the Vestry dissatisfied with their hero.

When the choir had shuffled out of the chancel, Boyce's Boy knelt down again. He remained kneeling for a long time. He had made up his mind to out-kneel Miss Tackle, who presently collected her umbrella, straightened her veil, tightened her goloshes, and made her way to the North Door. Boyce's Boy, following her at his leisure, was just in time to see Potter locking that door for the night.

"Way out by the West Door now," remarked the underverger.

"Why not by the South?" asked Boyce's Boy.

"Because the Dean and Canons ain't using it to-night. They're going to Minor Canon Row. West Door's nearest."

"If it's good enough for them, I suppose it'll do for me," replied Boyce's Boy. "But why can't you let me out of this one? You let Miss Buzz out. It would only take half a jiff to unlock it."

"Orders is orders," remarked Potter. "If you don't want to spend the night here, you'll get along quick to the West. Don't suppose you'd relish sleeping among the hassocks and the tombs."

"Shouldn't mind," answered Boyce's Boy. "Slept in worse places and more draughty places, as you know, and I ain't afraid of ghosts."

"Who said 'ghosts'? I didn't," snapped the verger.

"But you believe in 'em," jeered the boy.

"Don't," replied the old man irritably.

"There ain't much conviction in your 'don't,'" sneered the boy. "Bet you wouldn't sleep the night here. Bet you five bob."

"Shouldn't be so stupid," remarked Potter.

"Bet you ten bob."

"Prefers my bed."

Boyce's Boy produced a pound note. "Bet you a quid you don't to-night."

Potter regarded the note, mentally working out what he could do with it.

"Come on. Be a sport. Take it. You can hold the stakes," persisted the boy.

While he looked at the note Potter wavered. Then he glanced round at the dark building. He heard a door slam in the deep dismal crypt. He listened to the echoes—shuddered at the thought of spending half-an-hour there alone, and walking away from Boyce's Boy and the pound note, he muttered, "I never bets in Cathedrals."

Boyce's Boy, proceeding to the West Door, was saying to himself, "Good. That's what I was told to find out. The old 'un wouldn't spend a night here—no, not for nothing."

At the West Door Canon Beveridge was pinning up on the notice-board a list of offertories. The Dean was waiting for him, holding back the swing door.

Boyce's Boy hurried forward with gratitude on his face, and as he passed the Dean, said, "Thank you, Mr. Dean. Very kind. Feels like snow in the air. Wrap up well."

"Well, I'm——" The Dean did not complete the sentence aloud.

"What?" queried Canon Beveridge. "Did you speak, Mr. Dean?"

"Nothing," answered the Dean; "except that Boyce's Boy is getting no end of a wag."

"He behaved very well during Evensong. I was glad to see him there," and the old Canon followed the Dean through the swing-doors.

"I wonder why he came," remarked the Dean, drawing his Inverness cape round his surplice, for it was snowing.

Outside in the shadow of the arch stood Sergeant Wurren. He touched his cap to the clerics.

"Do you want to speak to me?" asked the Dean, thinking that the Sergeant was waiting to explain why he had left the chancel so abruptly.

"No, sir. I'm just keeping an eye on Boyce's Boy. I've got an idea about him, a kind of clue which, in fault of a better, I shall follow to the end. Excuse me sir," and the policeman walked quickly away towards the trees, the shadow of Boyce's Boy going ahead of him, flipping a twig against the railings of the graveyard as he went.

CHAPTER XVIII

MISS TACKLE DISAPPEARS

THE Minor Canons were not discovered the next day. They were not discovered the next week. The matter became serious. The Mystery of Dullchester was the leading sensational topic in the London papers. A thousand theories fantastic and absurd were put forward by people who knew nothing about it. Amateur detectives wrote and offered their services to the bereaved ladies. Newspaper camera-men snapped Minor Canon Row from every eye-line. In fact, Great London deigned to realize that there was such a city as Dullchester which owned a Cathedral, a Castle and a history as ancient as the Metropolis herself. But when the Minor Canons failed to put in an appearance, dead or alive, London began to think that Dullchester was overdoing it, and interest flagged. Pictures of the Minor Canons' wives which had appeared on the front page of the illustrateds gave way to the usual round of boxers, revue-artists, politicians, brides and *divorcées*, while the mystery of Dullchester remained as a mysterious jotting in the 'also ran' news-columns. Even the sudden arrest of Boyce's Boy, which caused the greatest sensation in Dullchester itself, failed to interest Fleet Street. But the startling disappearance of Miss Tackle awoke the general interest again. Here was a lady in the case. Two Minor Canons and a veiled lady. Poor Miss Tackle, in reality the most old-maidenish of spinsters, busy all day with her bees, so that she never remembered to remove her be-netted bonnet, became in newspaper fiction the beveiled beauty of an Eastern harem. Fleet Street would have taken no interest in Miss Tackle if she had not worn a veil. There was just the necessary *flair* in the veil. A slick journalist can do more with a veil than the most skilful milliner—for no milliner could have arranged Miss Tackle's butterfly-net to look anything else but a meat-cover. However, by a few dainty words the pressmen pictured the old buzzer—Boyce's Boy called her this—as a young butterfly within the net, and hey presto! the coarse anti-insect veil became the softest ninon yashmak of romance. *Clergymen and Veiled Beauty.* What a line for a jaded cap-tion-writer. *Deserted Wives Smile through their Tears and still Believe in their Wandering Husbands.* That sort of stuff makes any paper sell. Wouldn't you read details of such headings? Of course, and so would any other respectably-bored citizen.

Naturally the non-appearance of the Minor Canons was a great anxiety to the Dean, but it was even more of an anxiety to his wife. Mrs. Jerome was anxious about her husband. He had never explained to her why he was absent over that last week-end, and when questioned on the subject he not only declined to give an explanation but, contrary to his sunny and straightforward dispo-sition, became not only angry but the more secretive. Since then he had twice taken the train to London without telling her what he did there. As she reminded him of his meetings and clerical appointments, keeping his engagement-list for him, she knew that these sudden disappearances had nothing to do with his work. Neither did they seem to have anything to do with the missing clergymen, because when he returned he was anxious to find out whether there was any news, and confessed to feeling guilty that he should use any of his time on matters that had not to do with their recovery. Sergeant Wurren also had begged the Dean to tell him where he had been from that Saturday to that Monday, but the more he begged the more stubborn became the Dean.

"It really would not interest you in the least. You will soon know, and then you will realize what a fuss you are making about nothing. If I find it impossible to tell my wife, I certainly cannot tell the Police Station. It is something that I must keep to myself."

Jane had motored up to Dullchester on the Wednesday. She and Jubb had brought along a lorry-load of fish for the market, and naturally she was astounded at the extraordinary affairs that were going on in the Precincts. She got all the details from Kitty Beveridge, her particular friend in the Canon's household. Kitty was a very jolly girl, the same age as Jane, and the two had only to meet to go into peals of laughter over everything or nothing. They talked nineteen to the dozen. While Kitty, with her Dresden-china features and pink-and-white complexion, was certainly the prettiest thing in the Precincts, Jane was perhaps the most beautiful.

"Of course we are all dreadfully worried and puzzled about Quaver and Dossal, but my dear Jane, one really can't help enjoying Boyce's Boy's latest. Haven't you heard? He's locked up. Old Boyce is furious. He says no policeman has a right to arrest his errand-boy. I'm glad he's sticking up for the little beast."

"You shouldn't call him a little beast," said Jane. "You adore him as much as I do. But when did all this happen?"

"Why, on Monday night. To everyone's astonishment, Boyce's Boy walked in to Evensong, as good as gold. Of course, my dear, I've been kicking myself ever since that I didn't go. Just my luck. I always do go and nothing ever happens, and the one service I miss, all this excitement. It serves me right. Father asked me if I were ready, but I shammed a headache to finish a novel. After service Boyce's Boy was terribly cheeky to the Dean, so Father says, and then Sergeant Wurren followed him. Now here's the joke. I never knew this, but Boyce's Boy has formed a sort of Union Friendly Society of all the errand-boys in the High Street. He elected himself President, and went off after Cathedral to attend a meeting in Potter's tool-shed in the graveyard. Wurren thought this a good opportunity for arresting him, so as he came out of the shed he got collared for trespassing. He said he couldn't be trespassing on property he paid rent for, and it turns out that old Potter had let them the tool-shed for their meetings, on condition that they didn't make a noise or show a light. Of course, Potter was hauled up before the Chapter, but Father says they couldn't get any satisfaction out of him. He kept saying that he wouldn't be responsible for a lot of young ruffians, and that he wouldn't be responsible for the Precincts if the Dean and Chapter got up against Boyce's Boy. In fact, all he said was that he wouldn't be held responsible for anything under any circumstances, so long as the Dean and Chapter took away all his power. Nobody knew what he meant."

"What did Wurren have to say about it all?" asked Jane.

"You may well say that, because with him the plot thickens," went on Kitty. "He accused Boyce's Boy of having pushed him into the swimming-bath one night last week."

"Pushed Wurren into the swimming-bath?" repeated the amazed Jane. "Go on. This is glorious."

"So next morning," went on the fair narrator, "Boyce's Boy appeared before Mr. Watts, who came in last night and told us all about it. Simply killing. Boyce's Boy listened to all the Sergeant had to say, very gravely (can't you imagine it?). Then he said, 'Mr. Mayor, what I want to know is this. Is Sergeant Wurren within his rights if he arrests you for trespassing in your own dining-room?'

"'No, he would not be,' answered Mr. Watts.

"'Why?' asked Boyce's Boy.

"'Because it's my house. I pay the rent,' answered Mr. Watts.

"'Well then, so do I for the tool-shed. It ain't my fault if old Potter rents me Dean and Chapter property without telling them. That's their funeral, and I suppose my money's legal tender, ain't it? It has the sovereign's face on it like yours, I hopes.'"

"My dear," giggled Jane. "What a scream. Well?"

"Well," went on Kitty, "then Wurren got back to the swimming-bath. I suppose he saw that he had made a bloomer about the tool-shed. The pushing in the water episode apparently happened on that terribly wet night last week, at somewhere about eleven o'clock. Boyce's Boy listened to a long rigmarole story, which even Mr. Watts told us sounded an exaggeration, and then said: 'Mr. Mayor, now I ask you, do I look as if I could pick up that there sergeant and throw him into the swimming-bath? I wish I could.

Why, I'd go on the halls and throw policemen about for money if
I could. Would I stay here if I was such a Samson? No. I'd walk out
now into the High Street, with him under one arm and you under
the other. You wouldn't dare trump up cases against a Samson.
You wouldn't dare tamper with a Samson's liberty. Not that you've
done yourselves much good by tampering with mine, for I've had
the town posted'—and, my dear, he had."

"Posted? What did he mean?" asked Jane.

"Every hoarding, every shop-window on the outside of the
glass, every front door in the Precincts, even the backs of some
of the stalls in the choir, was pasted over with printing like this."
Kitty Beveridge went across to the mantelpiece and produced a
pink paper, discoloured by paste and torn at the edges. She held it
up to Jane, who read aloud:

> "BOYCE'S BOY ARRESTED.
> WHAT FOR?
> NOTHING.
> THEN LOOK OUT, ALL.
> WHY?
> AH!"

The "Ah" seemed to convey somebody was, in the vulgar ver-
nacular, "for it." The somebody turned out to be everybody who
resided in the Precincts, as the following chapter relates.

CHAPTER XIX

THE TRADES-BOYS RETALIATE

THAT night any of the Precincts folk who happened to be awake
might have heard strange noises in the chimneys. It was snowing
hard, and it sounded as if drifts of snow were falling through from
the roof into the fireplaces. When the servants went to do their
respective rooms in the morning they were astonished to find
vast quantities of soot everywhere. Curtains, ornaments, carpets,
everything covered with smuts. Now this was the more strange

because the sweep in the High Street, who was on contract to keep the Chapter chimneys clean, had only that week finished performing this annual office, and his cartload of soot all packed in dingy bags had been backed into the yard of the local florist, who always purchased the Precincts soot to sell to the Dean and Chapter for garden manure, a back-handed piece of graft that had never been spotted by the Cathedral treasurer, Mr. Watts.

This unparalleled fall of soot was not quite so mysterious when the florist discovered that every bag on the sweep's cart had been emptied. The sweep and nurseryman both took their oath before Mr. Watts that they had been full the night before. As each bag was tilted up to prove to the Mayor that the soot had indeed gone, a pink paper fluttered out with the announcement of Boyce's Boy's arrest.

Sergeant Wurren, with police penetration, discovered that a ladder usually hanging in the Deanery stableyard had been thrown into a railed-off corner of Minor Canon Row, where Potter always shot his barrow-loads of leaves. By examining the bushes that grew in this leaf-moulded dump-heap he proved that the ladder had been placed in the night against the last house of the Row, and by climbing up to the roof he discovered a sooty track amongst the snow path that ran from chimney-stack to chimney-stack.

Therefore some person or persons had with intent of nuisance deliberately clambered on to the roof and upset the bags of soot down the chimney-pots.

Boyce's Boy, having spent that night under legal lock and key, could not be accused in person, but that his organizing had everything to do with it nobody was in the least doubt, especially since the pink papers had fluttered out of the soot-bags. The errand-boy at the florist's was severely cross-examined, but by the help of his parents he was able to prove an alibi. Jim Stalk, as Vice-President of the Trades-Boys' Union, was not so stupid as to send one of his members into a point of danger if suspicion was certain to fall upon that individual.

Another way in which the Precincts was harassed occurred on the next morning. It was the custom of the dairymen to leave the milkcans very early in the Precincts. Upon this morning there were nothing but empty cans when the servants collected them before washing down the front doorsteps. The complaints became so bitter against the milkman that he complained in his turn to the Police Station. He took his oath that the milkcans were full when he left them outside the doors. Later in the day, when Potter went to feed the Deanery pigs, he discovered the drinking-troughs had been filled up with milk. Indeed, even the greed of the pigs had not managed to finish such a quantity. This also pointed to Boyce's Boy—but Boyce's Boy was under legal lock and key.

Another trick was played the next night which became rather more alarming. To the inside of every front door knocker in the Precincts was affixed a large gunpowder cap, so that the first persons who used the knockers the next morning were astounded at the mighty bang and flash they produced. Rhodes the toyseller and Huntley the gunsmith confessed that they had supplied a number of boys with boxes of caps the day previously. Evidently these had been emptied of gunpowder and repasted into powerful packets of explosives. Both these tradesmen were inclined, however, to forget the faces of any of their young customers. Perhaps they feared to turn informers during such a reign of terror.

Old Boyce, who was put to much inconvenience over the loss of his "errands," showed his disapproval by catching a cold and absenting himself from Cathedral. He even developed an acquaintance with Jim Stalk, who was condescending enough to organize his errands for him, on condition that the wages of his interned captain were put by till such a time as Boyce's Boy might be gloriously restored to liberty.

CHAPTER XX

BOYCE'S BOY IS CALLED IN QUESTION

FOR two days the prisoner had a cell to himself, his meals being brought to him by a policeman. On the third night the door was unlocked and a rough-looking tramp was thrown on to the floor. He was handcuffed and his legs were chained with anklets. He was dressed in dirty overalls, and although he continued scowling and cursing, Boyce's Boy, after eyeing him curiously for some time from the other end of the cell, began to perceive that this new prisoner had not such a bad sort of face as his scowl and bad language were trying to advertise.

"What the blankety-blank does that there policeman mean by calling me drunk and disorderly?" he ejaculated to the floor. "I've not had more than five pints to-day, so I can't be blamed well drunk, and I ain't disorderly. I just hit him gently on the nose. More of a tap it was than a hit. You can't touch a policeman now without getting jugged for it. Policemen are getting to be magistrates' darlings. The way they gets pitied and petted. Wish I'd chucked him in the river, I do. He could do with a bath could that fat, greasy, oily bit of blubber. Pinchin' me for slapping his nose indeed! Wish I'd had the courage to pitch him in the water."

"Well, why didn't you?" challenged Boyce's Boy.

"Hallo, kid!" exclaimed the newcomer with a friendly nod. "What are you in for?"

Boyce's Boy liked his friendly tone. "For doing what you didn't dare. I did chuck him in the water."

"No!" ejaculated the disorderly one, admiration giving way to incredulity. "Chuck him?" jerking his head towards the locked door. "You? No. Chuck it."

"It's gospel truth, anyway," and Boyce's Boy gave his new friend a full description of the swimming-bath incident, cautiously leaving out all mention of the Paper Wizard.

How the prisoner laughed, and how he congratulated Boyce's Boy on his scheme for avenging himself. They talked hard as they had supper together, and were about to form a lifelong friendship when the cell door opened and the manacled man was removed, leaving Boyce's Boy more lonely than ever, mourning over the loss of his companion.

The next morning he was taken once more before the Mayor. This meeting took place in Mr. Watts' magisterial office, much to the disgust of the prisoner, who considered it a slight not being put again into the prisoner's dock. Sergeant Wurren kept hold of his wrist as he stood in front of the magisterial desk. Beside Mr. Watts there sat a man with a handsome, broad face, young-looking, except for a mop of grey hair. Mr. Watts looked up at Boyce's Boy, then turning to the stranger, said, "This, Mr. Macauley, is our young ruffian. Ever since I have known him he has been employed by Mr. Boyce, who runs the fruit shop opposite."

Mr. Macauley looked out of the office window at the fruit shop in question. "I take it he's all right, sir? I mean Mr. Boyce himself."

Vaguely the voice of Mr. Macauley was familiar to Boyce's Boy, or was it his manner? or even his face? "Oh, I know," he said to himself. "'Tain't neither. It's his hair. Long and grey like that tragedian I saw outside Talkham Theatre last week. Yes, it's his hair. And his eyes. Oh, no 'tain't the tragedian. I knows. It's the Dean. Puts me in mind of the Dean."

"Oh, yes. Boyce is all right," answered Mr. Watts. "Most respectable. Sung in the Cathedral for years. Finest bass in the diocese."

"Does he know that this kid is Flagget's son?"

"I believe not. He got him at the Orphanage at Greenwich. He was apparently then called Jinks. His father left twenty pounds with the youngster, then disappeared. This boy was only two years old at the time. He was apprenticed to Boyce, practically adopted, and the name of Jinks not finding favour with Boyce, it was dropped, and the lad was called Boyce's Boy from that time."

Sergeant Wurren then took up the tale, which was all news to Boyce's Boy. "When Flagget called at the Orphanage, somewhat late in the day, he found that the boy had been put out to work in Dullchester. I presume that is why he came down here."

"That we must find out," put in Mr. Macauley. "Look here, Master Jinks, or Master Flagget, or Boyce's Boy, whatever name you choose to call yourself. When did you last see your father?"

"Look here, Mr. Macauley and Mr. Mayor and Mr. Sergeant," answered Boyce's Boy, with a fine imitation of Mr. Macauley's manner, "if you'll let me know what you're all a-getting at and what the object of all this kidding is, we'll understand one another better. I've never heard of Flagget nor yet Jinks, and I ain't got no father. Old Boyce is the only one who has ever troubled with me. I've lived with him as long as I can remember, and I don't see how he can be my father, 'cos he ain't married."

Mr. Macauley smiled. "Mr. Boyce has been your employer and your guardian, but your real father you may know by the title of the Paper Wizard."

"What?" exclaimed Boyce's Boy. "The Paper Wizard my father?"

Mr. Macauley looked at him steadily. "Yes. We've been able to find that out for you, and in return we should like to know what you think about it. Are you glad?"

Boyce's Boy could only repeat, "The Paper Wizard?" then added, "Well, I'm jiggered."

"Does 'jiggered' mean glad or sorry?" persisted Mr. Macauley.

"Well, I ain't ashamed of him, if that's what you mean," answered Boyce's Boy. "He's a free sort of man what earns his living like nobody else, 'cos nobody else cuts paper patterns like that, as I knows of. Besides, he's funny to talk to when he likes."

"Was he funny the last time you talked to him?"

"Not particular, I think," answered Boyce's Boy, mentally seeing the Paper Wizard holding Dr. Smith at bay with his revolver.

"Now, look here, kid," began Mr. Macauley, but he didn't finish the sentence because a look of horror and disgust had suddenly spread over Boyce's Boy's face.

The word "kid," and just the way he said it, revealed to the boy who his interrogator really was. He was the disorderly drunk in the cell, the man in whom he had confided the night before. Boyce's Boy realized that he had been trapped. The man was a police-informer. A dirty crimp. That was the reason that he sat now with the Mayor. That was why he was questioning him further.

"It ain't no use you asking me no more. I've got you fixed now. You're that drunk what came to my cell last night. Well, I think it a pity you're dressed up now like a gentleman. There's no harm in a drunk, but a *sneak*, a dirty sneak I holds no truck with but to spit at. There." Boyce's Boy suited the action to the word and was dragged back by the Sergeant growling. "Now then. You go steady. Don't you be vulgar to this gentleman. He's from Scotland Yard, London. He's come to teach you that it ain't wise pushing your betters into swimming-baths." The Sergeant blew his nose, to show that he had not got over it. The Mayor now took up the conversation.

"Assaulting the police is a very serious offence. I could give you a very unpleasant punishment for it, but that would mean passing you on to other hands, which for Mr. Boyce's sake I do not wish to do. I shall keep a strict eye on you for the future, so be careful. Will you promise me that you will try to be a good citizen? If you do, I will take your word and be lenient with you."

"Mr. Mayor, I should like to say that I have no quarrel with you,"
and Boyce's Boy bowed as if he were conferring a great honour on
the Mayor. "I should also like it to be recorded that I have no quarrel with the Dean. His organist and me had words when I was in
the choir, but that didn't have nothing to do with the Dean. I have
no complaints against either of you. As to Sergeant Wurren and
this gent from London—well, I prefers not to have anything more
to do with either of them. They're both policemen and twisters,
and if I said I had no quarrel with them, I should be putting myself
on their level. I hates policemen and twisters."

The culprit was dragged out of the room and locked up in his
cell.

CHAPTER XXI

MISS TACKLE REAPPEARS AND DISAPPEARS

THE mystery of Dullchester was still going very well with the London Press when an event occurred which completely took the wind
out of the journalists' sails and the gilt off the most gingery bit
of news. Without any fuss and without any warning Miss Tackle,
entirely ignorant of her notoriety, reappeared in the Precincts, and
attended Matins. Nobody had realized that she was there till she
rose from her knees in her usual stall, and opened the large prayer-
book. There was much whispered speculation amongst the choir.
There was a good deal of suppressed argument between the vergers. Canon Cable, who read the First Lesson, was so blind that he
did not notice her. If Canon Beveridge, who intoned the prayers,
did notice her, he was too courteous to show it, and the Dean,
who read the Second Lesson, seemed too absorbed by the service
to look her way. But the choir-boys noticed her very much indeed.
They were all agog with excitement throughout the service, being
of the opinion that the missing Minor Canons would be popping
up next. So the service went with an added zest.

At the conclusion of the Grace, Mr. Styles whispered to the
Dean. The Dean whispered back to Mr. Styles. Mr. Styles whispered to Mr. Potter, and Mr. Potter, to the great interest of the

choir-boys, crossed the aisle, went up the choir-stall steps and whispered to the kneeling lady of mystery. From behind her anti-bee veil Miss Tackle whispered that she would wait upon the Dean after the Vestry Prayer, and then the choir clattered out to the nave and down into the Crypt, to Mr. Trillet's accompaniment. Mr. Pot-ter waited behind in order to escort Miss Tackle with his silver poker to the Chapter Room. Had she refused to accompany him, he contemplated hitting her on the head with it. But she was docile enough even for Potter, who regarded her nevertheless with great disfavour. "Getting her portrait in the papers by false pretences," he muttered to himself. "After all the fuss we've made about her, if she wanted to reappear, she should have had the decency to turn up with her throat cut, her bee-net smothered in blood and her eyes popping out of her head." But all he said to her was, "You've been going it, miss, lately." To which she replied, "What do you mean, Mr. Potter?" Words failing him to explain at length what he did mean, what it was only natural that he could mean, he muttered, "False pretences," and shut her in the Chapter Room, towards which the Dean and Canon Beveridge, on the conclusion of the Vestry Prayer, hastened their steps. Canon Cable positively refused to accompany them, his plea being that women did not interest him and that he was hurrying back to his study to finish his new translation of the *Pesikta*, which he hoped to accomplish before lunch.

"No interest in women," remarked the Dean to Canon Bev-eridge. "And yet he has spent months resolving whether the ancient Hebrews countenanced the existence of harlots in their society."

It grieved Canon Beveridge to hear the Dean joking in Cathe-dral about harlots, when they were about to examine such an upright lady as Miss Tackle, but he was too dutiful to his Dean and too courteous to his friend to mention any distaste.

Apparently Miss Tackle had not seen a newspaper since they had given her such a boom. She had gone to visit an obscure friend of her youth who inhabited an obscure corner of that deserted region of Kent known as the Hundred of Wat. Into this good lady's cottage the London papers never penetrated, as the only news she cared to read was the local parish magazine. Therefore it became the Dean's duty to inform Miss Tackle how very famous she had

become, and he advised her to step around to the Police Station
and explain things to Sergeant Wurren. The prospect of such an
interview alarmed her. She had never crossed the threshold of a
Police Station in her life. She had been brought up as a good Christian and a Tory, and looked upon Police Stations with horror. She
declared that she would as soon be seen entering the Wesleyan
Chapel or the Liberal Club. She would rather die than enter any of
their doors. She would obey the Dean in all matters spiritual, but
this—— "Oh, my gracious!" Why, the Dean would be asking her
to a public-house, or the music-hall, next. So the Dean promised to
go for her.

Although the London papers announced, as it was their bounden
duty so to do, that their veiled lady had reappeared, and that in her
case there was no mystery at all, and that she had had nothing to
do with the still missing parsons, they were all of a mind to drop
the subject as soon as they could. But for all that, Miss Tackle,
who lived alone, with no servant but a daily char, was bothered
a good deal by strange men who journeyed from town especially
to see her and to take her photograph. "Men I have never been
introduced to, Mr. Dean," she complained. "It is all very well for
Mrs. Quaver and Mrs. Dossal to talk with such people, for they are
married, but for me to meet strange men in my own house and
before no third party, why, I feel that my dear parents are turning
in their graves. They were neither of them modern. My father, as
you are no doubt aware, Mr. Dean, distinguished himself at the
Indian Mutiny." Miss Tackle always referred to the Indian Mutiny
as a place where all the best people of that day were to be seen
gathered together.

"Well, Miss Tackle," advised the Dean, "if the bees will per-
mit it, and I understand that they don't do very much around
Christmas-time, I should suggest that you had better slip off
again to the Hundred of Wat, until this publicity has overblown. I
presume your friend there can put you up again?"

"Oh, yes, Mr. Dean. She will be delighted. I can go down to-
morrow, which will give me time to call round at poor dear Mr.
McCarbre's. I should like him to sample my home-made guava
jelly. Dr. Rickit sampled it before I went away, and pronounced it
excellent."

"But, my dear lady," answered the Dean. "McCarbre's house is all shut up. He is away on the Romney Marshes. Is it possible that you have not heard how he has turned off Dr. Rickit and taken to Dr. Smith?"

"What, to that odious man?" cried the lady. "Odious is the only word for him, Mr. Dean. He walks arm-in-arm with the defeated Labour candidate. Last summer he organized the 'outing' for the Wesleyan Choir and, returning in the brake, was overheard singing one of Mr. Trillet's anthems—derisively. He was inebriated, of course. Dr. Rickit declares the man is a squatter, but I say he is odious. What is a squatter, Mr. Dean?"

The Dean explained that, so far as he knew, a squatter was a free-lance doctor who put up a plate without buying a practice.

"Then we are both right," went on Miss Tackle. "He is an odious squatter. How in the world did dear Mr. McCarbre get into his clutches? Of course we shall get no more money, for the Cathedral. The squatter will get it all for the Wesleyans."

"On the contrary," said the Dean, "I have received a long letter from the invalid only this morning, praising Dr. Smith's treatment, it is true, but enclosing a fat cheque towards the Cathedral funds."

"Has Mrs. Sarle gone with them?"

"Yes, for the house on Bony Hill is shut up. He mentions the fact that his housekeeper was also being treated by the doctor, and that her rheumatism has been greatly alleviated by him."

"She's setting her cap at him, I expect," snapped Miss Tackle. "She must realize that she will never win a gentleman like Mr. McCarbre."

"Surely," laughed the Dean, "such an idea would never enter her head."

"I don't trust housekeepers," replied Miss Tackle. "She will have difficulty in winning the squatter, since he is in love with your beautiful Jane."

"Don't talk stuff and nonsense," commanded the Dean.

Thus reproved, Miss Tackle parted from the Dean and Canon Beveridge, after promising to return to the Hundred of Wat. She walked home by way of Bony Hill, in order to investigate whether it would be possible to squeeze a small pot of guava through the letter-box, though, if it were possible, she was not at all certain whether it was right for her to do it, now that her invalid, who shared more of her thoughts than she would have been willing to confess, even to herself, had gone away with the hated squatter.

A cold fog was sweeping down Bony Hill. Miss Tackle put her hand beneath the bee-net and adjusted a black velvet respirator over her mouth. She stopped at McCarbre's door. She looked through the letter-box. It was a large letter-box as letter-boxes go, but not large enough for the smallest of her jelly-pots. She sighed. She knew in her heart that she could forsake even her beloved bees to change places with Mrs. Sarle. She would rather look after McCarbre than insects. Perhaps Mrs. Sarle would not prove an impediment. Mrs. Sarle was merely a housekeeper, who lived in the kitchen. She could be so much more. She could grace the drawing-room, read to the invalid in a ladylike voice, and discuss the Indian Army, in which she had had relatives since the days of the Mutiny. Yes, she could discuss that and a hundred other edifying subjects that a man would delight in.

Meantime, with a suddenness only equal to the speed of her flights of fancy, the fog encircled her, black as pitch. No need for her to go to the Hundred of Wat to hide from Dullchester, if this lasted, for Dullchester was already hidden from her. Even the old front door against which she had been standing disappeared, and— hey presto! King Fog the conjuror had turned it into a black cavity. This magician then proceeded to do a better trick. He popped Miss Tackle up his sleeve. She was enveloped by something black which seemed to her a hairy cloth. She was whirled off her feet. She fainted. King Fog had enveloped his victim. This dread monarch brooded over the city for two days, causing destruction and dislocation. The tram service was suspended. Motor-cars were smashed against buildings. Horses knocked over pedestrians. The life of the city was interrupted. Business was at a standstill. The black necromancer had it all his own way until he was attacked by the superior forces of King Frost, who barraged him with snowstorms. Snow and ice proved too much for him, and he slithered ignominiously over the castle ramparts, over the old gables in High Street, over Dullchester Bridge, and plunged into the muddy waters of the river, on whose dirty bosom he floated away to the sea, victoriously pursued by the white forces of King Frost.

CHAPTER XXII

THE MAN FROM SCOTLAND YARD

WHEN the fog had disappeared the missing Minor Canons did not accompany Dullchester City when she chose to show up again with her roofs, her Castle, her Cathedral, her Precincts, her ruins and her gargoyles all clothed in white. No, they were still as great a mystery as ever, and neither Mr. Macauley from Scotland Yard nor Sergeant Wurren of Dullchester Police Station was any nearer an explanation.

Potter, noticing that Miss Tackle was not attending Cathedral, caused some excitement by announcing at the Police Station that she was "at it again" and had "re-hopped it," but the Dean was able to reassure them of her safety in the Hundred of Wat. Sergeant Wurren, in the name of the local police, accepted this statement immediately, and warned Potter not to be an alarmist. Macauley was more thorough in his methods. He took nothing for granted. Therefore he did not show any surprise when later in the day he opened a telegram bearing the Wat postmark, which said:

"Not seen Emily since she returned Dullchester Tuesday." It was now Friday.

"Potter's right," muttered the man from Scotland Yard. "She is 'at it again,' and this time her 'hopping' is more serious."

But he did not mention the telegram to Sergeant Wurren, who was quite satisfied, with the rest of the city, that Miss Tackle had returned to the Hundred of Wat. After the local paper had made a statement of her reappearance it referred to her no more, and her fame as a nine-days' wonder ceased. The London papers were no longer interested in her. She had let them down. Their romantic lady of the veil, having deliberately turned herself into a dowdy spinster who was annoyed at the publicity they had given to her, became to them a reproach. Journalists can let anyone down they choose, but no one has a right to let them down, and Miss Tackle had let them down badly. They were not interested that she had gone to the Hundred of Wat, because they considered she had no business to return to Dullchester. They would have been delighted to hear that she had gone to one place—and that was a hotter region than the marshland by the Hundred of Wat.

Sergeant Wurren had an instinct that Mr. Macauley was keeping something from him. This irritated him, especially when, next morning, he saw him looking out a train in his Bradshaw.

"Oh, and where are you going this morning?" he asked.

"London," the detective replied.

"Throwing up the sponge already?"

"No."

"Then what are you going there for?"

"On the track of those Minor Canons." The detective threw the Bradshaw down on the table. Sergeant Wurren picked it up and put it tidily on a shelf. It was a protest.

"They ain't in London," he announced with scorn.

"How do you know?"

"Well, I don't. But how do you know they are?"

"I don't. I'm merely going to follow a track."

"What track? Didn't know as how we'd got one. In fact, that's what I complain of with these Minor Canons—they've left none for us."

"Of course they have. They must have left a score. Nobody can cover up their tracks. It can't be done—not even by criminals. It's only we who are not spry enough to see them."

"Well, as I've given you all the help I can," grumbled the Sergeant, "I think you might mention what this track is you're off on."

"I was questioning Potter about McCarbre's fit in Cathedral. You mentioned it to me yourself, if you remember."

"Perfectly I do," rejoined the Sergeant, delighted to find that he had mentioned something that appeared to be useful. "I think you'll own that I've given you all the help I can. I've kept nothing to myself."

The detective ignored the interruption. "Also, about that window he went to look at. Now, you'll allow that the Minor Canons have a great deal to do with the Cathedral. We know that McCarbre gives a great deal of money to it. Also that he put up that window

THE MAN FROM SCOTLAND YARD

at his own expense. Does anything about that window strike you, by the way?"

For a moment Sergeant Wurren's face went blank. It upset him to be asked questions suddenly. He preferred asking them himself. Perceiving that some sort of answer was expected of him, he nodded his head wisely. "Yes, something does strike me about it. I consider it a very solemn bit of work."

"Nothing else?"

Sergeant Wurren was annoyed that more was expected of him. "Considering as how it was meant for a Memorial Window, I don't know as how anything else is expected of it more than what I says. A solemn bit of work—and so it is."

"Well, something else does strike me. It's solemn, as you say, and that makes it all the funnier."

"Funnier?" queried the Sergeant. "I don't see nothing funny in it, and if you do, well, you keep it to yourself, else you'll be getting unpopular with the bereaved parties."

The detective shook his head impatiently. "When I say funny, I don't mean comic."

"Well, if you'll explain what you do mean, I'll tell you what I think."

"I mean funny in the sense of strange. And you'll allow it is strange for a man to suggest a window, to pay for a window, to get a great man to design that window, to make a point of accompanying the Dean on a special inspection of that window, and then, when he has carefully looked at that window which he has set up—what does he do?" The detective leant across to the policeman, and repeated in a whisper, "What does he do?"

"What?" asked the Sergeant. He was deeply impressed, without in the least knowing why.

The detective set his jaw firmly, looking very grim as he stared at the Sergeant. This irritated the Sergeant more than ever.

"Well. Go on. What does he do?"

"Why," thundered the detective, bringing his clenched fist down on the table, "he screams at the damned thing, you owl. And where does that scream lead us?" he added.

"Bedlam," snorted the Sergeant. "That's why you're going to London, I suppose?"

The detective ignored that remark. "I've been talking to Mr. Gony, the Chapter architect. He has given me the name of the man who designed that Memorial Window. Mind, I don't say that it will help us, but as no other clue seems to present itself, I'm going to talk to that man. Perhaps he can help us."

"How do you know he will see you?" asked the Sergeant, thinking the detective deserved a snub after making such a fuss about nothing.

"Oh, he'll see me all right. Curiously enough, I know him very well. Philip Burgoyne. A very decent chap, too. If it's in his power to give us information, he will. I can but go and see."

"Meanwhile, I'll be getting on with the case," was the disgusted reply.

Philip Burgoyne, an alert little man with a skipper-trimmed beard, was very interested in Macauley's visit and gave him all the information he could.

"Ah, yes. Dullchester. I've been reading accounts of the disappearance of the Minor Canons. Yes. I designed the Memorial Window. I hope you haven't come to tell me that my work is responsible for the tragedy."

The detective smiled. "I think there's some connection somehow. The man who paid for it—what do you know of him?"

"Nothing, except the best from an artist's point of view, and that is that his cheque was not only a good one, but an honoured one, and he paid up pretty prompt. Only saw him once. Quite enough, too, as he struck me as a singularly ugly devil, and not at all interested in the work he commissioned me to do. He came here just to order the design and to assure me that he was good for a fair price."

"Didn't he come to see the designs?" asked Macauley.

"No. Neither would he go to see the glass people who executed the work, and I know they invited him. I was told he was ill by somebody who wrote from Dullchester—a Mr. Gony, who called himself Cathedral architect, or some such ridiculous title. I don't know whether he was ill or not but it's my impression that he wouldn't have come, anyhow. He didn't seem interested. He gave me a clear hand, except in one thing."

"What was that?"

"Why, I had finished the design except for the face of the central figure, which represented a dead soldier in khaki. I hadn't got just what I wanted, somehow. I was waiting for inspiration, of the right model. It was lucky for this fellow, McCarbre, that I hadn't done it, because I wouldn't have altered it, once done."

"Did he send you a suggestion, then?" asked the detective.

"He sends round a photograph, and says the face of the soldier was to be copied from it. It was a very old photograph. One of those things done on metal, like one used to get at the seaside. Very clear, though, and fortunately for all parties concerned, it was just what I wanted. A fine face. Young, English, and military."

"Have you got the photograph now?"

"Yes, somewhere. I'll look it out for you, and post it down to Dullchester."

"Did he bring the picture himself?" continued Macauley.

"Apparently. But I didn't see him. A model of mine, a fellow called Jinks, gave it to me with a verbal message. I knew it was all right, because the photograph was signed on the back, 'To my friend McCarbre, from Henderson.' I remember the incidents very well because this fellow Jinks was one of those fellows who stick in your mind. He had a curious habit of cutting patterns out of paper."

"What?" gasped the detective.

"Oh, a mad fellow I picked up to make some studies of. Used to earn his living cutting silhouettes. A music-hall stunt, most likely."

"Did he meet McCarbre when the Memorial Window was first discussed?"

"Let's think. I remember he was in the studio when my wife brought in McCarbre's card, because he repeated the name aloud and said, 'Queer,' and I remember thinking he was right, and that McCarbre was a queer name. He went into the dressing-room before McCarbre came in. I remember that."

"Would you say that your model gentleman—this Mr. Jinks—showed any desire not to see McCarbre?" queried the detective.

"Now you mention it," answered the artist, "I think it was rather the other way about. He kept peeping through the door while McCarbre was talking."

"Ah. Did McCarbre see him?"

"No; Jinks was keeping out of sight. He was quite a tactful fellow."

"I'm sure he was," laughed Macauley. "He wanted to see without being seen."

"I daresay. Never thought of it in that light. What's all this got to do with anything?"

"It's got a lot to do with the disappearing parsons of Dullchester, and I should be much obliged if you would look out that photograph."

"I'll do that for you now," answered the obliging artist.

On his way back to Dullchester, with the photo in his pocketbook, Macauley decided that he had not wasted his day. He had linked up a connection between McCarbre, the Paper Wizard, and the stained-glass window, which made the former scream and the latter grin.

"No, I don't think I've wasted my day," he said to himself. "I am perfectly sure that Sergeant Wurren has not got any fresh clue during my absence."

He was wrong.

CHAPTER XXIII

THE DISAPPEARANCE OF A HEAD

"AND have you found the missing Minor Canons?" asked Sergeant Wurren, when Macauley had hung up his coat and hat in the Police Station.

There was so much superiority oozing out of the Sergeant that for the moment the London detective thought he had been forestalled.

"Have you?" he asked, unable to conceal his anxiety. At that moment the last thing he wished to hear about was the safety of the parsons. Had they been rising for the last time in the waters of mystery, he would have thrust them under to their fate rather than accord to this policeman the glory of salving them. But if this frame of mind were reprehensible, it was only natural. That there is a given point where the policeman meets the criminal and becomes one and the same, is an accepted definition in the Euclid of crime.

"Have I found them?" repeated the police sergeant, losing a little of his assurance. "Well, no. Not exactly."

"But you are on the track?" Macauley was regretting his trip to town.

"That may well be. Can't say yet."

"What have you found, then? Come along. Out with it."

"Nothing. But we've lost something else which may be the next best thing."

"What do you mean?"

"Another disappearance in the Precincts—proved to-day."

"Another man gone?"

"No. Not a man."

"A woman or a child?"

"No. Only a head. But it's gone, clean as a whistle, because the wind shrieks over the shoulders what are left behind. You'd better come and look."

Sergeant Wurren led the mystified Macauley towards the Cathedral. As they came under the North Gatehouse, they saw the lights of Evensong shining through the stained glass and heard the sounds of an *Amen*, followed by the monotonous drawl of prayer. It was quite dark in the Precincts. They went round the West Front to the South side and passed through the door in Canon Beveridge's garden wall. They crossed the drive hedged with dismal laurel bushes and descended the stone steps that led to the lawn. Halfway down these steps—there were some twenty of them—the Sergeant stopped and pointed.

"What do you make of that?"

"Of what?" asked the detective. It was so very dark that he could not see anything but the great window that seemed to hang in space opposite them. "I can only see stained glass."

"That's all I want you to see," remarked the policeman. "It's the memorial window. The very one what made McCarbre scream. Look at the dead soldier's face."

"Can't see it," said the detective, coming down another step.

"Of course you can't. No more can I. 'Cos it ain't there. The bloomin' head's disappeared, you owl." Sergeant Wurren was triumphant. He felt that now he had got his own back. Macauley had called him "owl" that very morning. They were quits. "The whole section of glass containing the head of the central figure has been cut out, and if that ain't rummy, what is?"

"So rummy," meditated the detective, "that the solution should be simple. This makes four."

"Four what?"

"Disappearances," mused the detective. "Two Minor Canons, Miss Tackle, and this head."

"Miss Tackle ain't gone. She's gone to Wat."

"Ah, yes, of course. How stupid of me!"

Just as the detective was thinking how silly he was to have nearly given away information he wanted to keep to himself, a shriek arose in the silence of the Precincts. A long, piercing shriek that rose shrill and loud, and then died away in the blackness of the night. The Sergeant grasped the detective's arm. Huddled together, they stared at the memorial window. They somehow expected the missing head to come shrieking back to its place in the window. The terrible echoes of the scream were interrupted by the deep notes of the organ and a voice which came out of the darkness. "That warn't me, 'cos it come from across the lawn out of the Slype, and the Slype's haunted. Always has been."

"Who's there?" demanded the detective, flashing an electric torch down the steps and lighting up the form of Boyce's Boy. "Hello! What are you doing here?"

"Mr. Watts let him out after you had gone to London this morning," explained the Sergeant.

"What was that shriek, youngster?" asked Macauley.

"How should I know?" answered the boy. "I ain't a detective. Missing Minor Canons, I should think. It come from the haunted Slype."

"Let's go across to the Slype," said the detective.

"All right," answered the Sergeant, not relishing the idea, but resolving not to be left alone by that queer window, especially as the lights were going out behind it. To ensure close company, he pounced on Boyce's Boy and took him in custody towards the Slype, the detective leading the way with his torch.

But there was no one in the Slype. It was very damp there, for the snow had thawed into black slush and it looked more like a cattle-run than a short cut to Cathedral for respectable parsons. The thick walls were running with damp from the melting snow on their high tops. But of life there was no sign; only the sinister gargoyles vaguely showing in shadow against the sullen sky.

"I've a strong suspicion that you let out that scream," said the Sergeant to Boyce's Boy.

"Why?" demanded the accused. "I've something better to do than to scream. I don't like screaming. That's why I left the Cathedral choir. And why should I stand out in the cold and scream? What good would screaming do me, or frightening policemen? I came out, same as you did, to look at the missing window-pane, that's all. That scream's upset me just as much as you. I don't like it no more than you do."

"It wasn't him," snapped the detective.

"Oh, then, what was it?" sneered Wurren. "The missing head?"

"That wouldn't surprise me," answered the detective.

"I expect we shall soon find something, don't you?" remarked Boyce's Boy, kicking about the slush. "Most interesting on a winter's evening, I calls it, having a scream-hunt."

"There's nothing here," declared the detective. "We'll go back to the station." They left Boyce's Boy in the Slype.

"That boy ain't healthy," said Wurren, as they turned into Minor Canon Row.

"Why?" inquired Macauley.

"Being left alone in that Slype and not minding. I say that ain't healthy, at his age, and what did the Mayor want with letting the ruffian loose again?"

"My advice," answered Macauley. "If he's mixed up in this, and I think he is, he must be given sufficient rope to hang himself. But watch him! We must not let Boyce's Boy get far out of sight."

CHAPTER XXIV

THE DEAN DISAPPEARS

JANE had stayed on in Dullchester partly because there was nothing much for her to do just then in the fisheries, and partly because she perceived that the anxiety concerning the two parsons was telling on her grandparents.

Without Jane at Dingy Ness Daniel discovered that the place had lost much of its charm, and as he had collected the material he needed for his book, he wrote suggesting that he should come to Dullchester and help them in their search. The idea was welcomed at the Deanery, and Daniel was requested to call upon Mr. McCarbre at Littlepebble, to present the Dean's compliments to that gentleman, and then to hasten on to the Cathedral city with all dispatch.

Daniel packed up at once, sent his bag to the station and walked along the beach, thus taking in Littlepebble on his way.

This was a peculiar place, deserted and wild. Why it was deserted nobody quite knew. It had all the makings of a popular seaside. So much so that a wealthy philanthropist who wished to present another attractive holiday resort to that part of Kent bought up all the sea-front and erected palatial boarding-houses, an hotel, an arcade and a cinema, as well as laying out magnificent golf links over against the sea. Here was everything to make a resting-place for jaded workers. But somehow they did not take advantage of it. No doubt during the war the exposed nature of the place was sufficient to make people shun it, but it had never thrived before that. Very few people lived there, and its very pretentiousness made its emptiness the more apparent. There was something ghostly in the deserted curtainless windows of the lofty boarding-houses facing the sea. There was not so much as an invalid to be seen. Even trippers hurried through Littlepebble, glad to leave it behind them, as people who flee through a plague-ridden city.

Daniel knew this queer place well, but found some difficulty in finding Dr. Smith's bungalow, which he eventually located beyond the town, in the deserted sand-dunes. The house presented a shut-up appearance. Around the balcony was no sign of a living soul. The windows were shuttered tight. However, after a great deal of banging at the front door, he heard the back door open. He went round to find the door in question opened on the chain, and the scared face of old Mrs. Sarle regarding him.

"Sorry to have disturbed you," he said. "I suppose you are shutting up the place for the winter. I wanted to see Mr. McCarbre."

"He is away," faltered the old housekeeper. "He has gone with the doctor for a few days to the Continent, they told me. I will give any message when they return."

"Just tell him that Mr. Dyke called in passing to leave the Dean of Dullchester's compliments."

"Had I known it was Mr. Dyke I would have opened the door before, but I am so nervous by myself in this wild spot."

"You are quite right to be careful," replied Daniel. "I expect you will be glad when your master comes back. It's too bad leaving you all alone."

"I shall be glad to get home to Dullchester again," sighed the old lady. "Won't you let me make you a cup of tea, or something?"

Daniel glanced at his watch and discovered that he was running his train too fine, so, excusing himself, he hurried away. But for a long time he could not forget the look of fear that crept back into Mrs. Sarle's face when he left her. It haunted him in the train and did not fade till he found himself that evening in the cosy hall of the Deanery. He found the Dean winding up his twelve toy fiddlers on the floor. They were scraping away at their instruments like mad and walking across the polished floor as they did so. "My dear boy," cried the Dean, "I'm delighted to see you. I feel that you may be able to throw some light upon the extraordinary behaviour of my Minor Canons. That they are dead I will never believe. That they have gone cracked is much more likely. The difficulty is that one can't go on pretending to look for them, and one is not supposed to do anything else all day. I have turned to my twelve fiddlers as a recreation. They all rather blame me for not spending my every minute looking in wardrobes or collar-boxes, and just because I happened to have reason for going up to town on private business which I refuse to discuss, I am looked upon with suspicion. I give you my word that I haven't eaten my Minor Canons. Why should I? They don't suspect Cable of murdering them, and yet he goes on peacefully translating Hebrew as if the Minor Canons were living happily ever after. I go and see the two wives every day. That is, of course, my duty, but it is a very trying duty. Mrs. Quaver does nothing but weep, poor soul, and Mrs. Dossal, poor dear, shuts her mouth tight and looks heroic. It really is most distressing. Then, again, I find it exceedingly difficult to keep my face straight at the Beveridges', for I can see Kitty trying to stop giggling behind her father's back and Jane looking desperately solemn and not daring to look at Kitty. The discussions as to what might have happened to Quaver and Dossal are enough to make anyone hysterical. I wish to goodness I didn't see the funny side, but unless we discover their dead bodies, which of course we shan't do, I really cannot see anything in it that is not comical in the extreme. Styles has lately developed a habit of saying, 'No news of the reverend gentlemen, I suppose?' and Potter shakes his head at him. They do that regularly now before the vestry prayer. That alone upsets my equilibrium through service. Then Boyce's Boy, having been released from the Police Station, attends Cathedral regularly, which is most upsetting. His behaviour is so perfect that it becomes quite funny. I am afraid that young man has a sense of humour as great as mine. I daren't catch his eye. All of which is most trying for a Dean."

Daniel showed his sympathy by sitting on the floor and winding up some of the run-down fiddlers. Jane tiptoed in from the dining-room and kissed the top of his head; then, squatting herself down beside him, wound up another of the fiddlers.

"And how's my old man's book of smugglers getting along?" she asked.

"Famously," replied the author. "I've found out all sorts of peculiar facts about them. Old Jubb has been invaluable. I've got a lot of information out of him. Apparently one of his grandfathers was a riding-officer when he left the Navy, but the other was a regular free-trader. The preventer kept a logbook and the smuggler a journal. Both most extraordinary documents. The journal has a large pocket in its leather cover, and that was stuffed full of letters.

Some of them were from the famous smuggling parson, Dr. Syn, and others from his equally notorious sexton, Mipps, who escaped from Dymchurch the night his master was unmasked in the pulpit by the King's men. It's fascinating reading. You must help me sort them out. It's terribly difficult to make up one's mind what to leave out when there is too much material. But it's no use writing an encyclopædia of smuggling."

"Now then, you two bloody-minded pirates," laughed the Dean, "stop talking shop and help me put the fiddlers on the tray. There's one that's walked under the cabinet there. Twelve altogether. We dine early to-night. The dressing gong ought to have gone, but I expect Styles is looking for the Minor Canons again. Slip up and change. After dinner the order of the night is that we put on our great-coats and inspect Daniel's cottage in the stable-yard. It's all ready for you, my boy. Jane has decided that you don't return to the Ness till after Christmas. Jubb's got to give you both a holiday. I'm longing to see what Daniel thinks of his Dullchester home. How I do wish those wretched Minor Canons had not disappeared. It throws such a damper over everything. How I hope they'll turn up before Christmas. I never like anything spoiling Christmas. It's the one thing I'm thoroughly selfish about."

Styles eventually rang both gongs for dinner, and the Dean waited with the young people for Mrs. Jerome to join them in the study.

"Don't say your Granny's gone and done it now," remarked the Dean as Jane, dressed in a pretty grey evening frock, mixed Daniel a gin-and-bitters. "Give me one of those things to-night, please. In honour of the bride and bridegroom! But where is Granny? Sakes alive, if she's gone and disappeared, I won't forgive her!"

Just then Mrs. Jerome entered the study, and the Dean, gulping down his cocktail, mopped his brow with his handkerchief. "Catharine," he said, "you were driving me to drink. I thought you'd gone."

"I suppose there's no news from the Police Station?"

"No," returned the Dean. "But let's forget it if we can. I get nothing else all day. Drat the Minor Canons. When they do come back I think I shall sack them, or put them away into some remote country living. Anyway, I know I shall miss doing their work. I quite enjoy singing the responses. I was a very good Minor Canon in my day, Daniel. If you come and hear me one of these days I'm sure you'll agree. I never upset a Precincts but once, and that was when I announced my engagement to you, Catharine. The grief of the Precincts ladies was heartrending. That was at Trotbury, if you remember, my love."

"It's too long ago to talk about, Jonathan."

"Nonsense. Only seems yesterday to me! What a handsome young fellow I was, to be sure—that is, if one may believe one's early photographs. And you, my dear—well, if Jane would only oblige me by wearing a bustle, I couldn't tell t'other from which. Spin round, Jane, and let's have a look at that frock. Yes. Very nice! Granny had a grey one too. But the one I liked you best in, Catharine, was that red-brick thing with mustard spots all over it."

Now although the Dean did his best through dinner to keep the conversation away from the tragedy of the parsons, he did not succeed at all well, for Styles, when handing round the vegetables, announced that the gentlemen from the Police Station had heard piercing screams that evening from the haunted Slype.

Once Styles had broken into the ring of conversation he never ceased to chatter. He was a privileged person in this respect. He waited with Potter at all the dinner-parties in the Precincts, "by permission of the Dean," as he would say when settling his terms, and he considered that he had the right to break into any conversation on that score. The Archdeacon did not see eye to eye with him in this, for once when passing the cheese-straws to Mrs. Archdeacon, he had facetiously remarked, "A gasper, ma'am?" He never waited at the Archdeacon's table again.

"Don't approve of the Archdeacon," he confided to the Dean. "Why, you ain't allowed to help a dinner-party to go." Potter was much amused at this incident, for it might just as easily have happened to him.

There is a little corner off Dullchester Precincts tucked in under the Castle walls and shaded with ancient trees which is known as "The Quakers," and certainly the prim little houses which surround the paved court resemble the demure spirit of the "Friends," while the heavy foliage which screens the little settlement from too curious eyes bears striking similitude to a poke-bonnet.

In this little colony that leads nowhere save to a sheer drop on to the river-bank, there stands a house much larger than its fellows, and this is known as Satisfaction House, the name derived from Queen Elizabeth's reply, "Satis," to Master Richard Watts' apology for his poor abode, which he felt could not give the Sovereign adequate entertainment. Satisfaction House was rented from the Dean and Chapter by a Mrs. Furlong, a rich and worthy widowed lady who seconded every subscription list headed by Mr. McCarbre, and headed every one in which the restorer of the Cathedral's name did not figure.

While the Dean was yet at dinner upon this particular evening, this good lady sent an urgent telephone call, begging his reverence to wait upon her at his earliest convenience. No reason having been given for this summons, and the state of the Precincts being such that any message might be a solution to the growing mystery, the Dean announced his intention of running round there while the rest of the table were drinking their coffee.

"If I take you all round we shall have to stop and shall not get time to explore Daniel's cottage; so, if you don't mind, I'll run round there quickly and see what the old lady wants."

"Why not wait until the morning?" urged Mrs. Jerome.

"No, my dear," replied the Dean. "Mrs. Furlong is so polite that were she dying—which, of course, she might be doing this very moment—I am convinced that she would still call me 'at my convenience.' That is the worst of politeness. It must always be obeyed promptly, just in case."

The Dean accordingly left the dining-room. Styles helped him on with his Inverness, and insisted on his reverence wearing his goloshes, as there was not only snow on the ground, but more falling down. Styles went back to serve coffee in the study, and the whole household heard the front door bang. And that was the last that anyone was to hear of the Dean for a long time to come.

CHAPTER XXV

THE TWELFTH FIDDLER DISAPPEARS WITH THE SPECKLED PIG

THE Dean had gone. This time there could not be any question as to the possibility of his having gone to London. He did not possess a car and the last train had left. Besides, from inquiries made, his reverence had not been seen at any of the railway stations of Dullchester, Talkham, or St. Rood's, and the Dean was not a man you could miss even in a crowd. Why, he was a crowd in himself. He always talked to strangers. He couldn't help it. And strangers always talked to him. They couldn't help it. Therefore, although Sergeant Wurren had been suspicious at the Dean's lack of confidence in talking about a certain week-end already mentioned, that worthy policeman was the first to admit that Daniel and Jane had discovered the true cause of that secrecy. But let that explanation come in its proper place, and let us arrange the events of the Dean's translation in their proper sequence.

Half an hour after the banging of the Deanery front door, referred to in the last chapter, the telephone rang in the hall. "Mrs. Furlong had requested her butler to inform the Dean's butler that, as there was so much snow on the ground and as it had started to snow again, she would not expect the Dean to call till the next morning, and even then, had the snow not moderated, she urged him not to trouble, as all she wished to learn was the amount needed to make up the requisite sum for the widows of Dullchester's Sick and Needy Fund." Which message was all very polite, but also very alarming, for it meant that the Dean had never reached Satisfaction House, which was a mere three minutes' walk from the Deanery. When the police were informed, all traces of his footprints had been covered up. No one could tell how far he had walked in his journey through the Precincts, where he had stopped or whether he had met any body or bodies when he did stop. It was, of course, possible that he might have called in on some other Precincts folk. But no, neither Mr. Trillet, Mrs. Quaver,

Mrs. Dossal, Canon Cable, Canon Beveridge, nor the Archdeacon had seen anything of his reverence. Mr. Gony, the architect, was visited without result, and Mr. Watts, called up on the 'phone, could not throw any light on the mystery. It was not until they had exhausted all possibilities that Daniel and Jane thought of the cottage in the stable-yard. More than probably he had gone to put some finishing touches to his surprise present, and once there had miscalculated the time. This seemed to be the case, for when they reached it, they found the electric light shining from every window. They had then no doubt but that the Dean was inside. But if so, he was asleep, for he gave no answer to their knockings, ringings and calls. The door was locked, and it took some time to discover the key. They were almost deciding that the Dean must have put it into his pocket, when Mrs. Jerome discovered it hanging on a picture-nail in the study. They entered the surprise-house, but they found no Dean.

Now, although under the stress of this new anxiety most of the glamour had departed from this castle in the air, even then Daniel could not wholly ignore its beauty. Built into the old grey wall of the Slype, the little house had a solid appearance. Its ceiling beams were of the thickest, blackest oak. The walls were also oak-beamed, and although the two sitting-rooms were small, they contained massive carved stone fireplaces. The Dean had evidently visited the cottage before dinner and had turned on all the electric lights to give a cheerful welcome to the tenant. Had he visited it after dinner, the key would have been in his pocket, and Mrs. Jerome was positive that Jonathan had only one key to the front door, as he had remarked that very morning how necessary it was to have further ones cut at Huntley's, the gun shop.

The house had been fitted out with great care and taste, furnished throughout with old-fashioned but comfortable pieces. Glass-doored bookshelves were let into the walls between the beams and filled with all those volumes that Daniel most prized. It seemed that the Dean had made a note of all the books the young man had ever praised. Even the sturdy little wine-cellar was stocked, and a decanter of whisky stood beside a syphon in the library. Mrs. Styles had lighted the fires and the whole place was nothing less than a beautiful dream of an imagination house, but the absence of the great good-fairy Dean turned it into a sinister nightmare.

Daniel made no verbal comment on any of these details until he looked on the little table beside the reading-chair where the whisky was. A copy of *Chambers's Journal* lay on this table, and printed on the cover was his own name. In astonishment he turned the pages, and discovered printed the first of his essays that had been stolen from his room at the Dog Fish Inn.

Jane had meantime taken a cheque from the blotting-pad on the writing-table—a cheque made out to Daniel Dyke, Esq., with a covering letter pinned to it, stating that the twelve essays were bought and paid for. This, then, would explain the theft of the essays. The Dean was the thief. Also his mysterious trips to town. They were but to carry out these selling negotiations. But it did not explain this last mystery. The Dean would not have added to the general anxiety by disappearing for fun. A joker he was, but not a flippant one. Had he stumbled by some lucky chance upon the track of the Minor Canons? If so, Macauley was confident that they would be communicated with as soon as possible. He had a great belief in the Dean's wisdom.

The whole night was spent in searching and watching the Precincts, but with no success, and no clue as to his whereabouts was forthcoming on the next day. After two days' search the Dean was posted up as missing, and the London papers revived the Dullchester sensation.

On the morning following his disappearance a substantial cheque reached the Deanery, made out for the Widows of Dullchester's Sick and Needy Fund. This from McCarbre, posted from Littlepebble. "He has come back," thought Daniel. "Mrs. Sarle will be nervous no longer."

Mrs. Jerome did nothing else but stand in the hall. Every time she heard steps on the drive she would run to the window. But no communication reached her from the Dean.

Mrs. Quaver and Mrs. Dossal kept their vigil also at the Deanery window. They did their best to comfort the Dean's wife. They sympathized with her. They sighed over the toy fiddlers together.

"And to think, my dears," whimpered the old lady, "that he had been playing with these little figures an hour before he disappeared. That shows that he knew nothing of what was going to happen. Poor little fiddlers! How sad they look!"

"Just like the Apostles when the Master was taken," sobbed Mrs. Dossal.

Mrs. Quaver considered the likening of twelve funny toys to the Apostles was verging on blasphemy, especially before the Dean's wife, so she gently corrected her sister-in-misfortune by saying, "No, dear. There were only eleven who mourned His absence. Judas had hanged himself."

Daniel, who was awaiting a trunk-call in the hall, subconsciously counted the little fiddlers. "Hello," he cried. "Mrs. Dossal is right. So is Mrs. Quaver. There are only eleven fiddlers. One of them has gone."

"Nonsense," replied Mrs. Jerome. "I counted them last night, over and over again, for something to do. There must be twelve!"

There were only eleven. Just then there were steps on the gravel. The three ladies ran to the window.

"Only Boyce's Boy!" they exclaimed.

Boyce's Boy was swinging down the drive with a basketful of vegetables under his arm.

For no other reason but that it was something to do, when nobody knew what to do, a rigorous search was made for the twelfth fiddler. But the twelfth fiddler was not to be found. Styles was positive that the Dean had not taken it with him to Mrs. Furlong's. Mrs. Jerome was equally positive that it had been there for at least forty-eight hours after the Dean's disappearance. Not one of the servants could throw any light on the matter. Potter's explanation was that the little fiddler had set himself going and walked out into the snow to look for his master, but this was scouted as being too fanciful. The Deanery was searched from top to bottom. Not a mouse's hole was overlooked. Still no fiddler. He had disappeared as completely as his master the Dean.

And something else had disappeared, too, for Potter came round the back door, after feeding the pigs, and asked Styles if he had made way with the large speckled one.

"What? Not old Speckly? No! I ain't seen him," answered the amazed Styles.

"No more ain't I," continued Potter. "Not for the last three days, come to think of it. The Dean pointed him out to me the morning of the evening he disappeared. I says to him, 'Quite right, your reverence,' I says, 'Speckly's a good 'un,' and since then I haven't had the heart to think of pigs. No, I ain't noticed Speckly since. I just pitches their food over into the trough and walks away. Them pigs depresses me without the Dean in along of 'em. But to-day I just happened to think of what the Dean said to me about Speckly, and I looked about amongst 'em, and blowed if Speckly hadn't hooked it along of the rest of the Chapter."

When the news spread through the Deanery, a renewed search was made for the speckled pig, but to no avail. He appeared to have disappeared as completely as the Dean and the little fiddler.

CHAPTER XXVI

SNOW IN THE PRECINCTS

MR. POTTER did not like the snow. It meant too much sweeping in the Precincts. He was expected to clear a path from every Precincts residence to each door of the Cathedral, and the old man did not see why his boots should be wet through in order to keep the Dean and Chapter boots dry. If it were only the Dean and Chapter boots that he had to sweep for, perhaps it would not have seemed so bad, but his fairways were used by the tradesboys, the wayfarers and the vagabonds.

Winter was anathema to Potter. The whole year irritated him. The four seasons had been invented for the specific reason of heaping fuel upon the fire of his exasperation. Spring to him was impossible, with its falling blossoms; summer was irritating, with its dust-heaps; autumn was exasperating, with its fall of leaves; but winter, especially one with snow about it, was anathema. Even his clearings did not prevent worshippers' feet from kicking hard snowy soles all over the nave. Whenever Styles fell over the cocoanut matting in winter he would blame Potter for not having cleared away a piece of slimy slush that was often nowhere near the scene of his Waterloo.

About this time somebody started the silly rumour that the

bodies of the missing parsons might be discovered in the great snow-heaps at the corners of the Precincts. Heaps that Potter had piled up *after* the disappearance of the parsons. The curious and the morbid immediately attacked these tidy heaps with feet, umbrellas and walking sticks, and Potter was left to straighten them up when they were abandoned.

A most annoying practice of the snow was that it seemed to fall heaviest at night. If it had only fallen in the daytime Potter could have given a sound excuse for not sweeping it, but out of sheer cussedness it did nothing of the kind, and each morning the black paths of wet flag or cobble stones were covered with a white thick-piled carpet.

"What's the good of keeping Cathedral open in weather like this?" he complained. "Nobody goes except those what have to, and it's cruel to expect them. There's only one blessing about this snow, and that is that the blessed Archdeacon never wants to get about. He's in bed with one of his usual colds, so I don't go sweeping no path for him. If he didn't funk the wet I should be sweeping all night to get a clearing to his house," for the Archdeacon lived at the end of the Precincts, right against the Vines, and that part of the Precincts was now as completely cut off by snowdrifts as the South Pole by the Great Ice Barrier. It would need a thaw before the Archdeacon would bother the Cathedral, and that was the only thing that Potter could find in favour of the snow.

CHAPTER XXVII

THE TWELVE O'CLOCK GUN

Now once a day the Precincts of Dullchester suffers a somewhat startling occurrence. To the uninitiated it is nothing short of alarming. At noon a great gun is fired from the Fort on Talkham Hill. The noise of this ordnance never fails to make the visitor to sleepy Dullchester jump. The residents are so used to it that they would jump if they didn't hear it. As the loud report booms against the walls of the Castle, hundreds of pigeons rise from the roofless keep and circle in the air with a mighty fluttering. Seagulls join them, screaming, from the river-bed, and the peacocks on the Castle lawns utter their metallic cries. Dogs bark in the High Street and horses neigh. In fact, the twelve o'clock gun wakes up the entire animal population of the city.

Boyce's Boy and his colleague Errands would linger when the Cathedral clock began to chime that hour. It was the one excitement of the day.

On the morning referred to in the chapter before last, when Mrs. Jerome and her fellow-grass-widows were standing in the Deanery hall, and Daniel was considering the loss of the twelfth fiddler, Boyce's Boy departed from the back door, swinging himself and his vegetable basket along the drive. At the Dean's Gatehouse he was joined by Jim Stalk, who immediately began asking questions about Boyce's Boy's life in gaol. As it was nearly noon, they thought they might as well light a cigarette, sit down on the churchyard wall and watch the pigeons put up by the twelve o'clock gun.

"Nobody much stirring in the Precincts this weather," remarked Stalk.

"You're right," replied Boyce's Boy; "except that bloke from Scotland Yard what's hunting the parsons. He don't know what else to do, so he comes out and pokes the walls with his stick. Look at him standing there. Let's keep out of his sight and watch him jump when the gun goes."

"Tell you whom I saw just now," went on Stalk, "and that was old Tackle in her bee net. You said she'd gone away, but she was walking along, carrying a lot of poles—at least it looked like poles—tied up with string and newspaper."

"Gardening poles, I expect," suggested Boyce's Boy. "What's the good of thinking of gardening in the snow? She's potty. I did think she was away. Ain't seen her in Cathedral lately."

"Oh, yes," sniggered Stalk. "You goes there pretty regular, I believe."

"Never misses, if I can help it. I has my reasons, and they're good 'uns, believe me."

"Look, there's old Buzz-face. Up there on the Castle wall," cried Stalk, pointing to the lofty defences above him.

"Where?" demanded Boyce's Boy. "Oh, I see. Looking through that old window."

The tall figure of Miss Tackle was plainly seen, leaning out of an arched opening in a ruined part of the Castle outworks high up above the Precincts.

"What the devil's she doing up there? She looks as if she was pointing them sticks at us."

"Let's scoot round and see," suggested Boyce's Boy. "There's a good minute before the gun goes."

Jim Stalk shouldered his stretcher of meat and followed his companion. They ran up Bony Hill, turned to the right at the top and then raced up a steep path that led from Satisfaction House to the Castle Gardens.

Miss Tackle was hidden from their sight by the thickness of the arch, so that they were able to get into the next window recess without her noticing them. Their boots made no noise in the snow. By hanging far out across the stone ledge they were able to see the weird lady, though she could not see them, for her attention was riveted upon the Precincts below.

"Look," whispered Boyce's Boy. "There's that detective standing by old Beveridge's garden wall. What does he think he's a-doin' of?"

"He'll be a-jumping in two jiffs, if he ain't prepared for the gun. There's the chime."

The little bells finished chiming and the great bell began to boom out the hour.

They were hoping to see the detective start, but what did happen exceeded all their expectations. Just as the chimes began dear old Canon Beveridge had come out of his garden door. Macauley raised his hat. The courteous Canon raised his and walked along under the wall to meet him. He put out his hand to shake the detective's, when the gun fired from Talkham Hill. Up went the birds with a mighty scream, and down went the detective with a stifled curse. He did not start or jump! he fell heavily into the snow pile at the side of the pavement.

"Gosh! Knocked him over! Scared him stiff! And him a detective, too," cried Boyce's Boy to Stalk. They were delighted. So, apparently, was someone else.

A slight chuckle came from the next window-arch. Jim Stalk, being taller than Boyce's Boy, leaned out and looked. Miss Tackle had withdrawn from sight, but her parcel of garden rods was pointing out of the arch towards the Precincts, and from the end of the rods, where the paper was tied with string, there came a little—a very little—smoke. When Boyce's Boy looked, the smoke had blown away, so he put it down to his companion's imagination. "I know," he said. "It may have been her breath. It shows up to-day. Look. Ugh!" He breathed sharply and proved his point. Breath was very smoky on that cold morning.

The detective did not get up. He couldn't.

"Must have twisted his ankle," remarked Boyce's Boy.

"Who fired that gun?" demanded the detective angrily, sitting up in the slush and feeling his ankle.

"It's only the twelve o'clock gun from the Fort," replied the Canon. "I ought to have warned you not to be startled, but we are all so used to it here, except the pigeons, who always make a great 'to-do' over it." He pointed up towards the Castle at the clouds of birds flying round in circles.

"But why do they load the twelve o'clock gun with live shot?" asked the detective.

"Your ankle is hurt!" exclaimed the Canon.

"Yes. It's bleeding." The detective had been nursing his ankle with his hands, when he discovered that his fingers were covered in blood. His sock was saturated.

"You must have cut yourself on the pavement as you fell," suggested the Canon.

"I tell you, sir, that I have been shot," replied Macauley. "I must get a doctor."

"But it's impossible that the twelve o'clock gun was loaded," argued the Canon. "It is fired by the military. They are never careless with guns. Besides, had they wanted to hit you, they couldn't. Talkham Hill lies three-quarters of a mile behind this wall. It couldn't have hit you if it had been a live shell. We should have seen a bit of the Castle fall over."

"I tell you," persisted the detective, "that I have been hit by something. Someone must have shot at me deliberately. I was hit from the direction of the Castle. I can tell that by the way I was standing and the way I fell. Whoever it is concealed himself up there in the Castle. There are a hundred hiding-places. And that somebody is not afraid of murder."

"But why?" asked the incredulous Canon.

"Why should the Dean and Minor Canons disappear? Why should a toy fiddler, a speckled pig and a stained-glass head do the same? Why? Yes, indeed! There are many 'whys' for which I want the answers."

Just then Daniel Dyke came round the Precincts from Minor Canon Row, and was in time to assist the Canon in raising Macauley. They took him into Prebendal House and telephoned for Dr. Rickit, who, sure enough, extracted a bullet from the detective's ankle, bandaged him up and removed him in his brougham to the Deanery, where Mrs. Jerome insisted on his being put to bed in the best spare room.

Jane was a capable nurse. Assisted by her grandmother and old Rachel, a dearly-loved servant who had risen from family nurse to a general adviser, she soon made the invalid feel that his fate might have been a great deal worse, though Dr. Rickit told him that it would be six or eight weeks before he got about again. This was a serious blow to the detective. He did not wish to hand over this case, which had so far baffled him, into other hands. He had sent Daniel up to the Castle to investigate, and insisted on seeing him the moment he returned. Jane argued against this, saying that the doctor had forbidden him to worry about the case for a few days, but Macauley was equally insistent and carried his purpose to the extent of being allowed a quarter of an hour's conversation. So Daniel was admitted, and Jane left them alone after glancing at her wrist-watch.

"I've been doing some hard thinking since I asked you to go up to the Castle Gardens," he said, "and I may tell you that I have formed one or two conclusions. But first, will you tell me how you got on? Were you able to find out from the keeper who was up there at twelve o'clock?"

Daniel sat on the bed and talked. "The keeper couldn't help me any more than the two gardeners, for they were all together in the Dove House when the gun fired. From the Dove House, which they have rigged up inside the lower gate of the Keep, there is only a view of the centre path where the band-stand is. The seats were entirely deserted on either side, as they naturally would be in such weather. There were a few children snowballing in the band-stand itself. That was all they knew. It wasn't much. I then took a stroll round the path by the wall facing the Precincts. There are two obvious points of vantage there. Two archways—old ruined windows. I don't know whether you would have noticed them from below. They are cut into the solid wall and, looking out, you get a clear view of the Precincts. In one of these archways I found a raw Brussels sprout and a raw potato. In the other I found this," and Daniel held up a black velvet respirator on an elastic band. "All of these dropped recently, for they were quite dry on the top, which could not have been the case if I had left them there another half-hour."

Macauley smiled. "You have the right instincts for a detective. Splendid! Recent footprints in the snow, of course?"

"Yes," replied Daniel, obviously enjoying the statements he was making so methodically. "In the first archway—that is, the furthest from the Keep—there were two distinct sets of footprints, and the two people to whom they belonged leaned over the window parapet. These footprints were made by hob-nailed boots. Small men's size or large boys'. This suggested, of course, errand-boys, and when I picked up a sprout and a potato, I think even Scotland Yard will think me justified in having our eternal Boyce's Boy catalogued for one. Could he or his companion have had a revolver? You know what that boy is."

"No," declared the detective. "I was shot with a rifle-bullet. Look! Dr. Rickit put it on the table there. What about the other arch, where you found this antiquated respirator? I mean—the footprints there. Was there anything to learn?"

"Oh, yes," smiled Daniel. "One set of footprints that went in leisurely and came out hurriedly. I needn't explain why. That's obvious. You're a detective and I've read Sherlock Holmes. The size of the marks led me to believe that the owner was a man, but I noticed that the sole marks were either snow-shoes or goloshes worn over the boot, so that the size did not tell one much. This respirator suggests a woman, but then I have no idea who wears such a thing in Dullchester. Miss Tackle used to, when I was a kid. Indeed, hers is the only one I ever remember to have seen. I thought in these days they were condemned as unhygienic. Anyhow, she's away at Wat. It wasn't her."

"Go on," urged Macauley. "Anything else? I wish I could have searched that archway. I might have seen something else."

"Well, if your eyes had been very sharp, they might have seen this. Wait a minute; I must be very careful." Daniel took an old envelope from his pocket and shook it carefully over the white counterpane on the bed. There fell out a piece of newspaper, torn and jagged, about an inch long and half an inch wide. In one corner there was a dark mark, where the paper had been burnt.

"This was lying, quite dry, on a heap of leaves and slush. The occupant of the arch at noon must have dropped it then."

The detective looked at it carefully. "In my waistcoat on the chair," he said, "you'll find my lens." When he had made a further examination through the glass, he continued, "The black mark was made by that bullet on the table. Do you see? It is a segment of a circle. Why was it fired through paper?—unless—why, yes, of course—the rifle was hidden in a parcel."

"What?" cried Daniel, his eyes blazing with excitement. "If that's so, I know the would-be assassin. But I can't believe it!"

"Who is it?" demanded Macauley.

"Miss Tackle," answered Daniel, laughing at the absurdity of his deduction.

"Why Miss Tackle?" Macauley's eyes were shining with excitement now.

"Because," went on Daniel, "I challenged Boyce's Boy about being on the Castle wall, and showed him the vegetables he had dropped. All he said to that was, 'Oh, them two little veges ain't no good to me, thanks,' but he confessed to being there when the gun fired. I then told him that he would be 'wanted' again unless he told me who else was there at the same time. His answer was, 'Miss Tackle, with a parcel of gardening rods wrapped round in newspaper.' What is more, Jim Stalk, who was with Boyce's Boy, was convinced that smoke came out of the parcel. Boyce's Boy says that he didn't see any, and suggested that his friend was mistaking breath for smoke."

"That's clear enough," cried the detective. "And I applaud your thoroughness. It's obvious now that a rifle was in that parcel of gardening rods. That the bullet tore through the paper. That whoever fired it very cunningly waited for the big gun to startle the birds. The greater sound swallowed the lesser, and nobody would have suspected a rifle had not the victim been a detective."

"But how could it have been Miss Tackle?" persisted Daniel. "I know she's away again at the Hundred of Wat."

"How do you know?"

"The Dean told me."

"Then he told you wrong. Between ourselves, Miss Tackle never returned to Wat at all. She is no more there, I tell you, than McCarbre and his doctor are at Littlepebble."

"But they must have returned now, because the Dean has just had a letter from the doctor and a cheque from McCarbre."

"Written God knows where, and posted by God knows who. The only thing they care about is getting the Littlepebble postmark. What you told me about that old housekeeper being all alone and nervous made me suspicious of this McCarbre. His behaviour all along has been peculiar. I set the local police to watch Smith's bungalow, and no gentlemen have returned. Mrs. Sarle is still by herself. When they questioned her she confessed that the master was still away with the landlord of the bungalow, who was his medical man, but that she couldn't say where they were. The police are under the impression that there is something suspicious about the household and that the old lady knows a great deal more than she is willing to tell. She appears to them to be a simple soul, living in mortal dread of someone or something. They are watching her closely, and have got authority to intercept all letters, so that we should get definite information soon. Meanwhile the house on Bony Hill is empty."

"I wonder!" exclaimed Daniel. "Do you think it possible that——"

"The missing parsons were there? Yes, I did," continued the detective. "But I tell you in confidence that this is not so. Wurren and I, by the aid of a ladder, got into the place from the back. Nobody was any the wiser, as it was two nights ago, when it was snowing hard, that we made our raid. We got into the house, and searched it thoroughly. Empty!"

"But to get back to Miss Tackle before Miss Jerome interrupts us," said Daniel. "Do you mean to tell me that she pretended to go to Wat in order to stay here and commit a murder? But it couldn't have been her. To begin with, she couldn't shoot straight."

"She didn't," answered the detective. "You don't think it was me she was shooting at, do you?"

"Well, in God's name, whom else?"

"Canon Beveridge!" Daniel laughed, but the detective continued in a decisive voice, "He always takes a stroll in the Precincts at about noon. He has formed a habit of watching the birds when the gun goes. He told me so. Miss Tackle knew this, and waited. She trained the rifle on the door in the garden wall. But she missed the Canon and got me instead."

"But why on earth should Miss Tackle shoot at Canon Beveridge? It's fantastic!"

"Because he is a member of the Chapter. He'll be the next to go, you mark my words, or Canon Cable. Then the Archdeacon will be missing from his bed, and then her revenge will be complete, for I believe—and I state this quite solemnly—that in your Miss Tackle we have a fanatic and a dangerous enemy of the Cathedral."

"I won't swallow that," cried Daniel. "Why, man, she dotes on the Cathedral."

"She gloats over it, you mean. She strokes it and she purrs over it like a great cat, and every now and then she springs and her victim disappears. I should very much like to look at the face behind that bee-net. I should probably find the unmistakable look of a religious fanatic."

"Well, granting that possible, surely she would be the last type of person to attack the Dean and Chapter."

"Not at all, if she found that their views didn't coincide with hers," argued the detective. "According to Potter, she has already had one open quarrel with them which caused a good deal of scandal at the time. I suppose he is correct in telling me that there was an old saying concerning some Cathedral property in the High Street: that if it were ever sold into secular hands a curse would fall on the existing Chapter who parted with it?"

"Oh, that old wives' tale!" laughed Daniel. Macauley, ignoring the interruption, continued, "I expect you know the plot. The site of the New Inn. On that site used to stand some old half-timbered shops—a corn merchant's, a sweet shop, and a bootmaker's. Their picturesqueness is gone and a modern red-bricked and glazed-tiled public-house reigns in their stead. Personally, I don't see why the

Chapter shouldn't sell their own property if they were able to get
a big price for it, but Potter says there was a lot of bitter talk when
the sale took place, and that Miss Tackle organized a meeting in
the Corn Exchange and openly protested against the action of the
Dean and Chapter. I believe this caused a serious breach in her
friendship with the Deanery people, but it eventually was patched
up. How do we know that she has forgotten it? If she did bury the
hatchet, she could dig it up again. How do we know that she isn't
even now making the old curse to come true? What do you think?"

"I'm afraid I think your theory is as stupid as the old rhyme we
used to repeat in the nursery. It was carved upon the oak beam
that ran along the shop-window tops, and it went: 'If for secular
Lucre they sell this goodly tenement, May the Dean and his Chapter fall
by God His judgment.' Interesting as a relic of the Middle Ages, but
otherwise very stupid."

"Perhaps," assented Macauley. "But not stupid to a fanatic. And
what did the Dean and his Chapter sell this goodly tenement for?
To augment the stipends of the Minor Canons, and the Minor
Canons were therefore the first to go."

"I am sure the Dean would applaud your ingenuity if he were
here, Macauley, but personally I don't think there's anything in
your theory. However, since you do, I am willing to act upon it
according to your instructions. Here comes Jane, and, I believe,
your lunch. We will discuss this again when you have eaten."

Jane was admitted to the conference after lunch and she sided
with Daniel in scouting Macauley's notions of Miss Tackle as simply ridiculous. When she learnt of the telegram received by the
detective from Miss Tackle's friend Emily at Watt, she said, "If she
isn't there, she must be in Dullchester, because she's never been
anywhere else since we've known her. As for her being a wicked
fanatic, I won't for a moment allow. My instinct is sure about her.
She is all right. A little peculiar, but then so are lots of people. I
daresay she thinks we are. I know she thinks I am. Frankly, I dis-
believe Boyce's Boy's story. He's trying to make a mystery out of
nothing. Daniel's quite right, Mr. Macauley. Miss Tackle, bless her
heart, wouldn't know how to load a rifle, much less shoot one! If
she isn't at Wat, as you say, I'm going to find her in her house in
North Square, and when I have found her I'm going to get the truth

out of her and clear her good name in your mind, Mr. Macauley. In fact, I'm going now."

"Right!" agreed Daniel. "And I'll come too."

"No, you won't," contradicted Jane. "I couldn't talk to her tactfully in front of you. I must do it alone, and you must stay here with my invalid. And listen to me, both of you. By the time I get back I shall expect you to have hit upon a more sensible theory. We've got to find Grandfather quickly. Granny is keeping up so far most wonderfully, but if many more days go by in uncertainty she's going to break up. It's up to us to prevent it."

Jane put on her hat and went off. But the detective's suspicions against Miss Tackle were not shaken by her attack, and the moment the pretty girl left the room, he ordered Daniel to follow her, passing him his loaded revolver, and urging him, as he valued his fiancée, not to lose sight of her for a minute.

Daniel, however loath to disobey Jane, thought it was wiser to obey the detective, and directly he heard the bang of the front door, he slipped Macauley's revolver into his pocket and followed.

CHAPTER XXVIII

ANOTHER DISAPPEARANCE

AT the corner of the Cathedral Daniel caught a glimpse of Jane turning into the High Street, and was about to follow when he saw Miss Tackle hurrying in the direction of the Castle. Knowing, therefore, that his fiancée was going to North Square on a useless errand, and realizing that she was in no danger, he made up his mind to follow Miss Tackle himself and have a few words with her on the subject of the shooting. He would thus save Jane an unpleasant interview.

Although he walked quickly he only reached the East entrance of the Castle Gardens in time to see Miss Tackle disappear down the flight of steps that led through the North Gate down on to the Esplanade.

By the time he reached the wall above this gate, Miss Tackle was already walking along the deserted Pier.

"What on earth she's going there for I can't imagine," he said to himself. "However, unless she jumps off the end and swims for it, which she is hardly likely to do in this weather, I have her in a 'No Thoroughfare.'" So he went down the steps, passed through the arched tunnel in which the North Gate was built, and made straight for the Pier after her. To his astonishment there was no Miss Tackle now in sight. Unless she were hiding behind one of the penny-in-the-slot machines, she must have climbed down the iron steps to the water's edge beneath the Pier, a very dangerous thing to do in slippery weather. There was deep snow on the Pier planks. No one used it in this weather, so nobody had swept it. This was fortunate, for Daniel's boots made no noise, and a conversation going on below the Pier was consequently uninterrupted.

When Daniel reached the Pier-head he saw a small steam-tug alongside, with two men leaning on her bulwarks, talking to someone on the river level beneath him. He did not doubt but that this person was Miss Tackle, but she must have had a companion, for he only heard a man's voice in reply. What they were saying made him realize that at all costs he must remain unseen.

"We can pick up the Chink's boat on the lower river. If we ain't there on the tide he'll go, and then there ain't no use in us trying to catch him, 'cos there ain't no river craft to make the speed of that twin-funnel tug of his. It goes, and there ain't no denying it. So if you're late with your precious chest you gets left. And bring your cash with you, my hearty, or the Chink will half murder you."

"Not me," answered the male voice below the Pier. "I'm not to be browbeaten by any dirty Chink. I've knocked his type about before now. Sailed in ships where killing Lascars was the order of the day! Your Chink must watch his step with me, and if he sails without me he'll see which of us is for it!"

"Well, perhaps you're lucky," sneered one of the rivermen; "but for us, we don't care to go agin the Chink. It ain't so much brawn with him—though he's quick in a fight—as brain, and his brain is a bit his godfather the Devil had over and give him for a christening present. If you wants to rouse him, do it when we ain't around. We're for it already."

"How's that?" came the man's voice on the Pier steps.

"Why, you'd hardly think it, but that there John Chinaman is a rare one for the gals. Gets away with it, too. If he hadn't the knack of getting rid of 'em, he'd have a harem on that tug of his. Once he gets 'em, they don't want to leave him. If they is difficult to get for him sometimes, it's nothing to the difficulty of getting rid of 'em. Leastways, that's so when he passes 'em on to us, as he does when he's in the mood. What white gals see in him I don't know, unless it's the dope he gives 'em. But they never last above one voyage. New 'uns each trip is his fancy, and there's a good deal of money in them in some ports we touch at in the way of business. We're for it 'cos he's been too busy to get his own fancy this trip, and left it to us, and we ain't had no luck amongst the skivvies of this town nor the factory-gals of Talkham."

"I'm glad to know this," interrupted the voice. "This gives me a pretty hold on him. White slavery, eh? Ugly sound, that!"

"Silly sound," sneered the other river-man. "There's no slavery, for most of 'em wants to go."

"And some of 'em don't," laughed the other, winking towards the man beneath the Pier.

"Well, if I see one young and pretty enough for your precious Chink, I'll bring her along in my chest of explosives," laughed the unseen, and then added, "But I must beat it now, mates, and fix up those Talkham toughs."

"Wait a second. I'll get the life-preserver I promised you," and one of the sailors crossed the deck and disappeared below.

Daniel, who had remained unseen during this diabolical conversation, now realized that if he were to play a hand against these people he must act quickly, and they must have no suspicion that he had overheard them. Accordingly he raced back along the Pier, across the Esplanade, through the tunnelled gateway, up the Castle Gardens steps, and looked over the wall. From this point of vantage he could see not only the Pier and the full stretch of the Esplanade as far as the bridge and the High Street, but underneath the Pier as well, and the only figure coming up the iron steps from the water-level was the familiar figure of Miss Tackle. Her male companion, whoever he might be, had vanished. Quite possibly he had boarded the tug. That he was her companion Daniel could not doubt, because the iron landing of the stairway was small, and no man would have carried on such a questionable conversation before any but a colleague implicated deeply in the scheme. Macauley was right after all. Miss Tackle, despite Jane's belief in her, was associated with the vilest and most desperate characters.

As the lady in question came down the Pier, a closed car, which Daniel had already perceived behind the swimming bath, came round to meet her. She appeared to give an address to the chauffeur and got in, and the car moved swiftly down the Esplanade and turned into the High Street. Thus Daniel saw his prey escape without a chance of following. He blamed himself bitterly for not having made provision for the car, but he had had no time to consider the matter.

Now, if the car was going to Talkham, well and good, and Jane would be safe. But if to North Square, and the girl was still waiting—in that there was imminent danger. He set off running hard by the short way to the High Street. Going full-tilt through the Precincts, he raced down the alley by the Post Office, and at the corner bumped into a girl coming in the opposite direction. It was Jane.

"Thank God you're all right," he exclaimed breathlessly.

"Why shouldn't I be? Even though you did knock me into the middle of next week. What is more to the point, we score one up against Mr. Macauley, for Miss Tackle is all right, too. As right as rain. I knew she was. I've had a long talk to Mrs. Styles, who goes in every day to wash up. Old Tackle went out early to-day—she generally does—but she left Mrs. Styles her cheque for the month and a note, which I read, dated this morning, so it's all O.K. If I don't know her handwriting, I don't know my own."

Daniel was duly astounded at this news in the event of what had happened on the Pier, and was about to tell Jane of his adventure, when they were both amazed at the sight of Kitty Beveridge, racing towards the Deanery Gate, with no hat or coat on, bedroom slippers, in spite of the snow, her eyes bathed in tears and her hair all tumbled loose.

Jane shouted to her, and she stopped and then came moving towards them, but so great was her distress that she was unable to tell them what was the matter. All she could do was to give them a crumpled note, which she had been holding tightly in her hand. It was headed "Prebendal House, The Precincts, Dullchester," and was in Canon Beveridge's neat writing.

"My Dearest Child K.,

"I have received a summons which I cannot and would not disobey. What it means I am at a loss to explain myself—so how can I do so to you? If humanly possible, I will communicate with your dear mother as soon as possible, but break this news kindly to her that in disappearing, as I shortly must, I am thinking of others rather than myself or my family. This will be hard for you all to realize, but it is nevertheless my duty as I see it. In the event of the worst misfortune happening to me, my papers are all in order at the office of Mr. Watts, who has been my legal adviser and friend throughout a long life. I would write more, but there is haste.

"Trusting in God that we may be united again soon,

"Your distracted father,

"Edward Beveridge."

CHAPTER XXIX

THE SUB OF THE "SWEET WILLIAM"

They hurried with this astounding document to the Deanery and showed it to the detective, and when Kitty was sufficiently recovered from the shock to speak, she told them how she had found the note on the hall table, how she had rushed to her father's study and found that he had evidently left the room suddenly, for on his desk was a letter to the Vicar of Dullchester which he had abandoned not only in the middle of a sentence but in the middle of a word, and his pen, a quill, which was still wet with ink, was lying on the carpet. Also the brass inkstand had been overturned and a pool of ink was still dripping into the open envelope drawer. Whatever the summons referred to in his letter may have been, it must have been sharp and sudden, for the courteous Canon was a tidy man, and had he been going to execution he would have begged leave to tidy his desk first. The letter to the Vicar of Dullchester did not give any help to a solution, for when Daniel went round and examined it, on Macauley's instructions, he found it was about parochial affairs which the Canon had neglected for some days—so he said in the letter—owing to the trouble in the Precincts.

After examining the room carefully and making a plan of it for
Macauley to puzzle over, Daniel returned to the Deanery owning
himself as completely baffled as the detective, who was fuming
over his injured ankle which prevented him from taking a more
active part in the solving of the mystery.

Not having taken any food since breakfast, Daniel was persuaded by old Rachel to have some, and then hearing that Jane
had returned to Prebendal House, he put on his coat and hat and
went round there. He was determined, even at the risk of offend-
ing Macauley and Sergeant Wurren, to get in more help from
Scotland Yard, and he wanted to get Jane's support in the matter.
As he passed through the gate in the wall leading to the drive of
Prebendal House, he looked at the headless figure in the Memorial
Window. Was there some connection between all these weird happenings? Where was McCarbre? He was the man they ought to get
hold of. Why wasn't he at Littlepebble? And, as he wasn't, why did
Dr. Smith write as if he were, informing the Dean that his patient
was progressing there very well? McCarbre should be posted up
as "wanted" by the police. It had all started—all this peculiar horror—from McCarbre. He had paid for the window. He had sent a
photograph of a dear friend of his to be immortalized as the central figure of that window. When he saw this face of the man who
called him friend on the photograph, he screams with terror. He
nearly kills the Paper Wizard. The Paper Wizard was the man who
handed the photograph to Philip Burgoyne, with a verbal message.
The peculiar terror of McCarbre when Daniel first pointed out
the Paper Wizard through the railings. The little paper gibbet that
McCarbre had kicked into the drain. Why hadn't the Paper Wizard
been posted as wanted by the police? At all events, there was sufficient ground for them to question this man and McCarbre. Daniel
made up his mind that both of them should be advertised for. Also
the Precincts must have more protection.

He was disturbed in these thoughts by hearing the front door
of Prebendal House slammed to and brisk steps coming round the
drive. He walked in their direction, and met a young naval officer
whom, in spite of the gathering darkness, he recognized as Kitty's
youngest brother.

Unlike his elder brothers, Eddie and Arthur, who were both

fine, handsome majors in the Horse Artillery, Gordon had entered
the Senior Service and now, to his great pride, was commanding—
he was only a Sub—a species of launch used for running in and out
of the mud-banks below Talkham and for carrying orders from the
Dockyard to the various war-craft lying in the river-mouth. During a shortage of drifters she would convey officers ashore. In fact,
any odd job might at any time be thrust upon her. Gordon loved
this boat as Nelson loved the *Victory*, or as Grenville the *Revenge*. It
was his. To him it represented Britain's sea power. That there were
such things as battle-cruisers sometimes occurred to him when
their huge superstructures loomed above him in the lower river,
but for sheer efficiency, for which the British Navy has ever stood,
he wanted nothing better than his own *Sweet William*. True, he
might sometimes wish that she could be re-christened. There was
little imagination in such a title. His command was not a house-
boat on the Upper Thames but a gunboat of the Kentish Lower
River. Yes, "launch" be damned. She carried a gun, and a boat that
carries a gun must of necessity and by all the laws of reasoning be
a gunboat. The gun was mainly used for "blank," but then it was
quite capable of propelling a live shell. The Trafalgar for which it
had been shipped aboard the *Sweet William* was a regatta.

When he was "putting to sea," as he preferred to call "going
down the river," it was annoying to be chipped by his fellows with
such remarks as, "Hello, there's young Bovril"—Bovril was only
one of the many obvious nicknames for Beveridge. Then he would
be hailed by a passing drifter with such ribaldry as "Hallo, Bovril
Glaxo of Allenbury's! Going out to water your pet *Sweet William?*"
That kind of remark knocked the bottom out of romance. Certain
members of the Service did not take the *Sweet William* as seriously
as he did. To his seniors he referred to his "ship" as "the rotten old
'bus I run about the river in, sir." To his equals it was "My jolly old
gunboat, you know." To the snotties it was "The little fighting-
beast I run."

Yes, on the whole, it was better to be skipper of the *Sweet William* than a worse-than-nobody on the Admiral's flagship.

"That you, Daniel?" hailed the Sub. "Good. I say, this is an awful
state of affairs, isn't it? What the hell's the matter with the Precincts? The Governor can't be murdered. Do you think the London

papers have hit the nail on the head? Do you think it's just a joke?"

"A pretty serious one for the joker, if it is," answered Daniel. "Is Jane still here?"

"Yes. She's cheering up K., who is dreadfully upset. Look here, just stroll with me down to the Pier, will you? I've got to tell my bo'sun to lay by for me in the dinghy. Couldn't get alongside in the old gunboat. She's laying-off in deep water. These tidal rivers are a damned nuisance. You know, I can't fathom this about the Dean and the Governor. Believe anything silly I hear of those asinine Minor Canons. I always did think them merchants. But, you know, the Governor's a damned level-headed fellow, and the Dean, though he is a bit of a card, seems to have his head screwed down taut. What's your opinion?"

Arm-in-arm, they walked through the Precincts, and Daniel gave the Sub a rough description of the events prior to the first disappearance of Minor Canon Quaver. Gordon Beveridge not only agreed with Daniel that more detectives should be commissioned now that Macauley was out of the running, but that Scotland Yard should be moved into the Precincts en bloc. "I'll wire 'em, if you like. Perhaps coming from a navy chap would shake 'em up a bit. I've 'phoned through to Talkham Barracks for Eddie and Arthur. They're pretty sound chaps and may help us. But the blighters have had some posh show on to-day. The H.A. rode through the town this morning in full kit. However, they'll be over quick enough when they get my SOS. They were expected back before dark."

It was when they were hurrying down the Pier that Daniel told him of the conversation that he had overheard with the sailors, at which Miss Tackle was so mysteriously present.

"What's that?" exclaimed the Sub. "Did you say 'twin-funnel steam-tug'? And did you mention a Chink?"

"Yes," replied Daniel. "Why?"

Gordon whistled. "Come on," he cried, and ran down the Pier full-tilt. "Stay here," he whispered to Daniel. "I'll be back in a shake."

He ran down the slippery steps in style, sideways, as only sailors do, and Daniel heard him talking below.

"Aye, aye, sir," said a gruff voice, and then it sang out, "Ahoy, *Sweet William!* Lie fast till further orders."

Gordon then rejoined Daniel and, thrusting his arm through his, piloted him back along the Pier.

"Oh, so they mentioned a Chink and a twin-funnel steam-tug, did they? That bit of espionage work was the best day's work you'll ever do, my son. It's only a pity for them that the *Sweet William* got to hear of it—that's all."

"Look here. What do you mean?" asked Daniel, who thought it was quite unnecessary for his friend to swank. "Explain, will you?"

"Sorry, old man, but I can't. It's something I know through Service channels. Secret Service you might almost call it. You'll know all in good time. Meanwhile, don't worry. You may depend on my little girl doing her share in clearing up the mess."

"What little girl?" asked Daniel.

"Why, the *Sweet William*, of course," answered the Sub.

"But, look here," argued Daniel, "do you mean to say that this mystery is a naval secret?"

"I mean to say nothing, old man. It's safer," replied the Navy. "Your mentioning a twin-funnel tug has opened my eyes, and I shouldn't be surprised if you don't hear the bark of the *Sweet William's* guns." He always referred to his one gun as "the guns."

"What have guns got to do with Canons and Minor Canons?" asked the exasperated Daniel.

"Don't be funny," replied the Sub. "And puns aren't allowed in the ward-room these days, especially rotten ones."

"I didn't mean to make a pun, you ass," returned Daniel. "I merely ask you what the Navy has got to do with missing parsons."

"And I might as well ask you what rifles are doing in paper parcels, and why heads jump out of stained-glass windows, and why toy fiddlers wind themselves up and go for a stroll, and how a speckled pig can jump over a thirty-foot wall, and why screams fade away in the Slype. There's more in this damned business than meets the eye, but what the Governor's doing mixed up in it all, God knows."

"Or the Dean," added Daniel.

"Or any parson, let alone the stained-glass head, the pig and the fiddler."

"Miss Tackle, McCarbre and the Paper Wizard."

"Good Lord deliver us! It's a positive Litany List," said the Sub.

CHAPTER XXX

THE NAVY AND THE ARMY CONSULT

BY this time the two young men had reached the Precincts, and in front of Prebendal House they perceived a trooper in full uniform of the Royal Horse Artillery, holding three horses. Further up the lane, by Minor Canon Row, was a gun-carriage. The drivers had dismounted and were smoking cigarettes with the gunners.

"Hallo," cried Gordon; "the brothers are here with their guns."

As they hurried through the door in the wall, the horse-holder saluted Gordon, who, followed by Daniel, made straight for Canon Beveridge's study, where they found the two Major Beveridges in full uniform, medals and all complete, consulting with Sergeant Wurren. Mrs. Beveridge, Kitty and Jane made up the rest of the company, though Dorothy and Freda, the two elder Beveridge girls, tiptoed into the room during the discussion. They had been putting little Merial to bed—the youngest of the family.

Sergeant Wurren was completely at sea by this time, but did his best to assert himself, as he felt that, when all was said and done, in a matter of crime the police uniform should rank before the Navy and Army.

"One thing is certain," he remarked, "and that is that if the Cathedral is to carry on, Canon Cable should be given special police protection. He should not be allowed to stir without it. I would even go further, and say that he should not be allowed *not* to stir without it. Canon Beveridge was took within this room. If he had been took in the hall, he would have put on his hat and cloak, but he didn't, for they're all in the hall. As he was took, he upsets the ink and drops his pen. This indicates one of two things. A struggle or haste. There being no other sign of a struggle, such as a broken clock, or an over-turned chair, or a disturbance amongst the fire-irons, I think we may assume the pen and ink to be indicating haste. He was took while dipping his pen in the ink. If the Archdeacon is took, he'll be took in his night-shirt, because he's

in bed with a cold. The Cathedral won't miss the Archdeacon if
he is took, because it's used to him being 'took queer,' but Canon
Cable's different. He ain't everyone's taste, perhaps; he ain't got
the courtly ways of your poor father, who would always salute me
with 'Ah, Officer.' In fact, gentlemen" (bowing to the Navy and
army) "Canon Cable could learn a lot from your poor father in
matters of common decency. Canon Cable ain't my taste at all.
When I have heard him holding forth next door"——jerking his
head towards the window, through which loomed the Cathedral
across the lawn—"and, as you know, I am to be found next door
whenever there's a special 'do' on, attending to the Mayor, I am
bound to say his talk ain't my taste. There's too much scholar and
too little policeman about his talk for me, by which I mean that
his sermons give me no tips for my business. But, for all that I get
no benefit out of him, I do say that police protection he should
have, because he's the last one to keep the Cathedral on its legs, as
Mr. Styles has pointed out to me. When he's took, Cathedral must
shut up shop, unless it's a case of getting the Bishop himself, and
that 'ud stop him hopping about the Diocese, which 'ud be a pity;
or else it means getting the Archdeacon out of bed. Failing this,
the Cathedral won't be kept on its legs," and Sergeant Wurren only
stopped talking because he was looking out of the window and
trying to picture what would happen if the Cathedral sat, knelt, or
fell down on the snow-clad garden beneath it.

Just then the door of the study opened, and Mr. Cartwright, a
son of Mrs. Beveridge's by a former marriage, came in. He was
the only stepson of the Canon who was in residence at Prebendal
House, for this bachelor of forty went up to town every day on
business, preferring this daily journey to a banishment from home.
A good-looking man, but retiring and wanting the dash of the two
Majors and the impudence of the Sub-Lieutenant.

Mr. Cartwright, christened William, kissed his mother and step-
sisters, shook hands with everyone else in the room, and then,
perceiving Daniel to be the only man in the room like himself not
wearing one of His Majesty's uniforms, went over and grouped
himself beside him.

"I don't know what you've all decided to do," he said, "nor do
I want to delay you by asking details which you have probably

discussed. I have had the outline of what has happened from the station-master. But what I do ask you to do, is to tell me if there is anything that I can do, because it seems to me that something ought to be done at once."

"So it ought," agreed Sergeant Wurren, implying by his tone that he was delighted to find someone of his way of thinking at last, "Mr. Cartwright, so it ought. The only question we have got to decide is, what that something ought to be."

"If you don't mind my butting in," said Gordon, "I suggest that Daniel Dyke has hit more nails on the head than any of us. Daniel, just tell them quickly as you told me the sequence of events since the coming of the Paper Wizard."

When Daniel had done so, Gordon went on: "Now he thinks that more detectives should be sent from Scotland Yard. Isn't there a big four that we are constantly hearing of? If so, let's have the big four. Sergeant Wurren, it is not fair for anybody to expect you to do everything. Mr. Macauley wants to direct operations from his sick-bed. That's not good enough. He vows he'll be up and about to-morrow on crutches. Jane says he won't, and she's nursing him. You've got enough to do already, Sergeant, and the mystery thickens every day."

"Well, you see, Master Gordon—Mr. Beveridge, I should say," interrupted the policeman, "looking for disappeared parsons is not one's only duty. One has to keep the Station going and keep an eye open for other things too. I can't neglect my ordinary routine, even if the whole Precincts disappears. Murders are all right in their place, but they mustn't go upsetting the routine."

"You want help, and you shall have it. That's understood," said the elder Major.

"If we have to pay for the help ourselves, I'm game," put in Mr. Cartwright.

"Thanks, old man," loudly whispered the younger Major. The Beveridge family had a wonderful knack of making one another look heroic.

"Daniel also thinks that certain clues should be followed up," went on Gordon. "That Paper Wizard, for instance, should be laid by the heels. Nobody knows where he's got to, apparently. Then McCarbre. Where is he with that bounder, Dr. Smith? We are assured that they are not where they pretend to be. Then again, where is our old Miss Tackle?"

"You can leave her to me, Gordon," said Jane. "I'll get her before she leaves her house to-morrow morning. But, look here; it's quite dark. I must go back to poor Grannie. She wishes there was something she could do for you, Mrs. Beveridge."

"I wish the same for her," answered that lady. "We are both suffering from the same cause."

"If you are going back, Jane," put in Miss Dorothy, "I insist that Daniel goes with you. Do you know, I feel as if none of us is safe if left alone for a minute."

"I think that's right," replied the elder Major. "We've got to get to the bottom of this extraordinary horror; but for all our sakes and the sakes of those who're gone, we'll hunt in no less than couples. To be alone, even though it only be a question of minutes, is, as Dorothy implies, merely putting a chance in the way of this uncanny thing that is attacking us."

This speech, coming from a very dashing soldier, made a profound impression upon everybody, with the exception of Jane, who found herself thanking God that it had not been said by her Daniel, for Jane had no fear of anything, and was more annoyed than impressed by the uncanny thing referred to. However, she naturally raised no objection to Daniel accompanying her to the Deanery, and only when she found that Sergeant Wurren was to be of the party did she protest that she was perfectly safe going by herself, and that, as Daniel was to return with the Sergeant to the Police Station upon her safe arrival, it was quite unnecessary to drag them so far out of their way. However, the matter was compromised by Mrs. Beveridge.

"Since there are three of you, why not go by the Slype? The key is here. You can bring it back in the morning."

"I'll leave it on my way back from the Police Station," said Daniel. "Then I can leave you word whether there is any news received there or at the Deanery."

"But please do not go about alone," urged the elder Major. "Discretion, you know. The state in the Precincts is so peculiar that anything may happen, and it is worth noting that, so far as we know, each person who has disappeared was alone at the time."

"I shall be all right," laughed Daniel.

Jane liked the tone in which he said it, but immediately came to the conclusion that Eddie Beveridge was right. She did not want Daniel strolling about in the Precincts by himself. She was nervous for him in the very same situation that for herself she wouldn't care a rap.

As soon as the three had left for the Deanery, armed with the key of the Slype, William Cartwright took his mother and step-sisters into the drawing-room, but Gordon detained his brothers in the study. Producing a chart of the Lower River and switching on the reading light of his father's desk, he begged them to give him their attention.

"Now, look here," he began, "I want your advice. I oughtn't to tell anyone, but it seems to me that it's better you should know, and give me your opinion, rather than I should shoulder the whole responsibility myself and perhaps make a mess of it. I couldn't tell Daniel, though I wanted to, but you two being soldiers and broth-ers clears my conscience as regards Admiralty secrecy." He spread the map across the table and beckoned his brothers to examine it. "This is one of our charts of the river from below Dullchester bridge to the sea. Apparently, somewhere hidden in this labyrinth of mud islands and marsh flats, is lurking one of the most sinister figures of crime."

"Here, draw it mild. What have you been reading lately?" asked the eldest brother, smiling.

"I'm glad to say that long theatrical phrase was not mine. I'm merely repeating what the Admiral told me in his sanctum this morning. I expect he got it out of some book. Anyway, in plain English, there's no end of a dirty dog kicking around somewhere in this river, and I've been told to nose him out."

"But has this got anything to do with father's disappearance?" asked the younger Major.

"From Daniel's account, I think it has," replied the Navy. "If you remember, he overheard a remark on the Pier to-day of a twin-funnel tug and a Chink. I've got a warrant for that Chink in my pocket, which gives me power to work with the river police. I hand it over to a Scotland Yard man who will be on my boat to-morrow, or perhaps to-night. This Chink's wanted for the opium traffic. He passes the stuff to certain low lodging-houses in Talkham which the sailors frequent. Foreign sailors mostly, but they've been getting hold of some of our chaps lately, and that's just where we butt in. It's got to be stopped. My little show carries a gun and can nip in and out of the mud banks. She doesn't draw much water and is devilish fast. Now, the question is, has this Chink got anything to do with these disappearances, and if so, what the devil can his motive be?"

The elder Major shook his head. "I don't see what anything of all this has to do with anything else. It's a Devil's Kitchen nightmare. Nothing means anything, or leads us anywhere. However, old boy, it's up to you to get this Chink. It may help us, of course, but I doubt very much whether he's got anything to do with it. As to Miss Tackle—well, she may have gone cracked and got mixed up in the shady business somehow, but I don't believe Macauley's theory, which after all is only based on what Boyce's Boy told Daniel, and Boyce's Boy could invent any story which brought him into the limelight. I wish we could help you. I envy you being under orders to get on with something."

"You can help me," answered the Sub. "Your Colonel's away, isn't he? That means Eddie's in command of the regiment. If I go chasing in and out these mud banks and islands, there's one place where that damned twin-funnel tug can give me the slip. Look at the map here. This is a basin where we hid our submarines in the war. Some of the creeks would hide a battleship, with careful pilotage, but a small boat has a choice of a thousand ways to get in and out. But there's one catch in it, and it was spotted by an Army bloke in the war, and a damned good spot it was too. This point here, reached by a perishing bad road across the marsh, commands the whole sweep of that water. Right at the end is a concrete floor, cleverly camouflaged. The best gun-emplacement I ever saw. Now, it seems to me that you could—under the excuse of manœuvres, night practice, or whatever you like to call it——"

The speaker broke off and sprang to his feet. The two Majors did the same. From the garden, in the direction of the Slype, rose a scream, loud and piercing, ending in a blood-curdling gurgle.

CHAPTER XXXI

THE DISAPPEARANCE OF THE PIGS AND PIPE

THE suddenness of this sound in the still night paralysed the three officers, but they quickly recovered themselves when the study door was burst open and Mr. Cartwright and the ladies rushed in, asking what was the matter.

"The Slype. It came from the Slype," cried Arthur Beveridge. "Quick, you chaps, come on!"

The men made a dash for the hall, but on Mrs. Beveridge crying out that they should not all leave them, William Cartwright came back to the study, threw up the centre sash of the big bay window and, with one leg over the sill, prepared to drop down on to the flower-beds beneath if necessity arose.

Across the snow-covered lawn ran his step-brothers, only to find the Slype door locked.

"Daniel took the key. Can't we get over?" suggested Eddie. But they all knew, since they had used the garden from boyhood, that the thirty-foot walls were impregnable.

"There's someone in the Slype," cried Gordon. "Listen. I can hear voices." A low moaning was heard, which almost immediately died away. Then silence, save for a heavy lump of snow slipping somewhere from the old wall. As they waited, the Cathedral clock struck six. "Let's go round the other way and get the key," whispered Gordon.

"Listen," warned Arthur. "There's someone unlocking the other door."

"Going out through Minor Canon Row. Giving us the slip. Quick," whispered Gordon, clutching his brothers' arms.

"No. Coming this way. Listen!"

The footsteps stopped.

Eddie whispered to Arthur, "Run round to the other door. Give us a whistle, and then we'll beat at this one." Arthur raced back across the lawn.

Now, Daniel, followed by Sergeant Wurren, had taken Jane back to the Deanery, where he was surprised to find old Jubb, who had just taken tea with Rachel in the servants' hall. "Having heard of the trouble about His Harness," he explained, "I brought along some fresh dabs to console Her Harness, for we've been fishing for a few days in the lower river. Heard the news of His Harness on my boat's wireless, we did. Since when young Jones, your late servant and my son-in-law, has never taken the receiver off his ears, a-listening for His Harness to be found. We gets a rare lot of band-tunes at night on that machine, but 'give me news of His Harness,' says Jones, 'and dang your band tunes,' he says."

Daniel strolled with the departing Jubb as far as Deanery Gate and then returned to Sergeant Wurren, who was waiting for him in the hall, when the scream that so astounded Prebendal House reached his ears. Promising Jane to be back as soon as possible, he ran past the pig-styes, through the stable-yard to the south or top entrance of the Slype. By the time he had unlocked the door, Sergeant Wurren, puffing and blowing, caught him up and flashed his electric torch down the narrow passage. There was nobody there. Three distinct sets of footprints in the snow, which they had themselves made a few minutes earlier, otherwise no sign of life at all. Suddenly they were startled by a whistle, followed by a violent hammering on both doors which only proved to be the Beveridge young men.

Together they searched the Slype from end to end, Wurren's torch flashing into every crack and crevice in the walls. Suddenly the Sergeant astonished the young men by exclaiming, "I've got it. Sergeant Wurren's got it!" When pressed eagerly by the others to report what he had got, he continued slowly, "At least, I think Sergeant Wurren has." He beckoned them to follow him to the flight of steps at the lower end of the Slype, and then, turning round and surveying them as if he were Styles or Potter giving a lecture to tourists, he pointed to the high wall on his left. "Don't the Dean keep pigs somewhere over that wall? And don't pigs scream? Wasn't a speckled one stole only yesterday? That scream we just heard was another one going. We're on the track of pig-lifters. They're the trouble we must locate. Pig-lifters. They've took 'em all."

Although it seemed preposterous that pig-thieves should also take a Dean and Chapter to their iniquitous sausage-market, the young men were bound to confess that there was no harm in going to look at the styes.

"It didn't sound like a pig to me," remarked Gordon.

"Perhaps you haven't had much experience with 'em, Master Gordon," ventured the Sergeant. "I have. The Police Station backs on to the market place."

"How many pigs ought there to be in the styes?" asked Edward Beveridge.

"Blest if I know," answered Daniel. "There are such a lot. We'll ask in the house. Jane knows. And then we can come back and count them."

They went through the stable-yard and passed the styes, when Sergeant Wurren, who was bringing up the rear, said, "Is this where they keep 'em?"

"Yes; those are the styes," answered Daniel, thinking that his nose might have informed him of that fact. "We'll go to the back door and ask about these pigs."

"Just a minute," called out the Sergeant, flashing his torch triumphantly over the fence and into the pig-houses. "If this is where they lives, perhaps you can tell me where they are. For if any of you can show me a pig here, he can take it home and roast it."

It was quite safe for the policeman to dispose of the Dean's pigs in this large manner, for there was not a single animal left. On inquiry at the house they learnt that Potter had fed them at lunch-time. Potter, happening to be in the servants' hall, accompanied the party back to the styes. He could throw no light on the matter. He only knew that the styes were full before Evensong and afterwards, because, as Styles was coughing more severely than usual, Potter had volunteered to escort Canon Cable to and from Cathedral. During both these journeys he had noticed that the pigs were there.

Sergeant Wurren took out his notebook and wrote a few words in it by the light of his torch. Then, turning to his companions, he said, "Gentlemen, listen. This is the list of goners up to date:

"2 Minor Canons
1 Dean
1 Bit of Memorial window
1 Fiddling Toy
1 Speckled Pig
1 Herd of Pigs. Seven in all."

"I think you might add to the list," suggested Daniel, "one Miss Tackle and one Paper Wizard; and what about including McCarbre?"

"When I consider 'em proper goners, I'll include 'em," answered the Sergeant. "But not Miss Tackle. Under no circumstances. She's Macauley's job. Since he holds back information about that party, she's his affair. Had he told me about that telegram before, I might have located her by this time, but, thinking she was away in the Hundred of Wat, as the Dean informed me, I have not located her. Macauley is alone to blame for anything we may not at present understand concerning that party. Besides, she——" He broke off, hearing someone slam the Deanery gate. After flashing his torch in that direction, he announced, "Here comes Mr. Trillet."

The little organist came towards them hurriedly.

"Here's a go, Mr. Trillet!" cried Sergeant Wurren. "Have you stolen the Dean's pigs?"

Mr. Trillet looked indignant. He was in no mood for joking. "Dean's pigs?" he repeated. "No. Have you stolen my D-flat Tuba?"

"Whoever's that?" asked the Sergeant.

"My D-flat Tuba," shouted the organist.

"All right. There's no cause to swear about it, Mr. Trillet," urged the Sergeant.

"One of my organ-pipes, you ass. Taken clean away. Found it was dumb in the middle of the anthem, so after service got inside to tinker it up. No D-flat Tuba to tinker. Taken away as clean as a whistle pipe."

Sergeant Wurren added a note to his list, and repeated aloud, "An organ pipe. A herd of pigs and a speckled one. A mechanical toy and a head of stained-glass; and when you add four parsons to that, you have a very rummy collection, and the thief that makes such a haul must be a very rummy thief."

CHAPTER XXXII

THE DISAPPEARANCE OF MR. NORRIS

UPON this same evening Mrs. Norris, the pretty old wife of the curiosity dealer, was minding the shop while her husband was below in the pressroom, superintending the next issue of the *Dullchester and Talkham Weekly*. To do him justice, he was not thinking of the matter in hand so much as of his new romance which he was weaving out of old legends around his beloved Dullchester Castle. Even the disappearance of his great patron the Dean, to whom had been dedicated more than one of his historical novels, failed to stop the flow of the new plot which he had been inspired to write. Had an ancient Abbot disappeared in company with two friars and a Canon, the historian would have been given them a chapter to themselves. As it was, these modern events, startling as they were, rather annoyed him than anything else, as they were distracting his mind, and gave him more material to set up than he cared about, for the *Dullchester and Talkham Weekly*, being, as it were, the official organ of the crime, had doubled its issue and was assuming a bulk that would have done credit to an Annual. But since the crimes were being perpetrated only a few yards from the printing press, that is, the width of the narrow High Street, the great local had to take them seriously. The London papers, having been let down by Miss Tackle, could afford to joke about the mystery and head it as "Our Cathedral Hoax Still Going Strong." Had Fleet Street presses been as near the Terror as the Norris Printing Press, they might have shaken in their cellars as much as their little provincial brother was now doing.

It was with a desperate effort of cheering things up that the old lady crossed the rickety oak floor and, after fumbling for her matches, lighted the second incandescent burner in the crowded shop window. Not that there was much likelihood of any purchaser on such a wintry night, for the pavements were blocked with fast-thickening snow, but the pistols, the daggers, the South Sea idols, the sharks' teeth, et cetera, looked a little less grisly under the second light. But hardly had this piece of extravagance warmed to its work when Boyce's Boy, apparently at a loose end, popped his head round the corner, flattened his nose against the plate-glass, and pulled a most dreadful grimace. Mrs. Norris, whose nerves were more than frayed with the terrible happenings in the Precincts, let out a scream, raised the trap-door leading into the cellar where the *Weekly* was being knocked about with machinery, and literally fell down the ladder on the top of her husband, who at that moment was sitting on the bottom step, smoking a pipe and dreaming of Lady Abbesses, squires and knights. Fortunately, he broke his wife's fall, just as she unfortunately broke his train of thought.

"My dear, whatever——" he began.

"Boyce's Boy!" gasped his prostrate wife.

Norris forgot to raise her to her feet, forgot to pick up his fallen pipe, forgot, in short, to do everything that any reasonable man would have done. He dashed up the ladder with such impetus that the curios which always moved rhythmically to the printers' tune, positively syncopated to this Bull-in-the-China-Shop. Expecting to see his wife's enemy flattening his nose outside the window and preparing to run away, he charged up into the shop, looking in that direction, and was naturally surprised to hear the boy's voice the other side of the counter saying, "Shop."

"You——" began Norris, but not being able to find a modern word for varlet, he glared until he had recovered his temper, and then said, in an icy tone, "What do you want?"

"Spear," replied Boyce's Boy in the casual tone of one who bought at least fifty a day and consequently became bored with the mere mention of them.

"Spear?" repeated Norris, as if he must have been mistaken. "What do you mean? Spear?"

"Javelin, then," corrected Boyce's Boy, stifling a yawn and adding fifty per cent more boredom into the word "javelin" than he had to the word "spear," as much as to say, "I should have thought 'spear' was simple enough, but if you are so childish, thick and stupid, 'javelin' will anyhow convey something to you."

"Spear? Javelin?" replied the bewildered Norris. "What about them?"

"Them?" repeated Boyce's Boy. "No. It. That one there. Big blade with long handle. Spear and javelin's the same thing, you know, only I was trying to be more than clear, since you was being more than foggy. Call it what you like, or which you like, but how much?"

The words "how much?" brought Mrs. Norris through the trap again. If there were a sale in progress, she would be needed to support her husband and to help either to browbeat the customer or persuade him gently, according as things might go.

"That spear, my dear. Javelin, you know." Mr. Norris, in his confusion, was not quite sure which was the correct term. "How much?"

"Ah. It is a very beautiful lance," said Mrs. Norris, beginning to unhook it and knocking a tomahawk down in the process, which fell through the trap, just missed the compositor's head and stuck, quivering, in a pile of finished weeklies.

"Mind, my love. Look out, my dear. You'll knock that one over next"—pointing to a boomerang—"and that one will jump all over the place if you do, and keep striking back at us. Let me hold the boomerang while you unhook the lance." So saying, Norris steadied the boomerang while his wife extracted the javelin. "It's a very nice lance, this," she said, dusting it with her apron up and down, which caused her shadow to be reflected upon the ceiling by the light from the cellar, transforming her neat little figure into a gigantic monkey-on-a-stick.

"Mind my head, my dear, with that point," protested her husband, trying to avoid her without stepping upon the china plates that were heaped up on the floor. "Sure to be poisoned. And mind the gas-mantle, my love. How much is it? Can you see an indication of a price? It should be marked. No ticket, eh? No scratch? No indelible pencil?"

"My eyes are not good in gaslight," sighed the old lady, looking up and down the spear-shaft.

"And I can see next to nothing without my gig-lamps, which I left in the printing room," declared the old man, examining the blade. "Hallo. Wait. What's this? A mark, I think, on the blade. Here, you young shaver, your eyes should be spry, at your time of life. What's that mark?"

Boyce's Boy gave a cursory glance at the spot indicated, and said, still in his offhand manner, "That's nothing. Bit o' blood."

Whether it was the word "blood" or whether it was the sudden apparition of the policeman that made Mrs. Norris scream again was not apparent, for just then Sergeant Wurren, who had emulated Boyce's Boy and flattened his nose against the window-pane, raised himself on his toes in order to get a better view of the sinister transaction going on in the shop, which caused his nose to squeak as it ran up the plate-glass.

"It's only the Sergeant, my dear," said old Norris soothingly.

"There ain't no price on it at all," was Boyce's Boy's quick summing-up, after examining the spear which he had taken from the Norrises. "But Boyce's Boy ain't the sort to take advantage of that, so I'll give you three bob"—throwing the coins on to the counter as he spoke—"and I'll take away this 'ere 'orrible relic at once. Good-night to you both, and don't forget you dropped a chopper down the hole." Saying which, he stepped out on to the pavement, spear in hand.

"What are you going to do with that?" demanded Sergeant Wurren.

"Prod things," was the prompt reply.

The Sergeant was about to question him further, but Boyce's Boy, whirling the spear round his head—much to the policeman's alarm—leapt into a species of war-dance, and then, with a whoop, bounded over the snow parapet at the side of the road, and off down the middle of the High Street, the Sergeant being secretly glad to see the last of him, with such a formidable weapon in his hand.

"Whatever made you sell that rascal a thing like that?" he asked, entering the shop.

"Well, I did very little selling, Sergeant Wurren," replied the dealer. "He flung the money down, only three bob, too, and off he went, as you saw."

"What was the spear really worth?" asked the Law.

"Goodness knows," replied Norris. "Don't do much in the javelin line, do we, Mother?"

"No, and don't want to, when there's blood on 'em," assented Mother, wiping her hands on her apron, and shuddering like Lady Macbeth.

"Well, I mustn't waste my time talking of spears. 'Disappears' is more in my line at the moment," and laughing loudly at his own joke, he also sought the pavement.

Old Norris, in going to shut the shop door after the Sergeant, noticed a letter lying on the floor, and thinking it had been dropped by the policeman, picked it up quickly and was about to hail the majesty of the law back from the snow, when he read his own name upon the envelope. Tearing it open, he began to read. Mrs. Norris, observing him, was astounded at the way his eyes popped out of their sockets and at his frequently ejaculating, "Good God!"

"Whatever is it, my dear? A summons?" She knew that there were one or two bills overdue.

"Yes," replied her husband. "You've hit it right on the head. I don't make a habit of swearing in front of you, as you know, my love, but I really must say——" he broke off to look again at the paper and to say, "Good God!"

"If it's only a summons, we'll settle it all up to-morrow morning. You go into the parlour, and I'll go down and shut up for the night. Don't let a summons worry you. A summons ain't much. After all, lots of people get summoned. We're always printing about them in the *Weekly*, so they can't be very bad. We've only to pay it, and then the summons is powerless," and chatting in this comfortable vein, she disappeared down the ladder and told the compositor that he could knock off for the night.

"Ain't much, eh?" queried Norris to himself. "Only a summons! Well, there's summonses and summonses, but this ain't the kind you can get away from, even with money." He placed the letter in the pocket of his baize apron and looked round the shop with a tragic air. He then leant over the counter and peeped down at his wife, who was talking to the compositor and helping him on with his great-coat.

"All right, mum. To-morrow I'll be here a bit earlier, to make up for getting off a bit earlier to-night. Don't worry, though, mum. We're well in hand with the *Weekly*. Good-night, mum," and the compositor came up the ladder in a couple of strides, bringing with him an aroma of printers' ink.

Mrs. Norris waited for him to reach the top before turning out the gas-jet below. When she had done this she also came up the ladder. She closed the trap and bolted it, and was about to ask the compositor to close the shop door tightly when she perceived his face and the extraordinary expression upon it, and consequently asked, instead, whatever he saw to make him look so upset.

"Look," gasped the compositor. "It's blood. Wet blood, too. It's flowing down the slope of this board, and it's warm, and—O Gawd, Mrs. Norris, mum," he almost shouted, "what's become of the governor?"

They both looked round the shop, and through the glass-partitioned door of the parlour. Ah, indeed, what had become of the governor? They searched for him all over the house. With the help of the police they searched for him all over the town. Sergeant Wurren was more than ever at sea. What puzzled him most was the pool of blood. After gazing at it for some time, walking round it, and scraping up a little spot of it on an old envelope, he deigned to answer: "I make this of it. In all these disappearances there's something sticky and wet left behind. Why? With the Minor Canons we finds two throat lozenges. If you remember, they were picked up in the Precincts and came in for their full share in my report. I kept on mentioning them. With Canon Beveridge it was ink, and with your late husband it was blood."

At the mention of "late husband" Mrs. Norris burst into tears and became indignant with the policeman. "I won't have you say he's dead. Can't be. You're wrong, too, about the wet. When the Dean went, what was wet? Or the window? Or the toy fiddler? Or the pig? Or the pigs? Nothing wet."

"Thick snow," explained the Sergeant. "Their bits of stickiness wouldn't show, I quite see that. But this blood of your husband's puzzles me. Have you examined all these weapons?"

"There was nobody to use them," answered the wife. "Boyce's Boy had gone with the lance. I was down with the compositor in the print room. You was the last person to speak to him except myself, and I love him, so why should I kill him?"

"Now then, no more of that," warned the Sergeant. "No putting me into false pretences. No hinting that I clove his skull open with any of these things"—indicating the weapons—"'cos I didn't, and if I did, what have I done with the body? I'm a policeman, not a conjuror."

Mrs. Norris apologized, and after clearing him in her mind of all suspicion, she urged him to waste no more time but to go and look for her missing husband, which the Sergeant faithfully did.

He sought diligently, but the curio dealer could nowhere be found. The earth had opened and swallowed up Norris, and it was duly entered in Sergeant Wurren's notebook and in the virgin pages of the *New Weekly* as "Another Case of a Complete Disappearance."

CHAPTER XXXIII

JANE IN THE TOILS

JANE was determined to clear up the mystery of Miss Tackle. The more she considered the detective's theory, the more ridiculous she thought it. She was convinced that the queer soul was the good woman the Precincts folk had always thought her. She would prove Macauley wrong. A quiet chat with the old lady, and her character would be cleared. It must be done gently and with tact. Daniel was out of the way. He had left the empty pig-styes and gone with the Sergeant to the Police Station, and now this new rumour of Mr. Norris was abroad he would be amongst the zealous search party. Dinner could wait. In fact, meals at the Deanery had been grossly neglected since the disappearance of the Dean. She could not undertake an interview of this kind before a third party, Daniel especially. It would make her too self-conscious. In the excitement of this new development of the mystery, everybody seemed occupied. Her absence would pass unnoticed. Yes. She would go at once.

North Square was a "No Thoroughfare." It had two claims to its title, for it lay to the north of the Cathedral and surrounded a statue of Lord North, who would not have felt very flattered at the way his effigy was neglected. The garden around it was a jungle of rank grass, and the base that supported it had sunk on one side so that Lord North seemed to be perpetually suffering from a list to port. The little old-fashioned houses whose darkened windows surveyed this depressing outlook had seen better days. Miss Tackle lived there because it was her own house, left to her by her mother. Next door to her lived Dr. Smith, but this unpleasant fact she never recognized. He lived there because the house had been to let at a low rent. Most of the houses were empty, as there was a scheme for rebuilding on the site and the landlords would not renew their agreements, though the gloom of the place was not likely to induce any tenant to wish them to. Miss Tackle's outward dislike to her next-door neighbour would have compelled her to change her abode had it been a good time to part with her property, but she was going to hang on to it till the new builders gave her proper terms, and so she pretended to be ignorant of the fact that there was such a thing as a bounder who lived next door.

Jane reached the house and found old Mrs. Styles preparing Miss Tackle's high-tea. Miss Tackle always took high-tea about seven o'clock. Her bee farm was situated on the outskirts of the town, so that she never had time to get an early cup of tea in North Square. She lived on only two meals a day. An old-English breakfast with meat, and high-tea also with meat. The rest of the day she supported with bread and honey on the bee farm. The verger's wife prepared these meals and left them on the table. If Miss Tackle was not there to enjoy them hot, they got cold, because Mrs. Styles departed to time like the Continental Express.

Mrs. Styles was a kinswoman to the Dean's mechanical toys in that she worked by clockwork. She was stone-deaf and shortsighted. When she thought you wished to converse with her, she held out a slate and pencil, which both hung at her girdle. She read your writing by holding the slate close to her nose. Boyce's Boy said that she had formed this habit from watching Canon Cable read the Lessons in Cathedral. She worked almost as hard as that Canon. She was spotlessly clean. She explained to Jane that Miss Tackle had come back from the Hundred of Wat and that she was expecting her in to high-tea at any minute. Of course she might be detained by the bees. Seven o'clock was a very inconvenient time for Mrs. Styles, because Mr. Styles took his supper at seven-thirty, before retiring to bed to read the newspaper. Jane therefore dismissed the old lady by writing her dismissal on the slate. "You had better go. I will look after the kettle and wait for Miss Tackle." Mrs. Styles put on her cloak and bonnet and went. Jane took off her red overcoat with the ermine collar and her ermine hat, and waited. She sat by the fire in the front sitting-room. She did not light the gas. The fire gave a cosy light and the kettle was singing. She took the brass toasting-fork and gave the waiting crumpets a preliminary cooking. She would give Miss Tackle half-an-hour, and no more. The heat from the fire was comfortable after the cold air outside, and it was pleasant leaning back against the divan, with the comfortable cushions pulled on to the hearth-rug. Jane's eyes kept closing involuntarily. She was very tired. Since the disappearance of her grandfather she had had very little sleep. The heat of the fire and the comfort of the cushions were seductive. She was trying to think of the most tactful way in which to introduce the subject which she had come to discuss. But somehow her brain would not work. She could not keep her eyes open. Those persistent questions: *"What has happened to your grandfather?" "Where are the Minor Canons?"* went on repeating themselves in ding-dong fashion. Since there appeared to be no answer there was no stopping them and they took control of her tired brain, revolving there till even they seemed to tire of going round and round, for they turned themselves slower and slower until Jane wondered how many more times she would hear them before she fell asleep. *"What has happened to your grandfather? Where are the Minor Canons?"* At last the first word, *What*, became so lengthened out that Jane did not hear the final *t*. She was fast asleep.

How long she slept she could not tell. The fire still glowed in the grate, throwing a faint circle of reddish light to the edge of the hearth-rug. Beyond that—darkness.

The kettle was still singing like a choir of diminutive mosquitoes, soaring into unscalable heights of treble. Its last drops of water were being transfigured into steam, fine steam that scarcely showed, for it was not the kettle that was smoking. The smoke rose from the blackened crumpet on the toasting-fork which she had been holding while she slept.

When she first opened her eyes she was faced with the ghastly knowledge that she was not alone in the room, that invisible shapes were moving in the darkness beyond the ring of red, watching her and waiting for the net of fear which they had cast upon her to entangle her completely. Then they would materialize and take her as their prey.

She knew that by sleeping she had put herself into their power and that the opening of her eyes had startled and repulsed them for the moment. If she could only move she might yet save herself, but her limbs were cramped, her throat was dry and fear hypnotized her spirit. If she closed her eyes again she would be theirs, and the singing of the kettle was luring her to sleep once more.

Oh, God, her eyes were closing, and as they closed she saw the shapes—two of them—moving from the darkness towards the ring of light.

One of the figures resembled a gaunt woman, hugely tall and powerful. An exaggerated Miss Tackle, for a grey cloud of veil, shrouding her face and floating as she moved, hardly concealed the velvet respirator which looked like the black hollow of an open mouth.

The other shape had not fully materialized. All she could see of it was a yellowish face with slanting black slits for eyes. She dared not even try to look again. She could only lie still, waiting for them to take her. They were too strong for her. She must deliver herself unconditionally, body and soul, into their evil hands.

The tall woman was hovering over her. She felt the veil brushing her face. Fingers were carefully dragging the cushions from beneath her. She was sinking to the floor. A cold hand touched her throat. Thin fingers lifted her wrist. She opened her eyes. The veil was all round her like a vast spider's web. She could see the red glow of the fire through its folds. The smoke from the crumpet seemed to be creeping under the veil. A curious smell overpowered her. She was lifted up into the folds of the veil and carried towards the open window. She saw the snow. It looked green through the veil. She was conscious that it was now her turn to disappear. Had the others gone like this, and did that terrible vehicle come for them? A hearse-like-looking cab with shuttered windows. A massive driver on the box high up against the sky-line. His face was muffled up against the snow, with a peaked cap pulled down over his eyes. Behind him on the roof was a huge iron chest with handles. Of course, a coffin. Her coffin. The door of the cab was open. With its window shuttered it appeared to be the door of a mausoleum. It was only open because it waited for her to go into the darkness beyond. Then it would shut. She was sure of that. She was handed out of the window to the shape with the yellow face who reappeared in the snow. He must have placed her in the funeral cab, though she felt that she just floated there by herself. She had lost all sense of her own weight, and she thought, "Why have I never been able to float in the air before? I must teach Daniel how to do it, if ever I get back to him out of this nightmare. We'll have flying races down the drive in front of grandfather's pigs." The cab door was shut. The journey had begun. They seemed to be going very slowly. She wondered whether this was because of the snow or because it was a funeral procession. The folds of the veil were touching her face again. Sometimes ghostly tentacles gripped her tightly. At other times she floated through the dark. Then for a time she lost all sensation. Perhaps she was asleep again, or had they shut her into the coffin on the roof? No. She had been asleep, for she awoke feeling cold, and saw that she was being carried by the shapes across a dizzy bridge. She could see far down beneath her, ever so far, to where the dark water splashed around snow-covered posts. How bitterly cold it was. There were two great chimneys against the sky. No, they were the funnels of a ship. She was on the ship. A small red lamp got larger and larger, till it made everything red and warm. She was in a room. The walls were hung with red silk with great dragons worked on them. Was she back in Miss Tackle's room before the fire? There was a little column of smoke curling up beside her. Was it the burnt crumpet? No, the smoke was coming out of a little dragon's mouth. The smoke smelt very sweet. Cushions were under her again. Would she wake up soon in her own bedroom, and find that nobody had disappeared at all, that it was all a nightmare? Daniel's face appeared. Why was he calling to her through iron bars? or was he in the rose-garden, looking through the trellis-work? He had gone. Strange. He had disappeared into the floor. What was he doing there in the doorway? First he had a spear. Then he had a revolver. What a vibrating hum there was. "Is that a soldier in uniform riding at my side? No. It's a mixture of Dr. Rickit and dear old Rachel. I wish I could wake now, because this is my own room."

CHAPTER XXXIV

DANIEL IN THE TOILS

AFTER the discussion at the Deanery styes Daniel accompanied Sergeant Wurren to the Police Station. A lengthy conversation over the 'phone to St. Rood's and Talkham got them a promise of extra policemen. When these arrangements were satisfactorily concluded Daniel helped the Sergeant to draw up a full report for Scotland Yard, which was accordingly dispatched. He then returned to the Deanery to look for Jane. He couldn't find her. Nobody knew when she had gone out or where she had gone to, but it was obvious that she had left the house, because her red coat with the ermine collar, which she had been wearing for out-of-doors, was nowhere to be found. Daniel raced round to the Beveridges'. No. They had not seen her.

He then thought of Miss Tackle. Of course, he should have gone there first. He had every reason to regret that he had not done so, for those few minutes wasted made all the difference to Jane's peril and his own.

As he ran down the High Street towards North Square, a cab was coming slowly along towards the Bridge. Daniel glanced at it as he raced by, subconsciously thinking that the iron chest upon the top was a cumbersome piece of luggage, and wondering whether Boyce's Boy, who was hanging on to the back of the cab, was really contemplating helping the driver down with it when they reached their destination. The cab turned down a side street by the Bridge. Daniel hurried on to North Square. He rang the bell and knocked. There was no answer and there were no lights in any of the windows to give any promise of one. As he looked at the window on the ground floor he noticed that it was unlatched. Knowing that Miss Tackle was of a very careful and nervous disposition, he wondered whether all was right. It was not in her character to leave the house with a ground-floor latch undone. Nor was Mrs. Styles the woman to do such a thing. He went close to the window and peered in. The room was very dark, but there was just enough glow from the fire to show him a thing which made him open the window and climb over the sill. He picked up Jane's hat and coat. She had been in the house. Was she still there? If so, why were the rooms in darkness? He called aloud in the hall. There was no reply. He then went into every room in turn, lighting the gas in each. But no Jane. There was no gas on the top storey, so he lit a candle and, turning out the gas behind him, mounted the last flight of stairs. No one in the boxroom, or in either of the bedrooms. Upon the landing was a cupboard, with a door at the front and back. It contained one or two boxes and a heap of plaster and rubbish. He passed through this and found himself on another landing similar to the one he had left. Another staircase faced him. He had no idea the house was so large. He searched this side of the house more hurriedly, as it consisted chiefly of empty rooms. He worked his way down to the hall again, but the downstairs sitting-room seemed different. He did not remember these shelves of bottles. He lit the gas. It wasn't the same room at all. It was a surgery. How stupid of him! Of course, he had broken through into the next house, the house belonging to Dr. Smith. Immediately he thought of this man, he thought of his voice, and that reminded him of the voice he had heard underneath the Pier. So the two houses were connected by that cupboard on the top landing. That was the reason of the litter of plaster and rubbish. For some reason it had been necessary to join the houses. Another link between Miss Tackle and the mystery. These two had some secret connection. They had been together under very questionable circumstances beneath the Pier.

Daniel blew out the candle, opened the doctor's front door and rushed out of the Square, turning into the High Street. He had remembered the cab with the iron chest on the top of it. He had recollected the conversation about the Chink and the white girls. God! Was Jane in their clutches? The cab had turned to the right down by the Bridge. Yes, here were the wheel-marks in the snow. He was racing along, wondering how far he could go before the falling snow obliterated the track, when he saw the cab itself returning. It was empty of passengers, of course, for the iron chest had gone from the roof, but he could make the cabby give him the information he wanted. By keeping to the middle of the narrow road he made sure of stopping the horse. The muffled-up cabby swore and told him to get out of the way, but Daniel grabbed the bridle and ordered the man to get down.

"I'm working for Scotland Yard, my man, and I need some information from you, and my advice is that you answer truthfully, unless you want to see the inside of a prison."

The cabby realized that he was caught, and put the best face on it he could.

"Right-ho, governor. 'Taint my fault if I gets a shady fare now and then. Holt's gets all the respectable trade of Dullchester, and what Holt's don't care about gets took by Trace and Clockett's. They run taxis, so what chance have I got? This is my cab, but I'm a poor man."

"Good," thought Daniel. "He'll only want bribing." He produced his note-case and pulled out a pound.

The cabman looked at the note, and stood up on the box, unwrapping the heavy horse-rug from his knees. He put one foot down on the wheel. A heavy man who moved slowly. He spoke sulkily in his defence.

"It ain't none of my business what my fares do outside my cab. I own it looks bad for an elderly lady to be taking a young girl away at this time of night in company with a Chink. He may be their servant, for all I know. The girl was asleep or ill. That's a doctor's house where I picked 'em up. The more I look at it, the more aboveboard it seems. But I don't want to get myself into trouble."

"Of course you don't," answered Daniel, holding out the note. "There's another of these for you if you drive me to wherever you drove them."

"Give us the note, then, and get inside."

"I prefer riding with you outside, if you don't mind. I like to see where I'm being driven." Daniel had withdrawn the note from the cabby's reach while making this necessary condition.

"All right. Give us hold."

He put out his hand for the money, but instead of taking it he sprang from the top of the wheel, enveloping Daniel's head and shoulders with the horse-rug and bearing him to the ground.

Cursing himself for having been taken off his guard, Daniel put up a fight, but the cabby had the advantage and was too heavy to be shaken off.

Suddenly, from the folds of the rug he heard a dreadful cry from his antagonist. At the same time he was kicked viciously. Daniel lay still for a moment, sick with pain, but the cabby had got up, for the weight had gone from his chest. Perhaps the cabman was afraid he had gone too far. Daniel was summoning up all his strength for a final effort. He could hear the cabby cursing and then the noise of the cab moving away. He must not let it escape. He ripped the rug from his head and sat up. In front of his face a steel blade was shining, an ugly-looking weapon with a wet smear of blood on the point. The cab was being driven down the road, with the cabby on the box. He had had an accomplice inside. This person with the knife was holding him at bay. With a great effort he sprang sideways, using the rug as a shield from the blade, and down he went again, with his new antagonist, but this time he was on the top. The blade had been knocked into the snow.

"Shut it," hissed a voice from under the rug. "Don't you know a friend when you meets one?"

Daniel dragged the rug free and to his astonishment looked into the face of Boyce's Boy, who seemed to bear no resentment for his rough usage, as he was grinning. "Never mind the cab. Let him go. He'll be wanting a doctor. I stuck my spear a good inch into his flesh. Come up behind him, chose my spot and then pushed home. He didn't half holler."

"How the devil did you happen to be with a spear in this part of the town?" asked Daniel, helping the urchin to his feet.

"Just let me pick up that note which you dropped, and I'll tell you how I am going to earn it better than the cabby." He picked up the note in question, which had fallen in the snow during the attack, and pulling his cap crooked, which had been straightened in his fall, he told Daniel to follow him.

"There's dirty work going on. They've got Miss Jane. Give us that spear and let's bunk."

Spear in hand, he dashed along the road, with Daniel hard on his heels. Through dirty streets, across wharves, through deserted shipyards, in and out warehouses, a sordid labyrinth known well to Boyce's Boy, who made good speed, jumping over chains and rusty anchors half-buried in snow, never hesitating a second or seeming in doubt as to where he was bound for next. Daniel noticed that they were keeping the river as close as possible to their left. At last they reached a jumble of old ship-sheds and Boyce's Boy slackened his pace.

"Don't make a noise. We've got to trespass, and there'll be watchmen, I expect." He crept along towards the river, keeping under the shadow of a high wooden palisade. At the water's edge he stopped.

"If the police knew as much as me about the goings-on behind this fence, there'd be happy days for some of 'em," he whispered. "It's easier to get into the dockyard than here, but it's all right; I've got my own private key."

As he fumbled in his ragged pocket, or rather under the lining of it, Daniel looked at the fence in question. It was too high to scale and it ran out over the water in a defence of spikes. He wondered if this was the hiding-place of the twin-funnel tug. From a crowded ring of large keys his guide selected one which he inserted into the lock of a tiny door which was hardly noticeable in the fence.

"Stop here, Mr. Dyke. I'll scout for the watchman. It won't do to run into him, but if I finds he's in our way, you'll have to dispose of him. I'll stalk him while you look about for a bit of iron to knock him with." Boyce's Boy disappeared.

Had it not been for his fears regarding Jane, Daniel would have felt scrupulous in searching the heaps of old scrap-iron for a suitable weapon, but he was in the mood to knock twenty unsuspecting watchmen on the head if need be, and he would have done it, but it appeared that there was no need for anything so drastic. Before he had found what he needed Boyce's Boy looked out of the door and whispered, "Come on. Quick. All clear."

He followed him across a yard over a wooden bridge and along the side of a great shed. "There's boats here," whispered the guide. "You take your choice and I'll take mine. See that light in the river. That's where you've got to get to quick. Miss Jane is aboard of that steamer. You pull up-stream, then drop down on the other side of 'em. I'll pull out straight for 'em and I'll start saucing the fellow on watch. This may give you a chance to get on board. If they know you're coming they'll be ready for you—so you must look out. I'll

get their rag out while you slip it across behind 'em. Take this, if
you want a weapon. They'll be sure to scrap."

Daniel, having left Macauley's revolver at the Deanery, thought
the spear might come in useful, so he took it, asking the boy why
he was armed with such a queer weapon.

"Perhaps because I haven't a licence for firearms. Don't find fault
with it. You might be glad of it at a pinch. It's well made. Good and
strong. His head has looked into one or two queer places in his
time, I should think."

"I'm very glad of it," answered Daniel. "It's a good weapon."

"Deadly," assented Boyce's Boy. "Now you take that boat there.
Don't ship your rudder. Scull her from the stern. It's silent if you
knows how. I'll get in this one and row, and you just listen to the
noise I'll make. I'll keep saucing 'em as long as they'll stand for it,
then I shall cut and run, but I'll get the river police on your track if
I can find 'em. Ready?"

"Ready," whispered Daniel, who had unlashed the two boats.
He pushed off with his oar and started sculling. He was glad of his
recent training with the *Dog Fish* crew. He found he could manage
the boat swiftly and silently with the one oar. He whirled away
from his companion, whom he could hear singing and splashing
in his wake. Daniel took a wide circuit, Boyce's Boy made straight
for the tug. It was not long before the tug hailed him in somewhat
obscene language. Boyce's Boy replied with great spirit.

"What are you cumbering up the fairway for? Can't you move
your old puffing Billy out of my way?"

"Who the hell are you?" challenged the tug.

"Someone who objects to your language. You're in a Cathedral
town now, old Billingsgate, so trim your tongue according."

There followed such a loud and lengthy string of blasphemy
that Daniel managed to hitch his boat to the port-side of the tug
well aft, and by the help of a cable scramble on to the deck. He had
noticed that the main cabin seemed to be for'ard, so he crept along
under shadow of the bulwarks, under the wheel-house, towards
the door. It was pitch-dark, so he stood in the doorway, holding
the spear in his right hand and with his left flashed on his electric
torch. To his utter astonishment he lit up the face of a Chinaman,
who was standing close to him, with his finger to his lips.

"Quiet," he whispered. "If you value your life, don't speak above a whisper. Who are you? What do you want?"

"I want to search this ship. There's a lady on board that I mean to find."

"Is that all? Nothing else?" asked the Chinaman.

"All? Well, it's enough, isn't it?"

"I suppose it is," answered the Chinaman, who spoke perfect English. In fact, this was not at all the sort of Chinaman Daniel had expected. He was young. He was well-dressed in European clothes, and he wore a yachting-cap pulled jauntily over one eye.

"You are the young lady's lover, I take it?" he said, flashing a torch in Daniel's face. "You must forgive these portable lights, but the captain of this boat is lying dead-drunk on the floor of this cabin, and he must not be disturbed."

"I'm afraid he will have to be," answered Daniel, who could just see the form of the drunkard in question, covered with a sea-coat. "I must see this lady at once."

"Ah, yes. Of course. You fiancée, eh?" asked the Chinaman.

"I don't see what the devil that's got to do with you," cut in Daniel. "But if you want to know, yes. The girl who is engaged to be married to me. She has been kidnapped within this hour, and I know she is here on board, and I know that you or the drunken captain are going to show me where she is."

"Now, my dear sir, don't lose your temper with me." The Chinaman smiled charmingly. "This little escapade of the kidnapped lady has not met with my approval, I assure you. I warned the doctor that he was acting stupidly. I told him that if he did run away with a lady, a hue-and-cry would be raised, and, quite frankly, a hue-and-cry is the last thing I wish to be raised. I am glad you have come. It will show him that I was right."

"What doctor are you talking about? A fellow called Smith?" demanded Daniel.

"I believe that is one of his names," answered the Chinaman. "He has done business with me in all parts of the world. I met him when he was a very good ship's doctor. I belong to a firm of shipping merchants. A very useful man to me—this Smith—until he met this lady, your fiancée. She turned his head. When she left

Dullchester, what does he do? Why, he finds out where she had gone to and follows her, just to be near and watch. Buys a bungalow near her place of work. Watches for her all day, and when he sees her, he gets a closeup view through a telescope. He used to make me look sometimes, until I told him that she was not the type of girl who would fall in love with him. I believe my saying that put this mad scheme into his head."

"Where is he now?" demanded Daniel hotly. "Show me."

"I will, with the greatest of pleasure, and shall be glad if you will take the lady away with you," replied the Chinaman. "I want no more trouble. It's bad enough having to put up with a drunken captain. The girl is unconscious. He doped her with something. However, I'll help you put her into a boat, but it's up to you to have it out with the doctor first."

"Where is he?" demanded Daniel again.

"In the further cabin. I'll show you," answered the Chinaman. "But you'll leave this harpoon, or whatever it is, outside. I'll have no bloodshed, mind. He's unarmed. I saw to that. No weapons but fists on my boat."

"I've two good ones," laughed Daniel, "and your doctor friend will know it."

"It will not hurt him to be taught a lesson. His cabin is in the alley-way there. The door facing you."

The Chinaman had swung his light to the alley-way in question, and Daniel strode towards it, after leaning the spear against the cabin wall.

"Be quick about it, please," urged the Chinaman. "I'm only waiting for the captain to get sober; then I shall sail."

"Where's the door?" asked Daniel, entering the alley-way and looking for a handle on the iron plates.

"Further down," replied the Chinaman, behind him. "I'll switch on the lights for a minute and damn the captain."

"Is it a sliding door?" asked Daniel.

"Yes," replied the Chinaman. "It pulls across, like this. You're in the inner cabin now."

Daniel heard a door slide-to behind him. He also heard the Chinaman laugh. At the same time the cabin from which he had walked was flooded with light from three electric lamps set in handsome Chinese shades. But he was trapped. Cut off from the cabin by a steel-trellised gate.

"What's the meaning of this?" demanded Daniel sharply.

"I will explain everything," answered the Chinaman.

"Open this gate," cried Daniel, shaking it.

"That would be extremely foolish of me, as you will very soon appreciate," said the Chinaman suavely. "What do you think of my cabin? Silken hangings obliterate the iron of the ship's side, Persian rugs adorn the deck. It is heated by hot pipes from the engine-room, though this electric stove looks as if it were doing the work. The cage in which you are standing is a lift. It descends into the hold and is very useful for cargo that is small, which ours always is. It is an ingenious piece of nautical engineering. It is controlled from this switchboard. I told you that it descended to the hold, I think? That is immediately below us. But it will descend further. There is a watertight compartment through which it can pass into the water below the keel. We can keep the cage watertight by closing it—so." He pressed a button and a double steel shutter closed over the gate. Daniel was in the dark, but for a few seconds only, for the Chinaman released the shutters again. "Neat, isn't it?" he went on tauntingly, "and very useful. The bulk of a cargo that is profitable takes up so little room that in case of a search it is all stowed away here and dropped beneath the keel. If the watertight compartment gives the show away and I am forced to raise the lift, the floor slides open as it comes up and leaves the contents to sink. However, we have floats attached so that we can drag for them when we get a chance. I will not open the floor for you now, as I have no wish to drop you into the hold. I hope you don't find it damp? It has been under the water to-night. In fact, you disturbed me when I was examining the cargo. I called it 'the drunken captain' so that you would not disturb it. As a matter of fact, my captain is never drunk. He is on the bridge now and taking us down with the tide. This is the cargo I was examining." He pulled the sea-coat away from the figure on the floor, and Daniel saw the veil and hat, the old skirt and snow-shoes, the anti-bee gloves, and a glimpse of the black velvet respirator of Miss Tackle. The whole figure was water-sodden.

"What have you done to her?" cried Daniel. "Is she dead?"

"Yes, he is," answered the Chinaman with a chuckle as he tore the hat and veil from his victim's head. The velvet respirator turned out to be a black moustache and the staring eyes and distorted face revealed the corpse of Dr. Smith.

"Thus do I deal with my rivals," laughed the Chinaman. "When you have vacated the lift, he can go down. No marks of violence. If the body is discovered, a verdict of 'Found drowned.'"

"You devil!" hissed Daniel. "But you'll hang, as sure as there is a God in heaven."

"Which, after all, is very doubtful," commented the Chinaman. "I shall die, no doubt, when I deserve to, just as he has done. I have no regret for this man. If you knew his history, you would have done as I did. Besides, he was the cause of separating you from your fiancée, so you cannot feel pity, surely?"

"And do you mean to send me to this fate?" Daniel was surprised how steady his voice was as he asked the question.

"I will show you why it is lamentably necessary," replied the smiling Oriental.

He pulled aside one of the silken hangings and revealed Jane lying on a heap of rich cushions. A shaded lamp was fixed in the wall by her head, and two bronze incense-burners that stood upon the deck wafted their strongly-scented fumes across her face. Her eyes were closed. She was breathing as in a deep sleep. Daniel could not speak.

"She is exquisite," whispered the Oriental reverently. "You cannot blame me for killing that dog when you look at her. He taught me to love her. I used to worship her through that telescope of his."

"Listen to me," cried Daniel. "If you think you are going to escape to-night, you are mistaken. The authorities are watching for you."

"They always are," laughed the Chinaman.

"But they'll get you this time," retorted Daniel. "And as surely as you think I am in your power, will you swing for murder. Your only chance is to open this cage and to let me take the girl away. That would tell in your favour, I promise you."

The Chinaman chuckled and, crossing to the lift, pressed a button. The lift began to descend. In the darkness of the hold it stopped. There was a clanging noise beneath Daniel's feet. The lift descended another stage. It had entered the watertight compartment. A clanging noise above his head. The atmosphere was stifling. Another clank beneath his feet. An icy blast, and he felt the water rushing in. Over his boots. Over his knees. Up to his waist. He began to clamber up the trellised bars. The water followed him to the ceiling. Then the cage jerked up again. Again the clanging noises, and he was once more looking at the unconscious Jane and the devilish Chinaman, who came close to the bars and said, "Effective, isn't it? You must not imagine that I have brought you up again because I am bluffing. I have no need to bluff. I just thought, however, that you might like to take one more look at your beautiful fiancée before breaking off the engagement."

Suddenly there was a rush of feet on the deck outside and a violent knocking on the cabin door. "What is it?" called out the Chinaman.

"Open the door. They've got us in a searchlight. A damned cruiser's blocking the main channel." The Chinaman opened the door and admitted a burly member of the crew, a great rough seadog in sou'westers. Behind him streamed the dazzling rays of a powerful searchlight. The Chinaman appeared quite calm. "The British Navy, eh? They are taking notice of us on this trip. Well, we can steer for the side reaches. We can go where the cruiser can't. They dare not risk the mud banks. We have nothing to panic about. I will go on to the bridge myself. By the way," he added casually, "I shall need the lift to hide the lady in. When you have got it ready, put cushions inside. Get rid of that corpse on the floor there, after you have made that gentleman one. Then empty the doctor's chest—here's the key—and drop the damned thing after the bodies. You can pack the contents under the cushions with the girl. We must drop them all if the worst comes to the worst."

He turned out all the lights except the one over Jane's head; then, turning to Daniel, he added, "Good-night. Pleasant trip," and he was going when a dull roar resounded in the night. He stopped for a moment at the door. "Order to heave-to. What impudence these English have." The roar was followed by a sharp bark near at hand. "Another one. Come. We must show our pace." He went on deck. The sailor had been looking at the spear which leant against the wall. The moment his master had gone, he went over to it and examined it. He then looked at Daniel. "So it's you, eh? The gent from Scotland Yard who was so free with his notes. Where's the young spark who was so free with this, I wonder? I wish I had him in there too. However, you are something to get on with. I'll have a look at that pocket-book of yours in a few minutes, so I trust you'll oblige me by drowning quickly."

He was the cabman. Daniel recognized him, also noted that he limped badly as he walked towards the cage.

"Don't be a fool," urged Daniel. "You don't want to hang with that Chink, do you?"

"No, I don't," agreed the sometime cabman. "And what's more, I'll take precautions quickly not to." He pressed the lift button. Daniel carried a last mental picture of Jane, as she lay there on the cushions, down into the darkness. He could see her beautiful hair, every tress of it, and her young figure. He could almost hear her breathing, and he realized that the water was up to his neck. He drew himself right up against the steel ceiling and took a last deep breath as the water closed over his mouth. Oh, God! Death! What would it be like? A muffled roar and a rush of water. A dull pain, and then a blinding light and the dancing of a thousand stars. An icy coldness and then a feeling that he had left the water and his body. A scalding fire that shook him to the very soul. Somebody was pouring brandy down his throat.

CHAPTER XXXV

THE PURSUIT OF THE TWIN-FUNNEL TUG

"HELP! She's rammed us. We're sinking."

Men's voices were calling near to him. He opened his eyes and for a moment saw the night sky, which was almost immediately obliterated by a dark shadow that glided towards them.

"Who's there?" hailed a familiar voice out of the shadow against the sky.

"Jones, sir," came the answer. "Trawler Seven, Jerome and Jubb, Dingy Ness."

"Badly damaged?"

"Letting in water faster than we can bale. Don't want to abandon her, sir, but we're too heavy."

"Get your men aboard here, quick. That'll lighten her. Then, Jones, you and one other for baling, run down by the tide and reach her in the next slip. You can pull her in there. It's hard beach. Next point on starboard."

Daniel was lifted by three men.

"Hallo!" cried Gordon Beveridge—for the shadow was the bridge of the *Sweet William*. "One of your men, or the rascal's?"

"It's Captain Dyke, sir," answered Jones.

"Daniel Dyke? Good God, what's he doing here?"

"Swimming about, sir, unconscious."

"Careful, then. But quick as you like. We've got to get after that tug again."

Daniel was lifted on board the *Sweet William* and propped up against a bulkhead beneath the bridge. Jones, who had superintended his transfer, gave him another drink from his flask. This brought him back to reality and, thrusting the men aside, Daniel staggered to his feet, crying out, "Jane. She's there. In the cabin of the tug with that damned Chink."

"*Our* Miss Jane?" asked Jones, aghast.

"Jane Jerome?" demanded Gordon. "Do you mean *your* Jane?"

"Yes," gasped Daniel. "Gordon? It's you? For God's sake quick! Chase her. Set me aboard that tug."

The Sub sang out orders sharply and the *Sweet William* shot away from the damaged smack. "Beach her next slip starboard side," cried Jones, who was thus separated from his own vessel. But with Miss Jane's life at stake and Captain Dyke to the rescue, he would not have been anywhere else but on the deck of the *Sweet William*, who was now churning through the water at a stinging pace.

"There she is, sir," sang out a bluejacket from for'ard. "Not out of this channel yet. We're gaining. Must have damaged her, sir."

"It's a wonder she didn't damage us, like the smack," answered Gordon. "She came at us fast enough after our 'heave-to' shot. Then we fired a 'live' at her."

Daniel saw light. "Then it was your gunner who blew me out

of the iron cage," he cried. "I was being keel-hauled in a steel trap
beneath the bows. Quick, or Jane may come to the same fate."

"We'll rescue her," replied the Sub largely. "We got you out
pretty successfully, though it was a bit of a rough passage for you,
and a damned miracle you didn't get a worse one. In the war lots
of our fellows got blown about in the water without getting disfig-
ured. If we'd known the cage was there it would have been a good
shot. I daresay it was our round, but the old cruiser let off a couple
too."

They were driving down now with the tide at such a pace that
they could see the twin-funnel tug plainly. It was evident that
she was in distress. Her speed was slackening, while the Admiralty launch was gaining hard up under her stern. The Sub called
through the speaking-tube to the man at the wheel to come up on
her starboard side, thus driving the enemy towards the right bank
of the canal. "She can't get away then, Daniel," he added.

Daniel asked why.

"You'll see," replied Gordon.

They were now alongside, running neck to neck.

"We'll keep her to the speed of the tug now, and grapple." Gordon turned from Daniel again and sang out orders. The half-dozen
bluejackets laid hold on the tug with boathooks.

"Stop your engine, or I'll fire." The Sub was covering the man
on the tug's bridge with his revolver. The man called through his
speaking-tube and the pace relaxed. Another man, who had been
in the wheel-house, sprang up on the bridge and struck the man at
the tube in the face. Then, regardless of his own danger, he fired
three shots at the *Sweet William*, but Gordon fired back, and one of
the two dropped. Probably the man with the gun, because at that
the firing ceased.

The vessels were now close together. As soon as they touched,
Daniel jumped for the tug's bulwarks and scrambled on to the
deck, followed by Jones and three or four of the bluejackets.

At that the crew of the tug put up a fight. Revolvers spat in the
dark and hard knocks were given and taken, but Daniel did not
wait for any of this. Crashing one man under the jaw who was
in his way, he dashed straight for the bows. Jones followed, while
Gordon and the bluejackets went in and hammered the crew.

The cabin door was locked. "Help me to burst this in, Jones," cried Daniel. "Then you get on the deck above and watch the water. There's a way out of this cabin from beneath the keel. He may try some devil's trick with that."

"Take this, sir," answered Jones, handing Daniel a revolver. "It's fired in all six chambers. I pinched it off of the man you knocked out. He didn't get time to reload it. But they won't know. It's good enough to bluff with."

Daniel took the revolver and then threw his weight against the door. A second and third time, with Jones helping, weakened it but the lock did not give. Then, as Daniel went at it again, Jones kicked the lock with the flat of his foot, and it burst open.

The Chinaman was standing directly behind the cushion which pillowed Jane's head. She was still sleeping. She had not moved since Daniel had last seen her from the terrible cage. The outline of her slim body, the position of her limbs, the very curves in her tight-fitting jersey and the folds of her skirt had been photographed on his brain during that despairing moment when he thought Death was taking him from her. So far, then, he knew that she was safe—and that those yellow hands had not touched her pure body. She was breathing peacefully, and yet he knew, by looking at the Chinaman, that her life was hanging by a thread. His left hand was held above his head, palm outward and fingers stretched, an attitude of such command that Daniel instinctively paused in the doorway. Slowly the hand came down and the long forefinger pointed to his other hand, which held a nickel-plated revolver, the barrel pointed down within a foot of Jane's upturned face. Daniel had him covered with the useless weapon.

"We bargain," said the Chinaman. "Since you have managed to get back, we must come to terms. You are fortunate in being able to accept them. I am fortunate in being able to offer them. To-night I realize that my ship is doomed. I shall abandon her, then."

"If it's terms we are to discuss," replied Daniel, "you will perhaps oblige me by covering me with that revolver instead of the lady."

"The moving of my revolver before it blows out the brains of the exquisite creature beneath it is the price I am offering for my escape," returned the Chinaman. "So that, you see, until I have your word that you will let me drop myself quietly over the side, it would be foolish of me to do as you ask."

"If those are the terms, I agree," said Daniel, who would have agreed to anything in order to remove that deadly weapon from Jane's head. "But you must hurry up. Your ship will be in the hands of the British authorities in a minute, and if you are caught, you will hang."

"You give me your word that I shall be allowed to jump overboard without hindrance?" asked the Chinaman. "Also that you do what you can to help my escape?"

"Yes, damn you. But quick, give me that gun," answered Daniel.

"You will not fire at me when I am in the water?" went on the Chinaman. "You won't follow me?"

"No. But they are after cocaine. I suppose this ship's full of it. If you go without telling me where it is they'll scour the marshes for you, and I can't help that."

"They won't find any stuff aboard. When you queered my steel cage I had recourse to another trick. By the way, the doctor told me that the girl would sleep for many hours, but that when she awoke there would be no ill effects. I am giving you my gun. You may lower yours."

He raised his arm and tossed the revolver into his palm, holding it out to Daniel.

"Bring it to me," ordered Daniel, who was taking no chances.

The Chinaman looked down at Jane and sighed. Then he put out his left hand towards her hair and bent reverently, as if he would kiss it.

"Don't touch her," thundered Daniel.

"Beauty is a gift that the lowest creature may honour," said the Celestial.

"I prefer that you don't," objected Daniel curtly.

The Chinaman crossed the cabin, holding the revolver, handle first, to Daniel, who took it. The Chinaman grinned. "There is one thing about you English that all the world admires always and despises often. When you have given your word you keep it, even though you have been tricked."

"What's that got to do with it?" asked Daniel.

"Why," replied the Chinaman proudly, "merely that my revolver was not loaded."

"I see," retorted Daniel. "But you must not imagine that such cunning is peculiar to China, for, as a matter of fact, neither was mine."

This so tickled the rascal's sense of humour that he had to sit down till he had finished laughing, which nearly proved his undoing, for Jones, thinking that the villain was scoring off Daniel, rushed into the cabin flourishing an iron bar which, if Daniel had not seized it, would have descended upon the Oriental head.

Sobered a little by this, he got up and crept out on to the deck. The main fighting had taken place aft, where they were still at it, but by the continual cheering it was obvious that the bluejackets were giving the crew a good drubbing. The cheers gave place to the laughter of the sailors and the cursing of the Chinaman's crew.

"You hear how things are going," whispered Daniel to the Chinaman. "Well, then, my advice to a very dirty foreign rascal is, to get over the side without delay, unless the dirty rascal in question has a great desire to be lynched."

The Chinaman did not answer, but taking three long strides he vaulted over the bulwark into the dark water. The noise of the splash was drowned by another ringing cheer from the bluejackets announcing that their victory was complete, and a minute later the Sub, with a torn jacket and a magnificent black eye but otherwise very pleased with himself, hurried forward to tell Daniel that the tug's crew were overpowered and in irons. "But is Jane safe?" he asked.

"Yes, thank God and you, she is," answered Daniel, clapping him on the shoulder.

"You speak as if you had done nothing yourself," laughed the Sub. "Why, it was your first rush that did it. You set the pace magnificently. Any signs of that Chink this end? He's given us the slip aft. Hallo! What's that?"

"What?" asked Daniel innocently, as he watched the Sub gazing over the side. He could see the Chinaman's head, entering the main channel towards which the tug was swinging on the tide.

"It's a man's head right enough. Somebody's swimming there.

It's the Chink." Gordon's revolver was in his hand when Daniel seized his wrist.

"Don't fire. We've got to give the devil a chance."

"A fat lot of chance he deserves," retorted Gordon. "That is, if he's the Chink we're after. And he is, too. Look. He's been spotted by the searchlight from the cruiser."

The Chinaman, dazzled and surprised by the blinding shaft of light, turned in the water and looked back towards Daniel, who was wondering how he could best help the escape he had promised.

The tug and the *Sweet William* had now swung out from the shelter of the mud banks and were drifting down into the rays of the cruiser's searchlight. The Chinaman saw Daniel holding Gordon's wrist and arguing with him why he must not in honour shoot. The cross-current was washing the swimmer nearer to the vessels. If only he could get out of this blinding light he would be safe. He could then make the nearest bank, work his way back the way they had come, and collect the sunken packets he had dropped overboard. They were all marked with floats.

He dived and swam under water for what seemed an incredible time. He was used to this. He had fought shark in his younger days in his father's lagoon in one of the Pacific archipelagos. Armed only with a knife, with one's muscle and brain, the only salvation was quickness. But it did not avail him against the searchlight which picked him up again immediately he reappeared.

The tug with the *Sweet William* still alongside, but hidden behind her bulk, entered the shaft of light also.

Suddenly there was a lightning flash of fire from the blackness of the river bank upon their right, and the whole water in the vicinity of the swimmer leapt towards the sky as a thunderous report rolled over the broad river.

Before they could recover from their surprise, another flash, but this time the shell splashed a few yards from across the tug's bows.

"They'll hit us if we drift further," cried Daniel.

"My God, it's the Army!" ejaculated Gordon. "I forgot all about 'em," and making his hands into a megaphone, he shouted, "Hi! Chuck it, you blazing idiots. Cease fire. You'll blow us to hell. Hallo! Major Beveridge of the R.H.A.?"

"Hallo!" came the answer, "who are you?"

"Gordon, you cuckoo. Cease fire. We're aboard the tug. The war's over."

The *Sweet William's* dinghy was put out to search for the Chinaman, but no signs of him were found upon the water. If anything had remained it would have been carried out to sea on the running tide. But Daniel was of the opinion that the shell had struck him. While Gordon was dropping anchor from the tug, a river police motor-boat came splashing alongside, and the Navy handed over its capture to the Constabulary, which transaction the Sub managed in the traditional style of the Royal Navy.

But however awed the river police may have been with the Sub's patronizing manner, they had their own opinion about the night's work, as Daniel overheard. "Battery of Artillery, river police boats, a fishing fleet, a gunboat, not to mention a blinking cruiser, all after one Chink with dope, and then he goes and gets blowed to smithereens. Disgusting."

But Daniel, recalling the words of the Chinaman, was able to do the river police a good turn, for on his advice the river was dragged up along the course the tug had taken, and a number of floats were swept, to which were attached small watertight cases containing the dope for which the Chinaman had sacrificed his life. Had he been able to salve this treasure the loss of the tug would have been comparatively small to him.

Jane, still unconscious, was wrapped in Gordon's sea-coat and landed in Daniel's arms from the tug to the *Sweet William*, from the *Sweet William* to the dinghy, from the dinghy to the concrete platform where the guns were being limbered up, and from there to the gunner's seat of the fastest team, which made the journey back to Dullchester Deanery in fine style, so that within an hour of leaving the tub's cabin she was sleeping peacefully in her own bed, with Rachel and Mrs. Jerome on guard. It was not till the bedroom door was shut that Daniel began to shiver, and realizing that his clothes were thawing under the warmth of the house, he went to his room to change. He took the revolver from his wet clothes, and seeing that the Chinaman's was dry, filled it with ammunition, and slipping it into his dry jacket pocket, went downstairs to seek food and a hot drink in the dining-room, while upstairs Jane continued her adventurous dreams that had started before Miss Tackle's fire.

CHAPTER XXXVI

PANIC IN THE PRECINCTS

ALTHOUGH it was now well after midnight, the Precincts was very much awake. Lights burned in most of the downstairs windows, for everyone was anxious for the latest news. The disappearance of Norris within a few hours of that of Canon Beveridge had made a ghastly impression, and then on the top of that Jane had vanished, with the distracted Daniel after her. The news of their safety was received with great joy, but tinged with disappointment that the other victims were not also forthcoming. The presence of the blood in the curiosity shop had considerably frightened the bereaved households. Not only did hope begin to die, but fear of future horrors began to be born. On that night Panic was at its height.

People huddled together at downstairs windows which they left open to the cold night, in order that they could call out to their next-door neighbours or the policemen for companionship, each one fearful of being the next to be seized by the uncanny horror that stalked in Dullchester city.

To add to the general terror several persons reported the alarm of having heard ghastly shrieks from the Slype, each end of which was now guarded by special police. Sergeant Wurren, seeing that events were too startling to allow him to seek his couch, stood immovable on Canon Cable's doorstep, resolved to guard the last hope of keeping the Cathedral on its legs. How gratified Canon Cable's cook-housekeeper was by this attention and protection was shown by the numbers of cups of tea she kept handing out of the window to the gallant officer. He left it to one of the Talkham sergeants to do the rounds and bring reports. He would not leave his post. The constant activity of the policemen recruited from the three towns caused quite an excitement in the Precincts. People treated them as they had treated Tommies at the beginning of the war. They couldn't do enough for them. If they had withdrawn themselves from the Precincts on that night the inhabitants would have run mad. Scotland Yard, in the person of Macauley, was peacefully sleeping in the Deanery. Dr. Rickit would not allow him to be disturbed, for his ankle had caused so much pain that a fever had set in and a timely sleeping-draught was the result. The good doctor had stayed at the Deanery all the evening, doing what he could to comfort Mrs. Jerome. This was fortunate, as he was able to give an eye to Jane, by whose bed sat the faithful Rachel holding the girl's hand tight and resolved to do so till daybreak, in case the "Thing" tried to get hold of "her little Miss." The "Thing" was the name now bestowed by all the servant class of Dullchester upon the cause of the disappearances. They spent their time in speculating as to what the "Thing" looked like to its victims. The cook at the Deanery was in favour of a skeleton in a surplice and cassock. The underhousemaid thought it would be exactly like the weird man in the long coat with buttons who called himself the Paper Wizard and cut their "sillywets" for them at the back door. The Beveridges' scullery-maid, who had run over with a message to the Deanery and who was dreading to go back by herself, was of the opinion that it would be a tall man, very thin, dressed in Jaeger pants and vest, with an illuminated diver's helmet for a head.

"Just like that?" suggested Cook, pointing towards a flickering lamp-post. The scullery-maid screamed.

"You're all wrong," remarked Jim Stalk, who had joined the group to hear the latest. "I've heard from two or three reliable ones that the 'Thing' favours Sergeant Wurren in appearance and, funnily enough, is dressed exactly like him, in shiny mackintosh. I didn't believe it, but as I passed Canon Cable's I'm blowed if there weren't a 'Thing' just like that what I've told you, standing on the front door top step and waiting to pull the Canon out of his study window."

When the scullery-maid went back to the Beveridges' with a note from Mrs. Jerome, she ran all the way, with her apron over her head, which so startled Sergeant Wurren that he shouted "Hi!" Equally terrified, the girl peeped out from behind her apron, and beheld what Jim Stalk had just described. It was the "Thing." She uttered a shriek and fainted in the snow, while the Sergeant, thinking this female might be a siren to lure him away from his post, blew his whistle till assistance came, and the scullery-maid was

picked up by two policemen in mackintoshes and carried home in
hysterics.

Through all this excitement little old Canon Cable worked on,
his reading-lamp shining brightly and his brain translating from the
Hebrew. It is well to be deaf and blind when the Terror walketh by
night. Translations on paper were all-engrossing to him. He was
blind and deaf to these translations of the human flesh that were
going on around him, and which were putting everyone in such a
panic.

Not being allowed to hold a council of war with Macauley,
Daniel, knowing that sleep was impossible after all he had gone
through, changed into dry clothes, had a cold snack in the dining-
room, with a hot brandy-and-lemon, and then, lighting a cigar,
went out to talk to the policemen and any scared Precincts folk
who might be still awake.

The policeman guarding over the lower door of the Slype in
Canon Beveridge's garden remarked that, used as he was to lonely
night-watching and dangerous beats, he would prefer the loneliest
and most dangerous rather than change places with that "unfortunate Cathedral watchman. Is it Mr. Potter, sir, who has to go round
with a light amongst those tombs and empty seats?"

"What do you mean?" asked Daniel. "Potter would no more
stay in the Cathedral at night by himself than any of those frightened servant-girls that are huddled at the Precincts back doors,
afraid to go to bed. Why, I remember, when the Beveridge boys
and I were kids together, asking old Potter to take us into the
Crypt after dark, and he told us he didn't hold with youngsters or
adults dabbling in black magic."

"Well, then, Mr. Dyke," went on the policeman, "if it ain't Potter, I wants to know who it is what's been flashing a light about up
there in the Chapter Room."

The Chapter Room was the Cathedral library, where meetings
were held and where the canons robed when they did not wish
to do so in their own houses. Nobody had a right up there but
the members of the Greater Chapter. It was exclusively private
to them, exception being made in the case of Styles and Potter.
Daniel looked across to the great mullioned window of this upper
chamber of learning.

"How long ago did you see this light?" he asked.

"I see it now. Don't you, sir? There," replied the policeman.

Behind the mullioned window of the Upper Chapter House a light was indeed moving.

Daniel and the policeman crept through the snow along a derelict flower-bed which was backed by a ruined wall of the old Priory. At the end of this bed a grassy bank dropped down to the level of the Crypt. The light was on the floor above.

Backed with the experience of many climbs in boyhood days—a very laudable feat in those days to reach the Chapter House window, especially if the Deans and Canons were sitting—Daniel had no difficulty in getting up to the window-level now. With his feet in well-remembered crevices and his hands clutching the ivy, he looked through the stained glass. He could only see that there was a candle burning. The coloured glass was too dense to show anything else. But one thing he did notice. The catch of one of the windows was unfastened. He remembered that he had the Chinaman's revolver in his pocket. He drew it out, and with the barrel pushed the window open into the room. He was raising himself on his elbow to climb over the sill, when something struck his wrist and the revolver fell into the room upon the floor. The sharp pain and the suddenness with which it was inflicted lost him his balance, and he slid down the ivy on to the snow-covered grass beneath. The policeman helped him to break his fall.

"There's someone up there, Mr. Dyke," he whispered. "Look."

Daniel looked up. As the policeman flashed his lantern up at the open window, a large head was peering down at them. A dirty handkerchief was bound round the forehead. Blood covered the nose and cheeks, while the lower part of the face was hidden in a scrubby iron-grey beard. The brief glimpse they got of his face gave promise that it belonged to a body of ferocious brutality. Before they could challenge the hideous apparition it had vanished, and the window was hurriedly slammed.

Black rage seized Daniel. Had this blood-bespattered man got something to do with the Terror in the Precincts? Was he the cause of the screaming in the Slype?

"Come on," he cried. "Whoever it is, he has no right up there."
Again he scaled the wall.

The window was not fastened. He pushed it open again. Immediately over the candle he saw another wild face, which he recognized as the Paper Wizard. "Ah!" cried Daniel triumphantly. "I know you. You're wanted. What are you doing up here, and who is your bloody-faced companion?" The Paper Wizard blew out the light, and at the same time, from the cover of the open windowpane, the barrel of the Chinaman's revolver pointed straight into Daniel's face.

"Take your fingers from the ledge or I'll put a bullet through your dirty face," rasped a dreadful voice. "The bloodstained man," thought Daniel, who, having no desire to be a target at such a range, shifted his hold of the ivy. The window was promptly shut and fastened from the inside and the great hulk of the man with the revolver passed across the window. It was the man with the blood on his face, for Daniel could just distinguish the dirty white handkerchief tied round his head. As he walked from the window into the darkness Daniel tried to force the window, in order to question him. But this piece of foolhardiness was useless. The iron frame of the window was strong and the lead-rimmed panes unbreakable beneath their wire-protecting cages.

"We'll get in the other way, then," he called, as he scrambled down to rejoin the policeman. "We've got to get hold of these fellows. One of them is wanted by the police, and the other, I'll bet, is the prime mover in the mystery. I'll get the keys of the Crypt and Chapter House doors. They're kept at Canon Beveridge's back door."

The keys in question were handed to them by the terrified servants, and Daniel and the policeman raced back to the Cathedral.

"That fellow has got my revolver, but we can't wait to get another. We must trust to luck and do our best not to let the devils escape us." Daniel turned the key in the old door, and they entered the musty crypt.

CHAPTER XXXVII

THE RETURN OF THE TWELFTH FIDDLER

THE ancient Crypt was damp at the best of times, but this night it was worse. It was not only wet but flooded. In some places the water was an inch deep and there was a sound of continued trickling as if a pipe had burst somewhere. Daniel and the policeman splashed across to the steps that led up to the Cathedral. When they reached the Chapter House door, Daniel fitted in the key but did not turn it.

"They may fire on us as we open it," he whispered; "so wait a minute." He climbed the heavily iron-studded door, holding on to the massive cross-beams. "Now unlock it and push it half open quietly. They won't expect me up here. You keep under cover. I want to see what part of the room they're in. Then we can shut 'em up again if necessary. If they rush the door, you club the first, and I'll drop on the second."

The policeman drew his truncheon and turned the key without noise. Then, nodding a warning to Daniel, he began to push the great door on its hinges. Daniel raised his head over the top. The policeman stopped pushing. Then Daniel's electric torch flashed out into the room. In the large bare chamber there was no sign of a human being anywhere. There was the long, well-worn refectory table running down the centre. A dignified ecclesiastical chair at each end and oak benches at each side. The bookshelves were built into the walls solidly and were lined with large vellum tomes. The only place of hiding which needed any further investigation was the strong-room in the centre of the wall opposite the window. This was a roomy cupboard hollowed out of the solid wall and shut off by an iron door. "No one here," said Daniel, scrambling down and entering the Chapter Room. "Unless they're in the safe."

They crossed to the iron door and pulled it. It was unlocked, a fact which surprised them both, but when they pulled it open, there was no one inside. Suddenly Daniel recalled to mind the great chest which he had seen that evening, first on the cab and again in the tug. He now knew why it had seemed familiar. He had seen it before in this very strong-room. It contained the gold vessels of the altar. The space it occupied on the floor beneath the bottom shelf was empty. The shelves above were stacked with the ancient registers. These appeared to have been untouched. Yes, Daniel would take his oath that the chest in the Chinaman's cabin was the one missing from this safe.

"Well, they ain't here. Must have been nippy. 'Spect they had a key of this door and got away into the Cathedral before we got in," remarked the policeman.

"It's not much use looking for them, either," replied Daniel. "There are a thousand hiding places in this old Cathedral. What with the Triforium, the Nuns' Walk, the organ loft, the Crypt, the Nave, the Chancel, the Transepts and the Chapels, to say nothing of the Vestry cupboards. It would be hopeless. Hard enough to spot anyone hiding here in the daytime. Impossible at night. They may have used any of the doors from the towers on to the leads."

"No, a search ain't much good," agreed the policeman. "What's best to be done?"

"For you to go back and watch the Slype according to your orders," answered Daniel, "and for me to watch here till daybreak. Perhaps these thugs will come back. They were here for some purpose. I disturbed them. If they do come, I shall be inside the strong-room, waiting. Watch the window from the Slype door, and if you see a light flash twice, dash along, and if I call, give me a hand."

"You don't mind being left alone, sir, in this awful place?" asked the policeman, with a touch of admiration mingled with awe.

"I don't mind anything so long as we can lay our hands on some clue to this mystery," retorted Daniel. "If I feel too lonely, I shall creep to the window and flash my lamp."

"And I will answer you with my lantern," replied the policeman.

Thus it was that Daniel Dyke was left alone in the Cathedral. But was he alone? Where was the sinister Paper Wizard? Where was the big bearded man with the blood on his face? That they were neither of them in the Chapter Room was a certainty. Before the policeman had left him Daniel had examined every corner of the room. The flagstones were solid—built into the ceiling of the Crypt. The built-in bookcases were immovable and fastened to the masonry. The walls were solid stone and the ceiling groined with massive bosses carved into heraldic devices and queer faces of angels, devils, apostles and abbots.

The silence was intense, broken now and again by the policeman coughing in the garden below and by the big clock in the tower chiming every quarter of an hour. Daniel crouched on the floor of the strong-room, the door set ajar. If anyone came into the room, he could watch and listen.

The clock had struck the quarter for the fifth time. It was a quarter past two.

Suddenly he became aware that there was something moving in the room. A very slight sound—a sound that he could not place. A line occurred to him from an old Kentish ballad:—

> "A shuffling scuffle of skeleton feet."

Yes, that described the sound exactly. A regular tap-tap, as of bone on stone—*skeleton feet*—and a soft, whirring buzz—*a shuffling scuffle*.

He had his torch ready to switch on, and slowly opened the strong-room door. And now there came to his ears distant music, soft—ever so soft—but quite distinct. A jiggerty-tune, as if a hobgoblin was playing a diminutive instrument within the room. It seemed to be approaching him in the darkness. The shuffling scuffle was approaching too. He flashed on the torch. Now he had keyed up his nerves and muscles to meet anything. He was quite prepared to face whatever was lurking in the darkness—whatever would be revealed in the light. What he was not ready to face was Nothing. The Chapter Room was still empty. There was nobody there. He was alone. But the noise grew louder and nearer. This got on his nerves. It was horribly creepy. The ghostly atmosphere was making him feel jumpy. A cold shiver went down his back, and that unreasonable sensation only to be compared with the taste of sour lemons that grips a man behind the throat when awe becomes too great for flesh to stand. There was no doubt about it. The invisible thing, whatever it was, was moving in the room. Daniel could stand it no longer. He made for the door, meaning to make a bolt for it. His nerves were playing him up. As he did so he was conscious that the something was following him. Outside the door were some six or seven steps. He felt like taking them in a jump, but he called himself a coward, spun round and flashed his lamp across the flagstones. Yes. There. Something black was moving across the floor in his direction. Daniel thought it must be a bat that had fallen to the floor and was now crawling towards the steps. Whatever it was, he could crush it beneath his boot. It came on without fear straight for him. With an oath he strode towards it, and then, with a startled ejaculation, he perceived what it was. *The Twelfth Fiddler was walking in the empty room.* Just as he recognized it, the peculiar little man reached a crack in the flagged floor, tripped and fell forward on his fiddle, and the works ran out with a *whirr!*

The sight of this mechanical figure kicking on the floor was more scaring than if it had been a wounded lion. It was so unexpected. Daniel went to the window and hailed the policeman to come up.

"I saw your lamp flashing, and then I thought I heard you cry out. What is it, sir?" The policeman entered the room.

"Damned if I know," replied Daniel, pointing to the prostrate toy. "That walked out at me from the darkness. It was not in the room when you left. Nobody has been in the room for an hour and a quarter, so in God's name *what* wound up that toy and set it going on the floor? What can it mean?"

"The missing fiddler, eh?" queried the policeman; then, looking over his shoulder into the shadows, he added, "P'raps they're all coming back. All the missing ones—pigs and all."

"I wish they were," replied Daniel. "But there's no one here, as you can see. Had anyone been in the room I should have known immediately. I take my oath I've been alone since you left. But a mechanical figure can't wind itself up."

"But that's what it did do," retorted the policeman, thumping different parts of the wall with his fist. "Why, there ain't so much as a rat-hole. See? There's not a crack for a human hand to have got in anywhere. No one could have wound him up. So what does that prove? He wound himself up. Unless——"

"Unless what?" demanded Daniel, as the policeman paused.

"Unless——" The policeman looked fearfully into the shadows once again and suddenly seizing Daniel's electric torch flashed it at the bookshelves. He returned it, muttering an apology and looking more relieved.

"You were saying?" prompted Daniel.

"I'd rather not say, if you don't mind, sir."

"Why?" asked Daniel.

"Because it don't do for young policemen to dabble with the supernatural."

Daniel laughed uneasily. "I think it's time for both of us to go and have a drink." He took the policeman by the arm and led him to the steps, then, turning, closed and locked the door. When they had reached the entrance to the Crypt Daniel stopped his companion. "We must go back," he said.

"Why?" asked the policeman, not relishing another visit to the terrible room.

"We've left the Twelfth Fiddler. He's wanted by the police." They both laughed and went back to the Chapter House. But the Twelfth Fiddler had gone. They searched the room for an hour, taking out every one of the books and looking behind them, but there was no sign of the mechanical toy. He had somehow got up when their backs were turned and strolled off again with his whimsical gait into thin air.

CHAPTER XXXVIII

THE SCREAMING PILLAR

THE next morning it was snowing hard. Large velvety flakes that stuck wherever they alighted, and piled up thick. The policemen still guarded the Slype. There had been renewed screaming there in the night, but, as before, no sign of anything capable of screaming. The policemen kept shaking the snow from their heavy capes. Sergeant Wurren did not bother with the snow. His long coat was covered. If Jim Stalk's description of the "Thing" were true—that is, if the "Thing" which was so terrifying the minds of the kitchen-maids really resembled Sergeant Wurren—then upon this wintry morning the "Thing" must be a gigantic snowman. But this theory was ridiculous on the face of it, for the Sergeant could not be the "Thing" unless he were his own enemy, because nobody was fighting the mystery harder than this stalwart Britisher. There was something pathetic in his doggedness, for while the policemen at each end of the Slype were constantly relieved by their comrades, the Sergeant would not relinquish his post to anyone.

"Canon Cable shall not be took unless I am took with him," he declared. "From this top step I can see him through the window at his writing. The 'Thing,' if there is such a thing, will come up the front steps. At least, I hope so. On the top step the 'Thing' will meet the Sergeant of Dullchester's Constabulary, who will want a reckoning. If I win I shall have done my duty to the city and kept the Cathedral on its legs. If the 'Thing' wins, I shall have gone along of the Canon and the Cathedral won't be kept on its legs, but I shall still have done my duty."

"But if the master's took," suggested the Cable cook-housekeeper, "there's still the Archdeacon and the Bishop."

"For all we know," retorted the Sergeant, "the Archdeacon may have gone. He's been in bed a long time, to my thinking, and his house is cut off by snow. Potter reports that it's impossible to dig it out. That the Archdeacon must wait for the thaw. Certainly the tradesboys leave provisions there, at the expense of climbing and tumbling, but they never sees the Archdeacon. He don't take in his own 'orders.' He might well be murdered by this time and none of us none the wiser."

"I don't hold with that quite," argued the cook. "If he's been murdered the servants would talk to the tradesboys about it."

"Not if they was in league with the murderer," explained the Sergeant. "For my part, I was never much took with them domestics up at the Archdeacon's."

"Well, then, if the master is took—which heaven forbid!" went on the cook affably—affably because she had heard that the Sergeant was not partial to the Archdeacon's servants—"then the Bishop will have to be called in."

"But, as I've pointed out before," corrected the Sergeant, "the Bishop ain't our property. He belongs to Dullchester Diocese. He ain't merely Cathedrally. He ain't cemented on to the building like those gargoyles up there. Now the Chapter are. Just like them gargoyles, if I may say so, are the Dean and Canons."

Certainly old Canon Cable justified the comparison. In personal appearance he strongly resembled a gargoyle. This perfect bookworm, this ancient scholar blinked over his manuscripts with the fierce determination not to have his thoughts distracted from his life's task by all this uncanny idiocy that was going on around him. He realized that it was his duty to go to Cathedral twice a day for services because Mr. Styles or Mr. Potter called for him, but it seemed to him that recently he had taken more duty than was quite fair.

Where the others had all got to dimly puzzled him as well as annoyed him, but rather than argue about it with others or with himself either, he preferred to go to Cathedral and take the services and then come back and get on with his more important work. Any parson could take a service, but so few had the brains and application to cope with the dead languages. Therefore, considering that part of his career the more important, he regarded the other as mere drudgery which had to be got through in order to earn his livelihood. By rights he should not have been a parson at all. It was no love of Christianity that had made him one. He would have been equally happy as a Buddhist, but Buddhism flourished too far from the Charing Cross Road, that great playground of the bibliomaniac. So he had become a parson in order to get time for study. The only other walk of life for which he was fitted was a schoolmaster, but he was afraid of that. He thought he might murder little boys whose brains were not so far advanced as his own. There was no money in being an author of dead languages. He could not live on what he earned by that, for his works were so advanced in ancient knowledge as to be beyond the ken of the cleverest in that particular line, and very few bought them. Dean Jerome—a great scholar himself—had declared that Canon Cable, given the chance, could hold his own in any Hebrew Law Court with Moses himself, but for himself, the Dean preferred reading Moses to Cable, as he found the former gentleman more concise. In fact, Cable's monumental work on the Mosaic Law was to the Mosaic Law itself what the new edition of the Encyclopædia Britannica is to a penny dictionary.

Thus wrapped in his own thoughts, untouched by the Terror that clutched at his neighbours, Canon Cable was as impassive as the gargoyles that grinned down at his study window.

The Terror that stalked in the Precincts could not startle him because he did not see how worrying about it could help him with the dead languages.

On the way to Matins he showed no surprise at finding Sergeant Wurren waiting on his porch steps and following him into Cathedral. He seemed to consider this quite natural from all the notice he took of it. If the Sergeant had announced his intention of reading the Second Lesson, the Canon would not have bothered to question such a proceeding.

On this eventful morning he showed no surprise at finding that the lay clerks' and choristers' surplices were all spread out on the Chapter Room table, instead of hanging in the Vestry cupboards down in the Crypt. Potter tried to explain that the reason of this proceeding was due to the fact that some invisible pipe had burst in the Crypt and the Vestry was under water. He did not listen. He was not interested. He mumbled the Vestry Prayer as usual, and trotted behind the verger to his stall, just as usual. It took Styles some time to explain that it was up to the Canon to read the prayers as well as the Lessons. All he muttered back was, "Are the Minor Canons still absenting themselves from Cathedral? Kindly let me know if they return for Evensong. I shall be here for the Lessons, unless the Dean or the Canon in Residence think fit to look in. I presume the Archdeacon still keeps his bed? I shall be glad to be spared from Evensong if anything can be arranged. I have lost much time with this perpetual duty. I understand, by referring to my calendar, that I am not in residence. You may have to call for me at Oxford any hour. Some people forget that I owe duty to Oxford as much as Dullchester. If you meet any of our wandering dignitaries, you might inform them, Mr. Styles, that Canon Cable, you might even say Doctor Cable—that Doctor Cable occupies a professor's chair at the Seat of English Learning. However, I will be getting along with Matins now."

When it was over, the comic little procession of verger, scholar, and policeman started back to Minor Canon Row. It looked exactly as if the pompous Sergeant were some Roman Emperor returning from victory, for the verger with the silver wand was reminiscent of a Lictor, and the Canon might have been a dancing slave, for the little man walked three steps and ran two with the greatest regularity. If he had possessed the wind he would have resorted to a perpetual run in order to get back the quicker to his books, but the rest of his old organs had been neglected for his brain, so that he continued the dance of two running and three walking steps, which was as much as he could manage, and the Sergeant with imperial condescension regulated his steps accordingly, taking a longer stride whenever he saw the Canon being propelled forward.

On reaching the house Canon Cable showed no astonishment at the Sergeant following him up the steps and watching him as he fitted his latchkey to the lock, nor did he offer any apology to the Sergeant when he shut the door in his face, left him on the steps and returned to his book-littered table.

Another thing that Canon Cable had not professed to notice was the large congregation which had lately been attending Cathedral services. Normally the winter week-day attendance was scant in the extreme and recruited entirely from the Precincts, but since the Cathedral had become the centre of a popular mystery it was visited by gaping sightseers and curious police-news readers, the sort of people who queue up for murder trials and wait hours outside the prisons in order to read the official notice that some poor wretch has expiated his crime on the scaffold. This crowd was augmented by the local tradespeople, who were all agog to attend Cathedral now, quite expecting their patience to be rewarded by the sight of the last Canon being whisked into space before their eyes. Trillet, perceiving the multitudes, thought of the Cathedral's musical reputation. He knew that Canon Cable would offer no interference. He determined to enjoy himself at the expense of the choir-boys. He struck out the solemn Advent régime, and substituted rollicking anthems and more elaborate services, and in the midst of this noise he caused the works of Trillet to sound louder than any. Trillet in B flat, C major and F vied with Orlando Gibbons, Walmesley and Goss. "Praise the Lord," Trillet, "O sing unto the Lord," Trillet, "Sing praises unto the Lord," Trillet, "O give thanks unto the Lord," Trillet, were duly sandwiched in between "O clap your hands together," Green, Wesley's "Wilderness" (a great favourite of his), The Hallelujah Chorus of Handel, the Alleluia Chorus of Beethoven and—for no other reason but that he himself enjoyed it—the Coronation Anthem, Zadock the Priest. Yes, even if the choir-boys didn't enjoy themselves with all the extra practice for this exertion, Mr. Trillet did thoroughly, for he had no interests, no hobbies, no affection for anything in life except for the organ and Church Music, and so in face of the large congregation he took advantage of the absence of the Dean, Vice-Dean and Minor Canons, ignored the season of Advent as if it were never in the calendar, and ran a continuous Easter-cum-Whitsun-cum-Christmas Harvest Festival.

Canon Cable, as Trillet had expected, raised no objection to the extra noise that was going on, because he didn't hear it and fondly imagined that the choir were faithfully performing the usual Advent services.

The floods in the Crypt had continued to rise. Potter had gone down amongst them, waging war against them with his pudding basin by means of which he hoped to bale them out. But hours of work had no effect, so Mr. Gony was called to put things to rights. Mr. Gony did not find it so easy, but he certainly helped Potter carry the surplices and cassocks to the safety of the Chapter House. He then put on a pair of sea-boots, descended into the Crypt again and splashed about.

Potter had come to the conclusion that Dullchester Cathedral was more haunted than he had thought it, and he confided in his colleague, Styles. "Mind, I don't complain to you or of you. I suppose it's old Potter's place to sweep up water as well as leaves, dust and snow. With your chronic cold, you would just die in the damp of the Crypt. I don't expect you to come paddling and bathing with me, and it ain't so much the water as I'm complaining of, though that's bad enough pouring down from a crack in one of them fat Norman pillars. I'm used to dampness, dankness and darkness, but I don't like any of 'em when they're full of noises, and noises, mind you, what is worse than human."

"What do you mean?" asked Styles.

"I mean," went on Potter solemnly, "that every time Potter turns his back on that fat pillar, blessed if it don't whisper behind his back, mutter behind his back, groan behind his back, and rumble behind his back. That was bad enough, so Potter kept his eye on it, and then blest if it didn't start screaming straight into my face. Horrible screams, just like the ones we hear in the Slype. We always knew that the Slype was haunted, 'cos didn't I knock into a corpse there myself? Very well, then, so's the Crypt, and it won't be long before I knocks into a corpse down there. It's full enough of 'em, so Mr. Gony says, and what I says, is, A fat lot of good McCarbre spending all that money on restoring towers and roof and inside decorations. He should have started at the bottom. He should have cleaned up the foundations, and given them buried Abbots an airing. They've no relations left in the city what would make a fuss. Fetch 'em all out, I say, and let's see where we are. Goodness knows what ain't buried in that pillar. Some poor nun, perhaps, what got bored and carried on with a monk. Perhaps it's a thousand years to-day since they walled her up, and she's having an anniversary. I tell you, Styles, she keeps a-screaming."

"Couldn't be—after all them years," scorned Styles.

"Then it's the pillar itself," was the retort.

"Don't believe it," exclaimed Styles indignantly. "Stone don't scream. How can it?"

"This one does," answered Potter. "Come down and listen."

"With my chest it would be fatal," complained Styles, coughing to demonstrate how bad it was already. "I am afraid of the damp, but I ain't afraid of ghosts, because I don't believe in 'em."

"Well, if you don't believe in ghosts you'll have to believe in screaming stone, because something kept screaming, and it come straight out of that fat pillar."

"I don't believe in nothing dead that screams," said Styles emphatically.

"I'm going to persuade Mr. Gony to pull that fat pillar out of it to-morrow," declared Potter.

"Don't you tell him nothing of the sort," snapped Styles. "Leastways not when I'm about. You don't want this whole bag o' tricks"—intimating the Cathedral—"toppling down on our heads, surely?"

"Gony's men are down there now," went on Potter, ignoring his colleague's objection. "They're messing about locating the leak, but they don't know much about plumbing, 'cos they haven't found it yet. They have started pulling something down, by the noise they're making. I'd rather have a few stones cracking my head open than them shrieks cracking my eardrums. Bad as McCarbre throwing one of his fits is that old Norman."

"Get along with your old Norman," laughed Styles, poking Potter facetiously with his silver wand. "You said it was a naughty nun just now. Now it's an old Norman. Is it screaming now?"

"Sure to be," answered Potter. "Couldn't hear it except in the Crypt, naturally. Gony's men have heard it. It's getting their goat same as mine."

Styles was curious. "I'll come down with you after Evensong," he said. "It don't matter my coughing a bit if service is over. Yes, I will. I'll come down with you and hear for myself. I bet I'll explain it, that is if it ain't just imagination."

"Gony's men haven't got any, even if I have," replied Potter.

"I'll come down after Evensong and see," persisted Styles.

"It'll be dark then and everyone will have gone," faltered Potter.

"It's dark now, and there's men down there with lights," stated Styles.

"There ain't no gas down there. It's got choked or something," Potter objected.

"We'll borrow their lanterns, then," said Styles.

"There won't be no one down there. You realize that, I suppose?" Potter hoped he hadn't.

"There'll be three of us, anyway," chuckled Styles, who was now determined that he would go and score over Potter.

"Three of us? How?" queried that gentleman.

"Myself, yourself, and the naughty nun," laughed Styles.

"Chuck it," answered Potter.

"Well, the old Norman, then," retorted Styles. "Give me the nun for preference."

"It's easy to laugh up here in the Chapter Room. You wait," warned Potter.

"I will," laughed Styles. "Till after Evensong," and the old joker knew that Potter was wishing he hadn't mentioned it.

"I'll go over for Canon Cable. It's nearly service-time. Will you just sweep up that mess? It don't look very nice for Vestry Prayers, even if the Canon won't notice it." Styles pointed to a little heap of broken stone and mortar on the floor by the bookcase.

"Whatever is it?" asked Potter.

"Why, Gony came up here with a pickaxe and started sloshing the wall about," explained Styles.

"I'll sweep it up," agreed Potter. "But I wish Gony wouldn't go knocking the place about. What was he playing at?"

"Looking for naughty nuns, I expect," and old Styles laughed himself into a dreadful paroxysm of coughing.

Potter had procured a dustpan and brush from behind an old tomb outside the door. "You won't laugh so much after Evensong," he said grimly. "I'll show you something what'll stop you laughing for a long time to come."

The tears were pouring down Styles's face.

"Oh, stop!" he cried. "You'll be the death of me."

"I hope I shan't," said Potter, very grimly.

CHAPTER XXXIX

THE RESURRECTION OF THE CHAPTER

SNOW, snow. Thick, white, silent and heavy. Not a sound in the Precincts but the rumble of the organ and the distant singing in the Cathedral, where Canon Cable is worrying his way through Evensong. Trillet is giving them no festival service tonight. He knew there would be no congregation. The weather is too bad even for the Precincts folk to venture forth. It is the first time that Potter had ever given up clearing paths. He had deliberately downed tools in the face of such snow. If he had not done so out of his own exasperation he would have been obliged to out of necessity, for he could not shovel snow in the Precincts and bale the water out of the Crypt at the same time. The water is still coming in, and Gony's men have not yet located the leak. They still splash about with lanterns and strike the walls and pillars with mallets, but all to no purpose. The water slowly gets higher as they bale and pump. Gony in his pair of sea-boots walks about carrying a step-ladder, which he keeps setting up and mounting to shout directions from. A good deal of noise and splash and every now and then a muffled scream that seemed, as Potter described to Styles, to originate from the innards of the Norman pillar that was leaking. Through all this disturbance the distant mumble of Evensong in the Chancel up above.

Sergeant Wurren, tired and dogged, still keeps his eye on Canon Cable. He is watching from the nearest stall. He is ready for anything to happen, and hopes that when the cleric does disappear there will be some antagonist he can belabour with his truncheon. He wonders whether he can club the brass eagle in time to save the Canon's flight, if that bird takes it into his head to be aggressive. He finds himself frowning at the eagle, and is afraid the choir-boys notice him. Does the grim-visaged bird keep flashing his eye at the policeman, or is it merely the reflection from the flickering candles on the choir-stall desks? The little boys at the far end of the desks squash back into their next stall neighbours. There is too much gloom and mystery beyond the soft circle of the last candles. All those empty seats placed between them and the distant altar, where six vesper lights are flickering, made the Cathedral look like a London railway terminus in an air raid, so gloomy do the few lights showing make the rest of the black spaces. The two smallest boys are on the very outside, nearest to the darkness, and they feel their position keenly, for the right arm of the Decani one and the left of the Cantoris touch nothing but the great space that stretches to the altar. They would not have walked as far as the Credence Table to get the almsdish if the Chapter had promised them the contents of it after a Sunday offertory to reward them for their venture. No, for there is an old alabaster abbot lying on a tomb up there—a wicked old fellow with a battered face—who is always waiting to grab little boys' legs with his stone crook. The doings of this abbot were recounted by the bigger boys as they roasted chestnuts in the schoolroom on wintry evenings. You could also read of his doings in Norris's books, but the big boys' tales were more fearsome. Take, for instance, the legend of how the abbot lost his alabaster nose. Norris relates how a Cromwellian trooper knocked it off with a shoeing hammer and how the trooper fell next day in battle against the loyal men of Kent. But the big solo boy on the Cantoris side had a finer tale to spin.

The nose was struck off by the farrier trooper as in the Norris version, but when Dullchester slept the affronted abbot arose and left his slab in the Cathedral. When the farrier took his hammer in the morning, with every intention of knocking the mitre after the nose, imagine his surprise at finding his victim fled. But imagine his horror later in the day, when the battle was going against the Roundheads, on seeing an ecclesiastical gentleman mounted on a white horse detach himself from the Royalist squadron and charge down upon him. Recognizing his alabaster enemy and knowing that he would be unhorsed by sheer weight, the farrier turned his horse and galloped away, but the abbot, reining in his steed, was observed to take a pointed stone out of his saddlebag which he flung with a right accurate aim after the fugitive, who fell from his horse dead, with a cloven skull. They found the alabaster nose embedded in the wretch's brain, of course, but they could not find the abbot. Some said he had gone upon a pilgrimage to the Holy Land, but it was quite certain that during the Commonwealth he was not seen in the Cathedral, until on a certain night in May of the year 1660, when the Cathedral was thrown open to shelter the thousands of wayfarers who had turned out to welcome Charles the Second gloriously restored, a mighty tramping was heard in the Slype, and a great white abbot crossed the lawn of Prebendal Garden and entered the Crypt door. Up the steps he went to the Chancel, pushed a drunken sleeper from the slab in his niche, and lay down in his appointed place again. But his nose had been mislaid, and no man knoweth unto this day where it may be. They look inside every skull that is excavated in the neighbourhood, and perhaps some time someone may light upon the farrier's skeleton, when it can be detached from the abbot's nose.

The solo boy of the Decani had a more recent tale to tell, and this one is not mentioned in any of the Norris novels.

It was whispered that, years ago, the old fellow had said "Boo" at Mr. Styles when that gentleman—under-verger in those days— was extinguishing the last candle after Evensong upon a winter's night. This was the reason that Mr. Styles's hair was white. It had not always been white. Oh, Lord, no. It had been black and curly right up to the moment when the abbot had said, "Boo."

No wonder then that the little boys, as they file out of their places, hug the stalls closely so that they may not be grabbed when they turn their little backs on the east end. No wonder that as they walk under the Chancel arch the Cantoris close in quickly to the Decani, for in the dim nave and sepulchral transepts are many tombs with recumbent figures upon the top, suggesting that the corpses have risen for an airing, many carved faces and heraldic animals that appear out of the darkness all the way to the Chapter House.

And when upon this route they pass the great entrance to the Crypt, no wonder that the little boys are afraid that the bigger boys may lock them down there one of these dark nights. Then these two unfortunates are the first of the little boys to enter the gloomy Chapter House, which is lighted by a solitary candle that stands on the table, and as if these accumulated horrors are not sufficient for one journey, there is the added terror of never knowing for certain from which of the dark shadows Potter may not jump, in order to pick up his place in the procession as it moves upon its eerie way.

So it is with a great feeling of relief that the two leaders reach the Chapter Room. The bigger boys file in after them, the lay clerks after them, and the one Canon who, much against his will, was still keeping the Cathedral on its legs, totters to the candle-lit table, picks up the framed copy of the Vestry Prayers, applies it close to his face and his face close to the candle, and commences to read the form of dismissal. Styles stands just inside the door. Sergeant Wurren stands just outside it, and Potter, with his silver wand tucked under his arm, throws a shadow across the ceiling like Mr. Punch with his big stick. Then a terrifying thing happens. The little boys, who are glancing over their shoulders towards the dark end of the room where the bookshelves are, see the whole wall move. Then, with a crackling noise of split wood, the books part company from the shelves. They slide and crash in an avalanche of dust to the floor. A cold draught blows out the candle as shelves and masonry fall forward like the walls of Jericho. In the darkness a choir-boy lets out a scream. It goes echoing after the noise of the smash into the hollows of the Cathedral. Somebody strikes a match, which flares and goes out, for the man who was holding it has been knocked down by some creature that screams. Then everyone falls over. The choristers, encumbered in surplices and cassocks, struggle together on the floor, scratching and clawing one another in the darkness, while penetrating shrieks rend the air as they feel their bodies trampled on by heavy shapes with cloven hoofs. As they strike out in the darkness, their hands encounter clammy bodies with hairy skins. No wonder that their little minds are panic-stricken.

The lay clerks are in no braver case, for, struggling, swearing and kicking, they call out for lights. Lights suddenly appear from the end of the room where the books had crashed. Four brilliant lamps held amongst a strange group of people. Seven ragged, wild-eyed men, unshaven, unkempt and bloodstained, covered with dust from head to foot. In the midst of them a woman with grey hair blowing loose in the draught and dressed in a red blanket like a Red Indian. One of the men, a colossal fellow with a bloodstained kerchief bound round his head and a fierce iron-grey beard, appears to be their leader. He advances over the pile of wreckage to the table and places an acetylene lamp upon it. The eyes of the awe-stricken choir are upon him as he speaks. "An inopportune arrival, I fear, but when men are threatened by death they cannot afford to choose their time of deliverance in order to suit other people's convenience."

There is still a good deal of movement going on amongst the choir, owing to the Chapter Room being full of jostling pigs. Sergeant Wurren steps in and closes the door, exclaiming, "I believe we have discovered the Dean's pigs."

"And I believe," went on the colossal man with the handkerchief, "that the Bishop may have to re-consecrate this part of the Cathedral into which we have driven this herd of unclean flesh."

"I believe it's the Dean," said the puzzled Potter.

Canon Cable, with scarf and hood awry, for he had fallen during the darkness down amongst the pigs, bends his little body and gropes for the prayer-frame which he had dropped. He encounters the large snout of a pig which is under the table, and is a little surprised. "Will somebody inform me what is going on?" he asks.

"I believe it's the Dean," says the staring Styles.

"Names, addresses and occupations," demands the Sergeant, advancing with his notebook.

"Certainly, Sergeant," replies the big, burly villain with the kerchief, as he turns to his companions. "This gentleman with the fair, straggling beard is the first of Dullchester's mysterious disappearances, and although you may think that I am joking, I assure you that in this disreputable-looking fellow there is hidden the familiar spruce figure of Minor Canon Quaver. I can prove this by asking him to produce his Precentor's badge of office from his pocket. Quaver, your tuning-fork or pitch-pipe, please."

The scoundrelly-looking ruffian advances to the table, produces a red leather case from the side pocket of his torn jacket, and from it takes a two-pronged fork which he strikes upon his knee-cap and then holds upright on the table. A humming note is produced from which the Minor Canon sings three other notes, saying, "The common chord of C." To further prove his identity he fumbles in his waistcoat pocket and brings out a small silver pipe. This he adjusts from a wheel on one end of it, and putting it to his mouth reproduces the same note as that already given by the tuning-fork. He then retires to the group upon the debris, and the big man continues: "The remaining adventurers are easier to distinguish, though in this stalwart bravado with black beard and thick curly hair some of you may find a little difficulty in recognizing Minor Canon Dossal. Canon Beveridge, though I regret to say he is somewhat in need of a shave, needs no introduction. The gentleman in the sadly-bedraggled dressing-gown is the Cathedral's benefactor, Mr. McCarbre. The tall gentleman with brass rings in his ears is known as the Paper Wizard, and I think Mr. Norris's appearance has not undergone any very drastic alteration since his recent disappearance. Last, but not least, let me introduce this lady. Having been robbed of her robes of apiarian office—in plain words, somebody having run off with her bee-proof clothes—not even her greatest friend would distinguish Miss Tackle as she now stands before us. There is, of course, myself, Dean Jerome of this Cathedral, looking, I have no doubt, exceedingly unecclesiastical."

CHAPTER XL

THE DEAN GIVES ABSOLUTION

SERGEANT WURREN, who had been busily engaged in making notes, clears his throat and says, "Mr. Dean, there are some things which demand explanation."

"Their name is legion, my dear Sergeant," replies the Dean. "Why did we disappear? Where did we disappear to? Why didn't we reappear sooner? These are the first things you will ask, eh? Well, the answer is that we disappeared because we couldn't help ourselves, into a world of romance from which we couldn't return because of smugglers and pirates. And now you will, no doubt, think that I am talking through the piratical handkerchief upon my head. Believe me, I am not. But as the explanation, which it is necessary for me to make to you in full, is lengthy, may I ask that we be allowed to go to our respective homes, make ourselves respectable and get something to eat? Then, I propose, with your approval, that we all meet at the Deanery and tell our adventures. Shall we say eight o'clock. This will give you time to gather the clans together, and us to collect ourselves. It would be advisable for the Mayor of Dullchester to be present. Perhaps you would ring him up and inform him."

"Very well, Mr. Dean, but until then I would ask you all to decline any sort of interview with anyone. It is only fair to Inspector Macauley and myself, who have had charge of this case, and, I am glad to say, brought it to a satisfactory conclusion, that we should hear your accounts before they become public property."

"This we will agree to, I am sure," answers the Dean. "Indeed, to give you further security to that end, I propose that none of us leave the Precincts. If Canon Beveridge will take Miss Tackle to the ladies at Prebendary House, I will ask Mr. Norris to repair to the Deanery to acquaint my wife with the news of my return and to await me there. Mr. Styles can call at the curiosity shop and summon Mrs. Norris to join us for seven o'clock dinner. In this way, no one will leave the Precincts."

"And," added Sergeant Wurren, "we can place a cordon of police to keep everyone else outside the Gate Houses."

"Perhaps," went on the Dean, "when the choir-boys have unrobed, they will assist Mr. Potter in getting my pigs through the South door back to their styes. Then they had better wait for Mr. Trillet in the School House."

"I take it that you will not require me any further, Mr. Dean?" half queries, half states, Canon Cable. "I have lost a great deal of study with all this extra duty."

"I am afraid I cannot excuse you at eight o'clock, Canon," replies the Dean. "I think Sergeant Wurren will wish you to be there."

"It is necessary for all parties to be present," echoes the Sergeant.

"What a nuisance!" mutters the Canon. "Well, I'll be getting off now, at any rate," and putting the frame of prayers down on the table unused, he scuttles past the Sergeant and out of the door. So little do modern events interest him.

Within the next quarter of an hour all these mysterious adventurers, including the pigs, are in their Precincts homes with the exception of the Dean, Mr. McCarbre and the Paper Wizard, for the Dean has requested a private interview with these two gentlemen, before he is called upon to make his statement. This request Sergeant Wurren thinks fit to grant, and leaving them in possession of the Chapter Room, hastens out to close the Precincts from the curious.

Encountering Potter and Styles on the way out, he says, "I am going to place my men round the Precincts. When the Dean leaves the Chapter Room, will you kindly see that the door is locked and bring me the key? We shall then feel satisfied that no unauthorized person goes prying into that black hole from which the Dean and party appeared."

Styles and Potter, thinking this precaution very necessary, hasten their steps to the Chapter House and wait outside.

"Have you got the key?" whispers Potter to Styles.

"No," replies that old gentleman. "It's in the keyhole."

"Not this side, where I left it. I expect the Dean has taken it out to lock the door from the other side. Wonder what he's talking to them coves about?"

Styles applied his eye to the keyhole. He removes his eye to give place to his ear. He hears McCarbre speaking.

"Mr. Dean, you have repeatedly told me that you cannot regard my past life as vicious."

The Dean's voice answers: "This seems to be such an obsession on your part, Mr. McCarbre, that I begin to wonder whether you are hiding anything from me."

Again McCarbre speaks. "My past life has been an open book to you but for three damnable minutes. How they were employed for my soul's damnation is known to this Paper Wizard and to Dr. Smith, who took the secret from me during my recent illness. When he finds how you have duped him he will seek revenge on me by an exposure which will bring me to the gallows."

Mr. Styles gives a gasp. His eyes grow wider.

"What's it all about?" whispers Potter, feeling that Styles is getting the best of it.

"Sh!" cautions that old gentleman, for the Dean is speaking again, and Styles doesn't wish to lose a word. "Tell me the whole thing, then we will see how we can help you," says the Dean.

Styles hears a sob. Then he frowns, for the voice of McCarbre continuing is dropped to the tone of a whispered confession, not one word of which can he hear. At last the mumble ceases and he hears the Dean's reply: "You have told me everything now?"

"Everything," answers McCarbre.

"Then the position is this," says the Dean. "You are a very rich man. Our friend here is a poor one. I shall advise you to provide for him and for his son, and that provision will be earned by silence. When we have determined upon a sum which we all consider to be adequate, will you keep silence faithfully?"

"I will," answers the Paper Wizard.

"And the money shall be put in trust for you," adds McCarbre.

"As to the doctor's spite," goes on the Dean, "we need not fear it. You are the only witness. Without your evidence the police can prove nothing."

"They will never get that evidence from me," answers the Paper Wizard.

"And as I feel satisfied that you, James McCarbre, most truly repent and have most assuredly suffered for your great crime, I will now in this sacred building make your peace with God according to the laws laid down by the Church." And the Dean, lifting up his voice, prays, and the grand words of the Absolution as translated by Cranmer in the Visitation of the Sick do not need any keyhole to make them audible, for Potter hears as well as Styles.

"Hallo!" he utters in surprise. "Absolution out of the Sick Prayers. What are we coming to next?"

"Goodness knows," answers Styles. "Confessional boxes, I expects. The Cathedral is not what it was. It'll need a lot of persuading to get me to clear up that mess in the Chapter Room."

After pronouncing the Benediction, the Dean, immediately changing his ecclesiastical tone, says breezily: "Now the past is passed, and by God's mercy is buried for ever, but there still remains the future to be faced, and the immediate future happens to be 'policemen.' I see no good end that can be served by letting them into our secret, and so I advise you both to keep silent during the coming inquiry. Let the whole explanation come from me. These adventures are so bound up with the crime we wish to forget that, in order to keep the story clear of it, and yet clear without it, a very nice judgment will have to be utilized for selecting events and explaining motives, and since in my profession as a preacher I have gained considerable experience in knowing how to deal with a subject, what to engage and what to avoid, I flatter myself that of us three I am the most able to diddle the policemen. It will be no light task. It is going to be extremely awkward if unpleasant questions are fired at us. However, sufficient unto the day are the evils thereof."

His voice coming towards the door gives Styles sufficient warning to retreat with Potter, and as the Dean and his two companions come out of the Chapter House door, the two old eavesdroppers are innocently approaching it in the most unconcerned manner. The Dean locks the door and puts out the acetylene lamp, telling Potter in passing that he is keeping the Chapter House key himself, in order to hand it over to the police. Then, to Potter's amazement and to the increasing disapproval of Styles, he puts his arm about the shoulders of his ill-assorted associates, and Marseillaise-wise pilots them out of the South door.

Had curiosity but prompted Styles to look through the keyhole again, it would have shown him something else that would have given him further food for thought. In the darkness of the Chapter Room an electric torch is flashed on behind the strong-room door, which opens, revealing the bearer of the light. Detective-Inspector Macauley swings himself out of the safe by the aid of crutches, goes towards the fallen bookcase and examines it, then climbing with difficulty over the pile of debris, he enters the black passage behind it and disappears.

CHAPTER XLI

"LIKE AS A DREAM———"

JANE wished that she were awake. Her dreams had all been so terrifying that it was a comfort to be lying in her own bed, watching the serene face of old Rachel. But of course this was a dream like the rest, for now Rachel had somehow or other turned into Daniel and the sun was no longer shining through the window, the curtains having been pulled. The light was shining from the flickering fire. Was she back in Miss Tackle's room again? Was it that fireplace she was still looking at? Surely not. It seemed years ago—that part of her dream. She couldn't have found the fire still alight. Rachel's voice sounded in the room. "His Reverence would like to speak to you, Mr. Daniel, in his dressing-room." Daniel got up, looked down at Jane, then, stooping, kissed her forehead. Jane wondered in her dream how Daniel had got out of that terrible cage. She found that she could move her arms. They slid round Daniel's neck. She could feel him kissing her. Her grip tightened. He raised her up. She was awake. Yes, awake, and now Daniel has gone to talk to her grandfather, who is shaving in his dressing-room. Yes, he has come back, too, and he brought the other lost sheep with him. Norris had thrown the whole Deanery into excitement by bringing the news, and now Norris is kissing his wife in the hall. The kitchen is bustling over a plentiful dinner. There are guests expected, and dinner has to be finished before eight o'clock in order that the dining-room may be prepared for a meeting. All this news the serene Rachel tells Jane, but she will not allow Jane to stir until Dr. Rickit has seen her again. The old family doctor comes in. Jane persuades him that the relief from her nightmares is so exquisite that she never felt better in her life. She also explains that she has never been more hungry in her life and that he must allow her to get up at once, change into another frock for dinner and be ready to welcome her grandfather, who, she hears, refuses to see her until he has removed a terrible beard which he thinks would frighten her, after her nerves had been so tried. Half-an-hour later a very spruce Dean knocks on her bedroom door and she is in the arms of her grandfather, who never looked jollier in his life.

Nobody can get any explanation out of the Dean. He has given his word not to talk of his adventures until the meeting called for eight o'clock. McCarbre arrives with the Paper Wizard. Everyone else is turned out of the library but Daniel. He is the envy of the household, for he is evidently getting first-hand information before the proper time. He is locked in with the Dean, the Paper Wizard and McCarbre, until Styles sounds the dinner-gong. The library door is opened. Mrs. Jerome, Jane, Mr. and Mrs. Norris and Dr. Rickit are admitted, and the Dean makes them drink to the Restoration of the Chapter. They all promise not to question the Dean at dinner, but Dr. Rickit asks if he can throw any light upon the recent disappearance of his patient Macauley, who has been missing from his bed in the spare room. "Macauley with his sprained ankle? No, I know nothing about him," says the Dean. "I have quite enough people to answer for. Don't add to my burden. Hallo, what's this?" All eyes follow the Dean's in looking towards the French windows. There, leaning on his crutches in the snow, stands Macauley. The doors are opened and he is admitted. He declines to tell where he has been or what he has been up to, and after drinking his toast in gin-and-bitters to the Dean's recovery, he limps into the dining-room with the rest of the company. The meal is eaten almost in silence, for since the one topic of conversation which everyone wishes to indulge in is denied, anything else, however full of sound and fury, signifies nothing. Dr. Rickit has been prevailed upon to enter a temporary cessation of hostilities with McCarbre, the Dean assuring the medical gentleman that his one-time patient had been grossly imposed upon to quarrel with him.

Styles and Potter, impatient for the fray at eight o'clock, serve the company with the speed of an American quick-lunch restaurant, and no one dares to lay down knife and fork for fear of losing the plate belonging to them. Rachel spends her time at the telephone taking down messages which nobody seems to bother to read. In spite of Styles and Potter, everyone rises from table well satisfied with food and drink, and while cigars are going on in the library, the dining-room is cleared to accommodate the meeting which the Dean keeps referring to as the Gathering of the Clans. With the consent of McCarbre and the Paper Wizard, Daniel has been told the full facts of the various adventures, including the confession of McCarbre, and he is now helping the Dean to arrange his statement in Jane's bed-sitting-room, Jane helping Mrs. Jerome to receive the company below, who begin arriving well before the stipulated hour. On hearing from Daniel that Dr. Smith was dead, the Dean exclaims: "That is a dreadful thing, but I must say it makes my task easier. Had he lived McCarbre would have been greatly embarrassed, and I consider that he has suffered enough, been blackmailed enough, and made, when he has provided for the Paper Wizard, enough amends. Now his crime can be ignored in my statement, and I am glad that there is a chance of our being able to make the poor wretch a little happy. He can never be free from the burden on his conscience, but it will be lightened."

At five minutes to eight Jane interrupts them with the news that the Clans are gathered and requests that old Jubb may be admitted with Rachel to the meeting. She also gives the Dean Rachel's collection of telephone messages, and while he glances through these and is gathering up his notes, Jane manages to draw Daniel out upon the landing. "Since my nightmares were real, I want protection, Daniel. If you are still in the mind, marry me." "When?" is the eager question. "On Christmas Day, in the morning," laughs Jane as she kisses him. Then she breaks away with "Sh! Here comes grandfather." They think the Dean has not heard. If so, it is odd that in preceding them downstairs he hums, "O come, all ye faithful." Perhaps he is only thinking of the Gathering which is awaiting them in the dining-room.

CHAPTER XLII

THE GATHERING OF THE CLANS

"GOSH!" says the Dean, standing in the doorway and surveying the long polished table set out with quill pens, inkstands, sheets of paper and clean pads of blotting-paper. "This is going to be a super Chapter Meeting and no mistake, though the presence of the police makes it appear like a coroner's inquest, which I suppose it is, in a way, although the bodies to be examined have fortunately come to life again."

He takes his place at the head of the table and looks round upon the company, which includes Mr. Arnold Watts, present in many capacities—as Mayor of Dullchester, Constable of the Castle, Chapter Clerk and the Dean's financial adviser and friend. This important official sits at the far end of the table, with Sergeant Wurren and Detective-Inspector Macauley on his right and left, and two constables behind his chair. The two Major Beveridges are still in uniform, but the Sub of the *Sweet William*, much to the disappointment of Kitty, has changed into a dinner-jacket in accordance with the Royal Navy's extraordinary love of mufti. Canon Cable is still excessively annoyed at the waste that is being made upon his time. Canon Beveridge and the two Minor Canons are shaved and wearing black evening coats with silk-corded waistcoats. The Archdeacon has managed to rise from bed and has somehow crossed the Great Ice Barrier. The remainder comprise Mr. Norris, Mrs. Norris, Mrs. Jerome, Mrs. Beveridge with three of the daughters, Mr. Cartwright, Mr. Gony, Mr. Trillet, Mr. Boyce, Dr. Rickit, Mr. McCarbre, the Paper Wizard and Boyce's Boy, also Daniel and Jane, who have followed the Dean. Styles and Potter take up positions behind the Dean's chair. They wear their bobbled gowns and carry their silver wands. Places have been found for Rachel and old Jubb. The doors are shut and the Dean rises, arranges his notes before him on the table and then, abruptly looking at his audience, speaks briskly:

"Mr. Mayor, Ladies and Gentlemen, you are about to hear the details of an adventure which I think you will consider as unique in the history of crime as our Slype is in Collegiate Architecture. Indeed, the adventure is not only bound up in the Slype but it clearly resembles the Slype in form and atmosphere. We entered this adventure as we enter the Slype, through a dark door with a narrow passage, where there is no way to turn either to the right or to the left, a great wall being on either hand and a gloomy tunnel with broken steps ahead, steps that go down into darkness till the last obstacle is reached, the lower door. By God's grace we reached our last obstacle, the Chapter Room door, to-day, and opened it and are now as it were happy in the sunlight of Canon Beveridge's garden. Forgive this simile, but we parsons get in the habit of choosing texts, and I choose the Slype for mine. Now I promise you I am going to speak to the point and as briefly as possible, but as I talk bear the Slype in mind, keep its haunted shape before you, and then you will be in the right state of mentality to appreciate and share the terrors through which we have passed."

The Dean pauses for a moment to select a paper from the table in front of him. "According to Sergeant Wurren's extensive and careful report, which it has been my privilege to read, and from which I have taken, with his permission, certain notes, we find that certain persons in the Precincts of Dullchester have been causing the gravest anxiety, not only to this city but to the world at large. These persons include a Dean—myself. A Canon-in-residence— Dr. Beveridge. A Master of Arts—Minor Canon Quaver. A Bachelor of Arts—Minor Canon Dossal. A well-known antiquarian with celebrity for local literature—Mr. Norris. A gentleman of means to whom the Cathedral owes many benefactions—Mr. McCarbre. A gentleman who is an adept in the art of cutting paper—Mr. Flagget. And last, but not least, a lady who is well-known to the Cathedral and to all lovers of bees and honey—Miss Tackle, who, I regret to say, is too indisposed to attend this meeting. Sergeant Wurren's report here states that 'these persons, clerical and lay, caused great commotion and anxiety by wilfully disappearing'—I question the justice of that word 'wilfully'—'disappearing from the public gaze one after the other, with no attempt to explain cause or motive, thereby making themselves public nuisances by the commotion which they caused.'

"Now, as head of the Precincts in which these events have occurred, I think it incumbent upon me in the presence of my fellow-victims to state the facts before the Mayor and his officials, before the representative of Scotland Yard—Mr. Macauley, before the head of our city police—Sergeant Wurren, and before these relations and friends of ours who are entitled to be present.

"The first victim to disappear was our Precentor, Minor Canon Quaver. Perhaps he will stand up and briefly state before this assembly the true facts of his amazing experience."

"All in order, I think, Mr. Mayor," comments Sergeant Wurren. "Quite right and proper, in my opinion, that he should. Mr. Precentor, we are waiting, and I might add that I have your wife's deposition here in front of me, a deposition made at your house in Minor Canon Row before the Dean and myself, and in view of this I should advise you to make a clean breast of the whole affair, even though you may have to shame yourself in the recital."

Several people are observed to smile at this browbeating upon the Minor Canon, while certain others show their resentment against the Sergeant by frowning at him.

The Reverend Quaver himself shows neither resentment nor amusement, but turning to the Sergeant he nods his head sadly, saying, "You are right, Sergeant. I am not going to spare myself, believe me." He then rises to his feet and, bowing to the Dean, who has re-seated himself, begins his account in a melancholy strain. "That I disappeared was a judgment upon me well deserved. A punishment for leaving undone what I ought to have done. On a certain Saturday——"

"Was it the fifteenth of the month, or not?" interrupted the Sergeant.

"I think it was," admits the Minor Canon.

"Only think?" demands the Sergeant. "Can't we be sure, please?"

"Yes, we can," replies the reverend gentleman. "Saturday the fifteenth, because I now remember with pleasure that Mr. Trillet ordained that we should render the Quadruple Chant unaccompanied, and by the test of my pitch pipe I discovered during the First Lesson that we had not changed our pitch at the end of the seventy-three verses. Saturday the fifteenth it was, then, and it was upon that day that Canon Beveridge, out of his courtliness and consideration, had enjoined me to inquire in his name after the health of our benefactor, Mr. McCarbre. The counter-attraction of a choir practice obliterated this from my mind, and it was not until midnight, after completing a sermon on Lot's wife (never preached), that I remembered my order. I may say that Canon Beveridge's orders when he is in residence are always couched in the form of requests. He is so considerate. I remember blaming myself bitterly in the pages of my diary for having failed so good a master. It was too late to call at midnight, so I went up to bed. I could not sleep. In the small hours I felt that it was my duty to get up, to write a note of kind inquiry as from the Canon, and to take it round to the invalid's letter-box. I did not disturb my wife, but crept to my dressing-room, slipped on my trousers and jacket, went downstairs, wrote the note, got my boots on, also a scarf, my hat and cloak. I then let myself quietly out of the front door and walked briskly to Bony Hill. What was my surprise on approaching the house to discover a motorcar waiting and the front door open. As I came nearer, I saw a woman, well muffled up against the cold, come out of the house and enter the car. I thought it strange that a woman should be leaving the house at such an hour. I thought it stranger when I saw Dr. Smith about to close the door in my face as I stood upon the pavement. I knew that Dr. Rickit was Mr. McCarbre's medical adviser. What was Dr. Smith doing there? I thought. He changed his mind about shutting me out and requested me to step into the hall and wait for a few minutes, as my presence might be required. I could not imagine what for, at such a time, unless a clergyman was needed to attend to Mr. McCarbre. Wondering whether our benefactor was dying, I waited. It may seem strange, but I had never been in the house before, and so looked with interest round the old hall, while Dr. Smith went into one of the rooms, where a good deal of whispering was going on. Presently he came to the door and beckoned me to enter. As I did so, a wet cloth was dashed into my face. I remember struggling, and that was all until I woke up to find myself in a bare stone room, with no windows, but lighted by an oil lamp which stood upon the floor. I had no idea where I was except that I was lying on a stone floor very old and cracked, showing the soiled earth between the broken flags. I was conscious of a great pain in my ankles, and discovered that my feet were somehow fixed higher than my head and that, in consequence, the blood had flowed down towards my body. With great difficulty I raised myself on one elbow and found, to my utter amazement, that my legs were secure in nothing less than a pair of stocks. I examined this relic of the past with interest and perceived that it was one of six pairs, and so capable of holding five other criminals beside myself. But what had I done to be punished in this way? For failing Canon Beveridge I deserved a rebuke, but I had done my best to make up for that fault, and surely to be put in the stocks in a dark dungeon was too severe. I imagined that I was alone in the gloomy place. I also thought I was dreaming and that I should wake up in a minute by hearing the Cathedral bells and find myself late for early service. I got in a panic at this thought. I rubbed my eyes. I struck myself and it slowly dawned upon me that I was awake, that this was no dream, that I was in some prison, secured in ancient stocks, and, worst of all, that I was alone. I lifted up my voice and let out a yell. I then found that I was not alone, for there stepped into the circle of lamplight a curious-looking man who behaved in a curious manner."

"Don't describe him," cuts in the Dean, "but go on with your narrative."

The Minor Canon continues; "The man's description will no doubt be given to you later by the Dean. I am only to concern myself with what happened. The man had a revolver in one hand and a tankard of hot soup in the other. 'So you're awake at last,' he said. 'I was just about to empty this down your throat. Now perhaps you'll oblige me by doing it yourself.' This I did very greedily, for it came upon me suddenly that all I cared about was appeasing a terrible hunger. This I understood later, when I discovered that the day was Monday and that I had been asleep, or perhaps I should say unconscious, since early Sunday morning, and had in the meantime received no nourishment. Feeling better for the soup, which was most excellent, I got angry and demanded an explanation from my gaoler. He answered pleasantly that it was no use railing against him and requested me, for my own sake, not to make a noise, or it would be the worse for me, that he could give me no information but that I should find out all in good time, adding that very shortly I should need all my strength and was not to waste it with fussing. In other words, I was to keep quiet. I don't know why, but I obeyed him. Having nothing whatever to go on to account for the strange plight in which I found myself, I resigned my mind to holier meditations. I fortunately remembered that I had a copy of the *Daily Round* in my pocket. I read this and meditated upon it for some hours, until the pain in my ankles refused to let me concentrate. When I thought that I could stand it no longer, my gaoler, who had left me when he had taken away the empty tankard, returned, and I asked him if I could not be released, if only for a few minutes. He shook his head. I offered him my promise not to attempt an escape. He still shook his head, and again left me, but only for a few minutes. He returned with a piece of cord and told me that if I submitted to having my wrists tied behind my back he would let me walk about that room. Of course I consented, and the relief was heavenly, though it was some minutes before I could stand without pain. I was suffering from excruciating pins and needles. Presently I was put back into the stocks to eat another meal, but I managed to arrange my legs in a more comfortable attitude and was by that time relieved to get my wrists free again. The meal was excellent. A four-course dinner, admirably served. While I was eating it my gaoler became more communicative. He assured me that no harm would come to me if I did exactly as I was told, but that if I refused he would be forced to become unpleasant. As he fingered a loaded revolver all the time he was talking, I guessed that he meant what he said. He told me that I had been brought to do a certain work, and that as soon as it was done I should be released. He would not tell me where I was. When I asked him the nature of the work, he answered: "Clearing rubbish." I told him that the sooner I started the better, as I should then be released the sooner. He again left me, taking the lamp with him. During the few minutes he was away, I resolved to be utterly obedient, for the darkness was terrifying. It is a weakness to confess it, but I could have screamed. At all costs I determined to keep on the right side of my gaoler in order that I could persuade him in future to leave me with a light. When he returned he released me from the stocks and ordered me to walk ahead of him. He went through an archway, along a passage, and then turned into a tunnel in which it was only just possible to stand upright. The far end of this tunnel was choked up with dirt and stone, piled up loose right to the ceiling. He gave me a pick, a shovel and a wheel-barrow, and told me to clear the dirt and empty it in the large room from which I had come. He told me that he had work to do elsewhere, but that he would know if I stopped working, and that it was quite useless for me to attempt an escape, as I would only run into a ghastly danger which he was not at liberty to explain. Utterly bewildered I went at the rubbish with a will. I had no idea what I was doing it for, but it seemed to me that it was at least something tangible in the midst of so much vagueness. I worked for a long spell. I had cleared away a huge pile of the rubbish, but it still blocked the tunnel, and I wondered how far dirt and tunnel went. My guide reappeared at last and conducted me back to the stocks, gave me some cocoa and cold rice pudding, and advised me to get a little sleep, as I should be wanted again on another shift. I fell asleep immediately. When I awoke I was astonished to find Dossal looking at me. He was leaning on one elbow, trying, as I had done, to get relief from the stocks into which his ankles were fastened. At the same time he was looking at me as if he had never seen such an extraordinary thing in his life. I returned the compli-ment, I daresay, and stared at him, wondering how on earth he had managed to find me."

"Perhaps he will tell us how he did," suggests the Dean. "Thank you, Mr. Precentor. If you please, Mr. Sacrist."

Minor Canon Quaver sits down again. Minor Canon Dossal stands up. He pretends to blow his nose but in reality he removes a eucalyptus lozenge surreptitiously from his mouth to his handker-chief. He then is ready to speak. "When I knew Quaver was lost I went searching the Precincts backwards and forwards. I had been into every house, and in every house somehow or other I got into every room, and in every room I looked into every cupboard and poked my walking-stick up every chimney. I satisfied myself that I had looked twice at least into every receptacle capable of harbour-ing Quaver, but at both visits to each of the said receptacles I failed utterly to find Quaver. I become positively fantastic in my search, as you will imagine when I tell you that I made a plummet line and sounded for him down gratings of drains. There was but one house in the Precincts that had not received my attentions with walking-stick and plumb-line, and that was the house on Bony Hill. But Mr. McCarbre was away. As you know, it is impossible to see into any of the windows, because there aren't any that face upon the Precincts. The whole structure of that extraordinary house, as you all know, is hidden behind mammoth walls impenetrable, and by repute unscalable. But Rumour is a lying gossip and I have always had a passion for climbing walls. When the Dean criticizes my sermons I often feel I have mistaken my vocation. He would never criticize my steeplejackery. Why, a few years ago, during my reading for the ministry at Salisbury, the grey parrot belonging to the wife of the Archdeacon, at whose house I was residing, took it into his head one breakfast-time to fly out of the dining-room window and perch upon the upper reaches of the Cathedral steeple. They made a great fuss of me because I swarmed up and captured the erring bird, who by that time was swearing terribly upon the weather-cock. I was shown upon the screens of all the local cinemas. It made quite a noise through Sarum. Therefore, with such talents lying dormant, you will not be surprised to learn that they awakened at the sight of Mr. McCarbre's wall, reputed unscalable. The more I looked at it the more affectionate I felt towards Quaver. His spirit called upon me to get over that wall. If he should not be over there, then he could be nowhere in the Precincts. But, for the dignity of the Cathedral, I felt it was not seemly to be spied performing such a prank. I leant against the Cathedral railings and measured the wall with my eye. I knew each movement I should make by heart, for I had always longed to attempt it, but I figured it out all over again with my mind's hands and feet, as it were, because I knew it was a question of doing it very rapidly. It would never do to collect a crowd. That stormy young petrel, Boyce's Boy, begging his pardon, was hovering about Bony Hill. I waited for him to disappear, knowing that he carries catapults and pea-shooters about his person. As I waited, my clerical dignity urged me to give over the attempt. This left me very undecided. The clergyman wrestled with the steeplejack. I resolved to toss up. I had no loose coin in my pocket. Two lozenges I had, but they were the same both sides and were too sticky to throw. I got an idea. I put one in my mouth, to

keep me calm, and stuck the other on one of the palings. If it stuck
on for thirty seconds I would climb, if it slipped off before that I
would go home to lunch. The thirty seconds went. It stuck, and in
twenty more I was over that wall, and in ten more I was down the
other side. I found myself standing in a paved garden. It was very
full of snow, but in the centre a path had been recently swept leading to a French window which was open. I thought this a bit odd.
Family away, and yet this window open. I went up to it. It was the
drawing-room window, and there were many valuable pieces lying
about, china and silver, which seemed only waiting for the first person who cared to climb that way I had come. I knew that Mr.
McCarbre's household had gone with him. Very well, then, leaving
Quaver out of it entirely, I considered that I had every justification
in seeing whether there was anybody knocking about the house
with less right there than myself. I was in the drawing-room by this
time and was about to begin my search for burglars and Quaver,
and it even occurred to me that Quaver might be the burglar himself, when I saw a Napoleonic bronze which I think appealed to me
more than any other work of art I ever saw. I sat down in a comfortable chair by the pedestal on which it stood, and I looked at it. I lay
back in the comfortable chair and studied it. As I might never see it
again I resolved to memorize every line of it. I closed my eyes with
this concentration in view. I was going to photograph this work of
beauty on my brain. I opened my eyes again and was looking at
Quaver. I couldn't understand this. It was most puzzling and very
annoying. With all respect to my senior colleague, I preferred to
look at the exquisite bronze. I shut my eyes, hoping to discover that
Quaver was merely a mirage, but on opening them again discovered that it was Quaver as plain as a pikestaff. Another thing that
puzzled me was that my comfortable chair had vanished with the
bronze, that I was lying on the floor, while something was pinching
my ankles. Another thing that had disappeared was the daylight. I
was in lamplight, and gloomy lamplight at that. It failed to pene-
trate the gloom that surrounded me. It showed me nothing at all
but old Quaver's face. I was wondering what on earth he was playing at, when he opened his eyes, stared at me and asked me what I
was doing. 'Hallo! You're alive,' I said. 'Yes,' he answered. 'Are you?'
I told him I hoped so, for upon my soul I began to feel very doubt-

ful on the subject. I asked Quaver where we were. He hadn't the faintest idea. I was beginning to feel that I must have gone mad, when the idea became a certainty, for a most peculiar man stepped out of the darkness with a revolver and two steaming tankards of soup. This was the gaoler of Quaver's narrative, who fed us like turkey-cocks and worked us like navvies. How long this went on we had no idea. Quaver tried to keep a sort of calendar by the aid of his *Daily Round*, but the poor fellow had no stars to go by and the *Daily Round* muddled him as he wasn't at all sure what date he had started on. This seemed to worry Quaver. I don't know why. It didn't matter to me what the date was. What worried me was wondering whether Mrs. Dossal was keeping the Pop cartoons in the *Daily Sketch*. I couldn't bear the thought of missing those. Days and nights made no difference to us. They were all alike. After a time we became quite attached to our gaoler. He was such a pleasant fellow. I think he was equally attached to us, for he most generously accepted our word not to try to escape or show fight, and refrained from locking us in the stocks. He began to exercise quite an influence over us, and we behaved like a couple of small boys trying to please our schoolmaster. We dug, we shovelled, we wheeled, we slept, and, above all, ate, and we did all these things with amazing enthusiasm. Except for thinking of our wives' anxiety we really enjoyed ourselves. The worries of life were removed. When the *Daily Round* began to pall on me as literature, I petitioned for another book. At the very next meal our pleasant gaoler brought me a fine library edition of volume one, *Waverley Novels*. When I had read this without skipping a word, he took it away and supplied me with volume two. I intend now to read the whole of Scott through. I had no idea he was so entertaining. Owing to the success of my request and seeing the happiness it afforded me, Quaver made bold to apply for a Bible and a Cruden's Concordance. The gaoler was not able to locate these books, but brought Quaver an old Medical List instead. Apart from telling us briefly the life and accomplishments of our friend Dr. Rickit, Quaver and I found this book duller reading than the *Daily Round*. He was always trying to sneak my *Waverley Novel*, but I used to hide it. I'm afraid we quarrelled a good deal about this. Our lives did not vary at all. We lost all sense of time. Quaver had not got his watch and I had omitted to wind mine up. When I first asked the gaoler for the time he in turn asked me for the loan of my watch, as he pointed out, quite reasonably, that it was awkward not having one, as it tended to make our meals a bit irregular. In the face of that calamity, for we had grown to love our food, I handed it over. He admired the watch very much. He seemed to know quite a lot about clockwork. I thought I had seen the last of it; but here it is. A handsome one. A present from some good people in Derbyshire whose lad I had coached. So, as I say, we knew no time, but were comparatively contented, except that we missed the daylight. It was like living in the dark months of the Pole. In this way our lives went on, without change of either clothes or environment, and nothing happened worth recording until we met the Dean in the tunnel."

"Which he will tell you about himself," says the Dean, rising and motioning Dossal to be seated.

"The last that was heard of me was when I banged the Deanery door on my way to visit Satisfaction House in answer to a telephonic message from Mrs. Furlong. I walked through the Precincts by way of Bony Hill. It was pitch-dark there. You know how the ivy hangs over those walls in elephantine lumps, and there are a great many winter trees in the graveyard opposite, which make it dark. When I tell you that I could hardly see the whiteness of the snow falling in front of me, you will gather that darkness to your minds. I make a point of this in view of what followed. A small slit of vivid light suddenly startled me. Under those enchanted trees that creaked with the weight of their snow burden, this uncanny light became to my imagination the mouth of some fiery beast. To my credit be it said I advanced upon it. The beast's whiskers, wet and cold and spiky, brushed my face. They were ivy twigs. Long tendrils hanging from the wall lashed into me. I pushed them from me, seized the fiery mouth by the lower jaw, pushed his moving tongue to the roof of his mouth, and looked through McCarbre's letter-box into his lighted hall. What was a light doing in McCarbre's hall, when the house was supposed to be shut up? And what was Mr. McCarbre doing in this hall when he was supposed to be away at Littlepebble? As he will tell you, I called to him through the letter-box, telling him that I was only the Dean. He seemed relieved to hear this, for the fright which he had first shown on hearing a voice vanished. "Is it the Dean?" he whispered. "So pleased, sir. For God's sake, wait a minute." He took the lamp into his library, came out again without it, and shut the door, which plunged the hall into darkness. I heard him coming towards the front door. He opened it. I stepped into the hall. He shut the door behind me, and groping feverishly for my arm led me towards the library. I made some inane remark about being glad to find him returned from his holiday, but he didn't answer. When he had shut and locked the library door, he started speaking more rapidly than I have ever heard a man lay tongue to words. Billy Sunday's sermons were a funeral to it. Apart from my admiration for an elocutionary achievement, I was thrilled to the marrow with what he told me: a romantic yarn that concerned a little book that had come into his possession years ago." The Dean turned to McCarbre and addressed him: "Mr. McCarbre, may I trouble you for the little brass-bound book which you carry in your pocket? I think it is necessary for the company to know its contents now, in order to follow our adventures the clearer."

McCarbre takes from his breast-pocket a flat wooden case with brass bands on it, and hands it to the Dean, who holds it up for the company to see.

"Now, Mr. Mayor, Ladies and Gentlemen, I will ask you to switch your minds for a moment or so from Cathedrals and Cathedral folk to luggers and smugglers, from the present year of grace to the years about Trafalgar, and from Dullchester to the Romney Marshes. In introducing you to my friend Jubb here"—the old fisherman seems very surprised at being mentioned so suddenly, but he rises and bows to the Mayor and the rest of the company—"I make you known to one who resides in a region which was the hot-bed of the irregular traffic of smuggling. He will also tell you that no place enjoyed so much prosperity in this line of business as the little fishing village of Dymchurch-under-the-Wall, and this was due to the successful organization of a worthy Vicar called Syn, who was a doctor of divinity and a man of very wide experience and sympathy. His first lieutenant, according to local historians, was his sexton and verger, an old man called Mipps, who had served amongst the buccaneers in his youth as a ship's carpenter. This book which I hold in my hand is his handiwork,

and the letter which it contains has had, after all these years, a
queer effect upon the ancient Precincts of Dullchester. I am sure
Mr. McCarbre will give you all an opportunity later of viewing the
book at your leisure, but since there is so much to explain to-night,
I will tell you its contents, or the hour will grow too late, I fear.
We have here a little oak case protected by brass bands. Out of it
we draw this little book, roughly bound in leather, which you can
observe is well-worn and shiny. I observe that the case is a better
piece of workmanship than the book. These brass bands are thick,
let into the wood neatly, and the oak is well joined. This Mipps,
having been a ship's carpenter, knew the art of joining."

The Dean lays the case on the table and opens the book, turning
the leaves towards the company. "Rice paper, you observe, somewhat ill-cut, yellow with age and stained. The writing is neat and
legible in ink discoloured to this shade of brown. Upon this fly-leaf
we find three words which, no doubt, you can all read from where
you sit."

Everyone leans forward and those who can see whisper to those
who cannot: "Mipps, His Booke."

"Upon the next page," continues the Dean, "we have a very
spirited sketch of a coffin resting upon trestles, and underneath are
some rough notes concerning the prices of various woods. There
follow a few pages filled with a conglomeration of statements
obviously jotted down at different times. For instance, here is a
note to the effect that a certain 'Mrs. Whittle is very ill and likely
to become shortly a business proposition. She is fat but has put by
money in the tea-caddy to cover funeral expenses. Wood beyond
the average will be needed to cover this extraordinary woman.'
Again, I find reference to Mrs. Whittle in a receipt for 'payment
of funeral, including best pine coffin.' Mixed up between there is
a notice stating that 'the Owlers will meet a Tuesday night with
the full moon, in order to remove at Mill House Farm one who
has turned King's Evidence.' Two pages of accounts with Brandy,
Baccy, Wool or Silk as the items, followed by the words of two sea
shanties, too horrible to read to a select audience, and again we
find this written on a blank page." The Dean holds up the book
once more to the company, and they whisper, "Mipps, His Booke."

CHAPTER XLIII

MIPPS, HIS BOOKE

THE Dean turns to the next page and reads with obvious enjoyment:
"If this book should fall into the hands of any good Christian
what can speak the good King's English like as what I is now a-
writing in, let him forward the same to one Admiral Collyer of the
Royal Navy, which good gentleman was sometime Coast Agent
and Royal Commissioner at Rye in the county of Sussex nigh unto
the Romney Marsh situated in the county of Kent, him bearing at
that time rank of Captain, but who is now, as I hear say, commanding the Royal Dockyard of Talkham.* He what does this same shall
be doing a goodly service to his country by benefiting a brave and
worthy officer, and to me what is dying in the miserables far away
from any white man, but feeling a bit more comfort when I thinks
as how through the good services of some godly Christian this ere
book will reach the worthy admiral here above alluded to. And
now with a prayer that the good Lord will direct this book which I
have knocked up solid with my own hands in oak and brass for its
better preservation, I gets on to the matter in hand and addresses
the aforesaid noble warrior as if I was a-gossiping with him man
to man.

"How be you, Captain? Beg pardon—Admiral. I hopes hail and
hearty which is more than what I be. It's your old friend Mipps
what's a hailing you. Mipps what give you the slip off Dymchurch
Sands the night what saw a harpoon drove through the neck of the
bravest Englishman what ever sailed under the Black and White of
Jolly Roger. I speaks of Clegg the Buccaneer, what was feared on
the high seas as much as he were loved on Romney Marsh under his
other name of Doctor Syn, Vicar of Dymchurch-under-the-Wall.
Oh yes, I'm Mipps all right, Clegg's carpenter for many a merry

---

* AUTHOR'S NOTE.—This information was incorrect and probably explains
why Mipps, His Booke, never reached its destination. For Captain Collyer was
killed at Trafalgar.—(*See* DOCTOR SYN.)

year and Syn's sexton for many a happy one, till you hove along
and fouled our anchorage. Well, that's neither here, there nor
whatnot, for I'm an old man and although I've outwardly turned
Buddhist for my immediate convenience, I has still got enough of
the Christian Parish Clerk left in me to do you a good turn before
I goes to join old Clegg in Davy's Locker. I don't tell you the mark-
ings of my present log in case you might feel disposed to send a
frigate a dipping in my wake, and I'm too old for Execution Dock,
always supposing you could nab me, which I makes bold to doubt.
This much I will tell you. I'm very pleasantly situated thank you
very much in a Chinese Monastery what is built high up aloft over-
looking as pleasant a reach of sea as ever I struck. Considering my
age and my miserables I'm quite well thank you. I does no work,
me being an old sailor what's up to a trick or two, and I gets fed like
a Christian turkey round Christmas, and am generally looked up
to, not but what there's any news in that for I always did command
respects, me having been Clegg's Carpenter, but I must say that
here its rather more so, me being as it were a sort of Archbishop
among these yellow clergymen and what-nots.

"Well Captain when a sailor gets to the stage when he's
a-rotting ashore like an old hulk drawn up on the mud of Thames
or Medway, he begins wondering what little good turn he can
twist to make his peace with the world he is thinking of being
pitched out of, and as 'Love your Enemies' was always a familiar
text to me, cos my mother, what used to knock my father about
something shocking, nailed it up over my bed when I was a nipper,
I has decided to do you a bit of good before old Davy comes along
in his sea boots and sings out 'Mipps, show a leg. Look alive and
die.'

"Now then, never mind how I got it, cos it 'ud take a deal of
explaining and I ain't so free with the merry quill as I once was,
but if you dont believe me, well dont and be damned to you for
a suspicious old salt what's got too big to take the word from a
common sailor.

"Treasure. Aye, my hearty, that's the word, and don't your
fingers itch? Treasure waiting to be lifted and what's more waiting
within a walking distance of your noisy Dockyard of Talkham.
Treasure worth fitting out a frigate for to fetch. But there's no need

of frigates nor of voyaging and what-not. Shanks mare will take you to the location, and is it worth the lifting? Oh dear no. If you hadn't routed us out of the Romney Marsh that Treasure would have been ours, for Doctor Syn and myself was arranging to rent the place where we knew it to be from the Dean and Chapter of Dullchester City. Was there a cipher? I should just think there was but its no good passing it along. You'd never fathom it, or if you did, not till you was too old to crawl to the place. Syn worked the cipher out himself with me a-watching. It took him twenty-seven pipes of Virginia, one after the other, me filling while he smoked, and I should blush to say how many noggins of rum, him being a respectable parson. It was wonderful, not to say inspiring, the way rum cleared that marvel's head, but allay there Mipps, for if you begin talking praise of the captain you'll have stowed such a cargo of anecdotes under the hatches of this ere book that you'd never get room to ship what's its proper cargo. So without further beating up to windward here it be forthwith. Tack away my hearty from Talkham on your best belaying pins and head up Dullchester High. Look out for Holt's Famous Coaching House upon your starboard, this being worth registering as a handy cove for seamen to board a horse-chaise when too drunk to walk back to the ship. Hard a port into Dullchester Precincts where you'll find a full rigged Cathedral in dry dock amongst the tombs. Pilot yourself between two dangerous bits of graveyard what is like old Silly and Cribdish—for if you dont bang into one you'll run foul of tother—and you'll pick up Bony Hill ahead. On port side as you drives up against the hill is a house anchored so snug behind a bit of old wall that they had to make a front door through the wall to get into it. You'll see little of the house, I warn you, for its the hiddenest house I ever clapped eyes on, but you'll make out the little door right enough, hung over with a curtain of rank ivy full of moths and dusty spiders. Past them and through the door, you'll find yourself in a flagged hallway. Now if you dance a hornpipe on them flagstones you'll be dancing on top of tons of treasure what was put there by a knowing old Bishop when Dullchester City was besieged. This old bird escaped to Normandy but never got back to lift his treasure and there it lies to this day if one can believe the manuscript. Funny lingo it was written in. Saxo-Latin I think Syn called it. He pinched

it from the Chapter Library at Dullchester because he thought it a
pity that no one had troubled to translate it. He was a rare scholar
he was. Used to quote the Classics to blokes as they walked the
plank. He once saved a gentleman's life from the buccaneers in
the Caribbees simply because the gentleman gave him a line from
Vergil that he wanted. That's all I have to say. Goodbye Captain.
I mean Admiral. Best respects and please yourself about it. I'm
feeling dizzy. Come over sudden like a Typhoon in China Seas. I
can make out old Clegg coming round the Bay. Its damned funny
but Gospel truth, but he's under the water deep down, walking on
the coral. You can see very deep from this height. I can make him
out plain. He's coming up. Climbing fast. Why his hat's out of the
water. He's clear now. My Gawd he's looking aloft. He's spotted
me through his spy glass. He's climbing up the rocks. He's wearing his cock hat, the one that he always wore on deck, it having
belonged to an Admiral what walked the plank, and he's got his
sea-coat on, over—bless my soul—his parson's kit. I dont know
whether to hail him as Clegg or Syn, as Skipper or Doctor, as Captain or Vicar. His telescope's sticking out of his pocket. He's using
his cutlass for a walking-stick and his Bible is where his telescope
used to be, which is under his arm. He's coming quick now. Seems
to be floating up on a current of air. No one could climb as smooth
as that. He's hid now behind where the rock juts over. Forgive me
Admiral but I cannot write more. This has thrown me out of my
hammock. By Gawd I'm dizzy. I cant get up and he was my skipper. I must get up but I cant bloody well move. Everything's going
dark. The Captain's hat is putting out the sun. Is it Clegg or Davy
Jones? or am I going off my bloody rocker? Yes. By Gawd——"

The Dean looks up as he closes the book and puts it back in the
wooden case. "Here the quaint manuscript breaks off, and we can
imagine that the odd author is either dying or is about to suffer
with an attack of delirium tremens."

"Wrong, your Harness," cries old Jubb, smiting the table with
his gnarled fist. "Not your fault, of course, but, oh dear"—and
to everyone's amazement the old fisherman roars with laughter,
the tears trickling down his cheeks. When he is sufficiently under
control to be able to make himself understood without further
laughter, he whispers dramatically, "Your Harness, this 'ere Mipps

weren't dying, and he weren't getting no drink penalty neither."

"Then what was he doing, Jubb?" asks the Dean.

"Joking, your Harness. Just joking. If Captain Dyke would produce my grandfather's *Journal* which I gave him with my other
grandfather's log-book for to look at, he'll find letters to show us
in the pocket. One of 'em explains this proper, and it may just happen to tickle the fancy of this learned assembly as it has done me
already."

"Daniel, can you oblige Mr. Jubb?" asks the Dean. "Let us set
the table in a roar over this joke, whatever it is."

It is quite easy for Daniel to produce the book in question, for
it happens to be in the Dean's library. It is brought in and placed
before Jubb, who has borrowed Rachel's spectacles to read with.
He selects a page from many others in the portfolio, but when he
attempts to read it he laughs again so much that he is forced to sur-
render it to the Dean, who reads it out.

"And now that I have told you all my news I seem to hear you
laughing at the way I am settling scores with old Collyer. If he
ever gets that brass-bound book I have mentioned and which is
before me as I write he'll go sounding for Treasure where there
ain't none. I loves to picture him tearing up floors for nothing but
just exercise. The house I hit upon, though, like most old houses,
credited with a secret passage, which if he hears rumoured will but
excite him the more, has stone floors of great flags. How people
will laugh at him. They will think he's got the bats in his belfry.
Fancy that old bulldog being baited by a gang of creaky-boned
parsons. Life ain't much without jokes. I've had a lot. Some with
you and the other Marsh boys, but most with the Captain Doctor
Vicar. This is my last joke and it's a lonely one unless I share it with
you. Hope the point is reached. Suppose I shall never know, unless
you can somehow find out and let me be acquainted. Wish you
could have read my letter to him. Too long to copy out on chance
of it reaching you. Fair piled up the agony I did. Think it rang as
clear as a Bell Buoy. Made out I could see old Clegg coming for me
from the sea and I seasoned the gammon with some convincing
spinage. Greetings to my old friends, if there are any left, from
Mipps, sometime sexton, Dymchurch-under-the-Wall on Romney
Marsh, known as Hellspite among the smugglers and Clegg's Car-

penter amongst the buccaneers and now if you please a Buddhist priest which is a bit rummy aint it? P.S.—Write through usual channel though by the time you get this if ever you do I quite expect that Mipps will have a pound of gunshot tied to his feet and a ragged bit o' sail for winding sheet while instead of brass cannon these yellow idiots will be letting off Chinese crackers in a positive fifth of November over your old friend's noble corpse."

The Dean lays the letter down beside the brass-bound book. Jubb still shakes silently with suppressed laughter, but the rest of the faces round the table show incredulity rather than amusement. The Dean looks at Jubb and smiles. "I can quite appreciate," he says, "why Mr. Jubb sees nothing but humour in this situation. Apparently we have here a joke which has taken a hundred years or so to come off. The party on whom it was meant to be played is dead. The party who set the joke going is dead. This book, as you will hear presently, was discovered in the market of Penang amongst a lot of old junk. Let us suppose, then, that our sexton smuggler who had turned Buddhist was an inmate of the ancient monastery above that town. On his death his effects are dispersed, and this book is cast aside. Mr. Jubb's smuggling grandfather, however, receives his letter explaining the book which Mipps has neglected to dispatch. Had Admiral Collyer received the book and acted upon its advice, he would not have been scored off by the smuggler at all. On the contrary, he would have scored off the smuggler. Mipps evidently did not lay credence upon the legends of *Odo's Treasure*. We who have read your historical novels, Mr. Norris, are wiser. The point of our jocular pirate's joke was the fact that the Admiral was off on a wild-goose chase. By an amazing coincidence he was wrong. There would have been no goose-chase, and the only point of the joke would have been against the pirate. There was treasure there all the time, and Mipps should not have selected a house so likely to lead to it. Whether Collyer would have found it when he reached it is another matter. If he was as brainy and as courageous as the party you saw emerge from the tunnel behind the bookcase this evening no doubt he might have done. But let us get on. We can spend the next weeks in conjecture. To-night let us stick to facts. I must now tell you how Mr. McCarbre came to be in possession of this brass-bound book."

"Excuse me interrupting," says Detective-Inspector Macauley, "but is it necessary for you to break your very excellent plan of calling upon each member of your party for his own particulars? Their testimony, with your summing-up, gives us a clearer path to understanding. If the narrative is now turned to Mr. McCarbre, let us have it first-hand, and if your reverence can make anything clearer at the conclusion, pray do so. Forgive me, Mr. Dean, but please continue along the admirable lines upon which you started."

"I don't see why not, do you, Mr. McCarbre?" asks the Dean. "I was only trying to save our benefactor the trouble, but I am sure he will not mind explaining his adventure just as he did to me in his library that night I disappeared. My dear McCarbre, tell them just as you told me then."

"And not as you did just now in the Chapter Room. Is that what you would imply, Mr. Dean?"

Everybody looks at the detective.

"What do you mean to imply, Mr. Macauley?" asks the Dean.

"Only that I must warn Mr. McCarbre before he begins that every word he utters may be used in evidence against him," is the detective's answer.

"Explain yourself, please," says the Dean, doing some hard thinking.

"Certainly, Mr. Dean," replied the detective. "But let me first make it quite clear to James McCarbre that he is wanted on a charge of murdering Captain Henderson upon the banks of the Irrawaddy River."

"Murdering Captain Henderson?" gasps the Dean, appalled that his scheme for shielding his penitent has failed.

"Captain Henderson, sir. A handsome young officer attached to the Indian Army."

"Macauley, is this necessary?" asks the Dean. "I mean—what facts are you bringing up against our benefactor?"

"Ask James McCarbre if he has ever seen this face?" The detective hands a photograph to the Dean, who looks at it intently, but does not pass it to McCarbre.

"Show it to me, please," says McCarbre. "And let Mr. Macauley say what he has to say."

The photograph is handed to McCarbre, who looks at it, saying sadly, "Yes, it is poor Henderson, and this is my property. You see my name is on the back. I don't know how it came into the detective's hand." He lays it down on the table in front of him.

"Let me just run over the points quickly." Macauley has now risen to his feet. "I regret that I have not the gift of the gab like you clerical gentlemen—no offence meant. You seem to have a knack of spinning facts into narrative. My statement will be facts pure and simple. I shall leave it to the advocates later on to work up the embroidery."

"Mr. Macauley," interposes the Dean. "May I beg of you to keep whatever facts you know of to a private examination? You can serve no good ends in causing a scandal by bringing to light——"

"Let him speak, Mr. Dean," interrupts McCarbre. "It is better that he should."

"Mr. Dean," retaliates Macauley, "you can serve no good ends in your attempt to diddle the police. Forgive my slang; I am only quoting your own words."

"My own words in the Chapter Room," thinks the Dean. "Why has the Paper Wizard betrayed?"

The phrase also strikes McCarbre. He remembers it. "Why has the Dean betrayed me?" he asks himself. "It must have been the Dean, for it was too much against the interests of the blackmailer to do it." The detective seems to read their thoughts, for he addresses McCarbre. "The Dean has not betrayed you, James McCarbre. Your confidence in him was perfectly sound. He is a man of honour, though personally I think his ideas of it are wrong. Neither is the Paper Wizard to blame. It is hardly likely that a man of his type is going to throw away his chances of an annuity. No, sir, you are condemned by your own black deed, and the truth of the old adage, 'Murder will out,' which is again established, because it always will out, so long as the police know their business."

"What did I tell you?" whispers Styles to Potter.

"Well, what did you? You never told me nothing," is the contemptuous reply.

"Didn't I tell you 'Murder'? or wasn't you listening?"

"Sh. Let's listen now," says Potter, nudging his colleague.

"Has all this got anything to do with the matter in hand, Mr. Macauley?" asks the Mayor, speaking for the first time.

"Everything to do with it, sir," answers Macauley. "How the Dean would have explained the case satisfactorily without it beats me."

"Just a minute, Mr. Macauley," says the Mayor. "Although I am entirely in the dark, there seem to be graver issues in this case than I had anticipated. You are a comparative stranger to us. The Dean is known to us all. Therefore I intend to be guided by his wisdom and discretion." The Mayor rises and looks down the table at the Dean. "Jerome," he says quietly, "if you wish me to disperse this meeting, I will do so. We all rely on your judgment."

"Let it all come out, Mr. Dean. Don't think of me any longer," urges McCarbre. "Let the detective speak."

"It will only be a postponement if I don't, James McCarbre," says the detective. "If I don't speak here to-night I shall speak elsewhere to-morrow. It will make precious little difference to you. Mr. Mayor, I share your respect for the Dean's wisdom, but I maintain that he has no right to interfere with the course of justice, and I should like to warn you, Mr. Dean, that I regard any parson who harbours a murderer under the seal of confession as one who is aiding and abetting him. If you wished to diddle the police after hearing that confession of murder this evening, you should have looked inside the strong-room and knocked me on the head."

"I am well aware, sir," answers the Dean, "that to spy upon men is part of your unpleasant duty, but," he adds, his voice rolling out like thunder, "to spy upon God as you have done is presumption too awful for a man's soul to bear."

"Then the burden is mine, Mr. Dean," admits the detective. "I never shirk my responsibilities, though I own that this one is not light."

"It is so heavy," says the Dean, "that I am sorry for you."

"But I do not look upon it as a presumption. I am not a presumptuous man, and therefore I will not presume to argue upon theology with one of its masters. Instead, I shall continue to discharge the responsibilities of my duty by telling James McCarbre what I know of his dealings with that mischievous brass-bound book to possess which he killed Captain Henderson."

"Jerome, there is still time to dismiss this meeting," interposes the Mayor. "Either too much has been said or too little. Shall we call it too much and decline to hear more, or is it wiser to hear more of what sounds a very dangerous communication?"

"I refuse to have the Dean compromised further, Mr. Mayor," answers McCarbre. "It is better for me that the whole story should be told."

The Dean keeps silent, and Macauley takes up the story.

"James McCarbre, thirty-odd years ago, you were acquainted with Captain Henderson, whose portrait is before you. His regiment was stationed in Calcutta but he obtained leave to join you in an expedition upon the Irrawaddy in Burmah. You were an ardent entomologist. Henderson was as ardent a sportsman. He shoots game. You poison insects. In the native market of Penang he has picked up the little brass-bound book which lies on the table there. He reads you its contents. He doesn't believe that there is any likelihood of there being treasure in the spot stated. You believe otherwise. You persuade him to look for it. This he is willing to do in an open way. You do not approve of the open way. You do not wish to part with the treasure to the Crown. You try to get the book into your possession. Henderson, now persuaded by you that there may be truth in it, won't give it up. It was his find. You realize that you have no claim. You scheme how to get the book. Henderson gets fever. This gives you a chance. Peterson, the official doctor of the Irrawaddy Navigation Company, dines with you in camp. He takes a gloomy view of Henderson's illness and rides off in an endeavour to hasten the steamer, in order that Henderson may be conveyed to Rangoon where he can be given proper attention. A dreadful thought occurs to you. If Henderson were to die before Peterson's return, Peterson would testify that he had died of fever. Henderson is very ill, but he may recover. You listen to his groans. It is time for him to take the medicine Peterson has left for him. It is a different colour from the poison with which you are destroying your specimens, but the bottles are similar. Henderson's servant comes up to you. You are listening to the sick man's groans and hoping each one will be his last. The servant, not knowing the colour of his master's medicine, picks up what he thinks is the bottle. He asks you if it is correct. 'One to two spoonfuls of water?' You realize that it is the poison and also realize that fate is showing you a good way out. You nod. The servant—his name is Flagget, and he sits there at the table opposite you—takes away the medicine in all innocence and gives it to his master as you directed. What happens? In three minutes Henderson is dead. During three minutes your mental tension is terrible. You want him dead, and yet you fear your own conscience. Flagget calls you. His master is dead. You take the book you covet and tell Flagget to bury his master. Then Flagget terrifies you, for he shows you that he knows your secret. Some of the poison had been spilt upon the camp table by the bed. A large grasshopper lies dead in it. Flagget knows you are rich and he knows that you poisoned his master. He also knows that you have stolen the little book the contents of which are known to him. Your bluffing and blustering have no effect upon him. He has made up his mind to blackmail you, and you have no wish for an inquiry to be made. Knowing you are in his power, you begin to hate the man. He has a habit of cutting shapes out of paper which irritates you, especially when he cuts paper gibbets with men hanging from them. He torments your conscience with this trick. You repeatedly try to give him the slip. After many failures you succeed, owing to the fact that Flagget is arrested in Bombay. When he gets out of prison you have gone to England. You visit Dullchester and find that the house you covet is let on a long lease. You determine to wait till this expires. One day your plans are all changed, for on your bedroom door of the Bull Hotel, where you are staying, you find a paper gibbet sticking. You know that the blackmailer has discovered you. You leave that very day and book a passage to America. Once there, your money helps you to make more. You become a lumber king and it is many years before Dullchester sees you again. Meanwhile, what of Flagget?"

"I'll tell you what of Flagget," interrupts the Paper Wizard, springing to his feet. "Flagget was a scoundrel from the start. James McCarbre, the detective thinks he has nabbed a murderer in you. He'll find that he's only netted a blackmailer in me. You have confessed in his hearing to having killed Captain Henderson, and no doubt you think you did, but you think wrong. I am the only witness against you, but I can and do acquit you of murder, and by condemning myself, free your conscience, which I have imposed upon too long. Now, Mr. Detective, mark well what I say, for this is God's truth. McCarbre did not kill Captain Henderson, because

Captain Henderson was as dead as a door-nail before I asked McCarbre for the medicine. I picked up the poison purposely, in order to get McCarbre in my clutches. I needed money. I spilt the poison and killed the grasshopper for the same purpose. Whether he was tempted to kill Henderson or not don't come into the argument. Temptation's no crime, and you've got no case against him."

"Don't lie to shield me," shouts McCarbre across the table. "Tell me the truth. Can you, before God, remove this burden from my mind? Don't lie. I have suffered too much to want shielding, but to know that I did not do this dreadful thing would be to walk with God."

"I ain't lying, gentlemen, so help me Bob," answers the Paper Wizard solemnly. "If McCarbre likes to take proceedings he's got a clear case against me."

"I'm not a murderer. Not a murderer," cries McCarbre, with tears of gratitude running down his cheeks and his hands clenched before him in an attitude of exultation.

The Dean rises. "Paper Wizard," he says in a voice that shakes with emotion, "whatever your crime, you have made amends now, and I am sure none of us here would wish to proceed against one who has exposed himself to save another. McCarbre, I congratulate you on your freedom from a terrible bondage."

"As for me," adds Macauley, "although it always makes me happy to catch a murderer, it makes me happier to see him cleared. As for you, Flagget, since you have had the grace to clear McCarbre, you had better continue your history until he has recovered from his surprise. When you missed your victim that time in Dullchester, what did you do?"

"Took to a wandering life," answers the Paper Wizard. "Married a gipsy woman. She gave me a son and we all tour together, me picking up plenty of money by cutting sillywets. When the kid was two years old the wife dies."

"And you put the child into Greenwich Orphanage, eh?" asks the detective.

"Yes," says the Paper Wizard. "And give 'em twenty quid in trust for him."

"And changed your name from Flagget to Jinks. Why?"

"Because I knew that if McCarbre returned he would keep his ears open for the name of Flagget."

"Then you went to America after McCarbre, didn't you?"

"Yes, and always missed him. I followed him for years. But a rich man can travel faster than a poor one."

"Why did you return to England?" asks the detective.

"Because I heard McCarbre had gone there. Also I wanted to squint at my son. But McCarbre was the chief reason. I meant to run him to earth."

"You guessed he would return to Dullchester?"

"Yes, and since my son was working for Boyce's, I employed him to watch."

"But you did not tell him that you were his father."

"No, I thought it better to wait for that till I had nabbed McCarbre."

"Then you told him to rent the old tool-shed in the Precincts, I suppose?"

"Yes. It was a good spy-hole, that. No one went into it, and it commanded a view of McCarbre's front door."

"When McCarbre came to Dullchester, why did Boyce's Boy, your son, try to rent the old stable behind the Bull Hotel? You can't see McCarbre's front door from there."

"My son kept holding meetings in my tool-shed. He had formed a sort of union amongst the Errand Boys. I offered to finance their premises in order to get rid of them from the tool-shed."

"But why didn't you confront McCarbre sooner than you did, since you knew he was in the city?"

"Because I wanted to frighten him first. Boyce's Boy told me that my man was going to get a war memorial window put up. This gives me an idea. I find out the name of the artist who is designing it and——"

"You became his model," puts in Macauley.

"Yes but how do you know?" queries the Paper Wizard.

"And, by the aid of that photograph on the table there, you cleverly arrange that Henderson's portrait is the centre of the memorial window, which has precisely the effect upon McCarbre that you meant it to have."

"Yes, but I had reasons to repent it later; indeed, we all had.

That's so, ain't it, Mr. Dean? For all along of McCarbre throwing that fit and also all along of Mr. Styles not being able to locate Dr. Rickit, we get landed with Dr. Smith, who worms his way into all our secrets, and a more thorough-paced villain than Dr. Smith, especially when he was along of that Chinaman, I never wish to meet."

"You didn't know that Dr. Smith was wanted by the police of the world?"

"No. But I reckon that any of us would have taken anybody's word for that, don't you, Mr. Dean?"

"The whole company will think so when I recount how you saved McCarbre from his murder-trap, Paper Wizard," answers the Dean.

McCarbre looks up at that, and, smiling across at the Paper Wizard, says, "You saved my life there as you have saved my soul here. I am always your servant, Mr. Flagget."

"Let me explain," says the Dean.

CHAPTER XLIV

THE DEAN EXPLAINS

"TAKING up the narrative where I left off, I must tell you that when I understood the Mystery of Dullchester to be a Treasure Hunt, I resolved to be in it, partly to guard, if possible, the interests of the Cathedral, but chiefly, I must confess, to enjoy the hunt and to be in at the death. Not that I was given much chance of being out of it, for I was politely informed that if I started any hanky-panky I would get a bullet through me from the unscrupulous Smith. This information came from the Paper Wizard, the gaoler of the Minor Canon's narrative, whom McCarbre had admitted to the library. That threat put me into a good temper with the whole adventure, for the actual possibility of a large Dean having a bullet put through him in his own Precincts was delightfully droll. When Smith appeared, revolver in hand, which pleased me enormously, I could see that he resented my presence very much, but since one of his fellow-conspirators had admitted me, he couldn't blame me. Naturally he couldn't let me go free, and so I found myself being driven down below at the point of his revolver. I didn't want much driving. I was very interested in what I should find down below. The entrance was a gaping hole in the stone floor of the hall. A neat contrivance of a rug fastened to a thin piece of boarding was pulled over our heads when we descended, and then a great flagstone that slid in a groove closed the hole beneath it. I don't believe anyone could have spotted it as a sliding door, but we will examine that later. A flight of stone steps led us to a passage which sloped down in a long, gradual descent till we reached a very steep winding stairway. This brought us to a series of vaults through which we passed. How many vaults there were I couldn't say for certain, but we seemed to pass through a great many. It was very dark and we had only one electric torch with us. In one of these vaults there was an oil lamp burning and I was astounded to see Miss Tackle sitting by it, eating rice pudding. I wondered how she had got herself a place down there amongst the damned. She didn't see me. She was too busy eating rice pudding. The next surprise I had was to see two of the dirtiest-looking dogs imaginable at work on a rubbish-heap. I was informed that these were my missing Minor Canons. They *had* got themselves in a pickle. It was not long before I had got myself into a worse one. I need not go into details now concerning our life in those darkened halls of Dullchester. It is a world of its own, as you will all realize when I take you down. I was given a shake-down in a vault they called the Guard-room. I tell you the Catacombs of Rome aren't in it. It is a world of passages and vaults. Most of the floors were knee-deep in rubbish, some of the passages choked to the ceiling. Where it all came from beats me, but it was no doubt the accumulation of bygone centuries. It seemed to have been a depository for all the broken stones cast aside from the fabric of the Cathedral. We were puzzled by the quantities of dead seaweed about the place, but of that more anon. Our first duty was to clear the passages in order to locate the treasure. Now McCarbre and I were determined that if anything of value was found, it should be restored to the Cathedral Treasury. We knew that Smith would never agree to this, but we had hopes of squaring the Paper Wizard, who was more disposed to follow us than the doctor. The first thing to do was to find the treasure, and with this end in view we toiled in the rubbish, we scraped at the floors and ceilings and thumped the walls for hollow sounds. It was not long before there was friction in the camp. Smith had produced from somewhere or other a mysterious Chinaman. We couldn't find out much about him except that he was an old acquaintance of Smith's. They were always whispering together in corners, which put us on our guard against them. We guessed that they were in league together against us, but until the treasure was discovered it was essential for them to keep on more or less good terms with us. The only explanation we got regarding the Chinaman was Smith's assurance that he was as honest as the day and that his help was essential when it came to shipping our treasure abroad. He had a safe lie in Holland to hide it in. We said we would talk about that when the treasure was found. It struck us as being very comic that we should be expected to trust this Chinaman, though of course we had no intention of doing so. All the same, I was glad of the Chinaman. He supplied the right atmosphere in a fantastic adventure. It was not long before McCarbre, myself, and the Paper Wizard were leagued definitely against the others. Miss Tackle, by the way, lived and mealed by herself. Her duty was washing up and trimming the lamps. She took a turn at cooking now and then, but we dethroned her from that kingdom in favour of the Paper Wizard who, it transpired, had been a chef in a Paris hotel during his chequered career. The Minor Canons, I regret to say, had by this time degenerated into a couple of pit ponies. All they thought about was eating and sleeping, and all they did was to clear rubbish. When we did get a word with them, we couldn't get them to discuss plans of mutiny."

"Well, I was quite happy and didn't want to be disturbed," protests Dossal. "Quaver was fretting to get back to Cathedral and took no comfort from the fact that he was living in the very bowels of it all the time. Quaver doesn't really like Cathedrals. He thinks he does. But the word only conveys organ-pipes and choir-stalls to him; but to me it's massive pillars and dark places. It pleases him. It frightens me."

"Stop talking, Dossal," commands the Dean. "You were nothing more than a couple of blind pit ponies, and you know it. Your mention of organ-pipes brings me back to my story."

"Ah!" murmurs Mr. Trillet.

"While our gang was working on what we called the Lower Level, we kept hearing what first seemed to be the sounds of an organ-pipe—a deep one. The Paper Wizard maintained it was more like a steamer on the river blowing a siren. It certainly did sound very like it and I dismissed the organ-pipe idea, for if we could hear this one note so plainly, why couldn't we hear more? I concluded that Trillet in F must have been given once or twice since my absence, but never a note of it had we heard. If the noise were indeed a river foghorn, then we conjectured there must be a passage leading out to the river, or perhaps right under the river to the Old Palace of the Knights Templar on the banks of St. Rood's. You mention such a passage in your thrilling account of the Third Siege of Dullchester Castle, don't you, Norris? Indeed, I was telling the Paper Wizard about that book when we were startled by the most unearthly shrieks. Now McCarbre had gone to rest half-an-hour before, and——"

"Since I was the central figure of the scene that followed," says that gentleman, "suppose I take up the thread. I am sure you will not give yourself enough credit if you continue, Mr. Dean."

"Don't you believe it!" laughs the Dean. "There is no one who delights in patting me on the back more than I do myself. But to please the detective, and since it is your scene, you may continue, Mr. McCarbre."

The Dean sits down and McCarbre, already a different man since the Paper Wizard's revelation, takes charge of the chronicle.

"You cannot imagine how delightful it is, my dear friends, to be able to talk publicly and freely about things which half-an-hour ago would have stiffened me with terror. Since the Paper Wizard has cleared me, I cannot now think why I ever imagined myself guilty. He must have hypnotized me with his damning evidence as easily as he has just cleared me with his generous confession. I can now dismiss the torture of mind that was with me always, consciously or subconsciously. I am free. But I was not experiencing this freedom when I heard the note of the siren just described by the Dean. You must understand that my health has been badly shaken by my fit in Cathedral occasioned by seeing in the Memorial Window the face of the man I thought I had murdered. Can you conceive my horror on finding that I had paid a large sum of money to set up a stained-glass figure of the very man I was so anxious to forget? That painting seemed to have been created by the accusing finger of God. Flagget's ingenuity was marvellous, for since a figure in khaki was in accordance with a war memorial, it was also the colour and style of uniform which Henderson was wearing when he died. My glimpse of him dead, when I went into his tent to steal that book, was just as the window represents. Flagget must have suggested all those details to the artist which he knew would strike me. The bandage round the head, the tunic and shirt open at the throat and the figure lying on the stretcher in exactly the attitude of poor Henderson upon that bed."

"I posed for the figure myself," confesses the Paper Wizard. "You see, I was leaving nothing to chance. Mr. Burgoyne was astonished at my patience and enthusiasm, but I could have kept still till doomsday to get that figure right."

"Now, the sound of a siren," continues McCarbre, "never fails to make my blood run cold. It reminds me of the dreadful night when Flagget and I were sitting by Henderson's grave. From sheer exhaustion I had dropped into a sleep of nightmares, and was awakened to fresh horror by the siren sounding in the darkness. The dread of missing that boat was a panic, and this feeling came upon me when I heard the siren in the stillness of the Dullchester vaults. As the Dean was telling you, I was resting after my shift of work. I picked up a candle, meaning to join the others, and was on my way to the Lower Level when I perceived that Smith's working-party had cleared a tunnel which I had not explored. Expecting to find him at the end of it, I went along, the siren growing louder. This caused me to hurry. I wanted to get near some human being. Even Smith would have been a welcome relief. There was a draught blowing towards me, and fearful of being suddenly plunged into darkness, I was concentrating upon keeping the candle shielded with my hand and neglected to see where I was walking. Suddenly my foot went down into space. I fell forward, dropping the candle. Luckily my hand caught on something to which I clung in desperation. For a ghastly moment I supported my whole weight in this hanging position. I did not know how far I had fallen or what dark depths were beneath me. In kicking about for a foothold I discovered that I was hanging from one of a number of iron bars let horizontally into the wall of the shaft into which I had fallen. By the sound of water beneath me, I conjectured that this shaft was a well. My plight was not, then, so desperate, for my feet had found two of the steps, and I guessed that this ladder went from the top to the bottom. I felt above my head with my spare hand, and to my delight my fingers gripped the edge of the floor from which I had fallen. But just at this psychological moment the siren blasted out beneath me, loud and deep. I looked down, and in so doing lost my nerve, for beneath me, floating in the water, appeared the apparition of the man I had murdered. I gazed at this in horror. There could be no doubt about it. It was Henderson's corpse as I had seen it last, and it illuminated the water with a spectral light. The siren sounded again, deep and dreadful, and then the apparition spoke. 'James McCarbre,' it said in a ghastly voice, 'you have suffered on earth. You must now suffer in hell. Come.' The face of the corpse disappeared into the black water, and the siren, which I then took to be the trump of doom, shook my soul with its reverberation, while hideous laughter rang in my ears. 'Come down. Come down,' yelled maniacal voices. My fingers loosened their hold and with a shriek of despair I dropped into nothingness."

"Where you will remain quietly," says the Dean, rising, "while I continue the story. I hardly like to disillusion your minds with regard to this ghost in the well, for I don't suppose any of you could solve a mystery over which the penetrating Macauley looks so puzzled."

"Only over one detail, Mr. Dean," contends the detective. "I translate the phenomenon in this way. Flagget, having frightened McCarbre successfully with his stained-glass window in the Lady Chapel, thinks he will repeat the experiment in the vaults. No doubt he thinks he will get more money out of a scared man. He finds this well. He steals the head from the window and by the help of a box with an electric bulb inside has a first-rate apparition illuminated at will. When we know that a D-flat Tuba has been stolen from amongst Mr. Trillet's organ-pipes, we have no difficulty in locating the siren."

"Marvellous, my dear Holmes," laughs the Dean, "but you must suffer a mere Watson to set you right in one particular. The ingenuity of this trick does not belong to the Paper Wizard, who was now joined to McCarbre and myself in brotherhood, but to Dr. Smith, and it is my firm belief that he was trying to murder McCarbre, for on my arrival I distinctly saw him down the well, pushing McCarbre's body under water with the organ-pipe. Of course he pretended he was trying to save him. He assured us that the lantern was only a practical joke. Of course we disbelieved that, and agreed to keep our eyes skinned for treachery on his part. By the way, what was the point that troubled you, Macauley?"

"Why, I was wondering where the conjurer concealed himself. I suppose he was down the well the whole time?"

"Yes," answers the Dean. "There was not much risk of McCarbre knocking him off his perch if he clung on tight, flat against the wall. It's a wide well. We had a good deal of trouble in bringing McCarbre out, and we had more in bringing him back to life and in saving his reason, but to save his own face Smith accomplished the doctoring part of the job successfully, though the real credit belongs to the Paper Wizard, who dived into that ghastly black water and recovered the body. I came in handy when the lifting-out time came. I will not give myself the praise due to me. It would take too long; and after this tragic episode it is time you heard something funny which happened when the hated Smith discovered his Treasure Chamber."

"Do you mean to tell us, Mr. Dean," asks the Archdeacon, opening his lips for the first time, "that after all this rigmarole of pirates and passages, you actually have discovered something that can be turned into currency?"

"Why so mercenary of a sudden, Mr. Archdeacon?" parries the Dean.

"You would feel mercenary, in my shoes, Mr. Dean, with the funds of the Archdeaconry so low."

"You shall get all the help you want, if you don't interrupt," cries the Dean. "Your wretched coffers shall groan with gold of a bygone age. But you will have to pay me tribute for every doubloon you receive."

"In what way?" asks the Archdeacon anxiously.

"I shall probably ask you to hornpipe through the Precincts," pronounces the Dean solemnly, "and if you do not do it to our satisfaction we shall hang you in the Slype. But to return to Smith's find. He had cleared and clambered up the inside of a stone shaft which we thought at first was an air-passage. It was very steep, although quite simple to climb as there were ridges of stone to prevent one from slipping. It led up a passage that ran at right angles, which as far as we could see was a purposeless 'No Thoroughfare.' This seeming lack of purpose made Smith attracted to the spot, and when we abandoned it as no good, he continued up there, poking about. His diligence was rewarded, for by leaning his weight against a particular stone he swung open a secret door, which revealed a large room, in which he sees immediately an iron door let into a wall. This was locked, and as there was no key he comes to us for tools and help. If he could have got that door off its hinges by himself I'm sure he wouldn't have taken us into his confidence, but he had only one pair of hands, as that Chinese friend of his had done one of his many disappearing acts. So he fetches me along with the Paper Wizard. He was carrying the electric torch, and as soon as he passed through the secret door, which he had left open, he directs the light across to the iron door. 'We've got to get these hinges off,' he says.

"Now as soon as I was near enough to the iron door to examine it properly, I sat myself down on the floor, and as soon as I was on the floor, with my arms stretched out behind me, I started laughing. I laughed till I thought I should die of it. Smith flashed his light on to me. He thought I was being hysterical at finding the treasure's hiding-place, I suppose, for he ordered me, with an oath, to pull myself together. What he did not notice was that I was sitting on a thick Turkey carpet, beautifully swept and clean, and that there was a modern wastepaper basket beside me. 'Don't take off the hinges, you cuckoo.' I gasped between my laughter. 'We've got to get the door open,' he answered angrily. 'Then unlock it,' I suggested. 'Much easier than pulling it down.' I had taken out my key-chain by this time and untwisted a key from the ring. 'There's the key,' I said, handing it to him. 'How did you come by it?' he demands. 'The Dean always carries a key of the strong-room,' I explained. 'Didn't you know that you'd broken into the Chapter House?'"

At this point Mr. Gony, the architect, interrupts. "Was it the Chapter Room, then?"

"It was," answers the Dean. "I felt the carpet and I saw the wastepaper basket as well as recognizing the iron door. That's why I laughed."

"But in what part of the room was this secret door?"

"The bookcase at the far end was the door," laughs the Dean.

"But the Chapter Room is on the upper floor of the Chapter House, and there is the Rose window over the bookcase, which is against an outside wall. How in the world can a secret passage adjoin that end of the room without showing in the outside architecture?" The architect began to make a rapid sketch of the Chapter House.

"Exactly what struck me at the time," answers the Dean. "But, you see, it does show. In fact, the original builders of that secret passage made it so dreadfully obvious from the outside that nobody would think of noticing it."

"I'm afraid I don't follow you, Mr. Dean," puzzles the architect. "May I ask what is so very obvious?"

"What you are drawing in now," explains the Dean, craning his neck to look at Mr. Gony's sketch. "The great flying buttress that flies up from my lawn. The passage was built inside that, and if that isn't as unique as our Slype, well, I'll go and find a more original Cathedral."

"Was it quite wise, Mr. Dean," asks the Archdeacon in a tone of reproach, "to hand over the key of the strong-room to this man Smith? I mean to say—you knew something of his character, and although I quite appreciate the drama of your action, well—was it quite wise?"

"Mr. Archdeacon," answers the Dean, "you are too careful for this world, and you never risk a sprat to catch a mackerel, whereas I was risking a tiddler to catch a whale. I wanted Smith's attention directed to the tiddler, in other words the chest, while I gave my attention, uninterrupted, to the whale. I knew he wouldn't run away with the Registers and Records. I knew he would run away with the chest if I gave him half a chance, and to that end I told him of the contents. I spoke of the two great flagons of gold, of the jewelled chalices, and the silver plates given to our predecessors by Charles the First. Even before I had started to exaggerate about them I could see he had made up his mind to make off with them, which was just the frame of mind I wanted him in. And now comes a very important point in the story. I had a hole in my left breeches pocket. My keys had worn it and I had always meant to report it to my wife, but luckily forgot. I slipped the key of the chest from my key-ring while we were talking and dropped it through down into my gaiters, where it was very uncomfortable, but safe, for when Smith demanded the key I could truthfully report that it was not on my key-ring. He asked me who kept it. I told him to ask Dossal for it, as Dossal, being Sacrist, was responsible for the chest's safety. But Dossal hadn't got it. He had lent it to Canon Beveridge. Whereupon Smith makes me sit down and pen a letter to Beveridge, which Beveridge would feel obliged to obey. You have the letter on you, Beveridge. Would you kindly read it, as it explains your disappearance?"

Canon Beveridge takes a letter from his pocket and reads:

"November the Thirteenth and no address given.
"MY DEAR BEVERIDGE,

"If you wish to see me alive and in company with Miss Tackle and the Minor Canons, do what I ask you without fail. To-day between the hours of three and four p.m. make it your duty, your bounden duty, to walk up and down Bony Hill. As soon as you perceive the lane to be deserted, take out a white handkerchief and blow your nose, but be sure you are not overlooked by anyone. Tell no one of this letter. Bring it with you. If you inform the police, I am ordered to tell you, from a power which is stronger than us, that I shall never return with the others. Obey me and you will save all our lives. It will separate you from your family, but I hope not for long. When you blow your nose you will be given the means of disappearing, as we have done before you. We rely upon your courage.

"Yours desperately,
"JONATHAN J. JEROME, Dean."

"P.S.—Most important. Bring with you the key of the Communion Chest. Dossal gave you the key.—J. J. J."

"This note was sent," continues the Dean, "and its summons was obeyed with the fortitude one would have expected from the Canon. We watched for him through the crack of McCarbre's letter-box, Smith flourishing a revolver about to prevent any treachery on our part. I loved that. Certainly Smith could play the Pirate King very well on occasion. Beveridge was right opposite the door when he blew his nose. I opened the door and beckoned. He came in, wringing his hands with affection, but I fear the warmth of his greeting was somewhat chilled when Smith put the revolver to his head. However, before there was any bloodshed, I protested to Smith that I would answer for the Canon's discretion. I will give Smith credit for this. Whenever I gave him my word about anything, he took it with complete trust. Villain he was, but he did possess some qualities that called for admiration. Well, the Canon was marched below, and I must say here that he showed an excellent spirit, his only regret being that our friends Norris and Gony were not with us to share in these new mysteries of the Precincts. The chest had been placed in the Guard-room, and the Chinaman, who had returned from the outside world, was sitting on it, revolver in hand. At my request Beveridge surrendered the key, and with very mixed feelings we watched the Nonconformist and the Buddhist gloating over the vessels of our Cathedral. When Smith read out the text that is carved round the great almsdish and added a coarse rhyme of his own, I had difficulty in suppressing the Canon's righteous indignation, which increased when Smith informed us that we could stay and grope for a treasure that he didn't believe in any longer, but that, as far as he was concerned, he was decamping in company with the Chinaman and the chest, which he did believe in. Poor Beveridge nearly choked with anger, but I managed to convey to him that I had yet a trick up my sleeve which would diddle them."

"And thanks to the vigilance of the Navy and the promptitude of the Army," cries the Canon proudly, "we have diddled them, for the chest has been recovered."

"Excuse me, sir," says the Sub of the *Sweet William*, jumping up, "but there are two of my men waiting to bring it in, so that it can be unlocked and officially examined; but before this is done, I believe the Dean wishes me to make a report of our share of the business."

The Sub makes his report, which is substantiated by his brothers of the Artillery, and Daniel is then asked to tell of Jane's disappearance and rescue. When this is done, two sailors are summoned from the servants' hall, bearing the iron chest between them, which they put down in front of the great fireplace. The Dean's key is handed over to Mr. Dossal, who unlocks the chest and lifts the great lid. A cry of horror escapes him. Cries of horror escape from the whole company, for it is obvious to all the chest is full of rubbish.

"Well, I'm dashed," exclaims the Sub. "We're dished. That blinking Chink has done us in the eye. I expect he dropped the lot through that bogey trap of his into the river, before he jumped over with the key."

"Please don't get so excited," says the Dean calmly. "There is no need for any wool to be lost, let alone our sacred vessels. If you hadn't interrupted me you would all have been spared this panic, for I was about to explain why I had dropped my key into my gaiters and why I so tamely agreed to the kidnapping of Canon Beveridge. Smith, convinced that he had the only key, had no scruples in letting the chest out of his sight, and so I found plenty of time to fish out my key, to unlock the chest, to remove all the plate, to fill the chest with stones and rubbish for the requisite weight, and to relock it. The Cathedral plate is now taking a very second place in Odo's Treasure Vault, which I shall be very happy to show any of the company who possess sufficient daring at any time convenient." The company, by now entirely hypnotized with the fascination of adventure, all voted that there was no time like the present, even though the present was little short of midnight.

"Very well," says the Dean. "Mr. Jubb, what is the tide doing now in the river?"

"She's about three hours to the full, sir," the old fisherman answers.

"And that means that the next low tide will be—when?"

"As near nine o'clock to-morrow morning as can be, Your Harness," replies Jubb, looking apologetically at the members of the Royal Navy as much as to say, "I know you are man-o'-war's men, but I can't help knowing something about tides."

"Then the sooner we break up this meeting the better," says the Dean, "because we must all meet to-morrow morning in the Slype at eight-thirty. We have got to be on time, or we shall run the risk

of spending twelve hours in the Treasure Vault. And please dig out
your oldest clothes, though I don't suppose any of you ladies will
care to venture down the well."

"The well, my dear Jonathan? Sakes alive!" exclaims Mrs.
Jerome. "I should think not."

"It's safe enough, my dear," assures the Dean. "The iron rungs
are all sound, if they can stand my weight. A bit dampish it is, I'll
admit, and somewhat smelly, but lots of people like the smell of
seaweed."

"But this secret chamber—you haven't told us anything about
it," suggests Gony. "Is it in the well?"

"If you insist on an explanation, you shall have it," answers the
Dean. "On your head be it, Gony, if we get no sleep tonight. You
must know that the reason I laughed so prodigiously at Smith's
discovering the Chapter Room with the familiar treasure-chest of
the Cathedral was that I was just then feeling very superior, and
you shall know the reason. We had been to look at the well into
which poor McCarbre had had such a terrible adventure. By 'we'
I mean the Paper Wizard and myself, for nothing would make
McCarbre go near it, which was not very surprising. I remember calling to my companion, pointing down the well and saying,
'I had no idea we were such colossal heroes. Did we really get
McCarbre up from that level?' 'I know I didn't dive into that space,'
he answers. 'My rung was that one, and it was on a level with the
doctor's head. His legs were in the water.' 'What's that noise, that
tapping noise?' I asked. The Paper Wizard started to climb down
the rungs. He had an electric torch. I had a candle in a flat stand.
He went on climbing down, flashing the torch beneath him. I was
wondering when he was going to reach the water level, when he
whispered, 'Come down. Quick!' I confess I went down after him
with my heart in my mouth. It was not easy balancing the candle
every time I changed hands. I thought I was never going to reach
him, when I suddenly found him sitting on a stone ledge with his
legs dangling. The spooky box was floating about just below us
and bumping the sides of the well. This and the noise of running
water stopped simultaneously. The box had settled. The water had
all gone through a narrow passage that sloped away at an angle of
forty-five degrees. It was too dangerous to follow it without ropes

and air-tests, and when we reached the bottom we were careful
not to go too near to this opening, which was perilously slippery.
What looked much safer to explore was a Norman archway cut in
the wall on a level with the ledge. Into this we went. It was a short
passage, tall enough to stand upright in, though I had to bend my
head at the far end, as the floor sloped up. It led us straight to the
floor of a second well shaft. This had no drain off for the water
except the passage along which we had come. Up this shaft went
iron rungs like the others. 'Depend upon it,' I said to the Paper
Wizard, 'if the Treasure's anywhere, it's up there.' 'Come on,
then,' he answered, and began to climb. I put my candle on the
floor in the shelter of the passage, and went after him. The air was
deathly cold, but I suppose our blood was hot with excitement,
because we didn't seem to mind. We went up about twenty rungs
and found ourselves in a small stone chamber with stone niches
cut all round it to the ceiling. And, my dear friends, the moment
we looked at those niches by the light of the Wizard's torch we
were looking at Odo's Treasure, magnificent and of a value that
even Norris will not dare to estimate. There stood the gold and
the jewels still waiting to assist Robert of Normandy to the throne
of England. I kept on saying, 'Poor old Odo,' and I believe the
Paper Wizard kept on saying, 'Good old Odo.' I really don't know
how long we stayed in that wonderful Treasury Room, but quite
suddenly we nearly jumped out of our skins by hearing a loud
whistling in the place. We searched and searched, but couldn't find
anything capable of whistling in the room. We went to the shaft
and looked down. The candle I had left in the passage was slowly
moving towards the ladder. I shouted, thinking that McCarbre or
Smith had followed us, but as there was no answer, the Paper Wizard at last climbed down to look. I really shall never recover from
the fright I had when he called, 'It's your candlestick floating. The
water's coming back into the well.' Thank God we were tall men,
for it was up to our chins when we touched the bottom, and by the
time we had stumbled and splashed through the passage we were
submerged, but we got into the other shaft and swam about till
we grabbed the iron rungs. If we had tasted the water before we
should have guessed the truth, for it was brackish—not well-water
at all, but the river, which had changed guard every twelve hours

since Odo had given it his Treasure to watch over. The whistle we had heard in the stone room was a clever contrivance to warn anyone there that the tide was coming up the sloping shaft. It was a thin stone whistle pipe that runs up to the Treasure Chamber and is blown by the incoming water. They were clever enough in those days with their dodges. We should only have been imprisoned till the tide fell again, but by that time we might have gone mad."

"And Odo's Treasure?" gasps Mr. Gony.

"Yes, tell us," echoes the Mayor.

"No," answers the Dean. "If I start on that we shall get no sleep, and really we are in need of it."

"Very well, Mr. Dean," says the Mayor. "We shall only impose upon you a few minutes longer, but I am sure you will answer me on one or two points."

"Go on, then, Mr. Mayor," laughs the Dean. "I expect most of them can be answered in the two words—Boyce's Boy. You see, he was in with the Treasure Seekers from the start, and was their link with the outside world. I can answer for his usefulness during the time I was down there."

The Mayor referred to the notes he had been making. "I presume that Mr. Macauley was shot by Dr. Smith masquerading as Miss Tackle?"

"Yes. He was a first-rate shot with a rifle."

"But was Miss Tackle kidnapped for that purpose?"

"No. But for the details of her capture I refer you to the Paper Wizard as a more reliable authority. He was there. I wasn't."

The Paper Wizard jumps up and says: "Miss Tackle walked straight into us, sir, of her own accord. Smith was about to make a sortie to his house, under cover of the thick fog which you may recollect came along in advance of the snow. Just as it came down black enough for his purpose we opened the door, and the lady just was there on top of us. Smith had a coat over his arm which he promptly threw over her head and dragged her in. Once in, she had to stop, and then Smith saw the convenience of her costume for a disguise. When the fog disappeared he determined to try it on, but the announcement to a nervous unmarried lady imprisoned in a vault with a lot of men that she'd got to get out of her togs naturally sent her into them screeches what were overheard coming from the Slype. You see, there was an opening for the sound to get out of just the other side of the Slype wall behind the Dean's pig-styes. A proper archway it is, hidden under a great curtain of old ivy what we managed to lift up when we went to get the pigs down for roast pork. I daresay that more of your screams might be accounted for when we cut that speckled pig's throat. You should have seen me roasting him over a great fire. I even got the skin to crackle to a turn. So successful was it that when we'd finished him, the Dean says, 'Go and fetch the lot,' and we'd hardly got 'em safe through the arch when we got a proper landslide of stone and earth as near on top of us as pleasant, which cut off any more getting out that way, as we was afraid the whole Slype wall might come in on us."

"That explains the pigs, then, and the screams," says the Mayor. "I was going to ask about them and the Twelfth Fiddler."

"Oh, that," laughs the Dean, "was carried away under my wife's nose in Boyce's Boy's vegetable basket. He slipped into the hall from the servants' quarters when he was waiting for orders. I told him where he'd find the toys and he promised to try and prig one. I wanted one just as badly as Quaver wanted Cruden's Concordance, and when I saw Dossal glued to his *Waverley Novel*, I wanted it more than ever. Babyish—but there you are."

"Then, sir," says one of the constables behind the Mayor, "it was you what set it going and you what run off with it when Captain Dyke and me was in the Chapter Room last night?"

"Yes," answers the Dean. "When Captain Dyke got into the strong-room it was quite safe to open the secret door and let the Fiddler walk, and I rescued him later when you left him on the floor."

"But why didn't you declare yourself to Daniel Dyke?" asks the Mayor. "I mean, realizing what anxiety you were all causing by your absence, couldn't you have communicated with him? Smith had gone, with his threatening revolver. There was nothing to stop your return, was there?"

"The reason I resisted that temptation," answers the Dean, "is the same reason which explains why Norris disappeared."

"That's another of my notes," says the Mayor. "How did Norris disappear, and why?"

"Why? Because I wanted his expert opinion on the Treasure before we faced the Precincts with our story. I didn't want to make an ass of myself over my Treasure, if the stuff wasn't what I thought it. The means by which we got Norris were the same as we employed with Canon Beveridge. I wrote another note of desperate summons, which Boyce's Boy dropped in his shop when buying that spear, mentioned in Daniel's account."

"But the blood on the floor?" asks Macauley.

"Not my instructions, but a little humour of Boyce's Boy. Show them how you did it, my lad."

Boyce's Boy produces a toy water-pistol and grins. "Squirted it full of pig's blood."

"What for?" demands Macauley.

"Something for Sergeant Wurren to puzzle over," explains the ready urchin.

To save a passage of words, the Mayor changes the subject. "I suppose Norris had to interrupt his work because of the tide in the well. One tide wasn't enough for his decision, I suppose?"

"Oh, yes, it was, and we would have come out then if we hadn't been prevented, but whether it was the quantities of snow or not, I can't say, but for some reason or other the tide rose higher than the mouth of the well, and fairly flooded us out. If we hadn't managed to push the pigs up the Flying Buttress they would have drowned."

"That was no easy task, I should think," laughs Mr. Gony.

"It was not, believe me," answers the Dean. "We couldn't have done it without Boyce's Boy's spear, which was the purpose for which he originally bought it."

"What, to push them up the buttress?"

"No, but to prod them into obedience. They behaved very badly after poor Speckly's death."

"I'm looking forward to examining that buttress," says Mr. Gony. "Very unique. I had no idea such a thing was possible."

"I'll show you something else that will astonish you in architecture," laughs the Dean. "It's my belief that one of the well shafts is inside that fat Norman pillar of the Crypt. You probably sprung a leak with all your hammering about, just as you spotted our secret door in the Chapter Room. You evidently knocked a stone into the works. It wouldn't open."

"We did knock the wall about a bit by the bookcase, I admit. I was examining a water-pipe which I thought might have burst somewhere."

"And meanwhile we were cut off from our other exit and had to get the old bookcase off its hinges. That's why we pushed the whole show over during Vestry Prayers."

"And that explains all the points I wanted cleared," says the Mayor, rising. "Mr. Dean, Ladies and Gentlemen, you may go to bed, I think."

"And to-morrow you shall see the wonders we have brought to light." Saying which, the Dean nods to his wife, who superintends Styles, Potter and Rachel bringing in glasses and decanters.

When everyone is provided with a drink, the Dean proposes, "Odo's Treasure," which toast is drunk with relish, in anticipation of what they would see in the morning.

CHAPTER XLV

CHRISTMAS AT DULLCHESTER

For many days sleepy old Dullchester was very much awake. The Precincts teemed with experts who worked with Gony and Norris in the removal and cataloguing of the Treasury pieces. The "find" was so important and calculated to bear such far-reaching influence upon historical data, that the Government sent down officials from the great Museums to assist the work. The city teemed with London reporters, and for the first time in the history of the *Dullchester and Talkham Weekly* that newspaper was sold out before it went to press, so eager was the public to read the first official report. And as if all this excitement were not enough to keep the place awake, the police reported the amazing system of drug-trafficking which had been broken up by the death of a despised Dullchester doctor. But in spite of all this, the Dean did not neglect the preparations for Christmas. In fact, he neglected everything else. He never did let anything interfere with Christmas, and he wasn't going to begin to let it now, Odo or no Odo, especially as this was to be just *the* Christmas, terminating on Boxing Day morning with

the marriage of his adorable Jane to the young man whom he had
already loved as his own. But he wouldn't hear of them fixing the
wedding on Christmas Day. "Well, I do like that!" he had cried
when hearing the suggestion. "Anything else in a small way? You
can tell that to the Marines and Betty Martin. What a miserable
Christmas are you planning for me, all by myself, I should like to
know? All by myself in the dark, playing snapdragon? Choosing up
sides with myself for charades and setting to corners with myself
in the Lancers? Telling ghost-stories to myself all by myself? Musical chairs by playing the piano with one hand and running round
the music-stool with the other? Kissing myself under the mistle-
toe? And running away from my own handkerchief in Blind Man's
Buff? And how on earth do you suppose I am going to gather
myself for nuts in May, or ask for myself to fetch me away?"

"The wedding shall be on Boxing Day," laughed Jane in answer.
"I wouldn't leave you on Christmas Day even for Daniel."

"And I couldn't leave you, sir," echoes Daniel, "even for Jane."

Mrs. Jerome was as eager as anyone for a large wedding. She
thought of everybody who would like to be invited, even the
impossible people that everyone else had forgotten and whose
names when mentioned called forth howls of joyful derision. But
she did protest a little at the way the Dean filled up the sleeping
accommodation. He sent invitations broadcast to all sorts of jolly
people, not only for the wedding itself but for the entire Christmas
feast. "We'll put you up. Come as many days before Christmas Eve
as possible."

"You're quite ridiculous, Jonathan," was Mrs. Jerome's comment. "Christmas, as you always say, is a home festival."

"I know; that's why I've asked them. Want to fill the old home
up."

"But yours is not the only home in the world, you conceited old
man. They've homes of their own."

"Not so nice as mine, thanks to you, my dear, and they know
it."

"They'll all refuse, thank goodness, and they'll think you quite
cracked for having asked them."

"Well, that's where my dear clever pretty little wife is all wrong,"
cried the Dean, patting her cheeks. "They've all accepted."

"And where on earth do you suppose I can find beds for them all?"

"Where *I* did, I suppose, my love. At the bed-shop."

"What on earth do you mean?"

"Well, the furniture-shop, then. I've ordered a batch of camp ones that we can deal round to all the rooms and shove up in odd nooks and corners. Besides, Daniel has lent me his cottage. You leave everything to me."

And somehow or other, despite the rush to get the Deanery in order, Jane's trousseau ready, and the larder and pantry stocked, when the lights of the first car came up the drive in the early hours of Christmas Eve, Mrs. Jerome came to the open door in the hall, where her husband was standing with Jane and Daniel, to give his guests the old-fashioned welcome at the gate, and said, "We're all right now, Jonathan. Everything's ready, I do believe."

And everybody voted that everything was all right and that there never had been such a Christmas. Nothing was forgotten.

The procession of the Boar's Head, which the Dean, as a Queen's College man, always insisted upon, went this year through the snow-capped Precincts heralded by trumpeters and followed by the Mayor and Aldermen, robed, the surpliced choir, the Chapter in their academic gowns and hoods, Styles and Potter with their silver wands, Boyce's Boy resplendent in a livery-coat with silver buttons, and Mr. Boyce, dressed in the regalia of a cook and bearing the decked Boar's Head aloft on a mighty trencher, boomed out the Cantor's lines from the old carol:

"The Boar's Head in hand bring I."

The Dean brought up the rear with his own herd of pigs, decorated with:

"Holly, bay and rosemary."

Then, such meals, such games, such presents and such music and such a beautiful wedding on Boxing Day morning, with the sun shining on the snow-capped Cathedral and the whole of the three towns out to wish the happy couple God-speed. Amongst the guests we must not forget a motor-lorry full of Joneses, Jubbs and Joys, headed by old Jubb himself and little Joyce, which had left the Ness before sunrise in order to be in plenty of time to see Miss Jane and the Captain turned into Mr. and Mrs. Dyke.

When the bride and bridegroom had driven away to Dover for a Continental honeymoon, and when Boyce's Boy—now engaged as liveried page-boy at the Deanery—had closed the hall door behind the last of the guests, the Dean sat down in a chair, heaved a sigh and said, "That's that."

"You'll find it dull, sir, for a bit," ventured the page-boy respectfully. "I've a few minutes now, sir, if you want me to help you arrange those perks."

"Oh, yes," laughed the Dean, jumping up. "Come on. That's something to do. Get the hammer and nails. We will arrange the Museum of Perquisites." He led the way to the library, followed by Boyce's Boy with hammer and nails. "Now we've got to get these trophies hung together over there, so we'll move that picture. Let's see what we've got. There's the organ-pipe. I'm giving Trillet a new one. There's the rifle that shot Macauley. There's the two revolvers, Smith's and the Chink's. There's your spear which Gordon Beveridge recovered from the Chinaman's cabin and which, with your permission, I shall keep. This piece of stained glass is, unfortunately, not damaged, so must go back into the window. I don't think we'll keep the box belonging to it. It's ugly and cheap."

"Where's your handkerchief with the blood on it, sir?" inquired Boyce's Boy with relish.

"Oh, I buzzed that away in the laundry basket."

"Oh!" said Boyce's Boy reprovingly.

"It was pig's blood," argued the Dean, "not mine, and not at all pleasant for an ornament. It was very useful to keep my hair from getting in my eyes when I hadn't a comb, but its use is no more till it's clean. I think that's all the perks I've managed to get except, of course, this," and the Dean picked up the brass-bound book. "This is the most precious of them all, for this was the original cause of the mischief."

When these specimens were all hung, Boyce's Boy was asked to put away the hammer and nails. "Just a minute, sir—I mean your reverence. There's one more specimen to hang. It'll want two nails. I'll fetch it." He went out of the library, and returned with a red cloth-covered board, with two rows of brass hooks on which were hanging large keys.

"Whatever's this?" asked the Dean.

"Keys," explained the page-boy. "When your reverence agreed to take me on at the Deanery in order to go bail for me with the policeman, I thought it safest to give them up. I made the impressions from the originals, and young Snelling, the apprentice at Huntley's gun-shop, cast them in iron. Snelling's a member of my Trades Boys' Union, and a very bright specimen, too, sir. Them keys——"

"Those keys or these keys—not 'them' keys," corrected the Dean.

"Those keys or these keys, reverend sir," continued the page-boy, "can get you into most of the buildings in this old town. That one of the Cathedral North Door I consider very fine. My father used that when he and Dr. Smith took out the bit of stained glass."

"You must label them all for me. It's a very good collection," said the Dean. "But since you are now a law-abiding citizen, their day is done." They hung them up beneath the revolvers. Just then Mr. Dossal came into the library with a batch of papers for the Dean to sign. "I have received a most magnificent present, Mr. Dean. Mr. McCarbre has sent over to my house the Napoleonic bronze I so admired."

"The one that sent you to sleep in his drawing-room? Well, I never. Our benefactor is spoiling us all."

"He is, Mr. Dean, he is," and the delighted Dossal hurried home to have another look at his new treasure.

"Is that all now?" asked Boyce's Boy. "I promised to help Mr. Styles put away the silver."

"Good boy," said the Dean. "You'll live to cheat the gallows yet, for all Sergeant Wurren's ill opinion of you."

Mrs. Jerome came in to see what her husband was doing. "How quiet the house is, Jonathan," she sighed.

The Dean smiled. "Yes, but it's rather lovely, isn't it? You and I all alone. Come along. Let's go out into the garden. The sun's on the snow and there's a honeymoon feeling in the air."

CHAPTER XLVI

THROUGH THE SLYPE

THERE is nothing further to relate. The tale is told. Yet if there are any readers who take leave of Dullchester with regret, let us meet together once again at the Slype door and take a ramble round the Precincts before we say good-bye.

Yes. This is Minor Canon Row. The snow has gone. Of course. It isn't winter now. Look at the Virginia creeper. Those bright red leaves against the green. And don't you smell the jasmine? Several seasons have gone by since that severe winter when Panic reigned in the Precincts. Old Canon Cable has finished his last translation and lies with the abbots and scholars of the past. You can see his name upon the floor of the South Transept. He is not disturbed at his studies now with Matins, meals and Evensong. He is at home, conversing with the dead in their own language. Canon Beveridge has passed to a more courtly world. He had a peaceful end, surrounded by his beloved children of nature and of law. The Archdeacon has also retired. Yes, not only from his work but from his bed. A cold took him, and his brass plate in the Crypt needs continual rubbing to keep it free from damp. Styles too has handed back his silver wand to those that gave it. A bad chill took him off on the top of innumerable falls over the frayed piece of cocoanut matting. Potter still grumbles about that. "My friend was aggravated into his grave by that there bit of cocoanut." But Potter does not grumble at keeping his grave fresh with flowers and free from leaves, "for I was very fond of Styles," he says. "We had a lot of fun in Cathedral together, one way and another. What the Precincts is a-coming to now I don't know. It's not what it was. We gets preached at now by bits of boys from college. Disgustin', I calls it. And mark my words, when me and the Dean goes through them doors feet first, they'll have to shut up shop."

But the Dean shows no sign of going anywhere feet first. His grand old head is still erect in the Precincts, where he reigns supreme and jokes as usual. On Dr. Rickit's advice he has given up his Marathon against the pigs, but more to please the doctor than himself. He is very active in the rose garden, but his toys (with one exception) have been given to his great-grandchildren—the Twelfth Fiddler, whose technique has suffered since his fall upon the flagstones in the Chapter Room. This one is pensioned off for Services Rendered, and is given Alms-room on the library mantelpiece. A broken-down artist. A virtuoso who has had his day.

In the closely-packed bookshelves of that study there is one that seems empty by comparison. There are only five volumes there, but they all bear the name of the same author—Daniel Dyke. "I have given that shelf to that author's books and I am going to see it filled before my Will is read." And on the calculation of one book a year Mrs. Jerome measures the shelf with her tape to see how long it will be before she becomes a widow. And while Daniel Dyke is busy writing stories, the Dean is fond of telling them, and every Christmas it is becoming a custom for him to recount the great adventures in the Precincts when the parsons disappeared.

Trillet is no longer in the organ-loft. He has been put into a more important one. After doing so many good turns to the Te Deum and Jubilate, they reciprocated and got him recognized for his services. He is no longer plain Mr. Trillet but Sir John, if you please, and should you want to hear him play you can do so twice a day in London, where anyone hailing from Dullchester is welcome to a seat in his loft. He can make as much noise as he likes now. The Cathedral he has gone to is larger than Dullchester. There is no danger of his blowing that roof off, and the choir is too mighty to be drowned.

Dossal is no longer in Minor Canon Row. He has moved his Napoleonic bronze and his eucalyptus lozenges to a country living. His wife went too. Quaver cannot be tempted to leave the Cathedral which Boyce still shakes with Handel runs. This veteran chorister has given up the shop to Boyce's Boy, who got out of his buttons for a commercial life in which he is known as Mr. Flagget Junior. But you don't buy fruit there now. They haven't room for fruit on those great marble slabs. Those fish come up from Dingy Ness. Fresh? Yes, every day. You can smell the salt water as you pass. Mr. Flagget Junior is a good-looking young man. A mischievous face, hasn't he? That's because he still has a habit of pushing his nose into everything. He never waits to inquire whether his presence will be welcomed. It invariably is. A devil with the women? You might think so by his face, but you are wrong. This is his one tame spot. He has eyes for one girl only, and can you wonder, when you look at her? There she is, standing up on the fish lorry, looking like a boy in her driver's overalls. She drives the Jubb motors up from the sea. Have we met this delectable young girl before? Of course; for this is Joyce, and it was Joyce, backed up by Jane, who persuaded Boyce's Boy that there was more to be gained from fish than fruit, and Boyce's Boy, by the way he looks at Joyce and blushes, no doubt thinks so too. Sergeant Wurren watches his old enemy from the window of the Police Station. He is not in uniform, for he is not on duty. Indeed, he no longer does any duty in Dullchester and he is merely down here for the day, impressing his young successors by telling them that he is a Scotland Yard man. He obtained this situation through the good offices of Macauley. A highly-paid job, a highly trustworthy job, but—publish it not in the streets of Dullchester—it's not a job that calls for great mentality. He is not a detective, as he would have you believe when he tells you his address is Scotland Yard. He is a caretaker, and most of the caretaking is done by his wife, who is still of the opinion that the gallant Sergeant saved both her master and herself from terrors unparalleled during that romantic winter night when he chose their doorstep to mount guard upon. Yes, Sergeant Wurren has married the late Canon Cable's cook.

You must go and look at Odo's Treasure before you go away. The Crown did not press any claim to it, for the special High Court Commission that sat upon the subject came to the conclusion that as Dullchester had guarded it so long, that city should continue to do so. The difficulty of housing it was met by McCarbre, who once more put his hand deep in his pocket and purchased for the city that fine old timbered house over against the East Gate. Aided by Mrs. Furlong, he then formed a Trust Fund which provides the house with suitable custodians. Since the days of Richard Watts, Dullchester has not known such a benefactor as James McCarbre. And here is the very man, being wheeled in his Bath chair round by the Cathedral. He has asked the lady who is looking after him to stop a minute by the railings. He looks across the well-kept lawn to a certain window in the Lady Chapel. It is the War Memorial Window, restored since last we saw it. He bows his head and offers up a silent prayer for a young soldier who never lived to fight in the Great War but died of fever on the Irrawaddy's banks. Now the lady pushes the chair towards Bony Hill. She takes great care of him. Who is she? We have not seen that pretty old face before in the Precincts, have we? No. But she has been there for years and would be quite a familiar figure to you if she had not discarded her bee-net. Is it Miss Tackle? No. She was, but is now Mrs. McCarbre. Then has Mrs. Sarle departed from the house at Bony Hill? No, she is still there, and is Mrs. McCarbre's right hand. They are never jealous of one another, but they are sometimes of someone else for whom McCarbre can never do enough. Although this person is out of sight at present he can't be far away, for the fresh wind is blowing little bits of paper right over the Castle wall towards the river, which proves that our old friend the Paper Wizard is hiding hereabouts. Yes, there he is sitting on the wall between two children. The little boy might well be the miniature of Daniel Dyke and the little girl is the living image of Jane. Holt's cab is waiting to take us on our way, so we leave them learning the Paper Wizard's art, while the scraps of paper blow after us as we drive out of the Precincts with the old song of the Wizard ringing in our ears:

> "I cuts cafedrals out I does
> Wi' a pair o' scissors, and a wery little fuss."

THE END

ALSO AVAILABLE FROM VALANCOURT BOOKS